SHE'D THOUGHT THE LUCK OF THE IRISH
WAS GOING TO RUB OFF ON HER.
AND THEN SHE MET CARRICK FITZGERALD...

He had long legs covered in worn and faded jeans and Windsor blue wellies up to strong knees. An insulated rain jacket of raw sienna highlighted a broad chest.

Her pulse started racing.

No, no, no, no. Angie had vowed not to be sidetracked by another man, no matter how compelling. She was on a man-fast, and she was sticking to it.

She hit the button to roll the window up, wanting to tune out Carrick, but her sister grabbed her arm and stopped her. They grappled over the button, the window going up and down, before Megan pinched her like they were little kids again.

"Is your window malfunctioning?" Carrick leaned into the car, enveloping her in what she could only imagine a real man smelled like: the fields, sunshine, wool, and musk.

She pressed herself back into the seat to get more space.

"What is wrong with you?" Megan hissed under her breath.

I'm weak, Angie wanted to say, but that was pathetic so she sat on her hands—they might get a mind of their own and reach out and touch his colors and textures, God help her.

PRAISE FOR AVA MILES' NOVELS
SEE WHAT ALL THE BUZZ IS ABOUT...

"Ava's story is witty and charming."

"If you like Nora Roberts type books, this is a must-read."

"If ever there was a contemporary romance that rated a 10 on a scale of 1 to 5 for me, this one is it!"

"I could not stop flipping the pages. I can't wait to read the next book in this series."

"I've read Susan Mallery and Debbie Macomber... but never have I been so moved as by the books Ava Miles writes."

The Merriams grandparents' epic love affair...

Letters Across An Open Sea

Along Waters of Sunshine and Shadow

———

The Friends & Neighbors Novels

A feast for all the senses...

The House of Hope & Chocolate

The Dreamer's Flower Shoppe

———

The Dare River Series

Filled with down-home charm...

Country Heaven

The Chocolate Garden

Fireflies and Magnolias

The Promise of Rainbows

The Fountain Of Infinite Wishes

The Patchwork Quilt Of Happiness

Country Heaven Cookbook

The Chocolate Garden: A Magical Tale (Children's Book)

———

The Dare Valley Series

Awash in small town fabulousness...

Nora Roberts Land

French Roast

The Grand Opening

The Holiday Serenade

The Town Square

The Park of Sunset Dreams

The Perfect Ingredient

The Bridge to a Better Life

The Calendar of New Beginnings

Home Sweet Love

The Moonlight Serenade

The Sky of Endless Blue

Daring Brides

Daring Declarations

Dare Valley Meets Paris Billionaire Mini-Series

Small town charm meets big city romance...

The Billionaire's Gamble

The Billionaire's Secret

The Billionaire's Courtship

The Billionaire's Return

Dare Valley Meets Paris Compilation

The Once Upon a Dare Series

Falling in love is a contact sport...

The Gate to Everything

Non-Fiction

The Happiness Corner: Reflections So Far

The Post-Covid Wellness Playbook

Cookbooks

Home Baked Happiness Cookbook

Country Heaven Cookbook

The Lost Guides to Living Your Best Life Series

Reclaim Your Superpowers

Courage Is Your Superpower

Expression Is Your Superpower

Children's Books

The Chocolate Garden: A Magical Tale

BESIDE GOLDEN IRISH FIELDS

THE UNEXPECTED PRINCE CHARMING BOOK 1

AVA MILES

www.avamiles.com
Ava Miles

To Ireland and all that I love—dear friends, the land, the light, the water, rainbows, music, dance, storytelling, and chance encounters

ACKNOWLEDGMENTS

There are so many who gave me special snippets and thoughts for this book. Some were about sheep, horses, and farming while others were about how the Irish turn a phrase or think about a subject. Still others were about daily life and the comings and goings of people in village life. It's impossible to name them all but I would like to specially thank Martin, Andy, Emer, Shane, Ciara, Aidan, and Connor for some of my most heartfelt moments so far.

Every generation says a good man is hard to find.
And Prince Charming?
Well, he only lives in fairy tales.

But perhaps we women have been looking in the wrong
places.
With a little faith,
a willing and open heart,
and some help from a fairy godmother,
or the ghosts or fairies—
this is Ireland, after all—
a woman just might find him in the most unexpected of
places,
along with her happily ever after.

CHAPTER ONE

G*ood.*
    Be.
  Here.

Stopping in the middle of the narrow Irish country road, Angie Newcastle read the words in turquoise blue on the three individual sheep blocking their way. "Are you seeing this, Megan?"

"Those sheep have words on them," her sister confirmed beside her in their rented Volkswagen SUV.

"I want to see!" Angie's eight-year-old nephew called from the back seat, unlocking his seat belt and popping between them.

"Well, it's not like we can go anywhere," she said with a laugh, amused by their small titanium white faces and jet-black eyes and lips, which went with their puffy, buff white, barrel-shaped bodies. "They're kinda pretty, don't you think? Certainly a conversation starter. I can't wait to ask Cousin Bets why these sheep have words sprayed on them. Although the little lambs don't have enough room for words, it seems. Oh, they're so cute."

"She's just down the road once these sheep move," Megan said, leaning toward the dash. "Honk your horn."

Angie did, but the sheep only bleated loudly back at her. "I don't think they're impressed."

"None of the other sheep we've seen on the drive up from Dublin had anything but random markings." Megan made a shooing motion with her hands, which was met with even less interest than Angie's honking. "It's probably some teenage prank."

A little whiskey or Guinness and a spray can sounded like fun. Angie sighed, wondering who did it and whether they wanted company next time. Maybe it would inspire her. Because something had to kick her butt into gear.

Ireland, be kind to me, please. Be kind to all of us.

"It would be a pretty clean teenage prank," Megan said, shaking her head. "I can't imagine the kind of language a teenager would use."

"I can," she whispered, almost reverently.

Angie had been a rare bird back then—a rebellious A student and burgeoning artist, stifled by their father's ultra-conservative views and her high school's uninspired curriculum. Constantly in search of new and edgy ways of expression.

During the day, she was the dutiful daughter, cooking and cleaning for her sister and father while her mother worked twelve-hour hospital shifts as a nurse.

At night, when she snuck out, she came alive. Bohemian clothes and bold makeup were *de rigueur*. She didn't smoke because it gave her headaches or sleep with boys because she didn't want to get pregnant, but she *did* live. She'd had plans for her life back then. Big ones. About being a famous artist and living in Europe.

It was great—until her father caught her and punished

her. She'd been labeled *the wild one*. Her sister, who'd always been sensitive to criticism and rarely toed any lines, was *the good one*. The labels had stuck, and they were no more palatable now than they'd been then.

Megan turned away from the sheep and frowned at her. "Best not to think about things like that, Angie."

"Hard not to, given the state of things, Megan, but let's get back to the sheep. If I were going to spray words on a bunch of sheep, I'd go with something like *Focus, Ignite, Create* in fire engine red paint."

"Their faces look funny," Ollie said, grabbing her seat. "Like they used way too much black eyeliner, the way Aunt Angie used to."

Sadness rose in her heart. "Sometimes faces need paint too."

Not that she painted her face anymore or wore clothes she actually liked. Her wardrobe was probably indistinguishable from Megan's, and Megan had always dressed understated, first to please their father and then to please Tyson, her husband. Maybe her sister actually *liked* dressing that way, but it had never suited Angie.

The change had started years ago. Angie's ex-husband had given her lectures about "dressing like a kid," stressing that it was holding her back. The greater D.C. art scene was conservative, he'd said, and she'd never succeed there, either as a painter or a teacher, unless she looked the part. Given he was a successful artist and an adjunct art professor at Georgetown University, she'd believed him.

Her sister, of course, had encouraged the change, and a boring palette of neutrals had become Angie's staple. It had stuck around longer than her ex, actually, throughout her tenure as an art teacher and subsequent manager of the Baltimore Visual Arts League. But the serious look hadn't been enough, apparently, because she'd lost her job.

That was what artists called irony, although it felt more like tragedy.

First Tyson, Megan's husband and Ollie's father, had died eight months ago.

Then Angie's crappy ex-boyfriend, the one who was supposed to help her rebound from her marriage, had dumped her.

Then she'd lost her job.

On second thought, she should probably spray the sheep with something like: *No. Men. Ever*, because her own misfortunes could be traced back to the beginning of her dysfunctional marriage. *L'amour* hadn't been good to her. She sure as hell had never found Prince Charming. She'd promised herself she was off men until she could find herself and paint again.

"They're cute, especially the smaller ones," Ollie said, craning his tousled brown head to look over the dash, his hair still a mess from sleeping on the plane over. "I'd spray *Funny* on them." When one of the sheep emitted a loud bleat, her nephew let out a boyish giggle.

Ollie was giggling. He was actually giggling!

Emotion rolled through her, and she looked to see if Megan had noticed. Yes, there were tears in her sister's tired eyes, and for once they were happy tears.

That cinched it. Angie wasn't just going to ask Cousin Bets why these sheep had words on them when they arrived at her estate. She was going to find a local sheep farmer and ask him if she could spray more words on his sheep. Maybe he'd agree to parade them down the road to their new cottage every day.

They all needed to dig their way out of depression.

Thank God for Cousin Bets. If not for her offer to teach painting classes in her quaint village of Caisleán in County Mayo, Angie wasn't sure what she would have done. There'd been no job prospects at home after the closing of the arts center, not with her talent still deeply buried within her. Angie knew she had their mom to thank for this Hail Mary. She and Bets had been close friends since childhood, growing up in Baltimore together. When Angie was a young girl, Bets had been swept off to Ireland, a place she'd always loved, by her beloved Bruce, but the cousins had stayed close.

At first, Megan hadn't wanted to come along. Their parents had offered to take her and Ollie in, but Megan had refused, adamant that she wanted to stay with Angie, just like she had since Tyson was killed in the line of duty. So Angie had talked with Cousin Bets, and their cousin had agreed to host all three of them for her six months of employment. Bless her, she'd even arranged for Ollie's enrollment in a local school. Of course, he'd just gotten out of school in the States for summer holiday, and classes wouldn't start until late August.

The sheep bleated again—a loud, gravelly sound—and then changed places. The words rearranged themselves.

Here.

Be.

Good.

"Do you see that?" Megan's voice was whisper-soft. "I didn't get it before, but it's like a sign, Angie. I'm getting goose bumps."

Her arms did the same, sensing something in the air. "Does that mean you're starting to believe this place is going to be good for you?"

Because Angie sure did. From the vistas they'd seen on

the drive up, she couldn't imagine a more magical place. The verdant green hills rolled in waves of earth, mirroring the ones from the crashing blue and gray sea hugging the shoreline. Clouds drifted over those hills in puffs, streaks, and whispers in an array of whites and grays while the sky stretched out boldly across the horizon in blues ranging from cerulean to Prussian. Then there was the light...

She still hadn't processed its magic, but by God, she wanted to. She'd never seen light like this. Had she known, she would have visited Cousin Bets before, back in the glory days of her early twenties, when she was painting in Provence and Florence.

If she couldn't find inspiration here, she was screwed. And then there was the way Ollie had laughed—really laughed—after being here only for a matter of hours.

"Megan, what would you spray on the sheep?" she asked, revved with hope.

"I don't know." Her sister's face tightened. "I...wouldn't spray someone's sheep."

Angie deflated like a balloon.

"So here's where you girls have gotten up to," a deep voice called out, making her jump.

A large man appeared beside her window. His bearing was so powerful her brain captured his visage in an instant, and her fingers closed as if already holding her favorite paintbrush. Thick hair the color of vine black curled at the tips in an invitation to the wind or a woman's touch. Deep-set eyes best illuminated with Payne's grey to capture the mixture of humor and reserve there. His jawline was square and strong, requiring bold brushstrokes, and his rugged cheekbones would be a brushing of yellow ochre to convey the wildness about him.

A man like this wouldn't cower in the face of anything.

No, he'd stick his chin out and stand up to whatever life handed him. He belonged to the land stretched out before them as surely as the sea belonged to this island. Although he'd barely said a word to them, those truths felt unassailable.

Her belly burned. By God, she wanted to paint him. Bad. He was the first subject to ignite her like this since those years after college when she'd started to make a name for herself and sell her art in well-known galleries.

Before she'd screwed her life up with codependency and men.

He smiled at her when he bent at the waist to peer into her window. Her heart started to pound as she caught sight of his pitch-black eyelashes, the thickest, sexiest eyelashes she'd ever seen on a man. For a moment she wondered why her blood pressure was going up. Her doctor had told her an elevated heart rate while sitting was a worrisome sign.

Then the man smiled at her.

Shit. I'm attracted to him.

"Are you the owner of these sheep?" her nephew asked.

Angie realized he'd lowered the back window and was leaning out of it.

"I am at that," the man said, giving her another flash of a bold smile with what she could only call a twinkle in his eye before turning his head to her nephew. "I'm Carrick Fitzgerald. I would imagine you're Betsy O'Hanlon's relation from America."

"Yes, I'm Ollie, and that's my mom, Megan, and my aunt Angie. How did you guess?"

"Well..." He glanced back toward her. "Your Yank accent. Besides, your mom and aunt favor Bets, especially in the face and the mouth."

"Cousin Bets' mom and my grandma's mom are sisters," Ollie explained.

"Well, that explains it!" he said, leaning against the car. "I haven't seen Bets this excited in an age. Your coming to Ireland is all she's been able to talk about. The whole village is eager to welcome you."

"Really?" Ollie asked. "The whole village?"

"That's the story, and so it is," the man said with another winning smile.

God, his accent was as sexy as his sheer physicality. She could feel all her good intentions starting to cave inside her. Where was her willpower? She closed her eyes and repeated her alternate mantra. *No. Men. Ever.*

"Roll your window down!" Megan leaned into her lap and hit the button, knocking her out of her moment. "Who put the words on your sheep?"

He pointed to his chest as Angie's brain captured the rest of him. Long legs covered in worn and faded jeans and Windsor blue wellies up to strong knees. An insulated rain jacket of raw sienna highlighted a broad chest that contained a soulful and intriguing heart, if the words on the sheep were any indication. Her pulse started racing again.

No, no, no, no. She'd vowed she was not going to be sidetracked by another man, no matter how compelling.

She hit the button to roll the window up, wanting to tune out Carrick for her own self-preservation, but Megan grabbed her arm and stopped her. They grappled over the button, the window going up and down, before Megan pinched her like they were little kids again, thus winning like she used to.

"Is your window malfunctioning?" Carrick leaned into the car, enveloping her in what she could only imagine a real man smelled like: the fields, sunshine, wool, and musk.

He had his big strong hand on the window button before she could muster a reply. His presence overwhelmed her. She pressed herself back into the seat to get more space.

"It's probably a user glitch," Megan told him, giving her a pointed look. "We're not used to the steering wheel being on the other side."

He tested the window before smiling and stepping back. "Seems to be working fine. You're probably a little tired from the journey."

"No, I'm great," Angie responded, not wanting him to know he was getting to her. "It's only nine in the morning. Heck, I could drive another two hours."

His thoughtful gaze rested on her. "Seems you brought the sunshine," he said before turning to talk to Ollie.

Sunshine? Her? Her heart glowed at the compliment.

"What is wrong with you?" Megan hissed under her breath.

I'm weak, she wanted to say, but that was pathetic so she sat on her hands—they might get a mind of their own and reach out and touch his colors and textures, God help her. She looked straight ahead, trying to ignore the handsome stranger. Wasn't it her bad luck to meet a hot Irishman the moment she arrived? God, she *was* living in a Greek tragedy. She blinked when she read the sheep again.

Be.

Good.

Here.

Seriously? Okay, maybe it was a Greek comedy.

"Why did you write on your sheep, Mr. Fitzgerald?" asked Ollie.

"Yes, why?" Enthusiasm laced Megan's voice.

Angie bit her lip to keep herself from joining in the conversation. She started to visualize the things that usually tempted her as much as a man. She started with an image of a three-layer dark chocolate cake with chocolate shavings. Cake couldn't break your heart, and chocolate was an acclaimed healer. But his voice still came through, like the sexy baritone one might hear on a commercial.

"Well, it started on a sad and lonely night, let me tell you, but people around here—the tourists included—all seemed to like it, so it's become a thing. My wife was a poet, you see. The words are from her poems, so she's always around me."

Angie jolted in her seat, her imaginary chocolate cake falling off its table and crashing to the ground. *He's married?*

"*Oh.*" Megan put her hand on her heart, close to needing a tissue from the look of her watery eyes. She didn't need to ask why. Her sister and Tyson had exchanged dozens of letters early on in their ten-year marriage, when he was posted overseas, and sometimes Angie would find Megan asleep with one of them nestled in her hand. They used to joke about her married name being Bennet, like one of the sisters in *Pride and Prejudice*. "That's very romantic," Megan continued. "It would make an incredible movie."

Angie couldn't disagree, but she was stuck on the fact that she'd been attracted to a *married* man. How low could she go? No, she would focus on being relieved he was married. That made him strictly off-limits.

"I can't wait to meet your wife," Megan said, and Angie was stunned since her sister hadn't shown any interest in socializing. "You two must have a wonderful relationship."

For a long moment, her comment was met only with silence, and Angie finally chanced a look at Carrick, wrapping herself in the knowledge she was safe from him. His engaging smile was gone. As a painter, she knew the eyes held every answer, so she looked into them. She'd noted a certain reserve before, but her heart clutched at the barrenness she saw there now. His gaze was as empty as the stretches of rocky seashore they'd seen on the drive up.

"Ah, I wish you could have met my Sorcha. She was as beautiful as her name, but she's gone from us. Bets said you'd lost your husband as well. You can't know how sorry I am for you and your boy." He glanced back to Ollie, his face shuttered.

Her nephew drew back from the window and curled into the seat. God, she wanted to bundle him right up and put that smile back on his face.

"Thank you for your condolences," Megan said, the phrase rote. "We'll let you get your sheep out of the road. Bets is waiting for us, and I'm sure you have a million things to do."

His mouth changed, almost a polite smile. "Keeping busy helps. As does time. The poets got that right. I'm sure I'll be seeing you around the village. My land abuts Bets' on the west, and I'm building a house there. I'll be getting these troublemakers out of the way. The one with *Good* on her clearly doesn't seem convinced, does she? Well, that's sheep for you. Minds of their own sometimes."

Angie glanced at the sheep in question. Maybe it had been caught up in a good adventure. "She looks okay to me," she finally said, her mind capturing this new visage of him.

His skin wasn't vibrant with yellow ochre but pewter. She knew the colors of grief. While not all of them were gray, many were. He was wrapped in that color now, almost as if the Irish wind had brought mummy wrappings and encircled him with them.

Carrick Fitzgerald wasn't over his wife.

That made him off-limits too. She was not going to be

tempted by a man who was still grieving. She had enough on her hands with Megan and Ollie. Taking care of them for the last eight months, coping with the loss of her relationship and then her job...it had been exhausting, frankly, and she was looking forward to having some help from her Irish cousins.

Still, she found herself gazing at him with compassion. Megan was right. He and his wife must have had an incredible relationship.

What would that feel like?

Carrick put his hand on the top of their car and met her gaze. There was almost a challenge in it, as if he knew her thoughts. He widened his stance, silently communicating that he wasn't a man to be pitied. No, he stood tall in his loss and was unapologetic about the mourning cloths wrapped around him.

"Good luck with your sheep," she managed, putting the car into gear.

His mouth tipped up. "Good luck with Bets. That woman always has plans. Coming here, you'll be more than part of them, I'd say."

He strode off toward the sheep, pulling a crumpled white bag out from the inside of his jacket. She watched as he shook it in front of the sheep and then started walking away. They bleated loudly and trotted after him down the road, their bulky bodies awkward in motion.

"Are you okay?" her sister asked, touching her arm. "You usually talk a mile a minute."

"Maybe I need to eat. You know how I get when I'm hungry." Oh, the lie burned in her throat.

"Don't I ever!"

"Here," Ollie said. "Have my granola bar."

When her nephew handed her one, she made herself

eat it even though she had no appetite. She didn't want Megan to start watching her for signs of the Wrong Man Syndrome.

But she still couldn't take her gaze off Carrick. He knew what a broken heart was too. At the next gate, he shut himself inside with the rest of the sheep and strode across the verdant green hills while the three escaped ewes lowered their heads to the grass waving in the gentle wind.

She remembered that look in his eyes, blank of emotion. The man had shut himself away as much as he had the sheep, letting himself out of his impenetrable gates only when he must. Her heart sped up again, but this time there was worry with it. Would he be all right in the end? Megan clearly wasn't. God, she needed to stop trying to heal everyone. Becoming certified in art therapy had changed her into a bleeding heart painter, which had only made the compulsion worse.

Her creativity would continue to suffer if she kept doing things the same ol', same ol'.

She needed to focus on her art and not let anyone distract her. Goodbye, men, Carrick Fitzgerald included! And hopefully this spark she'd just seen in Megan would continue. Her sister had to figure things out sooner rather than later.

Not that Angie could wait for that, though. Coming here was maybe her last chance to shake things up and start over.

While she knew it wasn't going to be easy, she wasn't going to blow it.

CHAPTER TWO

L ove. Is. Here.

Carrick swore heartily in the wind as three sheep formed the message. He was still unmoored after meeting Betsy O'Hanlon's cousin—the one with the lush mouth who'd stared at him as if she could see into his soul. Unnerving, that. He'd have to avoid her.

"Stubborn as always," said a voice that had him jolting in place. "I've been trying to tell you through the sheep to prepare yourself, Carrick."

Jesus, his heart! He locked his jaw and swung around to face his wife, feeling as if the ground moved under his feet. She was wearing her favorite white summer dress, the one she'd had on the last time he'd seen her three years ago, when he'd kissed her goodbye like usual before she left to go for groceries. "So it is you again! It took me a while to suspect those messages were from you. I've been trying to prepare myself for another visit. How many times must I say it? I'm never finding love again."

"That's not how it works." She crossed her arms like she

16

did when she was vexed. "Hence why I've come back after a long respite."

At one time, he would have given anything to see her again, but the reason for her return made him ache to the core. "Well, I saw the messages, and they pissed me off. *Love. Is. Coming.* No, thank you."

"I wanted you to be aware," she replied.

He shook his head. "I don't want it, and I wish with all that I am for you to stop this. When we married, I vowed to never love another."

"But I died," she bantered back with a stubborn glint in her green eyes.

He didn't want their reunion to be about this tired old topic. "Like you have to remind me you're gone. Sorcha, when you died, I made another vow: to never love again. *On your gravesite.* I told you that when you first visited me six months after the funeral. The day you scared the spit out of my mouth by appearing in the mirror behind me as I dressed."

He'd always been able to see ghosts, but it was different seeing *her* this way. He'd stumbled into the dresser, knocking over their wedding photo and breaking the glass.

The same wind rushing over him played with her long brown hair and white dress. "And I told you to move on and not to be thick, but that would be like telling the wind not to blow. Then what did you up and do? You decided to start building me a dream house I'll never live in."

The wind rose up angrily as if she'd called it. "I promised you that house and all that goes with it."

"Death erases such promises."

"Not in my mind, dammit."

She'd often complained about having to go into town for groceries every few days since they only had a couple of shelves in a cranny and a half fridge to store them in. He'd told her their dream house would silence all her chiding, but something had always come up to delay it. The tractor had needed a new engine after rusting from the rain. He'd lost lambs when the weather had turned frigid for a few nights after the shearing in late May. He'd had to spring for improved fencing for the new pastures he'd rented.

If he'd given her the home he'd promised her, she might still be with him. She wouldn't have been on the main road that day going for milk and meat when an impatient lorry driver passed illegally and hit her straight on. The man had survived, damn him. And Carrick's Sorcha had been taken from him.

"Guilt doesn't become you, Carrick. My death wasn't your fault. I've tried to tell you again and again, but you're as thick in the head as ever."

He couldn't believe his hearing. "This is what you say to me after not speaking to me for almost three years?"

Her oval face softened. "I told you I would only visit you for a short time, to help you move on with your life and find love again. But it wasn't helping, so I left to see if *that* would help. We both know it didn't. Carrick, I won't have you keeping yourself entombed any longer. You're only thirty-eight. You can't live the rest of your life like this. I want you to be happy. You wanted a home, wife, and children. You're wasting away inside. Building that house for me is a stupid pursuit. You didn't even have the money to buy the land. You're lucky Betsy O'Hanlon agreed to let you use it out of pity."

"I don't want to listen to this!" He pounded his chest. "I promised you that house, and so it will be built. I know you won't be living there, but a promise is a promise."

"It keeps you focused on the past," Sorcha said.

"It keeps me occupied, which is what I like. I've found a rhythm without you. I tend to my sheep. I find side businesses to invest in or profit from. And I work on your house. I fall into bed tired every night, and that's how I want it."

"Your new pursuits—the building included—keep you busy so you won't have to move on and find another woman."

He wanted to growl at her pushing. "I've made my peace with you leaving."

"Don't lie—"

"Dammit, I've been with other women."

"Tourists! They come, they laugh, they leave. This is not what you want or what I want for you."

"What you want doesn't matter anymore! You're not here." He shook his head in frustration. "Why do you make me say these things to you?"

"You haven't opened your heart yet to another," she said, softly now after her earlier blasting. "In fact, you've shut it away. Carrick, I'm glad you've found enjoyment with some women, even if it's short-lived. But your heart has always been for love. I know that better than anyone. That heart and what's in it is why I fell in love with you when we were sixteen."

He kicked at a clump of grass, needing somewhere to express his anger. "I'm content enough, Sorcha. You're the one being thick. It's like I've told my family and my friends. I've lost the love of my life once, and I won't risk going through it again. I'm after peace now. I have my sheep and my extra pursuits. Soon I will have that house built, and my debt there will be repaid."

"I don't want—"

"With the sale of my prize ram at the fair in August, I'll finally be able to buy the land the house sits on as well as more pastureland from Betsy O'Hanlon. Call it pity if you'd like. I'm grateful she let me build that house until I could afford the land outright. Soon I'll be finished, and with those extra acres, I'll become the biggest sheep farmer in the county. I'll have the home to go along with it too."

"That home has seen more than its share of misfortunes since you started, and you know why."

He stilled, remembering the problems. Cracks in the foundation. Delays in deliveries. Surges of spring water through the ground, making the site engineer express concern about the site for building after the fact. The whole village had dubbed it Fitzgerald's Folly, a name he hated. "Sorcha, I want the truth. Did you curse the house?"

She shook her head slowly. "No, my Carrick. I would never do such a thing. But a house needs two hearts to make it a home. With yours shut away and mine gone, there's nothing to hold it together. Don't you remember how we'd remark after a solid stone cottage that went to ruin after the people abandoned it?"

Ireland was full of ruined cottages, something the tourists found charming. But he and Sorcha had heard an abundance of such sad tales and begun to believe them.

"You're wrong about my heart." He pounded his chest again, making his sheep bleat. "I have a passion for my sheep and my business. I will finish the house, and people from all around will praise it."

She glanced over her shoulder as one of the sheep came around her, sniffing, as if they could smell the orange in her hair, her signature scent from the orange peels she'd used in her wash water to bring out the highlights.

"Success will never fill your heart." She gestured to him. "You're not that kind of man."

"I am that kind of man now." He swallowed thickly.

"Leave me be, Sorcha. It's torture to talk like this. I would speak of other things with you. Like how you are and where you've been."

Seeing ghosts as he did, he'd often wondered what their existence was like, and he'd looked deeper after his wife became one. Even talked to the village priest. But no one had good answers, and it all remained a grand mystery. He'd think he was crazy if not for his mother and his friend, Kade, who also saw ghosts.

"Carrick, this talk is only torture because you have locked your heart away." She drew closer to him, so close he wished to touch her. When he'd tried in the past, his hands had only passed through her. How he envied the wind. The elements could touch her, but not him.

"It's my heart, and I'll do with it what I like," he said, locking eyes with her.

"True, but thank God it has a mind of its own, so to speak. You felt a connection with Betsy O'Hanlon's cousin. I've been trying to tell you through the sheep to prepare yourself. You two have more in common than you know."

He ground his teeth, troubled that she was privy to his feelings. "I don't care what we might have in common. She's Betsy's cousin and off-limits. Even if you weren't pushing me at her."

"And here you are, digging your heels in like an old mule. Carrick, you can do this the easy way or the hard way. Do it easy for once in your life."

He made a fist in the air to punctuate his thinking. "I'm not doing it at all, Sorcha, and that's the way of it."

She started to walk away, her bare feet gliding through the grass. "So the hard way then. What a surprise! Carrick, I'm here to help you. Don't fight me. Or your own heart."

"We had some of our best times when we pushed at

each other," he said, hoping reminders of their former days might soften her resolve. "You loved it."

"I didn't always, and neither did you. Life is short. We know that better than most. Go easy with this, man. I'm telling you."

"And I'm telling you!" He swore and glared at a sheep that bumped him rudely with its body. "I'm not doing it. *Love. Is. Coming. Love. Is. Here.* It's total and complete rubbish. Stop sending me messages!"

"Then stop spraying the words from my poems on your sheep."

Pain shot through his heart. "You know I can't do that. It's the only thing I have left of you besides my memories and photographs."

"And you say you've made peace with me being gone. It's time to let me go all the way, Carrick."

"If that's what you're asking, you should go back to where you came from and leave me be. Now I'm going to go work on your house."

"I can be as stubborn as you can." There was a smile on her face when she glanced back at him, a smile that portended trouble. She'd smiled at him like that before she'd spilled cold stew in his lap the morning after he'd stayed out all night drinking with his brother and friends and forgotten to call her. "Remember you chose the hard way. You can choose the easy road anytime. All you have to do is let me go and open your heart."

The wind surged up, making him brace his body so it wouldn't throw him off-balance, the kind of wind that could cause rack and ruin. The sheep next to him cuddled closer for shelter. When Carrick looked for Sorcha, she was standing next to the gate.

"Don't you dare!" he called, starting to run.

She laughed, that mischievous laugh he used to love.

The gate to the pasture blew open with an ear-splitting crash. His sheep bolted and started to run as the wind blasted across the land, almost as if pushing them out of the gate. They thundered onto the road and ran off toward Betsy O'Hanlon's estate, all twenty-eight of them. "You might delay me, but I'm still working on your house!"

Sorcha faced him as the wind died and the sun came out from behind a cloud, lighting the spot where she stood. "I told you, Carrick. *Love is here.* I won't let you squander it." Then she disappeared.

He swore heartily as the wind rose up again and then stalked to his truck, where he girded himself to chase down his errant sheep and likely encounter Betsy O'Hanlon's cousin yet again.

CHAPTER THREE

She'd been right to bring her cousins to Ireland.

Betsy understood what age and loss could do to a person, but Angie and Megan looked even less themselves, as they got out of their rental car. The cute little girls who'd begged her to braid their hair were as long gone as the young women they'd been. She'd seen them on a visit to the United States just three years ago, of course, so she'd known what to expect...or at least she'd thought so.

In her heyday, Angie had been as vibrant as one of her paintings, with henna red hair cut to her nape, bold eye makeup, dangling earrings and bracelets, a belly button ring, and flowing patchwork skirts. The woman she was now had mousy brown shoulder-length hair and wore baggy traveling clothes in tan and black. Saints preserve them! Their mother was right. Angie looked downright frumpy.

And Megan! Having a husband overseas for most of her marriage and childrearing had leached her, no doubt. Death had finished the job. Grief blanketed her wooden features, but Betsy knew that was to be expected. When her beloved Bruce had died five years ago from a heart attack as he was walking through the fields, she'd stayed in bed for three months mourning him, barely showering once a week.

The little boy Ollie was as downtrodden as his mother, Bets noted as they crossed the front garden. Not at all like she remembered her own son at that age. She glanced at Liam, now a man, standing beside her at the front door. Her boy was smiling, and she knew he was thinking the same. Their mother—Cousin Patty—had been right to talk to her about their situation.

Patty had worried about the burden Megan was putting on Angie, who was barely holding on to her own life preserver. They'd hoped Angie would come to Ireland alone and find herself again, giving Megan some space to grieve and make plans for the future.

Only Megan hadn't taken Patty up on her offer of shelter. Not that Bets blamed the girl. Their father, Dan, was charismatic in the way of many senior military men, something that had always worked for Patty, but he was a hard man. Still, Bets knew it had to be tough for Angie to help someone who was drowning when she herself was treading water. At least she and Liam could help.

"It's so good to see you," she said, hugging Angie and then Megan before kneeling down in front of Ollie, who extended his hand politely.

"Sorry we didn't pick you up at the airport, but we figured you'd need the extra room for the bags," Liam said, hugging his cousins. "Did you have a good drive up? You sure had great weather. How did you fare driving on our side of the road?"

"I took it nice and slow," Angie said, "but that worked for me since the views are so spectacular. I mean, I knew it would be beautiful, but it takes your breath away. I should have come years ago and painted."

"Yes, you should have, but we were glad your mom got away to visit a few times," Betsy said, knowing money had always been tight. "Every day, there's something new to grab your heart. But that's Ireland for you. I was just emailing Patty before you arrived. She's so happy you're here. So am I. I'm eager for us all to be together like it was when you two were little girls. But tell us. Did you experience a true Irish traffic jam on the way up?"

"She's asking if you came across any runaway sheep on the road," Liam said with a snort, as familiar with the joke as he was with her recent battle with Donal O'Dwyer's sheep.

"We *did* see some sheep on the road with words on them as we neared your place," Megan said, putting her hand on Ollie's shoulder. "We met their owner. A Mr. Fitzgerald. He said he'd lost his spouse as well."

So they'd met Carrick already. "Funny. His sheep don't usually get out. They're very disciplined for sheep, which is why he can spray words over them. Now, Donal O'Dwyer. That's another story. His sheep feast on everything when they break out, my prize roses especially."

"Mum loves her flowers," Liam said with a wink at their cousins. "She's won loads of awards and is getting ready for the big rose competition at the agricultural fair in early August."

"How wonderful," Angie said, glancing around casually. "I thought I saw rose petals on the driveway."

Sure enough, Bets caught sight of them and saw red. She wouldn't win any awards if Donal's sheep tore at her babies again, and Mary Kincaid—her sister-in-law, longtime competitor, and the town busybody—would sweep the category. God, that would piss Bets off. Mary had been a pain in her backside since she'd arrived with Bruce from the States, and her bitterness that Bets had this house and the land had grown worse after Bruce had died, even though it was the Irish way for the son to inherit the family land. "Donal's destructive brood was here yesterday, as is evidenced by the early rose petals."

"And here I thought you were lining our path in welcome with flowers like they do in Hawaii," Angie said, a sparkle in her eyes. "Maybe we should do it for our students on their first day of class. Thanks again for this chance of a lifetime. I can't wait to get started."

Good. Her cousin was psyched. Bets couldn't wait for the right time to share her full vision. The painting classes were only the beginning—she wanted Angie's help turning this giant estate into a community arts center. They had a ways to go, of course. Only thirteen people had signed up for Angie's painting class for adults and eighteen kids for the children's session. She was hoping Angie might be up for the challenge, but she hadn't said anything yet since her cousin was rightfully hurt and upset about losing her job and taking care of Megan and Ollie. But the opportunity would materialize soon. It always had when Bets went after what she wanted.

"I'm counting down the days myself. Only a week to go before our first class! I'm so grateful you're here. All of you," she added, smiling at Megan and Ollie. "Come inside. You must be thirsty. Maybe even a little hungry."

"I'll get your bags while you have a bite," Liam said. "Megan, we thought you and Ollie would like the cottage closer to the—"

"Separate cottages?" Megan sputtered. "But I thought I'd be living with Angie."

Bets tried to give an assuring smile. "Your mom and I thought it might be easier for you to start living on your own again like this. Your sister will be just down the road, and

Liam and I can get you any groceries you need in the village."

"That's very kind of you, Bets," Angie said softly.

"But I'm not even cooking right now." The pale woman turned to her sister and clutched her hand. "Angie, I'm not ready for this. I still need your help with Ollie."

The little boy hung his head, looking at his blue sneakers. "I'm fine, Mom."

"Ollie, you're not fine, and neither am I. We're grieving."

"My dad died too," Liam said, leaning down and tipping the little boy's chin up. "I still miss him. Maybe I can help you find a way to smile again. Like my mom helped me."

"We helped each other," Betsy said, hugging him with one arm. "Megan, I know everyone has their way of dealing with a loss, but we're here for you."

"But living on my own? It's too much. Angie—"

"Okay, you can stay with me," Angie said, rubbing her arm. "Let's not freak out. Maybe in a while—"

"I don't want to think about that," Megan said, her voice rising.

Betsy noted how Angie's earlier brightness had diminished, and she felt a wave of sympathy for both women. "Plenty of time for that."

"Time is your friend, Megan," Liam said. "Heck, I'm still figuring out what I want to do when I grow up. Philosophy, quantum physics, and self-help books and podcasts are my obsession. Considering my mom still hasn't figured that out for herself, I've decided I'm good."

She socked him, and he pulled her against him, making her feel as petite as her five foot three inches. "Can I help being a late bloomer? Besides, you're pretty handy to have around. Liam thinks he needs to rush around the estate to justify living here expense-free at twenty-five."

Liam turned to her and raised one of his sandy blond brows, looking like his father. Shifting his gaze back to their cousins, he said, "I love this time with Mum. Right now, I do odd jobs to save money, and then I travel to experience more of life. It's a blast. Sometimes Mum even comes along. She met me in Morocco on my last adventure trekking through the Sahara."

"As did your older brothers, who also have the travel bug," she added, smiling as she thought of Rhys and Wyatt.

"I remember the pictures," Angie said, doing her part to change the subject. "They were incredible. How are Rhys and Wyatt, by the way?"

"Still figuring their lives out too," Liam said with a laugh. "Wyatt likes to work at hotels with vineyards, and Rhys likes to make the wine."

"They're doing fine," Bets said, nudging him for good measure. "They're in South Africa right now."

"Personally, I'm not convinced anyone has it all the way figured out when it comes to life," Angie said, sending Liam a smile.

"No, just when you think you do, something happens to wreck it." Megan rubbed her nose. "Forgive me. I'm not jumping for joy these days. Ollie isn't either, are you, sweetheart?"

Then again, Megan had never done much of that either. She'd always struggled with the long separations from Tyson, or so she'd told her mother, who'd in turn told Bets. That wasn't much of a shock, all told. Betsy could never have married a soldier for that very reason.

"Maybe getting into a little trouble will improve your spirits and help you heal."

She kissed her son's cheek loudly to cover up the awkward moment. "Liam's middle name is trouble, courtesy of his mother."

Angie gave her a pained look. "Yes, I seem to remember hearing about a certain someone dancing on a bar regularly..."

Ollie's eyes widened, and Megan's mouth flattened. Angie would think it was good fun, of course, but that was the kind of fun she used to like to get into, according to Patty. Of course, their mother liked a good laugh, too, and Betsy had seen plenty of pictures of her cousin's antics back in the day when she was a young nurse in the veterans hospital, engaging in wheelchair races with the other medical personnel on break.

Megan was a different sort. Cousin Patty worried for her, as mothers did, and thought she and Angie had babied her too much to soften Dan's harder edges. Megan had always been a sensitive child, and she'd tried to please Dan and get his approval by being like her father wanted. Conservative. Her one rebellion, if it could be called that, was pursuing art, and even her pottery had been conservative, although lovely.

But that hadn't lasted long after she got married, and Bets was wondering if Megan might find strength and comfort from returning to her art. Although Patty hadn't disagreed with her suggestion, she'd mentioned that Megan had turned down Angie's offers to teach at the now defunct art league. Still, Bets would ask if the moment arose.

"When you work as a bartender," she said, "sometimes you have to shake things up. Those were the days!"

"As soon as you're feeling up to it," Liam said, "I'll take you around." He tilted his head, studying Angie and Megan. "Do you like pubs?"

30

Megan only shook her head.

"It's been a while since I've been in one," Angie said, "but I'm game. I'm here to shake things up too."

Bets laughed when Angie did a little shimmy. "I'm here to help as much as Liam on that score. I still manage to get into a little trouble myself."

"She's infamous in the village," Liam whispered playfully.

"I've been the eccentric Yank since I arrived some thirty years ago married and pregnant with Wyatt," she corrected.

"Dad worked fast." He laughed but she couldn't disagree. "Her three closest friends round out what the village calls the Lucky Charms."

"It's a long story," Betsy said with a laugh, "but in brief, I missed that silly cereal—it was my adult breakfast in the States—so my friends and I tried to make colored marshmallows—"

"And since Mum isn't the best cook, they turned out a mushy mess," Liam said, picking up the story. "So they went to the pub to console Mum. Only Dad came home and thought she'd made him some new-fangled American porridge and almost died from disgust when he tried it."

Betsy put her hand over her mouth as she started laughing. "Bruce showed up at the pub with green dye around his mouth, looking for a pint to counter the taste and to tell me he was never eating my American porridge again. I ended up telling him the story in front of everyone at the pub, and it spread around the village. We became the Lucky Charms. You'll meet Siobhan, Brigid, and Nicola soon. They've all signed up for your painting class."

"Wonderful!" Angie said, clasping her hands together.

"Of course, there's a bet in the village that Mum is going

to talk you into teaching a class on nudes." Liam elbowed her playfully for good measure.

This time Angie sputtered. "Ah... I've never taught one of those, but I've got plenty of stories from the one I took in college. Maybe I'll tell you later."

"He's mostly kidding," Betsy said, poking him back. "The village bets on everything, with Cormac O'Sullivan leading the charge. Oh, I'm running on like the Irish with my stories. Let's get you a drink and—"

Bleating sheep sounded in the distance.

Betsy went on alert. "Not again!"

Liam held up his hands. "You might step inside, cousins. Mum is about to lose her... Ahem. Mind."

She was already pulling out her cell phone to dial Donal. "Your sheep are out again and coming up my driveway, you eejit," she said as soon as he answered.

"And a fine hello to you too, Bets. I've finished making my rounds, and I haven't seen any missing."

"Donal, you'd better be here stat." She hung up and headed inside to grab her nine iron from the corner by the door.

When she came out, golf club in hand, her son grinned at her. "Mum, Angie looks to be fighting laughter."

"Laugh all you want," she said, "but you haven't seen what sheep can do. They're like walking lawn mowers that don't have an off switch."

"Isn't it kinda bad to hit sheep with a golf club?" Megan asked, coming out of her funk.

"Oh, I don't hit them. I wave it around like a stick, which all the farmers do around here to move them out. Plus, if they get too aggressive, I can poke them a little. The adults weigh a ton and are tough to move. Oh, hell, here they come."

Liam put his arm on the doorframe as the sheep ran up their driveway, a column of wild-eyed bleating weed whackers, some with their young lambs. "Mum, you should just go inside. There's too many of them."

"Donal has never lied to me about his sheep being out," she said, stepping into the yard and raising her club in the air. "This means war."

The sheep in the front suddenly veered to the right, and she spotted the words on their coats. *"Carrick!"*

"His sheep never act like this," Liam said, running up behind her.

She remembered her cousins mentioning they'd met some of Carrick's on the road. "Maybe there's a lunar eclipse or something. Oh, no! They're going for my roses. Stop! You beasts!"

Angie appeared beside her with a seven iron, God bless her. "What can I do?"

"Come on," Betsy said, grabbing her arm and pulling her toward the rose garden. "Station yourself behind the roses and make loud noises while waving your club in the air. We'll try and hold them off. Liam, call Carrick!"

"On the phone, Mum," Liam called from behind her. "He's on his way with his brother."

"At least he's bringing in reserves!" Jamie wasn't in sheep, but he was conversant. They'd need that. There had to be close to thirty of them. "Angie, brace yourself. They look sweet, but when you get between those fuzzy beasts and a meal, it's life or death."

Angie crouched like she was facing off against marauders coming to breach a castle, hands fisted around her club. "I'm too jet-lagged for life and death, Bets."

"That's when the sheep win. Don't let them. All right, you beasts. Back! Back, I say!"

33

"You sound like the officers in *Titanic* when all hell broke loose with the passengers trying to get on boats."

"Remember how that ended," she said, not taking her gaze off the sheep. *"Stop!"*

They froze at her yell.

"Way to go," Angie said, lowering her club like a rookie.

Betsy glared at the sheep. "It's only their first foray. Wait for it."

Like always, the most hungry and intrepid sheep lurched forward, and that's all it took for the others to follow. Herd mentality sucked.

The sweet-faced one in front started nibbling on the first blooms of her cream and coral Gemini hybrid tea roses, while a dark-faced monster ripped off the yellow head of her Julia Child floribunda. *Sorry, Julia.* She heard the revving of trucks thundering up her driveway and looked over. More sheep were scattering as the two vehicles circled them.

Carrick jumped out. "Sorry for this, Bets!"

"Don't be sorry. Just get them in the trailer."

Jamie exited and started to rustle a bag of lamb nuts, but roses were better than sheep food apparently because none of the beasts gave him the time of day.

"Okay, that's enough!" Carrick's yell could have been heard in the next county. "Girls, get in the trailer. I'm not chasing you around. I'm vexed, and I mean business. If you don't want to end up as a lamb roast tomorrow, you will heed me."

The wind rose up, twisting Bets' hair, and then died down. The sheep turned around and stared at Carrick and then started walking toward him. More importantly, they were walking away from her roses.

"Savage," Liam whispered, impressed.

Yes, very cool, Bets had to agree. Their response to him *was* incredible. She lowered her club slowly and gestured for Angie to do the same.

They watched as Carrick and Jamie opened the two trailers and herded the escapees inside. None bleated or tried to make a break for it like the troublesome monsters they were. No, the sheep were almost docile now, and when Carrick slammed both doors shut, a gentle breeze crested across the yard, this time carrying the scent of oranges. Gooseflesh rose on her arms.

"It's like the fairies are at play," Liam whispered.

Betsy had lived long enough in Ireland to believe in just about anything. She'd seen and felt things that had no logical explanation but were real all the same. There was something at work, all right, and as she watched Carrick walk toward her, she couldn't help but notice her cousin's shallow breathing. Angie wasn't that out of shape. And Carrick wasn't looking at Betsy, she realized. He was looking straight at her cousin, almost defiant.

"Heck of a day for you Yanks," he said, stopping on the other side of the roses. "Twice in one day. I apologize."

"What can you do?" Angie said, clearing her throat. "Sheep don't go to obedience school like dogs."

Liam laughed. "They've clearly learned something. Carrick, how in the hell did you do that?"

Jamie came over, ruffling Carrick's dark hair in bemusement. "Yes, brother. Do enlighten us. I've seen you formidable, but that made me think of a pishogue."

"What are those?" Angie asked.

"Pishogues are superstitions," Betsy said, tracking her gaze between her cousin and Carrick.

She felt something tap her shoulder and jumped. Even before she looked back, she knew she wouldn't see anything, and sure enough there was nothing but waving grass. When she turned back around, Carrick was frowning.

Had *he* seen something? Carrick had always seen spirits, like his mother. It was something her husband and her first-born son had in common with him. She smelled oranges again, and then she remembered. Sorcha used to smell of oranges from the special rinse she used in her hair. Gooseflesh prickled again on her arms, and she felt another tap on her shoulder.

Carrick growled deep in his throat. "Maybe the fairies are cross with me. Sorry, Bets."

"But if the fairies were cross, why would they help you get the sheep back in?" Jamie asked. "Ah, I'm talking like our mum. I need a pint. Anyone up for one?"

"It's barely ten in the morning, brother," Carrick said, casting him a dark glance.

"Isn't this Ireland?" Jamie bandied back. "Gavin will open his pub early to hear this tale."

Gavin would indeed, but she rather expected her friends, Gavin included, would show up later to welcome her cousins, which was the Irish way.

Bets waited for Angie's reaction. If her cousin wanted to go, they would go. Something other than the sheep had orchestrated this meeting, and if it was the ghost of Carrick's wife, she wasn't going to interfere. There were Irish tales of dead spouses helping their living mates find love again. It didn't defy belief that it might be happening now.

Of course, if that were the case, it would explain why the house Carrick doggedly worked on, in good and bad weather alike, had gone so wrong. Having lost Bruce, Bets had taken pity on the man when he'd asked to build Sorcha's dream house on her favorite spot on Bets' land before he could pay for the land outright, something he would soon have the money to do. Carrick's family and friends had expressed their concern, of course, but Bets understood wanting to keep busy in a life that suddenly held hours of emptiness. When her Bruce had died, she'd been lost. Carrick had been the same.

But perhaps there was a change in the air...

"I'll take a raincheck on the pint," Angie said, her hands locked around the golf club. "But you go on. I can see us settled if you point us to where we're staying."

She had planned for Angie to stay in the east cottage, but she reconsidered on the spot. "You'll be staying in the cottage right beside where some of Carrick's sheep pasture and the house he's building."

Liam, who'd known the original plan, swung his head in her direction.

Carrick's jaw tightened.

"Oh, good," Angie said unconvincingly. "Seeing your wordy sheep made Megan and Ollie smile for the first time since Tyson died. I was thinking about arranging for more messages with a local sheep farmer before I met you."

"I don't take requests," Carrick said in a more severe tone than Betsy was used to hearing from him.

Jamie shot him a surprised look before shifting his attention to Angie. "We'll leave you to settle in. I'm Jamie, by the way."

"Angie," she said, holding out her hand. "My sister and nephew are in the house."

Betsy looked back, and sure enough, they were both inside, pressed against the glass of the front window. Well, not everyone was easy with sheep.

"My future student." Jamie waved to them. "I'm sorry to hear of their loss. Hopefully my brother's sheep will put together more phrases to make them smile. Come on, brother. Let's leave Bets and Liam to their American relation."

Bleating sounded. Shrubbery rustled. Bets grabbed her nine iron in reflex as three sheep tumbled into the garden. They formed a straight line and headed to the trailer, ignoring her roses completely, thank God.

"Love. Is. Here." Jamie made a thoughtful sound in his throat. "Well, that's certainly a nice message for this happy reunion."

Bets didn't jump this time when someone tapped her shoulder.

Carrick glowered. "Indeed. We'll leave you to it. I'll have new rose bushes for you as soon as I'm able, Bets. I know how much you love to win the fair competition, and everyone in the village is talking about Mary Kincaid going to a new level to beat you this year."

"Don't bother," she said, watching the two men stride away. "Just keep your fencing tight."

Carrick put the three sheep in the back with the others and then opened his car door while his brother did the same. His gaze drifted to Angie for only half a second. "See ya, Yank."

Angie's wave was as tight and rigid as her mouth. So they didn't like each other. Well, that's how she and Bruce had acted in the beginning when he'd become a bartender at the place she was working in Baltimore. She thought of the phrase the last sheep had made in the yard.

Love. Is. Coming.

She smelled oranges again. This time she smiled.

Her cousins' visit was turning into even more of an adventure than Bets had imagined it would be.

After all, who didn't love a good romance?

CHAPTER FOUR

_____

Perhaps Angie should have expected the welcome party.

The Irish were renowned for partying, which was why Cousin Bets fit in so well. Certainly, the three other women who rounded out the Lucky Charms did. Nicola, Brigid, and Siobhan had shown up at Bets' house in what were apparently their signature feather boas—Nicola in canary yellow, Brigid in purple, and Siobhan in tangerine orange. Bets had grabbed her Kelly green one from the coatrack and made the introductions.

Honestly, she was happy for the diversion after Megan's mini meltdown. Her mom hadn't told her Bets was going to suggest separate living arrangements—likely in case Megan declined and became upset. Angie appreciated the gesture, though, and also how easily Bets had adjusted her plans.

Boy, they were a group. Bets and Nicola were the petite ones with short dyed hair—Bets' orangish and Nicola's blond—and bright clothes to match. Brigid and Siobhan loomed tall and nicely round with age, their gray hair a lovely accent to their light coloring and blue eyes.

"You're just in time," Bets said as she led everyone back into the parlor. "We finished a late breakfast and were catching up. I sent Liam into town for some more ice since the freezer is on the fritz again."

Angie's stomach was still stuffed from the full Irish consisting of fried eggs and tomatoes, black pudding, and oatmeal—all of which she'd loved. Ollie hadn't been so sure of the round black circles she'd devoured, and Megan hadn't eaten other than a few bites of oatmeal, per her usual. She didn't imagine this party was going to boost Megan's mood one bit. While Ollie was openly smiling at the women, Megan's smile was as fake as a spray tan. Which was too bad, really, because Angie needed a boost, and these women looked tailor-made to help her.

"We're so happy to have you all here," Nicola said, greeting them with a kind smile. "I run the bookstore in town with my daughter, and we have a small café. The village is glad to have you. It will be a good place for you and your boy to heal, Megan. I've always said we heal in community."

As an art therapist, Angie was of the opinion that it depended on the community, but she liked the notion. *Caisleán. Do your work!*

"They sure got me through Bruce's passing," Bets said, hugging Nicola. "I couldn't imagine what it would have been like without them—and my boys, of course."

"Speaking of..." Nicola continued. "Your boy is lovely, Megan. Hello, Ollie. We're all so excited to have you here."

Megan cuddled Ollie to her side, and he frowned as he tried to pull away. He and Angie shared a knowing look. Megan was babying him again. He'd complained about it before, and Angie was glad he knew he could vent to her.

"He's a bit shy with new people," Megan explained.

Actually, that was Megan, not Ollie, but her nephew restrained another aggrieved look out of politeness.

"My youngest, Kade, was like that," Nicola said, giving Ollie a soft smile before shifting her attention to Angie. "Bets says you'll have us painting like professionals in no time."

Angie made a face. "Gosh, I sure as heck hope so. Otherwise, she might kick me out."

Bets laughed, grabbing her beaded necklace. "Never. Your mother would kill me."

"Well, if you do find yourself wanting a change of scenery, you can stay with Seamus and me anytime," Brigid assured her. "I'd love the company."

"She's newly retired," Bets said, wrapping her arm around the taller woman with the gray hair in tight corkscrews. "Hence why she's taking your painting class."

"I always loved arts and crafts when I was a teacher," Brigid said.

Siobhan fingered her tangerine boa. "You two should sign up for a knitting class at the yarn shop to meet people. Bets and I own it, you know," she told Angie and Megan.

"Megan loves crafts," Angie said. "She used to teach pottery classes." But that had stopped when Tyson told her he didn't want her working, saying he would take care of her. Angie had never much cared for his attitude. Without her art as a method of self-expression, Megan had become even more neutral.

"Maybe you'll be inspired to teach pottery again here, Megan," Siobhan said. "I've always wanted to learn."

"Beats buying an overpriced mug at the agricultural fair," Bets said. "What do you think, Megan? Would you be game for some teaching as well?"

They all looked at Megan, even Ollie, but Angie already

knew the answer. She'd tried to lure Megan back to teaching years ago, after Ollie started school, only to be turned down repeatedly. Besides, her sister still wasn't ready to think about life after Tyson. While she was receiving financial support from the government's death gratuity program, which included a monthly stipend for her and Ollie, surely she would want to do something to pass the time. Ollie was getting older and didn't need her as much—despite how much Megan told him otherwise.

"I'm not in any condition right now," Megan said, drawing in her shoulders as if to disappear.

"Of course!" Siobhan said, rubbing her arm. "We'll dote on you and your boy while you're here. But you might consider taking a class yourself to help with your grief. I know crafts helped me after my mother passed."

"You know, Bets," Brigid said like a good co-conspirator, "maybe you and Siobhan might move your knitting classes over here as part of your new enterprise."

"Bets has become involved in some of the businesses in the village since Bruce passed," Nicola said, fingering her boa, "which is why we know her new idea is going to take off."

Bets gave her friends a look that Angie couldn't interpret. Huh. Their cousin was up to something. "I'm intrigued," she said, lifting her eyebrows. "What do you have cooking?"

"I'll go into it later," Bets said with a wave of her hand. "All you need to focus on is bringing out the inner painter in all of us."

Eyeing these women, she didn't think encouraging their creativity would be a tough assignment. They were wearing boas, for heaven's sake. "I'm sure we're going to do fine."

"Don't worry if you can't bring out the inner painter in

me, dear," Siobhan told her, a smile cresting her round face. "I pick up hobbies all the time. If it doesn't work out, I've plenty of other ways to pass the time."

"Hobbies keep us busy, and busy is good," Bets said. "I still want to learn how to make stained glass."

Angie felt the excitement of creating return, the way she imagined a butterfly would feel after traveling thousands of miles for spring flowers. "I used to love to go by that studio and see all the colored glass pieces. It's an amazing process."

"You can use stained glass in pottery," Megan said suddenly.

Everyone turned to look at her.

"Ah... The glass melts in the kiln and makes compelling patterns."

"I loved those pieces you did!" Angie exclaimed. "Whatever happened to them?"

"They weren't food safe or practical, and we didn't have the room," Megan said, "so Tyson had me give them to Goodwill when we moved into our place."

Angie had to bite her lip. He'd made her give her *art* to Goodwill!

"I didn't know about that technique, Megan," Bets said, making an interested sound in her throat.

"Sounds like you should start dabbling in pottery again, Megan," Siobhan said with a wink. "Nothing better to my mind. I'm a certified dabbler, and Bets is the doer. Then again, she's got the bucks to back up her plans."

"Did I hear you talking about your dabbling all the way in the entry?" a giant gangly man said, coming into the parlor unannounced.

Angie studied him. He had to be six foot seven at least. Tall as a bean pole.

"I had a feeling you were going to show," Bets said.

The man came over and kissed his wife's cheek. "I needed to greet Bets' American relation. Now it seems I must beg them for help. Please, girls, don't be encouraging Siobhan to pick up any more hobbies. I can probably withstand an interest in painting, but that's it."

"Like you have any say, Gavin," Siobhan told him with a swat. "You won't be eating in my house if you keep this up."

"I can eat in me own pub, can't I?" Gavin shook his silver head. "Bets' relations are going to think I'm a proper beast with all your clucking. Let me explain. Girls, this woman—the love of my very own life—can't pass up an opportunity to keep herself occupied. She dabbles in *everything*! The low points were the snail rescuing—"

"Okay, that wasn't my finest moment," Siobhan agreed.

"And what about the mushroom picking?" he continued.

"I told you not to eat those black ones until I'd heard back from my mushroom hookup on whether they were edible," Siobhan said, crossing her arms.

Angie found she was smiling again. Oh, how she liked these people.

"And, girls, don't be asking me about her obsession with making macrame owls and hanging those beasties with giant beady eyes all around the house," the man continued, slapping his forehead. "What a phase! When I got up to take a piss one night, I thought an owl had gotten inside when I wasn't looking, and I ran straight into the door to escape—"

"Knocked himself right out," Siobhan finished with a laugh their group shared.

Angie joined in, aware her laughter muscles were out of practice.

"Look at us telling these tales and without me properly introduced," the man said.

"You were the one who interrupted," Bets said with an eye roll.

"I was only adding my two cents. I'm Gavin McGrath, owner of the Brazen Donkey—the best pub in Caisleán—herself's husband—"

"'Bout time you got to me," Siobhan said with a huff.

He shot them all a playful wink. "Blessed with thirty-five years of wedded bliss."

"It's forty years, ye eejit!" Siobhan said.

Angie laughed again, and she was delighted to hear Ollie join in. Yes, these people were going to be good for them.

"Saints preserve us!" Her husband threw his head back and laughed. "So I forgot a few years. When you're married this long, girls, it's easy to forget a few. Don't you agree?"

Angie remembered every single year she'd wasted on her ex-husband: five stinking whoppers. "I wish I could forget, but then again, I'm divorced." And thirty-five. Sometimes she thought she'd wasted her best years.

He uttered another boisterous laugh. She imagined he was a great pub owner—quick to laugh and encourage others to join him.

"So neither one of you are married currently," he said, his gaze curious. "I seem to recall Bets mentioning that."

"All those blows to the head are finally taking their toll, it seems. You barely recall anything these days," Siobhan said in exasperation.

"Gavin doesn't forget everything. He texted me about the welcome party for Bets' relation," said a tall silver-haired man, entering the parlor with two bottles of whiskey in hand. Liam followed him and held up the dripping bag of ice, making Bets cluck about her rug.

Angie eyed the newcomer. His bearing was regal, what with the way his shoulders rested back and his chest lifted. Hard muscles were evident under his clothing, and from his tanned hands and face, she'd guess he worked outdoors.

"What are we talking about?" he asked.

"The relationship status of Bets' relation," Gavin said, crossing and taking a bottle from him. "You brought the good stuff."

"Of course! Bets' relation deserve a grand welcome. Regarding their status, one is recently widowed. The other is divorced and has what the poets would call a tempestuous affair with love."

Angie couldn't help laughing. "Tempestuous *is* a word for it. In the States I simply call it an affliction of the Wrong Man Syndrome."

"It's happened to the best of us," Siobhan said with a conspiratorial smile before gesturing to Gavin, who made a face in response.

"Not to my wife," said the man with the whiskey. "I'm Killian Donovan, Nicola's man. She's told you she owns the best bookstore in town, hasn't she?"

"It's the only bookstore," the woman said, shaking her head at him.

"Nice to meet you," Angie said, hoping she could remember everyone's names.

"Some days it's nice to meet him," Nicola said, playfully frowning at him when he leaned in for a kiss, which she laughingly dispensed moments later.

"She likes to make me wait for it, just like my horses," Killian said. "I breed them, you see."

After her encounter with the sheep, Angie realized she

was on the path for serious farm talk, so different from what she was used to in the city.

Bets gestured knowingly to the bottle he still held. "Well, I see you brought whiskey, Killian."

"It's customary to bring a bottle, and I brought one for Gavin too. Seamus sends his regards from the butcher shop. He's Brigid's husband, but he's tied to his meat counter right now. I heard you met their two sons today already."

Angie blinked. "We did?"

Brigid folded her hands at her waist, her lips twitching. "Our boys are Carrick and Jamie. Of the troublesome sheep. A rarity, I promise."

"It better be!" Bets gestured to the ceiling. "I have enough problems with Donal. If any sheep prevents me from winning the rose competition, I'll make lamb roasts of them myself."

"I keep expecting to see smoke come out of her ears," Liam said with a laugh.

"Those are your sons?" Angie exclaimed, studying Brigid again for any similar features, and that's when she saw it. He'd gotten his gorgeous thick eyelashes from her. Damn it, there she went again.

No. Men. Ever.

"They are," the older woman said with a smile.

Well, this complicated things, didn't it? Carrick's mom was in her cousin's inner circle, and his land abutted the cottage where they were staying. She could hardly keep away from him, inappropriate attraction or not. "Bets didn't say anything."

"I hadn't gotten to it yet," Bets said, patting her on the shoulder. "But let's circle back to your plans for that whiskey, Killian."

"I'm going to drink some with your relation," the man

said, "and welcome them to Ireland in a time-honored manner."

"Liam, let's be civilized and break out some glasses," Gavin countered, twisting off the top of his bottle. "I'll pour for the girls since I'm the professional in the group."

"*Girls* isn't meant to be an offensive or sexist term, although you'll hear it a lot," Bets told them. "Bruce had to explain it to me."

Angie touched her ear as if posing. "I decided to take it as a compliment to looking youthful."

"Pish, what's this?" Gavin elbowed Killian. "They *are* girls, aren't they? What could be wrong with calling them that?"

They both shrugged incredulously, which only made the Lucky Charms utter aggrieved sighs.

When Liam brought over a tray of whiskey glasses, Gavin filled the first one and handed it to Angie. "To the one who's tortured in love. You're already half Irish. Then you must be the widow."

"Yes," Megan said, clearing her throat.

"I'm sorry for your loss," Gavin said, gazing at her in an earnest way that bolstered Angie's impression that he was a good bartender/confessor.

"We all are," Killian said as the women murmured their agreement. "Losing love tragically at a young age is also Irish. It's like you two were meant to come all along. Here, have a drink."

Megan declined as expected. Angie didn't. The first whiskey gave a nice burn going down, as did the next one. Her body started to unwind, and she found a comfortable seat in the sun on the window seat in Bets' massive front parlor. Megan took Ollie and herself off to the bathroom.

Then someone put on Bon Jovi's "Livin' on a Prayer,"

courtesy of Bets' portable stereo sitting on the biggest side-board Angie had ever laid eyes on.

The Lucky Charms started to hoot and holler, rubbing their boas across their hips and dancing. Gavin and Killian kicked back and crossed their ankles, drinking whiskey with smiles on their faces. Liam left the room, pausing only to wave at Angie.

She swayed to the music, tempted to get up and join them, but they were a unit, and she'd just arrived. Would she be intruding?

No, probably not. Bets would love it.

She was on the verge of getting up when Megan and Ollie walked back in and sat next to her. "Oh, my God," her sister whispered. "It's like throwback ladies' night. Do you think this is how it is every day? I'm not sure this is good for me or Ollie. You may not mind things being wild, but we're grieving."

"It's only a little fun and isn't hurting anyone. Besides, some music might be good for you. I was thinking about joining them."

Megan grabbed her shoulders, making Ollie frown. "What are you thinking? You just got here. These are some of your future students. Business owners. You want them to respect you. Be smart, Angie."

She bit her lip as her sister's chiding stirred up feelings of anger. Why shouldn't she dance a little and enjoy life? Her sister needed to loosen up. For goodness' sake, Megan wouldn't let her listen to anything other than family-friendly playlists on Spotify when Ollie was around. It wasn't like she listened to anything filthy. She didn't like being told what she could and couldn't do in her own home. Annoyed, but not enough to defy Megan for the sake of it, she munched on the chocolate chip cookies Bets had made and tried not to be upset as she watched the older women have fun.

They were still dancing to Bon Jovi ten songs later, God love them.

Liam, who'd been in and out for the whole performance, reappeared and sat down beside Angie. "Mum and the Lucky Charms do love their Bon Jovi."

"Why Bon Jovi?" she asked.

"Mum said she thought she might kill herself if she had to hear another group of people sing 'It's My Life' when she worked at the bar back in the day, so she forced herself to listen to Bon Jovi for her entire day off. Dad swears she lost some marbles in the process. But after that trial by fire, Mum embraced Bon Jovi like a best friend. Her way of turning lemons into lemonade. She would dance her heart out and sing it at the top of her lungs. Always said she made a lot of tips that way."

"I'll bet," Angie said, wishing she could have seen Bets in action as a bartender. She'd been too young back then. But if this impromptu welcome party was any indication, it had been a hell of a good time.

"Wanted Dead or Alive" started to play, and Liam winced. "You've probably noticed that I keep retreating to the kitchen. Breaks are mandatory if you want to keep your head. Even with all my meditation training, it drives me a little batty."

"That would explain your long and frequent absences," she teased, bumping him. "I knew you weren't simply going back there to get us more water to chase the whiskey."

"I've appreciated it," Megan said, patting down an errant bang. "I'm so dehydrated from the plane ride. I thought about putting in the earplugs the flight attendant gave me, but I didn't want to be rude. Ollie's like his dad. He can sleep through anything."

He'd fallen asleep midway through the dancing. Megan stroked his hair, her face alight with that angelic motherly smile Angie hoped to capture one day.

Truthfully, she wished her sister would look at her with such uncomplicated affection. When they were little kids, Megan always used to tag along with her. They'd find seashells or build sandcastles. But growing up hadn't been good on their relationship. For a time, art had been a bond, even though their styles were completely different, with Megan being so careful and controlled, other than in those pieces with the glass, and Angie embracing a more Fauvist ideal. They'd driven to local art fairs together and helped each other set up their booths.

But when Tyson told Megan to stop doing ceramics, that bond had shriveled. Now all they had as a bond was Ollie and the fleeting hope of enjoying each other again. Or at least Angie hoped. It had been one of the reasons she'd suggested they move in with her. With Ollie at school, she'd hoped that she and Megan could perhaps comfort each other by spending quality time together, especially after Angie's boyfriend left and she lost her job. But Megan had only lain around, awash in depression. The status of their relationship made her sad. Ollie was a shared bright spot, though, and she never forgot that.

"Got a spare pair of earplugs for me?" Liam gave a mischievous smile.

"You can have mine," Angie said, shaking off her stupor. Her cousin was great—kind and a little soulful. Also, he looked like a pirate with his gold earring. It made her miss her gold belly ring, but her belly wasn't the same as it had been.

"Gavin and Killian don't seem to mind the music, incredibly enough," Megan said.

Angie looked over at the two men. "They look engrossed in whatever they're talking about." While they still glanced over at the women from time to time, they weren't staring at their wives like they had in the beginning.

"They're pros at tuning the music out over a long night, Gavin especially, from being at the pub. Unless the girls get devilish and play the song to end all songs, as the men are fond of saying, then all bets are off."

"Which one is *that*?" Angie asked.

"You'll know it when you hear it," Liam said, pulling on his gold earring with a grimace. "I won't ruin the fun. Maybe the men will get up to some good fun and play *their* song to end all songs. I didn't understand the byplay as a kid, but I do now. Oh, Gavin is gesturing for another round. Be right back."

After serving them, Liam returned with the bottle and held it out to pour. Angie didn't want to turn down good hospitality, but she was getting tired. Of course, it had been a long lunch hour after a long breakfast—post the crazy sheep incident Angie still hadn't processed—and this was her third whiskey. Bets' gold Victorian couch was calling to her.

"You Give Love a Bad Name" started to play, and Gavin and Killian rose to their feet and started booing as their wives sashayed over and playfully hit them with their boas.

"Oh, my, that's..." Megan trailed off.

Her sister meant scandalous, likely. Angie disagreed. The love and attraction between the two couples was obvious, and Angie found herself wondering, again, what that must be like.

Suddenly she was thinking about Carrick and the wonderful relationship he must have had with his wife. They must have loved each other very much for him to still be putting the words from her poems on his sheep. That kind of passion and commitment was foreign to her.

Stop thinking about him, Angie.

Really, she should be glad Bets and his mother hadn't talked about him more. The last thing she needed was to have more information about him. Actually, maybe he'd be less compelling and mysterious if she had details. A mother would know all of his flaws. Maybe he'd been a compulsive bed wetter or liked to tip cows. They had a lot of cows in Ireland, right? What else did kids do out here in the wilds of County Mayo?

"Angie!" Siobhan slapped away Gavin's hands when he tried to put them on her waist and dance with her. "What are you going to paint first now that you're here?"

Bets cut the music, and the parlor went silent. Everyone turned and looked at her. Their change in focus was so sudden, so intense, that Angie froze, her palms starting to sweat.

Carrick's tall, rugged form rose in her mind. So much for her no man mantra and attempt to drown her interest in chocolate. The urge to sketch him returned. Fire burned her fingertips, banishing the sweat, and she rubbed them together, longing for a paintbrush.

He could *not* be her subject. No way. No how.

"The fields!" she exclaimed in a good save. "They're golden in a way I've never seen before." And they were, by God!

"That's Ireland for you," Killian said. "Sometimes I go out to check on my horses, and I'd swear they're standing on a field of gold coins instead of sweetgrass."

"I can't wait to see it when you're finished," Brigid said. "Bets showed us some of your paintings. You're so talented."

"She used to be," her sister said out of nowhere. "We're hoping she can get it back after everything that's gone on these past few years. Right, Angie?"

Megan put her arm around her, as if in commiseration, and Angie dug her fingernails into her palms. She wanted to shove her away but didn't.

"You'll have to do a show when you have enough paintings," Nicola said, nodding enthusiastically.

"I already have the perfect spot in mind, plus a strategy for launching it," Bets said, her face suddenly glowing. "How about we show your masterpieces the same weekend as the Caisleán's agricultural show in August? That's over two months from now. Should be plenty of time. About thirty thousand people come from all over Ireland. There's always an arts and crafts bazaar, but some might like to buy paintings from a more serious artist. It would be a great time to introduce you to new patrons, make some money, and advertise our new art studio as you teach here."

"That's a great idea!" Siobhan said as others murmured their agreement. "Our village can sponsor you."

"You can show your paintings in my bookshop," Nicola said. "We have a prime location in town, and lots of visitors will come through that day as we have the best coffee."

Brigid clapped. "We can advertise your art show all over town and in the newspaper. People can pop by on their way to and from the campground. Oh, this is a great idea!"

Angie's hands grew clammy. An entire show sponsored by the village? Thirty thousand people? Dear God. That would mean producing a lot of paintings. Really, really good ones. She hadn't even done sucky ones in longer than she cared to remember.

Her blood pressure flew sky high as her heart rate kicked up. There was no way she could pull this off.

She turned and stared at her sister, who had a pitying look on her face.

Poor Angie, she could hear her sister think.

Pain shot through her chest. Was she going to keep letting fear run her life or was she going to make a stand and get her voice back? She wanted that for her sister... Didn't she want it for herself?

"All right," she said, standing up, feeling almost sick. "I'll do it."

CHAPTER FIVE

His brother's arrival at his cottage didn't come as a surprise.

Even though Jamie was younger, he'd always acted like a mother hen. That trait made him an excellent teacher, but it was also annoying as hell.

Carrick kicked out his feet, playfully threatening to trip up his brother, who only stepped around them, dripping from the cold rain falling outside. "Came to cluck at me, did you?"

"You weren't working at the house, so I swung by here." His brother dropped into a chair in the front parlor, stretching out his long legs. "I came to ask if the orange scent in the air when your sheep overran Bets' place was Sorcha? If you'd hung around after I helped—"

"Thanks again," he said, tipping his glass of whiskey in his brother's direction.

"I would have asked you earlier," Jamie finished, rising and grabbing himself a glass. "If we aren't going to the pub like I wanted to earlier—"

"We aren't." The village would be buzzing with news of

Bets' relation—the sexy Yank who'd wielded a golf club—as much as the rare breakout of his sheep. "I thought I'd have a touch of supper and then head off to work on the house. Want to come along?"

He should have gone earlier today, after the incident with the sheep, but he'd struggled to muster the energy after Sorcha said she didn't want him to keep building it. Just like everyone else around him.

"Not especially, no," Jamie said, pouring himself a drink. "The pub will be more entertaining than watching you struggle with that disaster. Donal O'Dwyer will be spouting off about having your head for Bets blaming him over this morning. I might have to buy him a pint for you by way of an apology."

Carrick dug some bills out of his pocket and threw them on the table. "Tell him it's on me. Although it's an easy mistake given how poorly his sheep have been behaving. There's something downright crazy about how many times they've been up at Bets' these past months. If I didn't know better, I'd say someone else was afoot."

"Speaking of... You didn't answer me, brother. Was that Sorcha's scent today?"

He tensed as his dead wife appeared in the doorway to the kitchen she'd so hated, a downright tempestuous smirk on her face, before disappearing again. That was not going to do.

"She did! I can see it from the look of you." Jamie downed his whiskey and poured another. "Oh, Jesus. She's here about the Yank who wielded Bets' seven iron, isn't she? I saw the way you looked at her despite how rude you were." He made a face. "Oh, for fuck's sake. I smell oranges again. I hate knowing someone's there and not knowing where exactly. Not that I want to see them. I don't envy you and Mum with the dead always popping up and appearing around you. Gives me the shivers."

Sorcha's laughter trailed into the room, and Carrick stared into his glass. "Shiver away then. I might as well tell you so you'll stop pestering me. Yes, I've seen Sorcha today—"

"But it's been nearly three years since the last time!" Jamie said, looking right and left. "Where is she?"

"I saw her in the kitchen doorway a moment ago," he said, putting his glass down. There wasn't enough whiskey in Ireland tonight, as far as he was concerned. On second thought, he couldn't wait to pound some nails.

"I'm still not sure if seeing ghosts is a blessing or a curse. Leaning toward the latter."

"Me too." He shoved the bottle toward his brother, whose face had turned green. "Don't lose your dinner."

"I've a stronger stomach than that," Jamie said, putting a hand to his unruly mop of brown hair. "So... Sorcha's back to push you toward the Yank. I must say, she was quite the woman, fending off your sheep with Bets."

He hadn't been able to dismiss the image of her waving that seven iron at his sheep. Her cheeks had turned an inviting pink with the exertion, and her clothes hadn't looked as baggy with her arms in the air. "She's Bets' relation."

"Off-limits." Jamie whistled. "Mum would kill you if you broke Bets' cousin's heart, you know. From all accounts, she and her sister have had a hard time."

The strain and grief were evident. The poor boy had looked whipped when the subject of loss had come up. He knew how horrible losing Sorcha had been, but he'd been an adult. What must it be like for a young boy? "I know it and have sympathy. The little lad—"

"Ollie," Jamie answered. "He'll be in my class, remember?"

He nodded. "There is no one better to teach him or any other child than you. Who else has the patience of Job?"

"Certainly not you," Jamie said, making a face. "Given your propensity for impatience—"

"It's called drive."

"Synonyms," Jamie said with a flick of a hand. "What I was trying to say, *nicely*, is that you're completely thick-headed about most things. Building that house for one."

Something crashed in the kitchen as if to punctuate his brother's point. Jamie flinched, glancing over at the kitchen with wide eyes. "I take it Sorcha agrees with me. The message on the three sheep who tumbled into the yard at the end said *Love. Is. Here.* Hard to ignore that. I expect it was by her hand."

"It was," he admitted crossly.

"What do you plan to do?"

His dead wife appeared in the doorway, arms crossed, as if waiting to hear his answer.

"It's like I told her earlier before she called the wind and blew the gate wide open to stir up the sheep," he said, giving Sorcha a look. "I'm not doing *anything*. The Yank—"

"Angie."

"Is Bets' cousin and off-limits. I plan to ignore her. From the way she tried to raise up the window in the car just after we met, she seems to be of the same mind." As he'd seen to his sheep this afternoon, he'd found himself laughing at the memory of the sisters grappling over the window.

"You can't ignore her, Carrick." Jamie put his hands on the wooden table as if he were explaining a difficult math problem to a slow student. "First off, she's Bets' relation. That would be rude and unlike you. Everyone in the village would think you two either had a tiff or like each other."

He growled. "Everyone needs to mind their own goddamn business."

"Plus, Mum would kill you." Jamie's mouth twitched. "Angie will be her painting teacher, and she's hot to trot about finding a creative hobby now that she's retired."

"Why can't she take up one of Siobhan's dozens of hobbies?"

"How the hell should I know what goes through Mum's head? Dad suggested she take up golf to spend time with him on the weekends when he's not at the shop. Do you know what she said?"

"I can imagine," Carrick said with a smile. His parents had a colorful way of communicating.

"She didn't care to spend an entire day hitting a man's *balls* for entertainment." Jamie crossed his hands over his man parts. "Imagine that! Dad said he'd never invite her again."

"Good for Dad. Back to the Yank. If I can't ignore her, I'll just have to treat her like a sister."

There was a long pause, and then they both started laughing. God, it felt good.

"A sister," his brother said, dragging his chair closer and whacking him on the shoulder. "That's a good one. And maybe angels will fly out of your arse."

That old turn of phrase only propelled them into more laughter, and by the end, they were snorting and wiping tears. "I've always thought it would be uncomfortable, having an angel fly out of my arse. God, help us, Jamie. Then I guess I'll have to have a word with her. Tell her I like her, but she's Bets' cousin and all that. Be direct with her."

"Yanks *are* direct," Jamie said cautiously, casting a look toward the kitchen.

"She's not there anymore," Carrick said, saddened he felt some relief at her absence. Seeing her was like having salt ground into a wound. It made him finally face the truth —what they'd had was gone forever. As he'd walked the fields with the sun shining on his back today, he'd admitted that to himself.

Even so, he intended to finish the house. He was already in so deep, and besides, he could use a newer, bigger home. He was tired of killing spiders in this tiny cottage wrecked with the damp. Dammit if he wouldn't enjoy a subzero refrigerator himself. He knew the village was laughing at him, but by God, Fitzgerald's Folly was going to be the best house in the area when he was done with it.

Jamie still scanned the room. "I expect Sorcha will be back if she's thinking Angie might be the one for you, right?"

"Probably." He hung his head, feeling the weight of his emotions. "It was hard to see her. Talk to her. Smell her. God, even the glare she gave me grabbed my heart and made it swell in my chest. But she's gone, Jamie. I can't touch her. I can't lie with her. She's only here to resolve her own guilt about dying on me. I realized that today."

Jamie's hand fell on his shoulder, a comforting weight. "She wants you to find love again. Have a family. We all do, Carrick. Maybe it's a blessing that you've accepted what you had with her is gone."

He could never look at it so. "It's merely a fact, one I'd be stupid to fight against. But I'm not changing my vow about never loving another woman. Jamie, I told you when she died that I wouldn't go through that kind of pain again."

"Even if you could have decades of happiness with someone else?" Jamie asked, studying him.

"This is old territory, and my answer remains the same. No person should ever have to grieve like that but once. Even Mum, in all her wisdom, doesn't understand. She and Dad have had each other for decades."

Jamie's heartfelt sigh filled the room and he patted Carrick's shoulder before removing his hand. "I can't say I understand either, not having loved a woman like that yet. If you're certain you won't change your mind, I think you're right to talk to Angie. Be clear about things."

Another loud crash sounded in the kitchen. Jamie cried out, and Carrick tensed as Sorcha materialized next to his chair.

"I smell oranges," Jamie said, looking pale again. "Is she back?"

"I am," Sorcha said even though his brother couldn't hear her. "You tell your brother I will haunt him to his dying day unless he helps you find love again."

He narrowed his eyes at her before turning to Jamie. "Sorcha says you look well, but you should pick up my bar tab more often at the pub."

"She did not!" Jamie said at the same time Sorcha crossed her arms, her eyes flat.

"Your thickheadedness will only encourage me to call in more help, Carrick." Her white dress billowed even though there was no wind. "Bets smelled my orange scent today after I tapped her shoulder, and I was pleased she put the Yank in the cottage by your sheep. I can visit your mother too. Or your friend Kade. He'd listen to me, I'm sure. Fair warning."

She disappeared before he could give her a firm talking

to. Terrific. This was just like her, trying to fence him in. Well, he was having none of it.

"Your face is thunderous," Jamie said, pouring them both another drink. "What did she say this time?"

"She's going to have other people cluck at me. She mentioned Mum, Kade, and Bets. The Lucky Charms getting involved wouldn't go well for me." Kade, he could handle.

"Kade will be on your side, but you might as well pack up your belongings and leave town if you plan on crossing them. I'd miss you, brother."

"And I'd miss you," Carrick said. "Most days."

Jamie snorted. They knocked their glasses together and downed the whiskey in one shot.

"You'd best clear the air with Angie fast."

He poured them another drink and felt the urge to work on the house slipping away. Suddenly he was tired of it all. His pillow called to him. A good night's rest had always enlivened him. "I'll find her first thing tomorrow."

Surely two people agreeing to be friendly and not act on an attraction would stop a ghost and the Lucky Charms in their tracks. Yes, that was the way of it.

When he heard amused laughter coming from the kitchen, he got the shivers himself.

CHAPTER SIX

—————

A ngie stared at the golden light seeping into her room when she awoke the next morning. Dawn. Her favorite time to paint. "It's now or never," she muttered to herself and rolled out of bed.

She pulled back the cream curtains in her room and sagged in utter bliss as the view rolled over her. A soft white fog covered the verdant pastureland, while billowing clouds danced across an open sky bursting with Persian rose, cerulean blue, and coral pink. The rain had stopped, but everything shone with dew. Sheep were grazing on the chromium green hills, the fog swirling around their feet, making them appear almost like mythical creatures from another place.

"*Wow*," she breathed out.

Here be good. Just like the sheep had said yesterday.

Carrick rose in her mind. She tried to banish him, but his thick dark hair seemed to billow in the image as his Payne's grey eyes locked on her. She tingled all over, dammit.

None of that, Angie.

Yanking open the window, she put her hand out to judge the temperature as much as cool off. Refreshingly glorious, she concluded. Irish weather was notoriously changeable, and Cousin Bets had told them dressing in layers was the key to being prepared for whatever weather one encountered. May had been mostly gray and cold, apparently, which was why the sheep hadn't been sheared yet. They'd gotten lucky, seeing those words on Carrick's sheep. She longed to see them again, but they were too far off for the writing to be deciphered from the cottage.

Angie pulled open a drawer in the dresser. She'd filled it with her things yesterday. Bets and Liam had shown them the basics in the small but quaint cottage and left them to settle in. It would have been nice to have more space, but Megan clearly wasn't ready to be on her own.

Her sister had shut herself in her room upon arrival, and Angie had helped Ollie unpack and made him dinner. They'd had an early evening, although they'd had to wait fifteen minutes for the water to heat up in the bathroom. Their shower had an immersion heater, something all too common in Ireland, Bets had said. Clean and showered finally, she and her nephew had been asleep by seven. Man, she'd slept hard, but she was refreshed.

Two months.

She had two months to get herself in gear and have enough paintings to do a gallery show in early August. She'd pulled a show together in less than a month, so it wasn't completely out of the question.

Of course, she'd had her voice then. It had been years since she'd produced anything she was proud of. *Years.*

Her solar plexus tightened, and she couldn't breathe. Nothing like the twin feelings of terror and pressure to shove her out of her funk.

She was here to turn her life around, and it started now. Good thing she was prepared to reconnect with the Angie she used to be, the one who could paint a gallery-worthy painting in three to seven days and sell it for five thousand dollars.

In high school she'd read in *The Baltimore Sun* that some Orioles baseball players wore the same underwear when they were on a winning streak. She'd created her own painting outfit along those lines in college, and it had rocked her world. So she'd decided to recreate it before leaving for Ireland, something that had required her to buy her first pair of jeans since she'd stopped fitting into her size sixes. But it was time to start letting pieces of frumpy Angie to go, and this was part of it.

Purchasing a pair in a larger size had been tough. She couldn't dance around the truth anymore. She'd gained a lot of weight since meeting her ex-husband, Randall, and she and her doctor had agreed that she needed to lose some of it because of her elevated blood pressure.

But Angie wanted more than that. She wanted to look in the mirror and like herself again. Feel sexy again.

She hoped washing her new jeans twenty times to make them soft like the ones she used to wear would help remind her of those days as much as the iron-on patches she'd transferred from her old ones. Creative Angie had rocked that single red rose on her right thigh as much as the winding flower tree trailing up her left leg, the theme working with her burgundy jacket from Florence embroidered with yellow flowers on the back, which she could throw over a comfy T-shirt. She didn't believe in painting in boring things. Her paint splatters added magic to her clothes and very self.

She tugged on her jeans, reminding herself to take it one

step at a time. The roads here would be great for walking, and she didn't think her brain would tell her it was exercise. Liam had mentioned bike riding, and back in the day, Angie had loved to bike through the French and Italian countryside.

When she left her small bedroom, she clipped her hair up and listened for sounds that would indicate anyone else was awake. Ollie was in the loft, which was more an attic with small skylights, only accessible by a ladder. Megan had taken the front room under him. Angie had the room by the one bathroom and kitchen at the back of the house. Never say Irish cottages were large, she'd decided yesterday. The kitchen had a half-fridge like she'd had in her college dorm and only a few shelves, so she was grateful Bets and Liam had offered to buy their groceries. Otherwise, she'd be shopping every few days! Then there was the parlor, which doubled as a dining room. It boasted a tiny wicker settee along with a small table tucked against the wall with benches.

But the white concrete walls were charming, she supposed, decorated with family pictures and a few pastoral paintings from local artists. The pot-bellied stove in the parlor made her think of *Little House on the Prairie.*

She turned on the tea kettle to make herself a cup and plopped a Lyons tea bag in her trusty aluminum travel cup. Striding over to the small portable stool she'd acquired from the main house, she grabbed her painting bag. She'd bought the woven bag at the market in Aix-en-Provence in college, and it bore oil paint smudges in turquoise, phthalo green, and burnt umber, which warmed her heart as she stroked them.

"I'm going to paint today," she told herself in an almost shy but excited little whisper.

Then she thought about Ollie. Who was going to get him breakfast? Megan hadn't made a meal since Tyson had died. Would today be a good chance to shake up their routine? Something had to give. She hadn't thought her arrangement with Megan would go on so long, or that Megan would stay this depressed—the grief as heavy as it had been immediately after she heard the news. They'd discussed antidepressants, but her sister said they made her even lower. She'd tried them before. When Tyson had gone on his first mission.

Angie struggled not to feel guilty for wanting things to change. She knew her sister was going through a lot, but so was she, and they all needed to dig their way out of this. Well, Ollie would find her if he was hungry. He had the granola bar stash she'd bought for him, and she'd pick up some cereal later. Obviously not Lucky Charms. That had been a great story.

Jesus, Angie, you're procrastinating. Are you painting or what?

"Yes," she said out loud. "I sure as hell am. *Focus. Ignite. Create.* Do it!"

Bets would give her a tour today, and Angie couldn't wait to see the easels and other equipment she'd selected online set up in the former shed turned studio. Teaching was as much second nature to her as was management.

More irony. Before, painting had been like breathing, and teaching and management hadn't interested her whatsoever. Then Randall had talked her into taking that initial teaching job at the visual arts center, saying it would help her grow as an artist.

She'd trusted him in that, too. He was her husband, after all. She'd thought he'd said it out of love. In hindsight, though, she realized Randall had been jealous of her success. Having her teach was his way of sidelining her.

At the beginning of their marriage, his paintings had made more money, but hers had quickly gained worth in the first two years. A memory flashed into her mind. "You can paint in your spare time, sweetie," he'd said as he frowned at his current canvas.

But that hadn't happened after she started teaching—which, yes, she was great at—and by the time she was promoted to director, she hadn't painted other than in demos in over a year.

Idiot.

His creative fire had guttered out too, and they'd both retreated into themselves. Spent less time together. He went out drinking and smoking and doing God knows what else while she taught her night classes. They made love less. Fought more. She gained weight from all the extra eating she did. He grew more sullen. Got high to "help his creativity," which she hated.

When he blamed her for silencing his artistry, his vision, and said he couldn't understand how he'd ever loved her or found her attractive, she'd been decimated. Hadn't she given up everything to help and encourage him as a person and an artist?

It hadn't taken her long to find someone else who'd claimed to support her art. Her two-year relationship with the charismatic corporate lawyer she'd taught in a painting class, Saul, had seemed so promising in the beginning. He'd thought her good enough to teach at the Smithsonian and had promised to introduce her to the right people.

In the end, he'd been in love with the idea of having a girlfriend in the arts, someone he could brag about to his clients at galleries and Smithsonian events in Washington,

D.C. He'd liked the way she dressed and how professional she came across, a boon to her rock-bottom self-esteem. He'd also expected her to paint, apparently, and when her inspiration failed to return, he'd left her.

Angie had made a lot of mistakes. She knew that. She'd changed herself to suit them, eager for love and the security of a relationship and a home. When she was young, her mother had told her that taking care of people made them need and like you, and her mother's life had seemed to bear that out. To this day, her mom received tear-jerking thank you notes and presents from patients and their families. It wasn't surprising Angie had fallen into the trap of believing her.

But love wasn't like nursing. Or at least it shouldn't be. In the end, when her exes hadn't wanted or needed her caretaking anymore, she'd been left with nothing.

That was over, she told herself as she left the cottage and wandered across the property. Trees lined the yard where the drive to the manor lay, some festooned with brilliant white flowers. It was like being surrounded by a magical forest. As she walked to the back, a wide expanse opened before her. This was the view from her bedroom. But now she could see a beautiful three-story white house on the hill above the pasture off to the left. Oh, what views it would have.

She assessed her own view before settling on a tall, windy sycamore tree at the edge of the pasture where Carrick's sheep grazed. She would paint that! She and trees had always had a good relationship, going back to her tree climbing days as a kid. She headed off, feeling a gentle wind caress her face. Goodness, the air smelled sweet. There was something almost citrusy about it.

She wouldn't care that these were Carrick's sheep. In

fact, she planned to enjoy the messages. God, she still couldn't believe his mom was one of the Lucky Charms. They would be running into each other all the time.

But not at dawn. This was her time.

Before going to bed, she'd given herself a talking-to about her attraction to Carrick. It meant nothing—she'd been caught up in the moment was all. She was in Ireland! Then there was the light and the countryside and those messages. If she'd met his brother Jamie on the road before him, she'd have been drawn to him instead.

She had nothing to worry about.

A few sheep trotted over as she reached the fence line and then turned sideways to show their words. *Light. Brings. Change.*

"Holy shit." She blinked in shock. "That's a little eerie. Okay, Universe, or whatever I'm supposed to call you... I might start actually believing there's something out there again if you keep this up."

The sheep bleated and turned around, their white faces regarding her while they chewed. A curious lamb came to the fence, its small head peeking between the slats. How adorable!

She set her stool down, feeling alive in a way she hadn't in forever. "What am I supposed to say to sheep? Good morning?"

One bleated, her dark black eyes staring at Angie, while the other two lowered their heads to tear at the thick grass.

"Great! Now I'm talking to sheep."

Setting herself up didn't take long. She plopped herself on the stool and pulled out one of her mid-size Arches paint pads. If any of her students knew their stuff, she'd have to explain that, yes, she used watercolor paper because she loved them for acrylics when she was painting *plein air*.

Her fold-up stepping stool from home doubled as a small table, and she laid out her travel-size acrylic paint kit and brushes. She unscrewed the lid of the small mason jar she'd filled with water yesterday, and *voila*, she was ready to reclaim her artistic brilliance. God, it felt good!

She studied the tree, taking in the finer details she needed to bring it to life. The thick trunk. The way it leaned slightly to the right. Taking a deep breath, she told her imagination to roam.

It didn't move.

She picked up her medium Golden Taklon paintbrush, hoping it would fire up her senses.

Nothing.

She feathered her fingertips with the bristles. This tree... What was it saying? What did it represent *to her*?

"I'm talking to myself like I'm one of my students," she said to the sheep, who chewed thoughtfully as they stared at her. "I need to just paint."

Looking back at the sycamore, she followed the body of the tree up, noting the thick branches, some covered in moss. Good, moss was green. Moss represented...

What exactly? She strained for the story she was supposed to draw, the passion, the drama.

Her mind didn't see anything but a tree.

"Shit."

Her imagination was still gone.

"Don't panic, Angie," she told herself, grabbing her tea and taking a desperate sip. "Oh, Jesus, that's strong. Note to self. Don't leave this tea bag in."

She set aside the tea with a pursed mouth, wishing she'd brought a bottle of water. Next time. Or hell, maybe she should start bringing a glass of wine with her like she used to when she'd painted in France and Italy. The first time one of her fellow artists had pulled a wine bottle and glasses out of his painting bag, she'd dubbed him a genius.

She snorted to herself. Megan would love that. Her sister didn't even want her to dance to Bon Jovi in their cousin's house.

"It's not that I'm an alcoholic. It's Ireland." She met the gaze of a munching sheep. "Don't people drink a lot here?"

"They do, Yank," a male voice said. "Most start at dawn, in fact."

She closed her eyes. *You have got to be kidding.*

She looked over her shoulder as he strode toward her...

Oh, Jesus, how did anyone roll out of bed looking like *that*? His vine black hair looked tousled from the wind, and his jaw sported a five-o'clock shadow like he hadn't shaved. God, her fingertips wanted to stroke the manly texture of his jaw as she fell into his slumberous Payne's grey eyes. *No!*

She gave herself a shake and reached for a paintbrush so she'd have something in her hands. "I figured you'd be milking cows or something this morning, Carrick."

His snort made a sheep bleat. "I'm in sheep. Not cattle. I start my rounds at dawn. I thought you'd be asleep."

So he hadn't meant to come upon her either. Good. He hadn't seemed happy about seeing her at Cousin Bets' place from the way he'd glowered at her before leaving. "I do my best painting at this hour. Which is why I didn't hear you coming."

He walked around her until he could look over her shoulder. "I can see that. A modern painting, eh? Minimalist. White only."

She swiveled on her stool to gaze up at him as the sheep trotted off. My God, he was tall and big. "You sound like you know art."

Oh, please don't let him.

"I've been to some art shows and museums and the like here and in Europe," he said, his eyes locking on hers. "I like art. I admit I was curious about you when Bets told the village you were coming. She showed us some of your paintings on her phone at the pub. You're good."

Pain shot through her chest. "I *was* good. I'm trying to get it back. I thought this tree might help."

He gazed at the tree, his profile capturing her attention. Her mind snapped the image. Aquiline nose. Square jaw touched with stubble. Thick neck. Full lips. God, she would need bold strokes to capture his essence.

"I was rather surprised to see you out by this particular tree. My wife used to come here to write her poems."

"I'm so sorry. Am I intruding? I can leave if it bothers you."

He didn't look at her, only kept gazing straight ahead. "It's Bets' land, and you picked a good spot according to Sorcha. In fact, you can see this tree from the house I'm building on that rise over there."

That was his house? My God, could she get any closer to him? "I was thinking it must have wonderful views."

"It does," he said, "and should give me the same when I finish it. I've been working on it a few years now."

"Your wife would have loved the view of this tree, I imagine."

"Yes, I asked Bets for permission to build on the land for that very reason," he said with a sigh. "Sorcha said the tree spoke to her. That the trunk looked like enormous hands clawing their way through the grass while the body of the tree leaned to the right as if it had been moved by a giant from times long past."

Suddenly Angie could see the fingers clawing their way

through the grass. She shivered. "Your wife's poetry must be very good."

He made a sound in his throat. "'Tis. What sheep message did you get today, or was it a garble of words that made no sense?"

He almost sounded hopeful of the latter. "No, it made sense all right." She closed her pad and set it aside, resting her elbows on her knees. "*Light brings change.* As a painter, we're all about the light."

He moved away from her. One of the sheep trotted over, bleating loudly, and he rested his foot on the low rung of the fence and petted it. She couldn't read the word on it from this angle.

"I thought about you last night," he said, surprising her.

"You what?"

"Let me finish." His glare was effective. "And since you're Bets' cousin—and a Yank, likely as direct as the rest I've met—I've decided to be frank about it."

She let out a slow breath. "That sounds ominous."

"Not ominous, I'd say. A storm as black as pitch over the land is ominous. You see one of those, find shelter. Right away. Don't tarry."

His accent was as crazy sexy as his directives. "Thanks for the tip. Ah... Should I remain sitting, or do we face each other while you get all direct with me?"

"You have a mouth on you," he said with some amusement. "I expect you have fire too, from the way you wielded that seven iron at my sheep."

Yesterday, he'd said she'd brought the sunshine. Today it was fire. This was good news. These past few years she'd felt tepid, beige, and disinteresting. Maybe her mantra—*Focus, Ignite, Create*—was working.

Then he leaned back against the fence. The sight of his

tall, rugged body in a green jacket, worn jeans, and black wellies made her mouth water. His sleepy eyes had her heart rate kicking up.

She couldn't allow it. "Well! Go on. Be direct. Only be prepared for me to do the same. About whatever this is."

He continued his lazy perusal with his smoky gray eyes. "What *are* you looking at?"

"You." He came forward again, his hands on his hips. "You look different than yesterday."

It was the outfit! Part of her wanted to cheer. "I'd just gotten off a plane and driven three hours. Give a girl some credit."

His mouth tipped up. "I do. More than I want to. But you're Bets' cousin, and even if me and my body have taken a liking to you, I want to tell you straight off nothing can come of it."

The way he said *me and my body* had her girl parts tightening in the most delicious way. God, that hadn't happened for a while. She decided to enjoy it as much as his compliments.

"Did you hear me?" He frowned at her. "I thought it best to lay it out. Should you be thinking that way at all. Avoid any misunderstandings."

The wind rose up at her back as she took a moment to form a response. He'd admitted any entanglement between them was off-limits. This was good. "Being direct works for me. You don't need to worry. You're still in love with your wife. I wouldn't mess with that for a million dollars. Well, I might for a million. I need to make money. Oh, never mind."

He rubbed his jaw in a very appealing way before saying, "Usually I'd be amenable to having a good time together. An occasional dinner or drink at the pub. Some sightseeing. Some quiet time alone."

"Is that an Irish way of describing something basic? Sounds like friends with benefits to me."

"Or simple fucking." He shook his head ruefully. "That's another word for it. Seems I was right about being direct with you."

"Yes, you were." She stood up at last. "Let me be equally direct. I might find you attractive, but I'm here to paint. Find my voice again. Men and 'spending time together' are how I got into this place. My canvas isn't mini-malistic. It's blank."

His mouth twisted. "I know you've had troubles, Yank. I hope you get your voice back. With an artist for a wife, I understand artistic temperaments as much as I do the need to create. It fills some part of you, like my animals and land do for me."

She could tell he meant it. That he really *did* under-stand. That was a surprise, somehow, but then again, the morning had been full of them. "I'm glad we're clear then. We can be friends. With no fucking. It's better than my other plan. I was going to avoid you."

"I'd thought about that too, but it's a small village. I like Bets and Liam, and my mum would kill me."

"She's a Lucky Charm."

"She is. I wouldn't be rude to Bets or her relation even if they were the Kardashians. Can you explain the American fascination with them?"

She laughed. "No."

"Well, then, Yank, I'll leave you to paint and see you around the village. Good luck."

He was already striding away.

"You too," she called and then dropped back onto her stool.

A stronger wind rushed over the land, and she watched

as it ruffled his clothing but didn't halt his progress. In fact, he seemed to lift his chin to the heavens as if to chide them for trying to slow him down. Her brain captured the scene—the way the white light coming from the Provence blue and Persian rose sky touched his hair. How the fields turned golden, the verdant green grass swaying in the breeze.

She was reaching for her paintbrush before she realized what she was doing.

She *had* to paint him.

The first brushstroke was as powerful as a lover's first caress. It was staggering, in fact, to feel the connection between her fingers, the pad, the color, and the image in her mind. She felt something turn inside her, almost like a rusty wheel. Her heart picked up as she went the next step and sketched him lightly with Payne's grey, striding away from her.

His body needed bold strokes. God, he was a bold man, telling her that he and his body had a liking for her. Her skin warmed.

She needed to paint his face. Now.

She tossed her paintbrush in the grass and reached for another, coating the bristles in yellow ochre. The angles of his face were strong, and she made slashes for his jaw, cheekbones, and brows. Then she settled into the very truth of him: his eyes. She threw aside another paintbrush and reached for a small, fine-tipped one and the Payne's grey again.

As they formed, she could feel the heat in them as they looked at her. She shivered, her whole body rising to answer the desire there.

She threw the paintbrush aside with force.

"No!" she told herself, sucking in a breath to calm her

wild heart. "If you paint him, he'll become a part of you. And that man cannot become a part of you. In any way."

Even if he had been the one to wake up her imagination.

She'd just have to find something else to inspire her.

Because if she let herself paint him, she would want to feel him. All over her. And that absolutely could not happen.

Good thing Carrick agreed.

CHAPTER SEVEN

S he was in Ireland.

Megan still couldn't believe it. Eight months ago, she'd been married and living in military housing with Ollie in the greater D.C. area. She'd known what to expect every day. Now her beloved Tyson was gone, and she was living in a small cottage in a foreign country, completely off-kilter. Bets' offer to give her and Ollie their own cottage had thrown her into a panic. She wasn't ready to be on her own with Ollie. Had her mother suggested it? Or Angie? Everyone kept telling her she had to move on, but grieving with a child was hard. How could she take care of Ollie when she couldn't muster the energy to take care of herself? Depression was like lying in mud, sedated with sadness.

Being with Angie made it easier. She didn't think her sister knew, but she was grateful for the support.

She eyed the short settee in their tiny living area. Lying around on it, depressed like she'd been in Angie's town-house, wasn't going to work. Even if it were comfortable, and it wasn't, she wouldn't fit.

She wondered if Angie had told Cousin Bets to find an

unfriendly couch, knowing her propensity to spend most of the day there, but she knew she hadn't. A large couch wouldn't fit into this parlor. They were practically on top of each other.

"Aunt Angie! There's a giant spider in my room."

Where was her sister? *"Angie!"*

When her sister didn't appear, she rushed to the ladder and quickly scaled it, wondering again if she should change rooms with her son. He came into view, pointing at a dark hairy spider dangling from the thatch ceiling.

"Ugh! That's disgusting."

"Squish it, Mom!"

Taking off her shoe, she swatted the long-legged monster, wincing. She realized it was one of the first active motions she'd taken in forever, and it felt strangely good. She swatted again. "We're okay."

A total lie. They weren't okay. They never would be.

Ollie tucked his arms around himself. His brown hair was sticking up on top of his head. His Superman pajamas looked even more wrinkled than they had coming out of the suitcase last night. "I hate spiders!"

"Do you want to switch rooms?" she asked again. "I didn't see any in mine. Why didn't Aunt Angie put you on the ground level? What if you have to go to the bathroom in the middle of the night?"

"I told her I can climb down the ladder," he said, sticking his chin out at her overprotectiveness. "I'm eight, Mom. Aunt Angie knows I'm not a baby."

"But I'm still your mother," she replied, kissing him on the head despite his bid for independence. "How about we have some breakfast and get dressed? Liam said he had a bike for you to ride. You can go by yourself if you wear a helmet."

Cousin Bets had told her it was safe to ride on their road. It was a dead end, so few cars came this way. More sheep used it than people, she'd said, muttering about Donal O'Dwyer again. Megan still couldn't believe her cousin—and her sister, no less—had chased sheep off with golf clubs yesterday. Then again, she couldn't believe she'd been to a welcoming party where everyone drank whiskey before five and their host and her friends wore feather boas and danced to Bon Jovi. Her sister had wanted to join *that* too.

She'd have to keep Ollie away from such wild antics and hope Angie didn't encourage their cousin. She didn't have the energy for such things. She didn't have the energy for anything, actually, and she didn't know what to do about it. Every day was a struggle.

Thank God for Ollie. He was her last link to Tyson, the lasting legacy of their love. "Let me go down the ladder first," she told him. "That way I can catch you if you slip."

"I won't slip, Mom. I can climb trees and the monkey bars better than any kid at school."

His frown was noticeable, but she ignored it. He was testing her more and more these days, pushing back whenever she got too close or overprotective. But he didn't understand his own grief. He was a little boy.

She made him wait until she went down the ladder halfway and then gestured for him to follow.

"Keep going, Mom. I can get down by myself."

"Indulge your mom, please."

He grumbled but started down, and they went down one rung at a time. At the bottom, he turned to her in the little hallway in front of her room. "I told you. Aunt Angie knows I can get down a ladder."

"But you still need an adult to kill a spider, so let's not get worked up. Where are your clothes?"

"Aunt Angie put them in a couple of her drawers since you were asleep."

A whisper of guilt asserted itself over the grayness around her. "Then find some clothes and come out for breakfast."

He ran to the back of the house and reappeared with his pants and shirt. She reached to help him dress, but he glared at her. "I can do it myself, Mom. Aunt Angie's bag isn't in her room. She must be painting."

"She should have told me," Megan said, feeling a twinge of anger.

Ollie's head popped through his green hoodie. "Mom, she needs to start painting again. Grandma told me to remind her every chance I get."

Her mother had always loved Angie the best, saying she took after her with all the caretaking and art therapy. Had her mother told Ollie to remind *her* to do anything? Stop being depressed? Her mom had mentioned she and her dad were worried about her depression. Why didn't they understand? Her husband had died. Of course she was depressed.

"Angie doesn't need you to be her cheerleader."

"Grandma thinks she does." Ollie sniffed. "Why does it smell in here?"

"Cousin Bets and Liam told us it was what the Irish call 'the damp.'" They'd also said that was why the furniture was about a foot away from the wall. That worried her some, truth be told.

"I still don't know what that means," Ollie said, pulling on a pair of jeans.

"Well, it rains so much here that things stay very wet. That's why the houses are concrete and stone, I think. Now, go and put your pj's away. Then we'll find you some breakfast." Angie wasn't here, so she was going to have to do it.

She wondered if that was why her sister had started painting so early. But Ollie was right. Angie *did* need to paint. Only Megan thought her sister teaching was more certain. Angie was good at that. She would have to try and find a way to do her part, even as her stomach flipped at the thought.

She knew Cousin Bets had only wanted Angie to come, and she didn't want to get uninvited, because her only other option was to move in with her parents.

She couldn't bear that—for herself or her son. With her mother still working full-time, they'd be home with her father all the time. Her dad would be hard on Ollie, but he'd be harder on her. He always had been.

You're scared of your own shadow, girl.

You need to toughen up.

Everyone needs to stop babying you.

Growing up, her mom and Angie had buffered her. When her mom was working, Angie had made her feel special with brownie and cupcake making after school. But those days were long gone. Even though Angie had cooked and made her eat since Tyson had died, it hadn't been the same.

Duty tasted different.

"*You're* going to make us breakfast?" her son asked, digging his feet into his shoes.

He sounded so surprised, her throat caught. Had she become that bad of a mother?

"I used to make it, remember?"

"Not for a long time." He ran past her to the kitchen. "I want to go see Aunt Angie."

Of course he did. She wondered how the painting was going. Her sister's agreement to do a village gallery show had shocked her out of her glassy complacency. Angie hadn't finished a single painting she was proud of since the third year of her marriage to Randall. While she admired Angie's overenthusiasm, she didn't want to see her sister crash and burn. Two months was a tight timetable.

"Mom! I can see her from the back door. Look! There's a whole bunch of sheep running like crazy in front of Aunt Angie. I want to go see."

He grabbed the latch and was out the back door before she could say anything. From the window, she watched him run through the grass. When he reached Angie, she turned and smiled, setting aside her palette to hug him. Angie and Ollie had always been close, but their bond had grown stronger since Tyson died. Probably due to Angie taking care of him when she was lying around.

A loud motor caught her attention, and then it stopped. A knock sounded on the front door a moment later, and Megan crossed to open it. She was surprised to see it was Liam. His matte black motorcycle was parked on the drive, which explained the black boots, faded jeans, and light navy jacket.

"Good morning! I brought the bike for Ollie since I was on my way out. And a helmet. I can bring down some bikes for you and Angie if you want later. Mom was still in bed, but she should be up soon if you want to tour the studio. Did you sleep well?"

"I was out cold," she said, glad she hadn't been kept awake by the squeaky springs in the mattress. "No idea about Angie. But she's been painting, so I expect she was up early."

"Yes, I saw her set up from the bend in the road at the top of the hill." He leaned the blue bike against the house and handed her the helmet. "You know, I got to thinking. Kade Donovan, Nicola and Killian's son, does pony therapy for kids going through rough patches. I thought Ollie might like to go riding. There's no one kinder than Kade, and it might even be fun. I can talk to him if you'd like. I'm doing some painting over at their farm right now."

"I... Isn't that normally for kids with special needs?"

Liam shook his head. "Not to Kade. He works with anyone who needs some healing. Even horses, especially ones that get hurt on the racetrack. He's a natural. People from all over come to see him."

"Ollie has never ridden a horse." Wasn't it dangerous? He could fall and get hurt, couldn't he? Die even. She started shaking her head.

"Not a requirement," Liam said with a careless wave of his hand. "Ollie looks like a smart, curious boy. I bet he's a fast learner. Besides, Kade has only the gentlest ponies around, and he is always there alongside the children. No one has ever gotten hurt. Trust me, Megan."

His earnestness touched something in her, his bright green eyes seeming to look into her soul. "Let me think about it."

"As you like." He paused, then added, "You know, when my dad died, I found it helped to do things that got me moving. It's easy to get stuck in grief. It's like a bog that way. I'll have to show you a proper Irish bog so you'll know my meaning. I was twenty when I lost my dad, and it was the hardest thing I've ever gone through or hope to go through. I can't imagine what it would be like to be so young. Anyway, you think on it. I'll be going now."

Emotion clogged her throat as she watched him stride off. He understood! This was what she kept trying to tell her mom and Angie when they told her not to remind Ollie he was supposed to be sad all the time. She couldn't count the number of times her dad had told her to "buck up" when she was a kid, and it had always made her feel worse. He may have praised her for being "good," but she knew what he really meant—weak.

Well, she was going to encourage her son to feel sad and not preempt his grief. "Wait!"

He turned around and smiled, saying nothing. Not pushing her. She appreciated it.

"Did your mother become overprotective when your dad died?"

"Is Irish weather changeable?" He laughed. "She had me, Rhys, and Wyatt go in for physicals. She didn't want us to drive our motorcycles anymore. She sent us emails about heart-healthy diets. She—"

"I get the picture," Megan finished, rubbing the tightness in her diaphragm. "That makes me feel better. Cousin Bets is usually so full of life. Fearless."

He shook his head slightly. "I love my mum, but she's human like the rest of us. Feeling vulnerable was a hard lesson for her. Personally, I'm glad I learned it young. Hurting doesn't make a person weaker. Hurting just is, and there are a lot of things in life we have no control over no matter how hard we try."

Raw pain was rising in her chest. Before hearing the news about Ty, she'd never imagined experiencing the searing, all-encompassing pain of grief. Strenuous forty-hour labor hadn't even come near it on the pain scale, and besides, labor had its rewards, didn't it? A child came at the end of it, but this... There was only more pain on the other side. "Does it ever stop?"

He put his hand over his heart and tipped his head up to the sky. "It lessens when you heal. I still miss my dad, but I don't mourn him anymore. I've made peace with him being gone. Mum is mostly there, save on her anniversary. I always try to distract her with some travel or fun to make up for him not being here."

She nodded. She was already a pro at making up for Tyson being overseas. What would it be like this year? There wouldn't be a special long-distance call with some of the guys in Tyson's unit singing happy birthday to Ollie. "Bets is lucky to have you."

"I'm lucky to be here," Liam said, gesturing to the house. "If you ask my older brothers, they'd tell you that I don't mind her babying so much because I'm her baby. Guilty."

"It's nice to talk to someone who understands."

He touched her arm. "Friends and loved ones make hurts easier."

Did they? Her mom and Angie usually made it harder, pressing at her to heal and move forward. When she'd heard Nicola talk about healing in a community, she'd recoiled from the thought. This wasn't *her* community. No one here could understand what she was going through. Except...*Liam* understood. He was the first reason she was glad she'd pushed Angie to let her and Ollie come. She hoped there would be more.

"If I think of anything else that might help, I'll let you know. Like I said, my search for inspiration and healing has driven me to read and listen to a lot of different things. Today's work accompaniment is Carlo Rovelli. He's an Italian physicist who writes about reality not being what we think. Living in Ireland, my favorite quote by him compares life to the spot where a rainbow meets the ground. 'We think that we can see it—but if we go to look for it, it isn't there.'"

Her brow wrinkled. "What does that mean exactly?"

His smile brightened his face. "When I was a boy, I

used to run through the fields until my heart was pounding in my chest, hoping to find the end of the rainbow—and yes, a leprechaun and a pot of gold. But I never did find it. So now, I only stay where I am when I see a rainbow and let its wonder fill me. I don't have to chase down beauty or magic. It's all around me."

Inside her chest was an ache she didn't understand. Beauty and magic all around? Where?

"Oh, listen to me go on." He laughed. "I love stuff like that because life can be really beautiful and really weird sometimes."

"It seemed pretty straightforward to me before Tyson was killed. I fell in love. I got married, and then I had Ollie. Now I don't understand anything."

"Exactly! It sounds like you might enjoy reading or listening to a few of the things that have helped me."

Would it work for her? She'd been good in school because it was expected, but she hadn't always liked what they'd taught. Who cared about past events or why an object was four-sided? Not her. She'd always been more drawn to art, where she could make and build things. God, she hadn't done that in forever. "Maybe."

He sent her a wink. "From where I'm standing, though, you and Ollie are doing pretty well, all things considered."

She stepped back in surprise. "We are?" It didn't seem that way to her. It felt like the merry-go-round of their life had stopped circling, the music gone.

"You're here in Ireland, aren't you?" He climbed onto his motorcycle. "I'd classify that as something that gets you moving, wouldn't you?"

He popped his helmet on and turned on the engine, giving a last wave before thundering down the driveway.

A shaft of sunlight broke through the clouds and lit the

trees in the front yard. The beauty stole over her, and she felt tears run down her face. Liam thought they were doing pretty well. Not just okay. *Pretty well.*

Wrapping her arms around herself, she considered his other advice. Movement. She thought of the impossibly short, uncomfortable couch. Yes, she would stop lying around, wrapping herself in memories of Tyson and her lost dreams of their future with their son.

She *was* going to make everyone breakfast, and then she was going to find a bicycle for herself.

Movement.

She would give it a try.

CHAPTER EIGHT

The painting wasn't her worst.

"I like it," Ollie said in his faithful way, hefting her stool back to the house as she carried her bag. "The fingers you gave the tree are super creepy, Aunt Angie. I could feel them tearing the earth open like in a slasher movie."

After she'd stopped painting Carrick, torn the paper from the pad, and folded it up so she wouldn't be tempted to finish it, she'd looked at the tree again. Carrick's depiction of how his deceased wife had seen it had risen in her mind. The sound of his voice describing it had moved that wheel inside her.

She'd run with it.

Her imagination had sputtered to life, although with less enthusiasm than it had about Carrick. *Not going there.*

"If you hung this on the wall, Aunt Angie, I'd be so scared."

Maybe her nephew was going over the top, but if Ollie was creeped out, at least she'd conveyed some emotion. Maybe she should paint her ex-husband. That composite would be both creepy and enraged—powerful themes for the viewer. Maybe exorcising him in such a way would make her feel a little better too.

But didn't she want to paint Randall. Or Saul even. She didn't want to give them the power to touch her.

No, she'd like *Carrick* to touch her. *Stop it, Angie.*

"When did your mom ever let you watch a slasher movie?" she asked, changing the subject.

His gaze lowered. "Dad did when she was visiting you or Grandma and Grandpa. He didn't want me to be a baby about scary things. Promise you won't tell Mom. Dad said it was our secret, although he said Grandpa wouldn't be mad. They're tough guys."

Her father had seen Tyson as the son he'd always wanted. Angie had jokingly asked her dad if joining the military and getting a buzz cut would have made him feel like that toward her. He'd only picked up a beer and told her not to sass. Fun days.

Megan didn't want to admit it, but part of her attraction to Tyson had been a Daddy thing. To be fair, Angie had her own issues—she'd always been drawn to men who supported her art, unlike her father. Too bad their interest, in her art *and* her, had never lasted.

Last year, Megan had actually admitted to her that she wasn't exactly happy in her marriage. The tearful call had come after Tyson decided to volunteer for another holiday mission.

Sometimes Angie wondered what might have happened if Tyson hadn't died. Would her sister have finally admitted the relationship wasn't fulfilling to her and Ollie? Ollie had certainly told Angie as much, saying it had made him angry that his father kept volunteering to go on tour. Tyson had preferred to hang around with his fellow soldiers and guys he'd grown up with rather than his family, and when he was home, he spent most of his time hunting or at ball games. Angie had disliked him because of it, even though she knew that he probably had trouble relating to homelife after war. But that wasn't an excuse. Plus, he'd been like that before his first tour. Why did a guy like him get married anyway?

Probably looking for love and security like the rest of the world, herself included. The world was really messed up. Time for it to stop in her.

"You know I won't tell your mom about the movies," she told her nephew, reminding herself it was time to forgive and forget her gripes against Tyson now that he was gone. That was going to take a while.

Unfortunately for her sister—and many Angie had taught in art therapy—it was hard to admit, least of all express anger, toward someone who had died. Certainly someone people thought of as a hero.

"You're the best, Aunt Angie."

"What do you think about the sheep?" she asked.

Ollie had stood near the fence for a while to watch them before sitting by her side and drawing on the small pad she'd given him.

"They eat a lot, don't they?" Ollie looked over his shoulder. "And they're pretty loud. I like the smaller ones, but they don't have any words on them. The big ones are like walking vocabulary cards."

"That's one way of describing them." They neared the house, and she smelled bacon. Had Megan actually *cooked*? "I used to hate vocabulary in school."

"Me too," Ollie said, setting the stool down and opening the door. "Do you think the new school will give me a lot of homework?"

"I hope not," she said, tapping him on the nose. "We're here to play and have fun."

"Speaking of... Liam brought a bicycle for you, Ollie," her sister said, standing in the kitchen with a hand towel tied around her waist.

She had cooked! That alone felt like a miracle.

Ollie jumped in the air. "Cool! Wait! Are you actually going to let me ride it?"

Megan's face fell. "Of course. Didn't I tell you so earlier?"

"Yeah, but you change your mind sometimes." He looked over to Angie with a grimace. "You wouldn't let me ride my bike anywhere at Aunt Angie's except in the garage. We don't have a garage here, Mom."

Angie kept her face neutral. She'd been walking on eggshells about Megan's overprotectiveness.

"You can ride it," Megan said, fingering the hem of her navy blouse. "With the helmet Liam brought. And when you see a car, you pull over to the side."

"I know how to ride on the street, Mom," he said, his determined chin thrust out. "Right, Aunt Angie?"

"Don't put me in the middle, Ollie. Why don't you show your mom what you drew?"

"He drew something?"

"Yes." Angie went over to the stove. "Thank you for making breakfast. It smells delicious. Ollie, your mom made bacon and oatmeal."

"Cool!" He ran over and grabbed her painting bag from her, locating his pad and flipping it open. "It's a ninja, Mom. He can do karate and everything. No one can stop him. Or kill him. Can I ride my bicycle before breakfast?"

Her sister clutched the hand towel tied around her

waist. "Sure. Take a piece of bacon. And don't be gone long."

Ollie ran out, the front door slamming behind him, and Angie waited to see how her sister would react.

"After Liam left, I was feeling good for the first time in a long time," Megan said in a harsh whisper. "Then my son tells me he drew a ninja no one could kill. Oh, Angie."

She hugged her sister. "At least he's drawing again. That's a good sign. He told me that he wanted to draw because I was painting. In art therapy, they tell you not to judge the subject of the painting. Expression heals."

"I know it does," Megan said. "I used to be a potter. But, Angie… Do you think he needs professional help?"

How ironic. Megan had bolted when she'd asked her that months ago. She held her sister's shoulders. "I think you need to let him play and explore. Let's see how things shake out."

Megan turned away and stirred the oatmeal. "He got mad when I made him wait for me to go down the ladder first."

Angie put the kettle on. "Maybe he needs to assert himself. It's a new place with new people. I always feel like I need to assert myself when I'm somewhere new."

"Just don't assert yourself too much," her sister said, spooning oatmeal into a simple white bowl and handing it to her. "You need this job, and you get in trouble that way. Your wild and willful tendencies rear up. Remember when you kept sneaking out and Dad caught you? He took your art supplies away."

For six months. It had nearly killed her.

Part of her wanted to tell Megan about her very direct talk with Carrick this morning. He'd asserted himself, and she'd done it right back. The two of them had handled the situation with honesty and maturity. Like adults. She felt like she'd turned a corner.

Was Meg too wrapped up in her problems to see Angie clearly? She hadn't acted "wild" in a long time.

Truthfully, she missed going where the wind took her. It had helped her art and made her happier.

"Why are you wearing your old paint clothes? I didn't notice before."

"I feel good in these clothes," she told her sister, caressing her coat. "I thought they'd help me paint again. I can wear my teaching clothes when I teach. Okay?"

She almost made a face to punctuate the words, but that would have undermined her point. Megan itched at her collarbone, probably because of the wool cardigan she had tied over her blouse. Or, more probable—her skin and the rest of her couldn't breathe.

Angie itched in response. "Come on. Let's make some tea. Eat breakfast. Then we can go for a walk and head up to see the studio."

Megan nodded, and they passed the morning more easily in the crammed eating nook, watching the light flicker over the countryside as a patch of rain came and then disappeared, turning to eerie, illuminated mist. God, she couldn't get enough of the everchanging light. The cottage didn't feel so small from this perspective.

When they finally headed up to see Bets, Ollie was smiling as he streaked ahead of them on the blue bicycle.

"Liam said moving was good for grief," Megan told her.

Moving was also good for depression, which Megan didn't like to talk about. God love their cousin. "Well, he would know. So would Bets. Look! Here she is."

Bets was waiting in the front driveway, animatedly

talking to Ollie. She pointed to a giant oak at the edge of the lawn, and he went running.

"Did I mention there was a tree house?" she called out to them, striding forward in purple yoga pants and a green hoodie with a shamrock on it. "My boys practically lived in it growing up. Angie, I love your outfit."

"How high up is it?" Megan interrupted.

"Not terribly, and the ladder is sturdy, I promise. Do you want me to call him back?"

Angie waited.

"I'm sure it will be fine," Megan said, clearing her throat. "You're kind to let Ollie have the run of your place. He's never had so much room."

"It's a good place to raise boys, Bruce and I used to say." She looked around, love and memories alight in her pale blue eyes. "I'm glad Liam brought the bicycle out of storage. Did he mention Kade?"

"Yes, the pony therapy guy," Megan said, tightening the cardigan wrapped around her. "Thank you. I need to think about it."

Angie didn't know what there was to think about. Ollie would love it, just like she would have at his age. But again, she bit her lip. Told herself to be grateful Megan had made breakfast and was out walking with her.

"Kade's a sweetheart," Bets told them. "Takes more after Nicola than Killian. Well, before I get carried off with that talk, are you ready to see your studio, Angie?"

Her hands grew damp. "Yes."

They took the path behind the main house, through a line of towering trees she would have to study later. Sycamores and oaks with some others mingled in that she didn't know. God, they would be beautiful to paint. She looked at their trunks, and sure enough, she could see an array of claws tunneling through the ground. Slasher trees, she would call them from now on.

The forested path opened up to a clearing with a beautiful two-story white concrete building fitted with rectangular windows and honey-colored wooden frames that matched the three large barnlike doors. "It's gorgeous! This used to be a barn?"

"We call them sheds in Ireland," Bets said. "Usually, they're bigger than a cottage and uglier than sin with all the corrugated metal. You don't see many concrete sheds with this kind of woodwork. Bruce found some old estate journals, and he discovered his ancestors originally built and used it to make whiskey, something that probably stopped when a steep duty was put on malt."

"That's so cool," Angie said, loving the history.

"Anyway, I've always loved this building more than any of our other outbuildings, but after I sold off all of Bruce's cows and fowl on the farm, I didn't know what to do with it. Until now. Putting the skylights in took it over the edge. Come over to the side here. There's another surprise."

She and Megan followed their cousin. Off to the right, a sandy golden shoreline hugged a calm indigo sea. The sky was a rich Windsor blue filled with puffy gray and white clouds. She inhaled the salt in the air. Oh, man, this place!

"I *love* your beach," Megan said, her voice laced with awe.

"Meg always wanted to live in San Diego," Angie said as Bets opened the middle door and led them past the empty first floor to a sturdy staircase.

Later, beach. I've got me a date with—

"Oh, my God!" She stopped short at the edge of the large horizontal room.

Bright new easels had been set up in three rows, waiting for her students. Canvases in varying sizes were stacked against the right wall. An open cabinet on the far wall held paints, charcoal, pencils, solvents, brushes, palates, and palette knifes.

"This is heaven, Bets!"

She strode through the rows, already imagining the people working there on their paintings. Pausing, she ran a hand over a smooth wood easel, savoring the delicious texture. Angling her head back, she studied the light coming in through the skylights and windows. "This light is perfect."

"I think it looks pretty incredible," Bets said, moving an easel a centimeter, "but if you want to change anything around, do it. This place is yours."

Her place.

She used to think of the arts league as hers in a way. She'd built it up from a decrepit community arts center, courtesy of some new paint and supplies from their fundraisers. But the community hadn't supported them enough in the end for them to survive budget cuts.

But this place? Bets owned it. No one could shut it down or take it away from her. "I love it! I can't wait to start teaching next week! Bets, how can I ever thank you?"

She ran over and hugged her cousin, jostling her off her feet and making her laugh.

"I'm so glad you love it! Maybe this is a good time to tell you I'm thinking about more than painting classes. Hell, I'm thinking about a whole bunch more than that."

Angie angled back. At last! Her cousin was going to share the plans she'd only hinted at yesterday. "What are you thinking, cuz?"

"I want to create an arts center here. A place people can

come from around the world to learn how to paint—or do ceramics if Megan comes out of retirement—"

"I said it wasn't a good time for me," her sister said in a terse voice, retreating to the edge of the room.

Bets followed her. "It's a long-term vision, Meg. Who knows where you'll be in a few months? Angie, I might even want to find artists to do a residence here."

"A residence?" Angie was getting goose bumps. "That's a great idea. More artists. More ideas. More people to come and learn from them. Oh, Bets, you could attract students from all over the world if you played it right."

"So you're game?" her cousin asked, cocking an orange-tinted brow.

She looked around the space, already smelling oil paint and solvent in the air. She wanted to open them and run her fingers through the paint. Brush her clothes with the colors to anchor her here and make it her own. "Am I? I haven't been this excited about something in forever."

Except for wanting to paint Carrick. This would balance that out, thank God.

"Good!" Bets clapped her hands. "Now all we need to do is gain more students and expand. Once we have the community on board, we'll apply to the Mayo County council planning authority."

Her stomach tightened. She hated to deal with local politicians, and that's what this group sounded like. "They have some say?"

Bets put her hands behind her back and nodded slowly. "They give the planning permission. I don't need to apply to change a part of my residence to a commercial property yet since I'm only holding two painting classes, and they're in my shed, which is unofficially covered. Once we start growing and more artists come in to teach, we're going to

have to make things official. Insurance. Fire and safety certi-
fication. That sort of thing. But that's putting the cart before
the horse... I figure your village gallery show will be just the
thing to get everyone in town on board."

Her blood pressure went up. The stakes around her first
gallery show in nearly eight years were going up by the day.

"Attracting visitors brings in money. The planning
committee wouldn't dare say no then."

"Why would they say no?" Megan asked. "There's no
harm in teaching art classes."

Bets' mouth tightened. "You haven't met my sister-in-
law, Mary Kincaid. She hates me living here on her family's
land, even more so now that Bruce is gone. Plus, she's a
regular tight arse about everything and likes to stir up trouble. She's good friends with Tom MacKenna's wife, Orla.
He's head of the county council presently."

Angie remembered her name vaguely. "Mary's the one
you compete with in the rose competitions, right?"

"Good memory. But I have a solid reputation, and when
you bring money into town, you're golden. That's what our
art center will need to do. So paint your heart out, girl, and
I'll work my magic."

A shiver ran through her. She was going to have to paint
better than a few trees with fingers clawing the ground to
get an entire community and county council on board, that
was for damn sure.

CHAPTER NINE

Carrick decided to enlist the Yank's help when he sighted her sitting beside the sycamore tree.

He'd become accustomed to seeing her in the mornings this past week. No, it was more than that. He'd grown eager for it, usually because she had something clever or witty to throw his way. The day after their *direct* talk, she'd asked if he thought of his ewes when he heard songs like "With or Without You." He'd responded that he was one hundred percent sure Bono and U2 had been near a sheep pasture when they'd written the song.

She'd followed up the next day with more sheep humor, this one courtesy of Liam, who'd shared it with her nephew.

"What do you call a sheep covered in chocolate?" she'd asked, morning sunlight touching her face as her lush mouth tipped up.

He didn't disguise his groan. "I thought I'd heard them all. What?"

"A candy baa," she said, laughing so hard she had to wipe tears away.

The following day she'd startled him with a surprisingly

earnest question about what asshole had started the story about black sheep being bad, something she knew to be unfair from personal experience. That had made him more curious about her, though he'd had to leave her unsatisfied. He wasn't aware how the story had begun. But, being Irish, he knew that was the way with tales... Still, she'd been vulnerable, and he'd felt a shocking flare of anger at whoever had spoken of her so disparagingly.

His sheep bleated as he crossed the field, making his steps heavier. The Yank didn't look up. He'd startled her yesterday, and the scream she'd given in response to his "good morning" had given him a belly laugh. God, it had felt good to tease her before she turned back to her pad, which had stubbornly remained mostly white this week. She was still having trouble but plodding on, something he respected.

Today she would start teaching art classes, and he wondered whether it was something she plodded at or sailed over. He hoped she was easy with it because, given the buzz in the village, today might prove interesting for reasons other than art.

Even from a distance, he could tell she was hard at it again. Her body curved as she bent over her paint pad like a capital C on the sheep who'd met him at the gate—she'd read *Courage.*

Two new sheep streaked in front of him, making him frown as he read their message. *Seize. Today.*

Soft laughter touched his ears, but he didn't see Sorcha. Part of him was relieved, and sadness touched his heart like the cold rain of last evening. He thought about detouring, but he had a mission. The Yank finally looked up as he reached the fence line. Her whole face looked pinched from the effort of trying to fill that blank page. She set aside a brush covered in red paint, a streak of which was visible on her jeans.

He wouldn't have imagined an embroidered coat or jeans with flower patches would appeal to him, but hers did. They hinted at a romantic, whimsical side while the streaks of paint portended a streak of rebellion. As did her hair, all bundled up with curls twisted about her ears and neck from the wind. The look was sexy as hell.

"Shall I start bringing you a cup of tea if we're to run into each other every morning?" she asked.

The challenge in her words had him smiling as he exited the gate and reached her.

"I had my tea before the sun awoke, but I wouldn't mind a second cup tomorrow if it's no bother."

She straightened on her short stool. "Of course! I'm happy to become a roadside tea stand for the whole village."

Damn, but he didn't want to like her. "Might make some money that way too."

"Good, because making money painting again—or attracting support for Bets' art center—is looking like a pipe dream." She rubbed the space between her brows, leaving a red streak there as well. "Why did I think I could do this? Don't answer that. It was rhetorical."

And yet he couldn't stand seeing her defeated. He fought against the urge to gently clean up her face and raise her chin. "You're made of stronger stuff than self-pity, Yank. You'll do whatever you have to in order to paint again. Claw it out of your very soul if you must."

The pinched look left her face, replaced by a stark vulnerability. "How the hell would you know?"

He thought about offering a pat answer, but his belly trembled in the face of her misery, a downright uncomfortable feeling. "Sorcha had what they call writer's block a few times, and I got good at helping her move past it. I've seen its legacy."

"I don't want to ask." She gripped her knees. "Okay, I do. How?"

He couldn't very well tell her he'd shagged his wife until she'd sworn she could hear the angels singing. He and Angie weren't talking or thinking about sex together. Ever.

Oh, he was lying to himself. He'd thought about them coming together as he was putting in the floor and working at his chores.

"We had our ways," he evaded. "You have yours. You're an artist. You have everything you need inside you."

"Thank you, Tony Robbins," she said, throwing her hair back after the wind blew it over her shoulder. "Do you listen to him like Liam does?"

His breath caught as a shaft of morning sunlight illuminated the long line of her neck. He forgot to ask her who this Tony fellow was. "Before I go, could you inquire in a stealthy way which rose bushes need replacing due to my sheep? I went to the co-op and realized I had no idea what to buy. Liam likes his philosophy, not gardening, and I'm trying to stay on Bets' good side."

He didn't think Bets would change her mind about selling him the land for the house his dead wife didn't want, but he wasn't a stupid man. That woman was mad about her roses. He understood the fire for competition, because he felt that way about Baron, his prize sheep. That young ram was going to win him big money at the fair this year—more than enough to buy Bets' land. That was something he needed, and yet he was still struggling to work on the house after what Sorcha had told him. He had to push through this current block as much as Angie needed to push through her own.

"What am I? A rose spy? Okay, fine. But I'll have to do it out of Megan's hearing. She'd know something was up for sure."

A rose spy. She was funny, this Yank. "Not into gardening either, eh?" he asked, leaning against the fence. "I might have thought otherwise by the red rose on your jeans. You're all Robert Burns."

She flashed him a wry smile. "My love is more like a volcano than a rose, according to my exes. I love to paint them, but no, I don't care for the weeding and watering. That's Megan."

He didn't want to ask, but he did all the same. Seeing that little boy grieving had gotten to him. "How are your sister and the boy settling in?"

She put her elbows on her knees and cupped her face. The pose as much as the new look made her appear years younger. "Better, I think, but it's early. Liam gave Ollie a bicycle, and he's tearing up the driveway and the side roads. Megan has been making breakfast with me painting in the mornings, and we've started to take a walk after dinner. Although I missed it last night because I was fussing over my lesson plan. Your *mother* is excited to see it—she told me so yesterday when she came by to visit with Bets. That made me nervous since she was a teacher for decades."

He laughed. "Don't worry. She's curious but supportive. Part of her probably misses teaching, though she keeps busy enough. Seems she can't spend a whole day without one or more of the Lucky Charms around. My dad and I aren't sure the village will survive it. Turn them down if they ask you to paint a Bon Jovi mural on the side of Gavin's pub."

Her faint chuckle told him she wasn't used to laughing much. Like him. "Is a rock star mural on their minds?"

"They love that band."

"I know. They welcomed us with a dance party."

He made a face. "One night at Gavin's, Siobhan might have mentioned wanting a mural to celebrate their favorite band, and the others gave up a cheer. The rest of us live in terror of them spray painting their best attempt at depicting Jon with his guitar. Now they have you, Yank. We might be done for."

"I have work to do," she said with another chuckle, "although it might be fun. I could be Banksy to Caisleán."

"Fun is a pint at the pub with your friends. Try that, Gavin might call the Garda—the law—on you."

"Even better." A twinkle appeared in her eye. "Of course, Megan wouldn't like it. Do you break out into hives when you hear Bon Jovi, or can you ignore it like your dad does?"

"I'm more on the hives side." He could admit that, if only to hear her chuckle again. "It was craic in the beginning, when I was a kid, but there are other bands. My dad and I still can't understand why they don't idolize U2 like the rest of us."

"I get it," she said, her smile as tempting as her lush mouth. "It helps them recapture part of their youth."

"But they're not young anymore, girl. Might as well accept it."

Her face fell. "It's Angie," she corrected. "And neither am I."

He disagreed, but he wasn't sure how she'd take it—or how he wanted her to take it—so he rushed on to say, "My friend Declan keeps telling Siobhan—that's his mum—that she can't pester him about getting married and having grandbabies if she's going to dance around with a feather boa and gyrate her hips like a snake charmer. Not very nanny like. My own mum might kill me if I said the same, even though I think it every time that infernal purple boa comes out."

Her crestfallen expression disappeared, and she uttered her first heartfelt laugh. He felt like he'd had a victory.

"Your mom has been very nice. All of the Lucky Charms are when they stop and chat as they leave Bets'. I didn't know you Irish just pop in like that."

"Easier to pop by when you have time than have to cancel something planned due to a farm issue and the like," he said, thinking he should move along. "Best mind yourself with the Lucky Charms, though. That's how they lure you in, Yank. You have enough to focus on with the paintings."

He turned to leave and nearly swore. A lone sheep stood a few meters away, rubbing her body against the fence, the word *Stop* painted clearly on her fluffy body. He knew who was to blame.

"I need a little fun or I'll go crazy," Angie said, rearranging her wild mess of hair with a clip. "Overwork is what landed me in this mess."

"I thought men had. If I can be direct."

She lifted her brow, making her paint smear move. "It *was* men, and me burying myself in work so I wouldn't have to face the fact that I couldn't paint anymore. And to pay the bills, of course. Shit, I should stop talking right now."

He gestured impatiently. "Don't stop on my account. Get it out. Maybe it will help."

Her throat moved, and an answering lump appeared in his own.

"I didn't want to admit that I'd become someone I'm not proud of," she said softly. "I didn't used to look like this."

"Like what?" he asked, blinking at her. "I don't see anything wrong with you."

She shook her head at him. "You didn't know me before.

I was thin and pretty and spirited and... You wouldn't understand."

He couldn't help but cross to her and put his hand on her shoulder. She looked up at him in surprise.

His fingertips itched to touch the curls bouncing around her nape in the gentle breeze. "Life changes us. Sometimes we let it by ignoring it, like the English ivy strangling all the ash trees here in Ireland. Sometimes it simply wrecks us like a storm blowing the roof off a well-built shed. You get up and keep on."

She pursed her lips as if gathering herself. "I appreciate you saying that. I guess I need to do some pruning and rebuild my roof then."

He wanted to rub her shoulder in comfort, so he forced himself to drop his hand. "Ah, Yank, you're still pretty as a picture, if you don't mind me saying, and a woman who wields a golf club at a three-hundred-pound sheep is certainly spirited."

Her eyes glistened. "You didn't mention me being thin."

He held up his hands. "I've never been accused of being a stupid man, but if you mean you were rail thin like those Americans I see on the telly, I'm glad to see it's behind you now. You look like a real woman, and that's how a woman should be."

She wiped her eyes. "Aren't you full of surprises?"

Wasn't that the truth of it? "I must have woken up in a generous mood."

"Then can I ask you something else?" Her voice was almost hesitant now. Struck with the thought that he'd always know the shades of her mood by that expressive voice, he knew he needed to leave. "Make it quick, and then I'll be on my way."

"I... Ah... Shit. I wondered what else your wife said

about this view. What you told me about that tree having fingers to claw through the land really helped. I guess I need to see this place through fresh eyes."

Wouldn't hers be the freshest? But it was rude to ask, and she was only doubting herself. He studied the land. The house he was building had a view of another of Sorcha's favorite spots. "Do you see that raised hill over there to the west? The one with the gorse on three sides?"

"Is gorse the big bush with the yellow flowers?"

"It is," he answered, resting on his haunches beside her, pointing to the very spot. "That's a fairy fort. You'll also hear locals call them raths or lios. People believe fairies live there, so those spots are left to themselves. Only the animals graze upon them, and some aren't even touched by beasts, depending on how jealous the fairies are about sharing their home. There's a lot of superstitions about them, but then again, there are a lot of superstitions in Ireland period."

She had a half smile on her face, like she was amused. He realized she didn't wear makeup, and his eyes took in more of her features. Her mouth was lush, he already knew, but her eyebrows were also strong. Not plucked and waxed into a thin line like on some of the women he knew. Then there were her eyes, shining brown with flecks of gold and green. Beautiful eyes, they were.

How could she not think she was pretty? Oh, women! They were so hard on themselves.

"You were talking about superstitions," she said, clearing her throat.

"What?" he asked, startled out of his study of her. "Right. Has anyone told you to wear your jacket inside out on the way home from the pub so the fairies won't recognize you and mess with you as you walk?"

Her smile crested across her face before she covered it

with her hand. "No, but I'll keep that in mind. Only... Wouldn't wearing a hat better disguise you?"

"You have the way of it," Carrick said, smiling in return. "The forts are in circles, Sorcha used to say, because the fairies run circles around any person they find disagreeable."

Rather like Sorcha herself.

"Those circles would turn into the center of a storm, and soon the person would disappear from sight. Never to be seen again. Only their true love could call them back, and only then on the night of a full moon. But if the fairies like you... Well, that particular fairy fort has seen many a secret rendezvous between local couples growing up around here. With three sides of gorse, it's mostly protected from human eyes."

"An outside love nest? I love it!"

He laughed again. "Sorcha fancied them romantic fairies—ones who keep watch for the couple in love. Getting caught fooling around isn't always easy on the woman, especially for those from my mother's generation. They like to help couples in love."

"Have you been up at that particular fairy fort?" she asked boldly.

He met her gaze and had a flash of them wrapped around each other with the white light of the full moon streaming over her naked body. "I have, yes."

She turned her head away. "I'll have to stay far away then. I'm on the no-sex-for-decades plan. Or at least until I start painting like a master again."

Decades. He whistled. "That's a long time, Yank. You must have some willpower."

"No comment." She started to pack up. "This conversation is veering out of the friend zone."

Indeed. "I'll be leaving you then. You should stay and see what other inspiration strikes you. There's no rain to interrupt you after the heavens had their way last night, according to the weatherman. Have a good first class, Angie."

It was the first time he'd said her given name, and the power of it surprised him.

She gaped at him like a prize salmon. "Ah, thank you. That's...nice and unexpected."

Yes, he definitely needed to leave, but there was one final nugget he felt compelled to impart. "Don't be surprised if you have spectators show up. Even some in the village who have no interest in painting themselves might want to watch this first turnout."

Should he tell her about the buzz in the village? From what he'd heard, people had been betting whether the painting class would involve nudes. No, if he said that, his mum and likely others would kill him.

"Thanks, Carrick." She reached for the red-splashed paintbrush, her mouth already twisting as if it were torture to begin again.

He wanted to help assuage the torture and reassure her, but it wasn't for him. She had to find it herself. "Good luck, Angie," he said, wanting to feel her name on his lips as much as hear it on the wind.

As he headed off, he sighted two sheep with another message. *Surprise. Hero.*

He shook his head. Sorcha was wrong. He was no one's hero. Not anymore.

CHAPTER TEN

C ars lined the driveway up to the manor house when Angie left for her first class.

She liked punctuality in her students, but the class didn't start for another thirty minutes. Carrick had cautioned her about spectators. How many could there be? Was Caisleán really that hard up for something new and different? She'd walked its charming streets, and while it was small, the town had a fun, vibrant vibe that she looked forward to exploring further.

"Aunt Angie!" Ollie called out, racing after her. "I want to come with you. Liam said it was going to be something to see."

She stopped to wait for him and righted the rigid bun she'd pinned on her head, which had been twirled around like a Tilt-A-Whirl by a strong gust of wind. Wild strands escaped and blew in her face. No amount of tucking would right the damage. The wind clearly had ideas about her looking professional for her class.

Part of her had hated to wrap up her hair the way she had in Baltimore. In the small mirror in the bathroom, she'd faced her old nemesis: her dumpy self. Carrick's compliments had been stark in her mind as she'd changed out of her morning painting clothes and donned her tan slacks and a simple brown top. He'd said she was pretty and spirited and looked like a real woman was supposed to.

God, that's how she wished she could see herself. But they needed to trust her as a teacher, didn't they? Her paint-splattered jeans wouldn't convey authority. She'd met tons of art professors and teachers through Randall, and he'd been right about one thing—everyone in that world, or at least the Baltimore subset of that world, favored a professional look, even in a paint smock. No "wild" jeans or coats with patches, that was for sure.

Except her old clothes didn't feel right against her skin. In fact, every stitch of clothing she'd brought, save her throwback painting attire, looked unappealing in her dresser drawers.

"I like what you had on before," her nephew said as if reading her thoughts. "You looked like you did in that picture Granny has of you at the state fair with my mom when you were my age."

She did her best to smile at him and stop counting the cars they passed. "You love that photo because we're eating funnel cakes. Your mom and I had a powdered sugar war that day." Those were the days when she and Megan had felt like girlhood friends, something that still felt out of her grasp. Megan was making breakfast and going walking with her, and on the beach by herself. All of those things were improvements, but she still eyed Angie's paint clothes with a frown when Angie came into the kitchen every morning.

"Powdered sugar wars are the best," he said, "but I mostly like it because you and Mom look so happy."

"We're working on being that happy again. That's why we're here."

"Yeah, I guess." He kicked a rock on the driveway. "How many people are in your class, Aunt Angie?"

She eyed the endless lines of cars packed in the driveway in front of the house. "Not this many."

"Well, it's herself at last!" a thin older man called, waving and running toward them like a small bird. "The turnout is better than could be expected. Even Bets' busy-body sister-in-law has come, although I expect it was a chance to see the state of her roses up close and personal."

"Mary is here?" she asked.

"With her nose in the air like usual. It's an event not to be missed, even by the disapproving likes of her. We had a few from the next town come in."

"From the next town? I'm sorry. Are you in my class?"

"No, I'm Cormac O'Sullivan," he said, holding out a thin hand, leathery with age. "I'll be keeping the book today. On the betting. You'd best get up to the studio, girl. Nothing will happen until class starts. Do you fancy a bet yourself?"

"On what?" Dear God. This is what Carrick had tried to warn her about. Well, whatever it was, she'd best send her nephew away until she could get a handle on things. "Ollie, why don't you head back to the cottage?"

"Probably for the best," Cormac said, giving a trill of a laugh. "If you change your mind about the betting, I'll be outside the studio door waiting for ye."

But Ollie stayed put as the older man hurried off in that strange walk. What now? She couldn't just march up there with her nephew. She eyed her watch. She could walk him back to the cottage and still make it.

"Angie!" Liam came running across the lawn toward her. "I hope you have a good sense of humor, cousin. Like you Yanks say, 'Shit is about to get real.' Sorry, Ollie. Even my aunt is here, and she and Mum do *not* get along."

"I've heard people say shit," her nephew said, frowning. "Aunt Angie, I want to stay."

"I suddenly want to leave," she said, making a scary face designed to make her nephew laugh. "Liam, would *you* like to teach today?"

"I could lead everyone in yoga or meditation or a discussion of philosophy, but I'm all thumbs with drawing. This isn't painting houses, cousin."

"No, it's not. Ollie, go back to the cottage, please."

He stuck out his chin, showing signs of resistance. Usually Angie would welcome the sight—anger was better than no emotion, after all—just not right now.

"That's my best offer, Ollie."

"You'd best go," Liam said with a hand to the boy's shoulder. "Trust me on this one, from one man to another."

He kicked another rock. "Fine!"

She watched as he jammed his hands in his pockets and started to storm off in a tiff. Later. She would make it up to him later.

"Liam, do you want to tell me what's going on?"

"Mum said to keep an eye out for you." He put an arm around her shoulders and started to lead her toward the studio. "We had no idea so many people would come out. Don't even ask me how mad she is about Aunt Mary using this as an excuse to check out her roses."

Which still wasn't an answer. She stopped and faced him. "Liam! Why are they here?"

"They've come to see if anyone will volunteer to be a life model."

She pressed her hand to her temple. "I thought it was a joke about us painting nudes."

"It was, mostly, but a few people at the pub talked big over pints this week, and it raised everyone into a fervor. Hence Cormac. He used to be a jockey. Now he's what you would call—"

"A bookie," she answered slowly. "I'm in hell. Wait! Maybe I'm looking at this all wrong. Please tell me there's going to be a parade of hot naked Irish guys my age volunteering to model."

She might be off sex, but she could look.

His shoulders started to shake. "Sorry, cousin. For familial harmony, I'm not showing my stuff to you or anyone in that class. Mum made me promise. The only likely candidates will be over sixty, I expect."

She was going to go blind. Today. All her painting hopes would be gone.

"Come on!" Liam grabbed her hand. "Mum and the Lucky Charms have a plan if anyone tries to strip, don't worry."

"Why would I worry?" She laughed as they wandered down the path between the trees. "I used to be a semi-respected teacher in America. Now, people are placing bets on whether old men are going to streak through my class."

"Technically it's volunteering, but it's craic, all right."

When they emerged from the tree line, she was sure her mouth popped open. People were sitting in everything from dinner chairs to patio furniture in front of the studio!

"That's Aunt Mary under the oak with her one friend, Orla MacKenna, who's to her right," Liam said, tilting his head in their direction. "I'd keep away from them."

"Good to know." She glanced over. A short, round, silver-haired woman in a brown rain jacket and wellies looked to be Aunt Mary. Her friend—also silver-haired—was a shade taller and thin as a rail.

"Liam O'Hanlon!" the first woman yelled.

"We shouldn't have made eye contact," Liam said in an undertone, grimacing as his aunt barreled over with Orla. "Aunt Mary, how are you?"

"My brother and my parents are rolling in their graves at what might transpire today on O'Hanlon land," she said, her face shimmering with dark emotions Angie would paint, the bitterness wrapped around her like a sticky cocoon.

"Oh, Aunt Mary, it's all a good bit of craic if anything happens," Liam said gently as Orla stared at them like they were bugs. "You should get out of the sun. Your face might burn."

He pulled Angie away as the woman sputtered, the lack of introductions telling.

"They're a barrel of laughs."

"Yes, but everyone else here is great craic," Liam said, waving as the bystanders sent up a cheer as if to assure her. "It was standing room only inside, but the Irish come prepared. As you can see, people anticipated the turnout and brought their own chairs. If anyone shows up to model, you'll be talked about in the village for years. Decades maybe. This is big stuff, cousin."

She braced her shoulders and walked through the bystanders, who had thoughtfully left a path to the main door. Strangers of all ages patted her on the shoulder and shook her hand like she was the MC for a parade.

"We're so glad to have you," one woman said.

"Oh, what a day for the village," another man told her with a wink.

When she entered the building, people lined the stairs to the second floor. More of them came forward to greet and congratulate her.

"What in the hell will they do if nothing happens?" she

asked Liam. People who lost money didn't always react well.

"Ah... It's no bother. People had a chat. A bright spot in their day."

God, she loved the Irish.

When she reached the studio, Liam kissed her cheek. "Good luck, cuz."

She surveyed the bodies lined against the wall and the people sitting in chairs beside the students at the easels. Everyone was staring at her expectantly. Liam hadn't been kidding. It was standing room only.

Bets rushed forward—or as much as she could, winding around the acre of people. "People have gone absolutely mad, Angie. This isn't how I wanted to start off, but I know you'll get everything under control."

Her cousin didn't sound happy about their crashers, and her diaphragm tightened. Would this reflect negatively on the arts center her cousin wanted to start? On her? Were they behind before they even began? "I'll give it my best."

"We're really all excited to paint. Aren't we?" Bets had raised her voice to be heard.

A few people murmured in response.

"You bet!" Nicola called out and gave them a thumbs-up, looking especially serious in a bright white paint smock.

"Don't worry," Bets said, leading her to the front. "We're here as backup."

She nodded to be encouraging, but the theme music from *The Twilight Zone* was playing in her head.

At the front, Bets leaned in and kissed her cheek. "If you want to place a last-minute bet with Cormac, now is the time. I can have someone run it down for you. I bet against a showing. They'd be daft to do it."

She forced a smile and shook her head. "I'm good."

Facing the class as Bets found her spot in front of an easel, she took a breath and went for honesty. In teaching, she'd learned to assert her authority, something she couldn't possibly do if she tried to ignore the elephant in the room.

"I'm Angie Newcastle, Betsy O'Hanlon's American cousin, and I have to say this is the first time I've presided over a class where streakers were a distinct possibility."

People laughed, and she felt more anchored to take the situation in hand.

"Personally, I've taken classes with live models. It's part of art training. So if anyone shows up, they might find themselves with a permanent job if they're not careful." Total bullshit, but no one needed to know that.

"If it's some of the men we think might show," a woman said, "they'd be delighted to unveil themselves on a permanent basis."

Great. She was dealing with aging perverts. "All right, this is a painting class with a little sideshow. I'm going to start teaching, and since prospective nudity is on people's minds, let's begin there. How many of you have ever drawn a naked person?"

A few people gasped while others laughed nervously.

"Does a baby count?" asked the woman whose easel was next to Bets. Her expression was surprisingly earnest, and she wore a blue top. "I painted the baby Jesus for a church play once."

"It was a fine depiction," someone in the crowd called out, causing more murmuring and sounds of assent.

"A baby does count," she said slowly. "Since all of my official students are women, let me be specific. Have any of you ever painted a naked man?"

Her answer was met with wide eyes and more laughter, some embarrassed.

"I can't imagine getting one particular appendage right," the student in blue said. "It moves around a lot, don't you think?"

"I'd just try painting a garden hose," another said. "That's about the same way of things down there."

A debate ensued among the people in the room over the bobbing and rising of said appendage and whether a garden hose would do it justice.

Angie fisted her hands by her sides. *Kill me. Kill me right now.*

Cormac appeared at the top of the stairs, black book in hand, a smile of evil delight on his thin face. "Girls, you're about to have your chance to paint naked men."

A woman in the back called out, "Cormac? How many models have shown up?"

"Five, Saints be praised! All wearing the town's boxing club robes. And most of them are pissed!"

Drunk. Great. This was going to be fun, she thought, as everyone pulled out their camera phones. Of course, they were going to film this. Who needed to pay money for a movie when you had this kind of entertainment?

The sound of laughter began from below. People called out indistinct phrases. There was a clamor on the stairs, and some people spilled out into the second floor as if to make way. The laughter grew, an infectious sound even to Angie's ears. Despite herself, her mouth twitched in response.

The first man appeared in the doorway, his emerald green robe with a shamrock hanging off him rather badly. If he was sixty, he'd had an incredibly hard life, because he looked closer to one hundred. He gave a broad smile, showcasing a few missing teeth. Then he dropped his robe. She bit her lip. He was so short he resembled a leprechaun, mostly bald, with wrinkled skin—*everywhere*—and only wearing a red bow tie.

"I'm here to apply to be a life model," he said in his whisper-soft Irish accent.

"You're not hired," a woman called out. "But you would save on the paint with that carrot."

"Oh, don't be listening to the old biddies with their harsh tongues," said the barrel-chested man who came in behind him.

He was a giant spectacle and had thick, lustrous silver hair and strong features. He was downright handsome and more in the sixty-year range she'd been expecting.

"I'm here to apply as well." He dropped his boxing robe. A collective gasp went through the room, and Angie couldn't blame them. He would be one hell of a subject to paint.

"They're simply jealous not to be lying down beside a real man like us," he continued, gesturing to his appendage.

"It's as I always thought," a woman whispered from the front row.

"*Jesus, Mary, and Joseph,*" another breathed.

"You're a strong possibility," Angie called out, deciding if the theater had arrived, she would play her part. "Next, please."

"Well, now, the Yank has better taste than the women in this village, it seems," the man said. "Seamus, you're up, man."

"Not my Seamus," Brigid squeaked.

"Don't worry none," the well-endowed man said. "We had to get them all pissed to make a showing."

Sure enough, Seamus appeared. And then Gavin and Killian. The Lucky Charms had been outdone by their own husbands.

"Here we be, girls," Gavin said, holding his arms out. "Your own personal inspiration."

Killian looked green, but he puffed out his chest. "You'll be making masterpiece after masterpiece now."

"Won't be able to keep their hands off us," Seamus said, a wide lopsided grin on his face.

They dropped their robes, and more gasps sounded.

The Lucky Charms sure as hell were lucky, Angie thought. But they didn't seem to feel so lucky just now. They were all sputtering.

"You're all hired," Angie said, calling their bluff. "Ten euros an hour. No breaks. And you have to stand completely still the whole time. Okay, come to the front of the class now. We've held class long enough waiting for you. Line up, please, on either side of me."

"Oh, the Yank is a fierce one," Seamus said, walking toward the front, almost proudly.

This was Carrick's father, Angie suddenly realized. In the flurry of naked men, she'd forgotten, or at least failed to make the connection. Oh, God, if he were anything like him...

She so didn't need to be thinking about that.

"I'm Angie, and yes, I'm fierce. Are you taking the offer?"

He gestured to himself. "Your offer is low, I think. This fine body is worth more than ten euros. Goodness, girl, I have striploin steaks that cost more."

"Let that be a lesson to you, Seamus," someone yelled. "Your steaks cost too much."

The rest of the men joined him at the front. The elderly man with the red bow tie was grinning from ear to ear.

Gavin cast Angie a glance and winked. "Would you

consider a hundred euros an hour? With this gorgeous body, I don't think I can work for less."

"What rubbish!" his wife exclaimed.

A sluice of water hitting Gavin's chest had him crying out, "What's this?"

More water hit him, and then the rest of them. Angie put her hand over her mouth as the rest of the Lucky Charms pulled water guns out from behind their easels and started soaking the men.

Like the sheep who'd rampaged Bets' garden on the day she arrived, the men scattered, crying out at the tops of their lungs.

"Run for it, men!" the giant of a man cried. "Forget the robes!"

The spryest of them made it to the doorway, only to get shot with more water in the backside. Gavin rubbed his butt and disappeared from view, and the remaining naked backsides disappeared quickly from sight.

Laughter crescendoed downstairs as more people called out to the streakers.

The Lucky Charms, headed by Bets, ran after them. Angie went to the open windows and watched with the remaining bystanders and students as Bets, Nicola, Brigid, and Siobhan shot them with the water guns until they reached their car doors.

"You'll get my Mercedes wet, Bets," the well-endowed man called as he fumbled with the door.

"Like you don't deserve it for this stunt," Bets said, running at him, "talking the men into it."

"It wasn't too hard," he said before slamming and locking the door.

"Oh, what a day!" The old man with the bow tie ducked

as water was shot his way, and then he waved and let himself into the passenger seat of the Mercedes.

Angie watched as Brigid chased down Seamus, who opened the side of a blue Berlingo and yelled, "Come on, men. Run for your lives."

The remaining men rushed across the yard to the van and climbed in, buck naked, as the Lucky Charms pelted them with the remaining water in their guns, right out of a scene from *Ghostbusters*.

"Drive! Drive!" someone inside the van yelled, and then they were navigating their way back down the driveway as people rushed after them. Class was obviously dismissed, since eighty percent of her students were downstairs, so Angie went down to join them. Women were talking animatedly. Cormac was looking into his book and handing out money as people leaned in to speak with him. Mary Kincaid and her friend's dour faces were visible when she looked over, but they were the only ones with that expression, thank God.

The Lucky Charms were talking to a group clustered around them. Bets raised her orange water gun in the air and the crowd cheered. People Angie didn't know patted her again on the back, shook her hand, and told her she'd been *brilliant*.

Her first class here in Ireland had ended in absolute and complete mayhem, and without a single paint stroke, but she realized she was smiling, happy even, maybe as happy as that day Ollie had mentioned at the state fair all those years ago.

And nothing had gone as planned. She hadn't handled the situation the way a "professional" would, or at least that's what Randall would have said, but no one seemed to mind. In fact, they were treating her like she was one of them.

Liam appeared beside her. "Pretty memorable day, eh, cousin? Even Aunt Mary can't complain. You did great from what I heard. Ten euros! That was brilliant."

Brilliant. She'd done nothing but talk smart to a bunch of streakers, yet she was being treated like a hero. "I'm really starting to like Caisleán."

"You need to come to the pub for a drink, cousin," Liam said, putting his arm around her. "The whole village will want to buy you a pint."

"Sounds good to me," she said, stepping away and tearing down the last of her ramshackle bun.

She shook her hair out and then shrugged out of her jacket. Forget the dumpy clothes. They'd liked her even though she'd utilized none of her usual professional techniques. She was going to ride this train for as long as she could.

"I might even get a little pissed." Forget Megan and her opinions. "And I want to change. Liam, it's about time I let my hair down. Past time, in fact."

He waggled his brow. "I'll be your wingman. Mum's going to be apeshit all night from the looks of it. I was afraid this was going to happen."

"What do you mean?" she asked. "I thought you said your aunt couldn't complain."

"That's not the reason," he said with a sigh. "Seeing someone naked changes things. Although I agree with my brothers. She's going to fight it like hell."

"Fight what? What are you talking about?"

"Well, if you must know—"

"Liam O'Hanlon!" Bets shouted, charging over. "Next time I need a bigger gun. Did you see that odious man bring his very own father to make a spectacle of himself? In front of the whole village, no less. And he talked Nicola, Siobhan, and Brigid's husbands into coming today to interrupt my first class. Sorry, Angie. *Our* first class."

"Yes, Mum," Liam said, keeping a straight face.

"It's outrageous, and I plan to tell him so when next I see him. I have a mind to drive to his house right now."

"You do that," Liam said. "I'm taking Angie to the pub."

"I'm going to have a stiff drink," Angie said, miming the action of taking a shot.

"Everyone is headed there," Bets said with a flick of her hand, gesturing to the cars leaving while other people carried their chairs off toward the driveway. "I'll see you shortly. Angie, you did wonderful, all things considered. Ten euros! When I'm not so hyped up, I'll probably laugh until my belly hurts."

Bets strode off, her hands pumping vigorously, stopping only to fill up her water gun at the outside water faucet.

Angie punched Liam lightly. "Okay, what in the hell were you talking about before your mom came over?"

His mouth twitched. "Donal O'Dwyer. He was the one in the Mercedes who brought his very own father."

"The sheep foe?" she sputtered. "The very well-endowed... Ah..."

Liam shook his head. "I heard some women say that, yes. Male size remains a hot topic, but you'll remember who Donal is to my mother."

"Her mortal sheep enemy." She whistled. "I didn't know mortal enemies looked like that."

"He's also on the county council."

"You're kidding. Then isn't it good he made a showing today, so to speak? It suggests he's supportive, right?"

"Mum won't see it like that, since she's keeping her plan

close to the vest." He muttered something under his breath, looking heavenward. "You should know he's also a man my brothers and I think she fancies. And he her. I can't begin to tell you how much! His sheep had never overrun our place until a few months ago, and he's been paying calls with presents to make up for it. An excuse to see her, of course, although she'd never admit that's what's going on."

"*Oh.*" She spied another look at Bets, who was red in the face.

Liam's shoulders started to shake. "You might chat with him tonight at the pub after Mum rakes him over the coals. Might help smooth things over, both for her future happiness and her dreams for this place. She's been known to stick her foot in her mouth when she's vexed, and my brothers and I approve of the match."

"Liam, I'm terrible when it comes to politics. I'm even worse at being in relationships and helping other people into them."

"Then this will be good practice for you."

She thought of Carrick. After their last conversation, her temptation was deepening into more than a simple attraction.

"If only."

CHAPTER ELEVEN

Seeing Donal O'Dwyer *naked* ranked up there with having the chicken pox when she was a kid.

Annoying, to say the least, and certainly not comfortable.

She pounded on his bright blue front door, happy to see his black Mercedes was still gleaming from her water gun attack. Maybe she'd gotten lucky and hit his leather interior. That man did love his car.

The door opened, and there he stood, an amused smile hovering over his mouth. A white towel was wrapped around his rather fine form, and he was towel-drying his messy silver hair with another.

"Are you planning on shooting me again with your water pistol?" he asked.

She raised it at him. "I'm seriously considering it after your stunt today!"

He didn't move a muscle, only grinned. "If you'd brought a water pistol for me, Bets, we could have had our own private war."

She thought of his sheep. "We already do, remember?

Donal, you have the most incredible cheek, answering the bell in this getup! What if some kids had been at your door instead of me?"

He chuckled. "You're only sore because you finally got to see the goods, Bets."

She wanted to smack him. "What are you talking about? I swear a horse must have knocked you in the head. And to include your poor father in your little stunt—"

"Dad wanted to come along," he said, resting his meaty hand against the doorframe as he stopped towel-drying his hair. "He's ninety-three, Bets, and said it's the most fun he's had since he and his friends streaked through the pasture beside his mother's May luncheon when he was a boy, making the leader of the women's club faint dead away."

"You're from a line of streakers then." She waved her gun in the air. "Why am I not surprised? Donal, you made my first art class a laughingstock. I have big plans for that studio."

"Oh, come now!" He shot her a cajoling smile, the same one he used when he brought a trinket after his sheep devoured her roses. "This from the head of the Lucky Charms? Bets, you're always up for some good fun, and so is the village, which is as I expected. Besides, tell me you weren't thinking about having your Yank cousin teach painting nudes."

"That was for me to decide."

"Bets, it was the buzz of the village these past days. You must've known what we were after." He nodded to her water gun. "You were ready for us."

His superior brow rose, and she almost shot him again for good measure. "We didn't have names."

"Like you couldn't squeeze them out of someone?"

She let out a frustrated sound. "How long have I lived

here? Like we could stop you eejits. Donal, these classes are important to me. It's a chance to start something meaningful for the village."

"I admire the hell out of you for the business pursuits you've created since Bruce died, but let's be honest," he countered, pointing his finger at her. "They won't feed your soul completely—keeping you busy and occupied and not thinking about living alone for the rest of your life. Trust me. I've been working my whole life, so I know. You're not meant to, girl, and neither am I."

She tightened her grip as the same confusion covered her. He'd talked like this before on a stormy day in early April, standing in her parlor, dripping on her rug with a bouquet of gorgeous red roses, ones he'd said were to make up for the damage his sheep had done the day before. "I don't want you to talk like this. I've already told you that."

"What are you afraid of?" He threw the towel in his hand aside. "I'm not giving up until you see sense. I know how you've looked at me since you grieved Bruce. I know how I've felt about you since I grieved my Margaret. Why do you think I haven't been sewing up the holes in my fencing these past months? Girl, I've been courting you. Even my father and my two girls in Dublin are cheering me on. They've always liked you."

She stepped back, almost dropping the water pistol. He'd spoken to his family about her? "*Courting me?* That's a fine excuse for your sheep getting out."

His eyes narrowed. "Bets, my sheep have never gotten out this much, and I swear to you it's over now that your roses are starting to bloom. Did you think I was bringing by gifts only to apologize?"

Sure, she'd been suspicious at first—the problem of the sheep *was* a new one—but she'd persuaded herself there was nothing to it. Oh, why hadn't her girlfriends said anything? "But I knew your Margaret."

"And I knew your Bruce. Both were fine people, but they're gone from us now, girl."

She still hated hearing that, even if it was true. "I don't want to get married again, Donal. I loved Bruce with all my heart, but I don't fancy taking care of another Irishman. You know how you are."

His brows slammed together. "Saints preserve us. All right, even though I'm not proposing marriage, I'll ask you. How are we?"

"You want someone to cook and clean for you," she continued. "You threw that towel on the floor, for heaven's sake."

"Which I'll pick up when you stop picking at me like a hen—"

"I want to do more than take care of another man in my final years. I want to travel, which you can't do as a farmer. I also want to do something with all this space I have. I have *ideas*. You're right about me wanting to keep busy, but I don't see anything wrong with that. I like being busy."

"You've got your opinions, I see, but you always did." He scratched his jaw. "I'm not sure today is the day to address them all save one. I've managed to cook and clean just fine without a woman around. Not that I don't appreciate everything Margaret did for us. Our agreement was that she'd take care of the home and kids, and I would take care of the sheep and make a living. It doesn't have to be like that with us, Bets—although let me say again that I'd only like to spend some time with you to start. You're the one talking about marriage. I mean, I know I'm irresistible—"

"Widowed men don't like to be alone—"

"Carrick Fitzgerald is an exception then," he countered.

"Oh, let's put this to bed for the moment. I'm sorry if the scene at your painting class made you cross. Bets, I honestly thought it would make you see me in a new light."

Her eyes flew down to his crotch. "Did you, now?"

"Oh, Jesus, Mary, and Joseph! Yes, I wanted you to see me as a man."

She sure as hell had. After that, there'd be no forgetting he was a man and then some.

"But more," he said, leaning closer to her, "I wanted you to see I could get into some fun like you and the Lucky Charms do. That I could fit you in that way. I know it's important to you."

Her legs seemed to weaken under her as if the ground had given way. She hadn't expected him to be so sincere, so intent...

"I also needed to know if I *liked* getting into that kind of trouble," he said, his serious gaze touching her face. "Know what? Despite the nerves I've had all week, thinking about our stunt, I liked it. And I sure as hell like that you charged over here to poke at me for it."

She lifted her water gun again and shot him straight in the chest, making him laugh, damn him. "Then here's me poking you one last time. Now, I'm leaving. Keep your sheep in your pasture and away from my roses."

"I gave you my word—"

"I want to win the top prize at the fair this year."

"You will if I have anything to say about," he said, prompting her to shoot him again.

"And stay away from my painting classes."

"Go out with me then." He followed her to her car in his towel, not caring that people were walking on the road, their eyes locked on the spectacle they were making. The village was going to be clucking for days.

"I won't go out with you. Certainly not after today. Not for all the tea in China!"

"I'll ask you when I see you next," he said, reaching her car first and opening the door. "I can be patient."

The easy way he said it conveyed his resolve, and it made her belly quiver. She'd always wished for patience in a man. The last man she'd expected it from was Donal O'Dwyer.

"I don't want you to be patient. I want to forget we ever had this conversation." That she'd ever seen his naked body. How was she to forget *that* when they ran into each other at the pub or a store in town?

"Instead of forgetting, you might ask yourself why you're so opposed to the idea."

"You have some cheek telling me what to do!"

"You already said that," he told her, an amused smile hovering on his mouth.

She got into her car and glared at him. "I don't like you like that."

He planted his feet, but thankfully the towel didn't fall. "Your eyes tell me something different. I might have been married for thirty years, but I still know when a woman wants me, and Bets, you surely do."

"Maybe I'm just horny," she shot back.

His laughter came from deep in his chest, an engaging sound that called to something inside her very heart. Oh, she didn't want to feel like this. She had plans. A man would only get in the way.

"I'm horny too," he said, gesturing to the area wrapped in the white towel. "But that's not the reason I want to go out with you. Of course, I'd like to have sex with you when the time is right for us. I have a feeling we'll both be surprised by how good it is. I mean what I said—I'm not interested in you because I want someone to keep house for me. I can do that for myself. We can just enjoy each other."

She didn't want to think about having sex with him, and she certainly didn't want him to tempt her by not tying the privilege of it to washing and ironing his clothes like some of the idiots from the pub. "I'm leaving now."

"I'll be seeing you later on," he said, closing her door carefully. "Put your belt on."

"You put some clothes on!"

His hand went to where the towel was secured, threatening a mischief that made her heart bounce in her chest. She turned on the car and jammed the gear into reverse, almost running off his driveway and onto the lawn like a drunkard. How embarrassing.

If she went out with him, she would be going backward for sure. Tied down to another man who couldn't travel or didn't want to. Who was content to stay at home, watching the telly after dinner or going to the pub with his friends.

She'd loved Bruce—she had. But their relationship had changed after the move to Ireland. They'd been adventurous once. Wild. But living on O'Hanlon land had changed him. He'd fallen back into the routine of working with his dad's cattle, taking care of his parents, and attending family events with people he didn't like, Mary Kincaid topping the list. She'd hated spending Sunday after Sunday like that.

Raising the boys had kept her from noticing how many things she'd given up. Sometimes she'd even used them as an excuse to opt out of something she didn't want to do. She knew she'd babied Liam because of it, and at times she felt ashamed of that. No question: marriage had changed her and restrained her spirit some, even though she'd had the Lucky Charms.

That's why she understood Angie's struggles. She was determined to help her with this new project, as much as be helped by it. And Megan... Hadn't her cousin settled into a predictable life? Only she wasn't sure if Megan wanted to change, especially given how adamant she'd been in turning down the offer to live on her own and teach ceramics.

Bets wanted to change. This was her chance to start living large again. Making and contributing to something more.

A man would try to stifle that, certainly a man from this village. Donal might have said he wanted something else from her, but hadn't Bruce said the same in the beginning? He hadn't expected her to become a farmer's wife, and yet she had.

She rolled down the window to cool down her heated face. She couldn't show up at the pub like this.

But as she drove past Donal's sheep in the pasture on the way back to her house, she couldn't stop thinking about what he'd said.

Especially the part about liking her brand of trouble. Bruce had found the Lucky Charms amusing, but he'd been more of a bystander to their shenanigans than an instigator.

No, she couldn't forget that, and of all the things Donal had said, that was the one she needed to forget the most.

CHAPTER TWELVE

The Brazen Donkey had the allure of intense hops, heated conversation, and loud music, alongside a cluster of amusing paintings and caricatures of donkeys, apparently an animal many Irish were nostalgic about.

Angie loved it from the moment she stepped inside.

Of course, the cheer that went up when the patrons spotted her helped, drowning out Coldplay. She'd never been cheered before. Her mind was so heady from the praise, she might as well have had three whiskeys.

"It's herself, at last," an old man said, stepping forward and taking her elbow and leading her to the bar. "I'm Eoghan O'Dwyer from earlier, and I'd like to be the first to buy you a drink. You're not like one of those American women on the telly who only drink white wine?"

"God, no," she answered as people made room for them in front of the scratched-up bartop. "I love whiskey."

"Then you're in the right country, you are." He signaled to Gavin what she imagined was a sign to pour her a drink and gave a naughty wink. "You don't know me, do you?"

Liam snorted beside her. "She might wish she didn't remember you."

When he pointed to the unmistakable red bow tie displayed between his gray cardigan, she laughed heartily. "Oh, I didn't recognize you with clothes on."

A few people around them laughed, including Liam. "Never do we want to see you without your clothes on again, Eoghan. You'll give me nightmares about aging."

"It *is* a nightmare, Liam O'Hanlon," the man said, "so you'd best enjoy your youth while you have it. But we aren't here to speak of aging. We're here to speak about me posing naked on a permanent basis for this fine girl here."

"Jesus," Gavin said, extending a whiskey to her, "that's enough of that talk, so it is. Siobhan was threatening to put me own clothes in the spare bedroom after today's craic."

"Ah, she'll get over it soon enough," Eoghan said, picking up his whiskey and clanking their glasses together. "We don't have enough craic anymore. Everyone seems to be bothered by a little bit of this and that. I swear! What's the point of living if you don't have fun now and then?"

"Well, you'd be knowing it," Gavin said, "given that you're in your ninety-third year."

"You're ninety-three?" She catalogued the age lines flowing like tributaries through his oval face, along with the twinkle in his Van Dyke brown and verdant green eyes. "Good for you then for showing up today and auditioning. I'm buying *your* next drink."

He turned around and held up his whiskey and yelled, "The Yank congratulated me on auditioning today for the life model position and is buying *my* next drink."

Another cheer went up.

Leaning in, he gave her a cheeky grin. "Am I hired then?"

"No," she said with a laugh. "But things could change."

"Around here they don't change much," he told her. "I think sometimes the weather has more fun than we do, what with all its ups and downs. Days like today remind us we need to stir things up more. Like Bets loves and Mary Kincaid hates. You watch that one, girl. But I'm keeping you from the others. Liam will be introducing you to the village proper like. They're mad to meet you."

She kissed his cheek. "Thanks for the drink, Eoghan."

"Anytime, girl, anytime." The old man righted his bow tie and gave her another grin.

"Gavin, his next one is on me." She dug out some bills and laid them on the bar before Liam tugged her through the crowd. He introduced her to table after table and to those mulling around with their ears cocked to overhear their conversation.

Gavin came out to fill her glass, saying everyone was vying to buy her a drink. How many did she have in her? She shrugged and knocked the whiskey back, inciting another cheer. Forget her doctor and her worry about her blood pressure. What she really needed was a night to blow off some steam. Let out all that pressure in her blood. Yes, that was it.

"I like whiskey," she told Liam after some whiskey fairy had put another in her hand. "But I think I love Irish whiskey."

"So I see," he said, putting his arm around her sweetly. "We couldn't be related otherwise."

She studied his features. The sedge brown hair. The green eyes. Strong granite jaw. The gold hoop in his left ear. "You know what, cousin? You really look like a pirate."

He cheered her glass. "I'll take that as a right fine compliment."

"It looks as though someone might need a chair," she heard a familiar voice say.

Turning around, she wobbled a bit, spilling her drink. "Dammit, Carrick. Look what you made me do."

"In for a few whiskeys already, Yank? I heard you had a day."

He was standing with Jamie and a few other men she didn't recognize. They were all the same towering height as the Fitzgerald men with dark hair in various shades of brown, massive shoulders, and well-defined facial features. Glorious subjects to paint. "You all might be the most gorgeous men I've seen in a long time. I wish I had a paintbrush right now to capture you." Even more so in this moody lighting—the pub was all dark wood, with mellow yellow streaming from brass fixtures above them.

"I can come tomorrow to pose, if you'd like," one of them said. "I always thought it would be wonderful to be painted. I had an artist outside Notre Dame in Paris make a portrait of me. I'm Brady McGrath, Gavin and Siobhan's eldest. This here is my twin brother, Declan. He's a butcher—"

"Where's the baker and the candlestick maker?" she asked with a laugh, glad they weren't identical twins.

Carrick's lips twitched. God, he was way too beautiful for words, and she was feeling a little tipsy. Damn if it didn't feel good.

"The baker is sitting in the corner over there under the proud Mayo GAA football flag," Carrick answered. "The candlestick maker, I'm sorry to say, went out of business in the eighteenth century."

"Oh, you're funny," Angie said, analyzing his eyes. Yes, they were Payne's grey, but flecks of blue peeked through them today. They would be a delightful challenge to paint. Except she wasn't supposed to paint him.

But it was hard to ignore the temptation. Sometimes at night, she dug out that first and only painting she'd done of him. Her whole body tingled when she touched the paper. His very being seemed alive, and she hadn't even finished it. What would happen when she captured his humor?

"No, he's mostly not," Jamie told her with a quick flash of a smile.

"He is," Brady insisted. "I'm the postman—at least until Dad retires and lets me take over this fine pub."

"Since we're making introductions, I'm Kade Donovan," said the fifth man. His eyes were Van Dyke brown and positively soulful.

"You run the pony therapy farm for kids with emotional and special needs." An image of Ollie holding his sad little blanket after his father's funeral rose in her mind. "Ollie is going to love it if Megan agrees."

"Tell her to come by and talk to me. We all need friends, especially when we're new to a place and going through a rough time."

"And losing someone you love is the toughest," Carrick added, capturing her gaze. "Be silly to pretend otherwise."

She knew it all too well, which only reminded her of her responsibility to them. "Oh, what am I doing? Getting tipsy when they're at home. I should call Megan. She's going to wonder where I am."

"Already handled," Liam said, squeezing her shoulder. "I texted her where we were headed and asked if she wanted to pop by. Told her I could look after Ollie for a time if she wanted to join the festivities. She declined, but maybe we'll convince her next time."

She felt the pull of duty. She should be home so she

could read Ollie a story after his bath. Megan couldn't muster the energy to do the voices in his favorite books anymore. She used to read so creatively, and it had been a delight to listen. It was like a younger, happier Megan came to life alongside the characters in the storybook, a Megan who used to catch her if she tried to skip over pages.

Tears burned her eyes, and the hopelessness of it all came over her, the kind of hopelessness no amount of whiskey could help. "I worry she's never going to heal."

"Hush now," Carrick said, his face darkening. "She'll heal."

"You haven't." She slapped her hand over her mouth, spilling more whiskey. "I shouldn't have said that, Carrick. I'm so sorry. I should leave."

"Ah, forget about it," Jamie said. "You speak the truth, and we all know it."

Kade nodded to Liam, and the two steered her to the right before Carrick could say anything. Brady rushed ahead, leaning down to whisper something to the large group of men around the closest table. The next moment, they were all rising from their chairs, taking their drinks with them with a few parting salvos.

"You shouldn't have moved those people," Angie said as Kade pulled out a chair for her and sat down beside her, Liam sitting on her other side. "I can stand."

"You're a hero," Kade said gently. "Enjoy the privileges. Now, you don't need to be apologizing to Carrick. Jamie's right. Truth is truth."

She looked over to where Carrick had sat down, directly across from her. "You're not mad?"

"You don't think my friends mention this 'truth' to me every few months?" Carrick reached for her whiskey and drank some. "Sorry, I'm parched. Hell, Kade's even offered me a pony ride."

"Winston couldn't handle your brute weight," Kade said, "but Eve—one of my ponies for adults—would manage you just fine."

"I offered to cleave his heart right out of his chest one time like I did when my own fiancée called off our wedding," Declan said as Brady brought a tray of glasses filled with whiskey to the table. "Sorry, that's bad butcher humor."

"Butcher humor is really awful," she said, inhaling deeply to stave off more tears.

She studied Carrick again. He was smiling. No, he wasn't upset about what she'd said. That was good. The thought of hurting him had almost put her in a panic. He caught her looking at him and gazed right back. Her chest grew tight. She didn't want to like him.

"You had a hell of a day, Yank," he finally said.

Indeed, but it had started very pleasantly with him, just like every other day this last week. "I've had a lot worse."

"That sounds like a good story," Brady said, leaning over the table. "Did you leave some Yank heartbroken when you came to Ireland?"

She huffed a bitter laugh. "That would be the day."

"Then you're not in a relationship?"

"Leave her alone," Carrick said with another glower. "She's here to paint and help her sister and nephew. Not be getting into the thick of it with you."

Brady whistled.

Carrick shoved a drink at him. "Let's change the subject."

"I'll help you out there," Liam said. "Kade, I wonder where your dad has gotten off to. I don't see him here. Or

Donal. But that's likely since my mother went and henpecked him for today's antics. Oh, she was mighty cross."

"So I heard from Cormac O'Sullivan and a few other bystanders who witnessed the show," Kade said, shaking his head. "Me own mum didn't seem too cross. I saw her and Dad yelling at each other and then slipping into the shed to make up. I expect that's why they aren't here yet."

"Oh, God!" Angie said suddenly, her mind whirling. "I just realized. I've seen your fathers naked. Is that weird?"

Declan laughed. "Only if it happens again. Our mother will be less forgiving next time."

"Dad told me she made him swear he'd never do it again," Brady said, "and he refused, saying *never* was a long time. Look at Eoghan O'Dwyer. Unveiling himself at his age. Donal was a genius to ask him."

"Speaking of himself," Kade said. "Donal is here. Liam, is your mother still refusing to see that he's courting her?"

"I suppose we'll find out," he said with a grimace. "Here he comes."

A giant hand touched her shoulder, and Angie turned her head. Donal towered over her, his hair still a touch wet, making its usual silver look more like mercury in an old thermometer. All conversation in the pub stopped.

"Yank, if you require an apology like your cousin, I'll give it."

His mouth was tight, but his shoulders seemed even tighter. Like someone had screwed the bones and sinew together with pliers. Somehow she knew it hadn't gone well between him and Cousin Bets. "I appreciate the offer, but it's like your father said earlier. If we can't have a bit of craic from time to time, then where are we?"

He held out his hand to her, and she shook it.

"Thank you," he said, his shoulders relaxing a touch. "My father does have his moments, God bless him. Age isn't great on the body, but it's good on the soul."

Angie loved that. She hoped she'd remember it in the morning.

"She give you hell?" Liam asked.

"With the four horsemen as her companions," Donal said, running a hand through his hair. "She brought her water pistol. Shot me upside the chest again. Liam, I told you the regard I had for your father—God rest him—and your mother when we spoke a few months ago. But after today, maybe I should up and forget about everything I told you. The opinions she has..."

He'd spoken to Liam about his interest in Bets? Liam hadn't let on that it had gone so far. She thought it a sweet gesture, endearing, although she didn't want to be disloyal to her cousin.

"Let her cool down, Donal," Liam said, lowering his hand in the air by degrees like a temperature gauge. "Mum's mad usually burns through her stubbornness around an issue."

The door of the pub crashed against the wall, and the conversation died again. Cormac O'Sullivan appeared in the doorway, his book in hand. "We've had us a fine day of craic, and since I was involved, I've conceded to introduce the next bit, God forgive me. Killian, if you'd be so good as to do your part."

The large man stepped into the pub, red in the face. "You're to remember I did this under duress. Gavin, step aside. I need your music player."

When Killian pushed behind the bar, Gavin tried to head him off, but he stepped back when the man gave him a healthy shove.

Angie leaned forward in her chair like everyone else. The opening of "You Give Love a Bad Name" began to play. Part of the pub groaned. The other part started laughing.

Then the cheering started as Bets, Brigid, Nicola, and Siobhan entered the pub wearing emerald green boxing club robes identical to the ones the men had worn earlier, although theirs were paired with feather boas. They walked toward the bar, people scattering to give them room. Bets pulled out a chair as Bon Jovi's guitar wept and then used it as a stepping stool to climb onto the bar.

This is going to be fun.

Oh, she envied them their freedom, their self-assurance.

"We're in for it now," Liam said, holding his head.

"You don't think they're going to show the village their lady bits, do you?" Brady asked, grimacing.

"Good God, I hope not," Carrick said, pressing his hand to his eyes.

Angie started to laugh along with everyone else as the women took up positions on the bar and started to dance. Well, Bets gyrated like a punk rocker from back in the day. Siobhan and Brigid mostly shimmied. Nicola wove her body like a belly dancer in a sultan's tent.

"Are you planning on tearing off your clothes for us?" Eoghan shouted out.

A cheer went up from the men—save the cluster of sons around Angie, all of whom groaned.

"Don't you wish?" Bets called out, but when no one made a move to strip off anything, the crowd settled down.

"Mind if I sit?" Donal asked, grabbing a nearby chair and pulling it up to their table. "Liam, forget what I said earlier. I'm not giving up on your mum. How could any man give up on a woman like that, who's breathing a fiery challenge at me in front of the whole village?"

"Angie!" Bets called out, motioning to her. "Come on up here, girl!"

People turned their heads and looked in her direction. A cheer went up. A surge of excitement rose within her.

"Maybe the Yank will give us a real show?" someone shouted.

That froze her like a deer in headlights. "Not on your life."

The crowd started to clap, encouraging her. Megan's face swam in her mind. She could already hear sister's chiding. *A few whiskeys is one thing, Angie. Dancing on a bar in the village pub is another. Would a teacher dance on the bar? No students equals no money. You want people to respect you, remember?*

"Oh, go on!" Liam encouraged. "This is why you're here, isn't it?"

No, she was here to paint and teach. She couldn't afford to alienate the people in town who thought like Randall and her dad and Megan—the ones who wouldn't understand or approve of what she was trying to express.

Better to play it safe, Angie.

Bets called her name again, and the crowd gave a groan when she shook her head. Her cousin stopped motioning to her though, and the crowd turned back to the show.

She hunched down in her chair, reaching for her whiskey, only to realize Carrick had it. When she lifted her gaze, she noted his eyes weren't on the women dancing on the bar, but on her. In them, she saw compassion and an eerie sense of understanding. Her heart banged against her rib cage. She thought he was going to speak, but his jaw tightened. After a few moments, he silently slid the whiskey to her. Then he looked away.

She'd disappointed him as well. Hell, she'd disappointed herself. The artist she used to be wouldn't have given it a thought, but the party had gone out of her.

Hanging her head wasn't the way, so she pasted a smile on her face. The better to cover up a hard truth: she was still letting other people dictate her expression, and a true artist didn't do that.

In any form.

CHAPTER THIRTEEN

S he'd wanted to join them on the bar.

Carrick had seen the green fire that had lit up Angie's hazel brown eyes. Green fire was a sign of the unstoppable force of nature, his granny had always told him when they had a bonfire around summer solstice.

But the Yank had stopped herself. She'd frozen up like a frightened animal and then bowed down to her fear. He'd almost given her an encouraging word. Pulled her out of her chair and helped her onto the bar even.

But Jamie and his friends were watching him too closely. She wasn't his business.

Hell, she wasn't his woman, and he'd do best to remember it.

And yet, he continued to keep track of her as the evening progressed, all the while noticing how lovely she looked with her hair tumbling down around her shoulders. She didn't drink any more of the whiskey offered her, saying she wasn't in proper drinking shape. The smile on her face was as fake as the rhinestone tiaras women wore to hen parties.

He loathed that smile.

When she sent it his way as Liam walked her around to give her goodbyes, he ground his teeth so hard he feared a toothache later on. She looked about as animated as a wooden pigeon, for heaven's sake. As she left, a cheer went up to see her off. He didn't join in. He couldn't look away from her sunken shoulders of defeat before the door closed, stealing her from his sight.

Kade leaned close to his ear as Bon Jovi came on again. "You want to go after her."

"He does," Jamie said, leaning in close as well. "Has Sorcha visited you again?"

"Sorcha is back?" Kade grabbed his shoulder. "How is it I'm just hearing this now?"

"Because it's none of your damn business," Carrick said, trying to rise from the squeaky chair.

Kade pushed him back down, an unusual move for such a gentle man. "You one of my oldest friends, and it's not my business? What did she say?"

Jamie opened his mouth to speak, and Carrick spoke his name in warning.

"There's no hiding it." Jamie knocked back his drink. "You know why she's back, Kade. Same reason she came before."

Kade turned his chair to face him full on. "She likes the Yank for you then?"

Jamie—the traitor—nodded.

"I'd be seeing it," Kade said, rocking a little in place as he mulled it over. "Both a little lost. Both a little stubborn. Both a little craic."

"I'm going to head home unless you shut your mouth," Carrick growled.

"You desperately need a pony ride," Kade said, "but you need something else more."

"Don't we all," Jamie said with a hearty sigh.

"Not only *that*," Kade said with a pointed look. "Something to fill your heart and soul again, man."

"I don't need anything to fill my heart and soul," Carrick said with an edge. "Oh, why do I bother arguing with you? When you have that puppy face, there's no talking to you, Kade. You'd heal the whole world if you could."

"One pony ride at a time," Kade said, loosening his grip from Carrick's shoulder. "And I'll always put in something extra for friends."

Damn. That was why Kade was Kade, and they all loved him. "Look, me and the Yank have already talked this through. She doesn't want me any more than I want her. She's here to paint and find herself again—whatever that means. I told her how I want my life. We're not compatible. Simple as that."

The front door slammed open suddenly, smacking the wall. A couple of people cried out in fright. One said, "Jesus," and another shouted, "The fairies must be out stirring up trouble."

Carrick knew who the real culprit was.

"Do you see her?" Jamie asked Kade.

His friend, who also could see and hear ghosts, shook his head. "No, but I'll have her visit me. Best to get on the same page. I know you have your ambition, Carrick, but it won't keep you warm at night."

"Unless you're thinking about taking up with one of your ewes," Jamie said with an audible snort. "There's stories about men and their sheep. Don't be a cliché."

He elbowed his brother and then forced a smile as their mothers came over to the table with Bets.

"And what did you boys think of your fathers parading around naked as jaybirds at my first painting class today?" Bets asked, twirling her green boa.

"I plead the fifth, as you Americans say," Jamie answered first.

"Where did you hear that saying from?" she asked.

"An American TV crime show," Jamie answered. "Don't make us answer, Bets. It's best when we're not in the middle between our mothers and fathers."

"I couldn't agree more," Declan said, knocking back his whiskey.

Kade set his hands on the table. "I think the men had something they needed to express, and I for one admire them for it."

Nicola shot him a look. "Son, usually I love your compassion, but while your father and I have reached a truce, I have to wonder what showing off their naked bodies like eejits helped them express."

Brady shrugged. "Maybe they were looking to spice things up."

Siobhan put her hand on his shoulder. "And what might they be wishing to spice up? Answer carefully. Your spot at my dinner table might be in jeopardy."

"They clearly lost their minds, Mum," Brady answered quickly. "You should beat them with thistles to teach them a lesson."

Carrick wished he could put his hands over his ears and blot out the whole matter, but his mum nudged him, and she wasn't a woman to be ignored. "The Yank seemed to handle the whole incident well, so there's no harm. She even managed to garner the respect of the men without shaming them for their visit. I heard people talking right and left about joining the painting class—despite Mary Kincaid's chiding. Bets, I'd say it's a win."

"You do, do you?" She stared Carrick down, twirling that infernal feather boa. "Then why didn't she dance on the bar? I thought she wanted to, and with Megan at home—"

"She's still finding her way," he said, feeling strangely protective of her. "It's a new town. Give her a break, Bets. She's got a lot of pressure, what with needing to paint again for the gallery showing around the agricultural fair."

All eyes zeroed in on him. Kade was smiling. Jamie was trying not to smirk.

Oh, for fuck's sake. He'd gone way too far in Angie's defense.

"Heard you ripped into poor Donal but good, Bets," Brady said, changing the subject like the good friend he was. "Wish I could have seen it. But not the lot of them in nothing at all, of course. From what I hear, some of the women fainted."

"They did not," Bets said, smacking him with her boa.

But Carrick noticed how her gaze tracked to the bar, where Donal stood talking to his father and some other men.

Brady hooked his thumb in Donal's direction. "My dad was telling me he might start feeling less of a man around Donal. If you know what I mean."

Good God! They were not talking about Donal's size, were they? Carrick rose in his chair.

"Your father is a fine specimen of a man," Siobhan said sharply. "I'd never want him to feel lacking."

"Then be kind to him, Mum," Declan said, glancing at his brother. "Don't make him sleep in the spare bedroom."

Even though Carrick knew they were only trying to help their parents make peace, he didn't want to hear it. "I'm going. Early morning."

"Brother, it's always early for you, between your sheep and your building," Jamie said, but he stood in solidarity. "I'll walk out with you."

"Me too," Kade said, joining them.

The McGrath twins agreed, rising and kissing their mum. Carrick followed Jamie, and they kissed their mum goodnight too.

"Off with you," Bets said. "We have one more song to play."

"Are you going to talk to Donal?" Siobhan asked as Carrick and his friends were leaving.

"Not even if he were on fire and needed a blanket to quench the flames," Bets said as they walked away.

Poor Donal. He wasn't going to have an easy time of it. Taking pity on the man, Carrick and the others made the rounds to bid goodbye to the remaining patrons from the village, which included making a visit to the front table where his father sat with the rest of their streaking group. Eoghan was asleep in his chair, snoring, but with an almost childlike smile on his face.

Seamus gestured to the old man. "If he dies in his sleep, he'd have had a grand send-off."

They nodded and all crossed themselves.

"I suppose we should be grateful Bets and her crew didn't spray us with water pistols from atop the bar," Gavin said. "For a moment there, I wasn't sure what they were planning. I feared for my bar glasses as much as my eyes. Me own wife excluded, of course. She's a goddess."

"Take the win today," Kade said, gesturing to the men. "You expressed some inner desire to be seen as men. Walk proudly these next few days while the talk in the village is red hot."

"Son, I always walk proud," Killian answered, removing his hand. "We don't all ride ponies."

Carrick bit his lip at the jab. This old line of talk from Killian about Kade liking pony therapy and animal healing instead of stallion breeding angered all of them.

They all hustled out of there before anyone came to Kade's defense and caused bad feelings. The McGraths offered a quick goodbye, leaving Carrick, Jamie, and Kade.

The street was blessedly quiet, thank God, and a gentle rain had started to fall. Carrick took a breath to clear his head as they moved along.

Jamie hunched his shoulders as the rain danced off his waterproof jacket. "I wouldn't be a very good example to my students if I clocked your father, Kade."

"You've all spoken up before. It won't change his mind about things. I've told you to leave it be."

"I'd have punched Killian for you," Sorcha said, appearing on the street.

Carrick jumped a mile. "*Jesus.*"

Kade elbowed Jamie. "You were right. She's back. Hello, Sorcha. Thanks for wanting to defend me, but it's not necessary."

"So you say. It's good to see you, Kade. You're doing well, they tell me. I was going to call on you."

She smiled, untouched by the rain, her white dress billowing in a wind they didn't feel in their place and time.

"Then we're of the same mind, as I was going to ask you to come for a visit," Kade answered.

"You can *ask* them?" Jamie whispered.

Carrick gave him a little shove.

"Back to why I'm here," his dead wife said in a pointed tone. "You should have helped her, Carrick. She needed it tonight. More than you know."

Guilt swept through him as he remembered the wooden look on her face. "Leave me be, Sorcha."

"Kade, help this stubborn man find his way back to his heart. The Yank is the key. I know *your* heart, even better from where I am now. I know you won't disappoint me."

She kissed his cheek and then vanished.

"Why did she kiss you and not me?" Carrick asked, his jaw tight. But he knew. She wouldn't want to torture him that way.

"They can kiss too?" Jamie asked with a gasp.

"She always did like me," Kade said, meeting his gaze. "And she wants you to move on, doesn't she?"

"What did she say this time?" Jamie looked back and forth between the two of them, looking pale. Kade answered, but Carrick barely paid attention. The smell of oranges was so strong he wouldn't have been surprised if the patrons in the pub noticed it. He hoped no one would recognize it. The last thing he needed was anyone knowing Sorcha was back in ghost form, trying to set him up with the Yank.

"As I live and breathe," Jamie finally said, ending with a whistle. "She's mighty determined."

She always had been. And they hadn't always been of the same mind. He thought of what she'd said about his plans for the house. Certainly, they weren't of the same mind about that. Anger burned in his chest.

"Did she say anything about me needing to pick up Carrick's bar tab?" Jamie asked.

Kade only looked puzzled and shook his head. "Well, I guess I have my orders, Carrick. What time will you come by for your pony ride?"

"Up yours, Donovan."

CHAPTER FOURTEEN

D ammit, she should have gotten up on that bar and danced last night.

As Angie got dressed, a litany of regrets played in her mind, like they had for most of the night. Her retro painting clothes felt like sandpaper against her skin, reminding her of all the ways she felt lost and voiceless. She eyed her mousy brown hair with disdain and put it into a ponytail. If she couldn't express herself without fearing judgment and punishment or losing people's respect, she couldn't create anything more than the stilted demos she painted in her art classes.

She had to push through these feelings, or she'd seriously backslide.

Picking up her phone, she noticed a text from Bets.

People are clamoring for art classes after yesterday. Who could have imagined that scene would inspire such an interest in art? Hope you're game for offering more classes?

She sat down on the bed as her knees gave out in relief. After gathering herself, she crept into the kitchen and cried out. Her sister was sitting at the kitchen table in her tan robe, her hair unbrushed, per her usual grief routine.

"You're up early," she said, noticing the unwashed dishes in the sink and the remnants of dinner.

"You were out pretty late."

She was so not up for this. "I got home at ten o'clock, Megan."

"Ollie was asking about going to the pub to join you—and Liam," Megan continued. "Angie, I saw some of the videos people posted on Bets' Facebook page. My God, you had a bunch of naked men overrun your first class. *Old* men! How absolutely mortifying!"

Angie crossed to make herself tea. "It was a bit of craic, like the Irish say."

Her sister stood and put her hands on her tiny waist, accentuating the weight she'd lost in the past few months. "Bets and the others wouldn't have used water pistols if it had only been a bit of fun. She was so mad her face was red."

Her head started to throb. "Megan, she was mad for other reasons, which is why she and the Lucky Charms ended up dancing on the bar in Gavin's pub and giving as good as they got."

Her sister sank into the chair and took a sip of her tea. "I saw that too. I thought they were going to drop their robes for a moment, and I was appalled. Thankfully better sense ruled, if you can call it that. I was happy to see you refused to participate. When Bets started calling your name in the video, I wasn't sure what you'd do."

She had to bite her lip to hold back her anger, some of which was still for herself. "Megan, I need to get painting. The light is really great right now."

Her sister glanced out the window. The mist hovering

over the fields was almost a pinkish gray. Angie had the sudden urge to be swallowed up in it so no one could find her.

"I don't want to table this." Megan crossed the room to her. "You're changing, and not in a good way if you think public indecency isn't a big deal. Ollie isn't himself either. He's growing angrier by the day. When I was putting him to bed last night, he shouted at me for babying him. He even threw his blanket at me."

Angie rubbed the back of her neck. Her headache was gaining speed. "You brought it?"

Her sister nodded, her cheeks flushing.

She sighed. "Megan, I know you brought it out after Tyson died, but that's his baby blanket. He hasn't used it since the funeral."

"I know what my son needs." Megan fiddled with her robe's sash. "It gives him comfort. He just doesn't know it. But you're missing the point. I needed you last night, and you weren't here."

There it was. Her sister *needed* her.

She could hear Randall telling her how much he needed her at the beginning of their relationship. How he didn't know how to do anything without her, meaning he didn't want to try.

Maybe it wasn't fair, but she was sick of it after eight months.

She fisted her hands to gather her strength. "Megan, I can't always be here. I need to live my life too."

Her sister turned a darker gray. "But I can't do this alone. I can't be both mom and dad to Ollie. My husband just died."

No, your husband didn't just die. He died eight months

ago. But she couldn't say that. "Megan, you took care of him alone when Tyson was gone."

"But I wasn't depressed then!"

She pressed her fingers to her temple. "We've talked about other ways to help you overcome depression, Megan. I don't know what else to do. I've been trying to see your new breakfast routine as a win, plus the way you haven't been lying around as much, but I need you to do more. Maybe you should have moved in with Mom and Dad instead of coming to Ireland."

Her sister gasped. "But you know how Dad is. He wouldn't be soft with me or Ollie right now. He'd tell us to buck up and move on. Not dishonor a fallen war hero by acting like crybabies. If it were only Mom... She'd take care of us and make us feel good. Mostly."

Yes, she would. Angie knew the pattern all too well. She'd been doling out the same kind of caretaking her whole life. "Then you have a dilemma. I'm going to go and let you think, but regarding Ollie, I think it's healthy that he threw that baby blanket aside. Megan, he's eight—"

"He lost his father," her sister said, staring at her accusingly.

"Yes, he lost his father. And you lost your husband. I 'screwed' up my life with Randall and Saul. It's time to own our problems. Figure out a way to move past them. Maybe Dad's partly right. If we don't buck up, we'll be crippled for the rest of our lives. I mean, do you really plan to live with me forever?"

Her sister's eyes filled with tears. "I don't know. I'm so lost, Angie."

She couldn't stand to see her pain any longer. She grabbed Megan in a hug. "I am too, but I'm digging my way out. There's support here, Megan. I feel it. I've found it. In Bets and Liam and Carrick."

Megan pressed back. *"Carrick?"*

Oh, God, she'd included him. But it was true. Still, she rushed on before Megan could probe. "And I met the man who does the pony therapy last night. His name is Kade, and he's wonderful. I think you should talk to him. He can help Ollie. I just know it."

"I'm still not sure about that," her sister said, taking her hand. "Angie, I need you to *promise* me not to do anything impulsive. It scares me that you included Carrick on your list. I thought you'd sworn off men for the time being."

Oh, God, not this!

"Now I'm really going to leave before I say something I'll regret. Megan, I know you're hurting, but you might remember I'm trying to help you and that I don't exactly feel great about my life either. I wish you'd understand you're not the only one going through things."

"Stop arguing!"

They both turned. Ollie was standing in the doorway, red in the face.

God, he'd heard them. She should have left before it got this bad. "Ollie, I'm so sorry—"

"Go back to bed," Megan said, crossing to him. "I'll tuck you in."

"No," he yelled. "Stop treating me like a baby. No one does that but you!"

Angie gazed at her nephew, but he was staring at his mom, who held out her hands to him. "But honey, your daddy died."

"Dad was never home!" He pressed his fists to his little legs. "It's no different than when he was alive except you're sad all the time and won't let me do anything."

Megan sucked in her breath. "Ollie—"

"No! You keep telling me to be sad, and I *am* sad. But not all the time. I just want to be like other kids and ride bikes and climb down ladders without you hovering over me every minute."

Megan got on one knee before him. "But you aren't like other boys. You lost your father."

"Stop saying that!" He stomped his foot. "He was never home. He never played ball with me or took me to my soccer games or came home for my birthday. He wasn't like other dads." His voice rose to a shout. "I hate him. I've always hated him."

Megan pressed her hand to her mouth as Ollie charged past her and wrapped his arms around Angie's legs, his whole body trembling.

"Tell her, Aunt Angie. Tell her to leave me alone."

She met Megan's anguished eyes. Caressing his hair, she comforted him as best she could. Part of her understood Ollie, but this couldn't be about her. "You know I think you should be allowed to play and ride your bike all you want, but I'm not your mom."

"I wish you were," Ollie said, clutching her leg.

Megan turned her head away, and there was no denying Ollie's arrow had found its mark and dug in deep. *Shit.*

"Aunts are more fun by definition," Angie said, trying to be the peacemaker.

"I want to ride the pony I heard you talking about," Ollie said, lifting his tomato-red face. "And I want to ride fast."

Angie glanced over at Megan, but her face was still averted.

"Fine," her sister said, rising slowly. "You can ride the

pony. I'm going back to my room now. Ollie, feel free to play wherever you want."

That was it? She was just going to give up and scuttle off to bed? Angie wanted to call after her, *He's your son. Not mine.*

Well, so be it. If Ollie wanted to move forward like Angie did, they would do so together. She couldn't force Megan to engage with the world.

"How about you get dressed, grab something to eat, and then get your bike?"

She rubbed the back of his head gently, and he nodded.

"I'm going to paint while you ride by the pasture. If you decide you want to paint or, I don't know, chase the sheep, then you tell me. We're going to have a good day."

"And see Liam," Ollie said, rubbing his eyes. "I'm mad at my mom."

She nodded. *So am I.* "We're not going to let that ruin our day, are we?"

Eoghan's wisdom about life rose in her mind.

"There's way too much fun to be had," she told him. She was going to have some fun and forget other people's judgments. *God, please let it help her art.*

If she didn't figure out how to do it, she would never find her way back to being someone she was proud of again.

CHAPTER FIFTEEN

The bedroom was foreign with its plain concrete white walls and old windows.

The only familiar items were her favorite tan jacket draped on the bed and the framed picture of her, Tyson, and Ollie that sat on the side table. The quiet around her was unsettling to her frayed nerves. Ollie had never yelled at her like that, and she and Angie never quarreled as they just had.

She looked longingly at the bed. The white down comforter would wrap around her and drown out the world. Brushing at the tears running down her face, she walked over to it. Touched the softness. How she wanted to shut out the world and everything in it, a world as foreign to her now as this place she found herself in.

Ollie's angry words ran through her mind. He'd said that he hated his father and wanted Angie to be his mother. God! Even if he didn't really mean it, he'd meant it in that moment. What had she and Tyson done to make him say such things?

If she got into bed, she'd be a failure as a mother and a

sister. Maybe Ollie wouldn't be as angry if she met with Kade and arranged a pony ride. As for what to do for Angie... She would have to see. Her sister's mention of Carrick still troubled her. She'd seen her sister enthralled with a man before, and this had all the markings. Had she picked another bad egg?

Although Megan hadn't really spoken with Carrick since that first day, she'd liked him well enough. He'd seemed like a solid sort of man. But he was clearly still caught up with his deceased wife. Was there more?

The rumble of Liam's motorcycle sounded. Liam. He could tell her how to reach Kade. She rushed to the front door and flagged him down as he appeared on the driveway, visible from their cottage.

He cut the engine and took off his helmet. "Morning, cousin. How's everything?"

Everything is crap, she thought, but said, "Ollie is a little upset, and I was hoping you might tell me how to reach Kade and set up a pony ride."

He grinned and swung off his bike. "Perfect timing. I was just going over to his place to start painting some fencing. Why don't you get dressed and come with me? I keep an extra helmet with me at all times."

Sure enough, he popped the small container on the back of the bike and pulled out a sleek black helmet like the one he wore. "Ah...I've never been on a motorcycle. I probably shouldn't. I'm a single mom now, and it's not very safe, is it?"

Oh, how she hated talking about herself like that, but she *was* a single mother now—and widowed. She hated those labels. Every time she filled out a form, she was reminded that the life she'd planned was gone.

"Do you trust me to take care of you, Megan?" Liam

asked, coming toward her. "I wouldn't invite you or anyone on my bike if I weren't completely sure it was safe."

She looked longingly at the cottage.

"Come on," he said, holding out his hand. "There's nothing like seeing the countryside on a bike and feeling the wind around you. If it weren't for all the rain, I'd drive my bike all the time. But it's another glorious day out. Mum and me were just saying that you guys had brought good weather. It's been mostly dry since you arrived. Come on, Megan. A good ride clears the head."

Her head needed clearing, that was for sure. Tyson never would have approved of her taking such a risk, but she found herself saying, "All right, I'll get dressed if you promise not to go too fast."

He crossed his heart, and she rushed inside to change. When she returned, he took her hand and led her to the bike, helping her with the helmet. "Now hang on to me, and when we go into a turn, lean with me."

She climbed onto the bike after he did and wrapped her arms tightly around him. Nerves barbed in her belly when the bike thundered to life, and then they shot forward. The hedgerows and trees were a green blur as he drove down the remainder of the driveway until they reached the main road. Then the engine seemed to growl ferociously, and they started flying.

An open blue sky dotted with white clouds and the first shafts of sunshine stretched out above bright green pastures filled with sheep painted with words. A few caught her eyes. *Power. Magic. Music.*

There was a certain loud music to the ride, she realized, and it drowned out everything else.

She was shocked by how much she liked it.

The wind rushed over her clothes, making her feel

almost electrically charged, like someone might touch her and get a shock. They came to a T in the road, and Liam signaled for her to lean with him to the right. Her hands clutched him as they dipped in the direction of the ground before leveling out and racing down a narrow Irish road overtaken by brush and bramble. She watched it all race by, and it dawned on her that that's how life felt to her now—rushing by too fast for her to touch.

They rounded another corner, and she saw pasture after pasture of horses. A large wooden sign saying The Donovan Farm sat at the end of the driveway. They turned onto the road. If they hadn't slowed down, she might not have seen the smaller sign saying Pony Therapy Ahead closer to the ground.

They passed a white two-story house on a small hill, and then they were traversing a dirt road past a trio of large gray sheds. At the back was a smaller shed, this one bright red. A tall man with curly brown hair was leading a black and white pony out of the large doorway, but he stopped and lifted a hand in greeting. The pony nudged him playfully, and he laughed, cradling its head in a way she could only interpret as loving.

This had to be Kade.

Liam pulled to a stop and cut the engine. The man walked over, leaving the pony where it stood, and extended his hand to her. "You brought an extra helper, Liam?"

She tugged on her helmet, and then those same hands were helping her remove it.

"No, this is my cousin, Megan," Liam said after taking his helmet off. "She wanted to meet you and make an appointment for Ollie."

Kade studied her, taking his time, and she had the notion he saw everything. His regard wasn't awkward—the opposite, in fact. Maybe it was the ride that had cleared her head, but she felt like she was seeing clearly for the first time in months. His brown eyes were kind, and were it not for the gentleness about him, his large size and stature would have made him look quite tough.

"It's good to meet you, Megan," he said, extending his hand.

She took it and felt her hand engulfed in a gentle clasp.

"I'm Kade, like you know, and I can't wait to meet your son. This here is Winston."

He made a clicking sound with his teeth, and the pony came trotting over. When it reached her, it bent its foreleg and bowed its head to her.

"It's almost like he's meeting royalty," she said with awe, then sputtered, "but of course, I'm no royalty or anything."

Liam laughed. "If you ask most Irish, they'll say we're all the descendants of kings and queens. Right, Kade?"

"That's the story, so it is," he said with a smile. "I taught Winston and some of the horses a few tricks like that, but we haven't mastered hand shaking."

A Jack Russell came running down the path behind the shed, its bark bigger than its little body.

Kade scratched the little dog behind his ears when it reached them. "This one does shake, and he's clearly excited to meet you. Duke, this is Megan, Liam's American cousin."

The dog uttered a short bark and extended his paw. "Oh, look at you," she said, bending over and shaking the foreleg gently. "You're obviously great with animals. If you're this great with people, you must be a miracle worker."

When she stood up, he was gazing deeply at her again. "Do you need a miracle worker, Megan?"

He was asking in earnest, she realized. "Yes, I suppose I do. Losing my husband has put me in uncharted territory. I'm not doing a great job of helping my son. Or anyone, for that matter."

"Oh, you're being hard on yourself, Megan," Liam said. "You'll remember what we talked about. Movement. Time. Friends."

"They're all great healers," Kade said with a decisive nod. "The hard part for most people is accepting that something can't be undone. We only call it a loss while we're healing. After that, it's just a detail about ourselves we sometimes share. It might change us, but it doesn't have to define or limit us."

Her throat thickened as she remembered thinking about those new labels attached to her. "I can't imagine feeling like that right now."

He put his hand on her arm, the touch as comforting as his gaze. "No, I imagine it hurts a lot. For you and Ollie."

She nodded, feeling tears burn her eyes.

"And your sister, Angie, too. I met her at the pub last night. I like her. I was actually planning on bringing Majestic by today to take her riding."

He *like*-liked Angie? First Carrick and now Kade? She stiffened. "She's not supposed to be interested in men at the moment. She's supposed to be painting."

His mouth moved as if he were fighting a smile. "I heard she was having a little trouble on that score, so I thought a ride would help. I don't have that sort of interest in your sister, Megan. I only planned to be her friend. Like I hope I'll be with you and Ollie."

Oh, how embarrassing. She glanced at Liam, and he raised his brows at her, suggesting she was on her own with this one.

"I'm so sorry. I misunderstood. Well, I don't want to keep you from your day. Can I make an appointment for Ollie?"

"How does today sound?" Kade asked. "Now, in fact. I can collect a few horses and take you back to Bets."

"You make house calls now?" Liam asked.

"Sometimes," Kade said with a mysterious smile. "The fairies told me a house call was just the thing. I'll take Angie and Ollie on a ride. You, as well, Megan, if you've the mind."

"I've never ridden a horse."

"It's a lot like riding a motorcycle, Megan," Liam said, patting his bike's sleek frame.

That intrigued her.

"Except bikes are more sanitary."

Kade made a rude sound and laughed. "Don't let my father hear you talk like that. You've met my dad, Megan."

"Killian, yes."

"But she didn't meet *all* of him," Liam said with a chuckle, "like most of the village did yesterday. Oh, what craic!"

She didn't say anything, but Kade was smiling. His father had been involved in that? Wasn't he embarrassed? Maybe she didn't understand the Irish. *She* would have been mortified.

"You wouldn't believe the interest their stunt generated for the painting classes," Liam continued, shaking his head.

The deviancy had helped attendance?

"Mum is going to talk to Angie about adding more classes. She might have been as angry as a hornet yesterday, but today she's over the moon."

That was good. Teaching had been stable for her sister when her creativity was dying, which was why Megan had encouraged her career shift and helped her settle into the role. Also, keeping out of each other's way for a while might help repair the damage of the harsh words they'd exchanged.

"How are you planning on keeping yourself?" Kade asked. "What do you like to do?"

"She used to teach pottery," Liam said. "Am I remembering that right, Megan?"

"Yes, I used to do that. But it's been a while."

She wasn't even sure she could center her clay now, when she wasn't centered herself. The other day in the village, she'd gone into a secondhand shop and come across a set of local pottery. The glaze was unlike any she'd come across, and she'd asked if the owner knew what had been used. She hadn't, and Megan had felt oddly deflated. But she'd bought a pitcher on impulse with some crazy idea that she might figure it out one day.

"Interested in helping Liam paint the fence, Megan?" Kade asked softly. "It would go faster with two people."

He and Liam shared a look, and she knew they were banding together to help her. Her throat clogged at their kindness. Angie had mentioned they had friends here. Maybe it was the clear head from the ride over, but she was starting to see it. "Angie's more the painter in the family."

"What about me?" Liam rocked on his heels. "I imagine every one of Kade's fence posts is the Mona Lisa."

"I sometimes swear I see her eyes following me when I walk by," Kade said, sending an amused look in her direction. "Well, Megan, we're here to help however we can. Aren't we, Liam?"

"We are," her cousin said with a smile. "I'll start on my masterpiece. Can you run her back, Kade?"

She motioned with her hands. "I hadn't thought about that. Can I call a taxi? I don't want to impose."

They both roared with laughter.

"Guess not."

"As you say." Kade made a clicking sound, and Winston trotted off. He grinned at her. "He's going to start the truck for us."

"After the bow you taught him, I'd almost believe you," she said, feeling an unfamiliar smile rise on her face. "I can see why you're good at what you do. I'm glad you'll be helping Ollie."

"Perhaps you'll let me help you too," Kade said, picking up the Jack Russell when it barked. "Do you like dogs?"

He was placing the dog in her arms before she could reply. Suddenly it was licking her face. Unbidden giggles rose to the surface as the dog showered affection on her. She ducked her head as it went for her ears.

"Oh, stop that," she told the dog, but it only gave a *ruff* and peppered her with more dog kisses.

"Looks like you're a pro," Kade said, crossing his arms.

"I'm not." But the truth was, she'd always wanted a dog. Tyson had thought it would be too much for her to take care of Ollie and a dog, so she hadn't gotten one.

Her husband hadn't thought she could do anything useful, really, and she knew he'd stayed away because she disappointed him. Sometimes she wondered what he'd ever seen in her. The day they'd met, at a restaurant along the Chesapeake, he'd said she looked like the kind of girl a man settled down with. Only he hadn't settled down.

And now he was gone.

"Come on, Megan." Kade started to walk off in the direction Winston had disappeared. "You can bring Duke. Maybe he can convince you to take a ride with us."

The dog looked at her with big brown eyes. She really should put him down. He was getting dirt on her favorite jacket. But she couldn't make herself. Didn't want to, in fact, and her little spurt of rebellion cleared her head more.

His affection was uncomplicated. *He* didn't know that her world had fallen apart.

Ollie's words came back to her mind. *I just want to be like other boys.*

He wanted to be normal. In the moment, she'd only felt the pain of his words, like a raw wound, but now she understood.

"Kade?" she asked.

He was leading a larger pony out of the shed. "Yes."

"Do you rent out your dog? Maybe for a few hours a week? I think Ollie would love him."

His thoughtful gaze rested on her again. "I think we could arrange something."

"Good."

She hugged the dog to her.

CHAPTER SIXTEEN

Angie was finally sitting in her usual spot.

She hadn't been there earlier, when he'd started his rounds, and truth be told, he'd tarried in his work. He'd been worried about her, dammit.

Perhaps she was late because of her nephew. Ollie was racing back and forth in front of the fencing, making his sheep bleat. A blue bike rested against the fence line.

A sheep raced toward him with the word *Urgent* sprayed on her body, and he nearly cursed.

"Original, Sorcha," he muttered, and the wind rose up around him strong enough to blow open his jacket. "I bet you wouldn't bully Kade like this."

He couldn't shear his sheep fast enough this year. He'd been waiting for the weather to steady out a little. One year he'd jumped the gun and sheared them in late May, only for a cold and wet spell to hover over the land for weeks. He'd lost some lambs. He now waited until mid-June unless the weather was scorching during the day, which rarely happened. Truth be told, he usually delayed the shearing to keep Sorcha's words around him.

This year, he was eager to stop her interfering messages.

A sheep sporting *Thick* ran in front of him.

He heard her laughter and looked around. She was standing beside the gate, her white dress billowing as it always did. She gestured toward the Yanks with an impatient hand before touching the metal slates. He understood the implication. He could go willingly. Or she would take matters into her own hand and let his sheep out again.

There was no choice.

Or at least that's what he told himself as he headed across the pasture. When they saw him, his sheep made a beeline for him, bleating for food. "Oh, you're a greedy lot."

The sheep closest to him annoyed him to no end with their messages. The words they sported were all of a romantic nature. Clearly from one of Sorcha's more passionate poems.

Kiss.

Embrace.

Beauty.

Desire.

"Rubbish!" he called out to her.

He watched as the sheep with *Thick* on its belly joined them. How did Sorcha do it?

He nudged them away. "Go on with you. Shoo!"

They scattered and he fixed his gaze on the Yanks beyond the fence. Ollie spotted him and waved. Angie lifted her head, her hand poised over the pad in her lap. He felt the grass give under his wellies, as if he were sinking into the very land, the closer he came.

A sheep with the word *Surrender* ran in front of him before trotting over to the fence line. Angie's brows shot up to her hairline.

Their eyes locked as the message hovered between them.

He could feel the pull of her, as if an invisible silken cord already bound them together. She didn't seem to be faring much better from the way her hand crept up to her throat as if she had a fishbone stuck in it. Ach, they were a pair.

"Hi!" Ollie called out. "Do you remember me? I'm Ollie."

Good. Let the boy be the distraction. "Of course I remember you. How could I not? Your family is the talk of the town."

The boy stepped up onto the low rung of the fence as he neared. "I like your sheep. Their words are funny. Like *Kiss*. Yuck!"

Carrick chuckled. "Poets like that word, but when I was your age, I would have said 'yuck' too."

"How many sheep do you have?"

He stopped and rested against the fence, nodding to Angie by way of greeting. "This week's tally is five hundred and thirty-eight."

"Wow! That's a lot. There doesn't seem to be that many."

"I have a number of pastures for them. They all need space and a bit of grass. Soon I'll have more sheep than anyone in this whole county. What do you think of that?"

Angie pursed her lips together like she was impressed, and he swore he stood a foot taller.

"Cool," Ollie said, bobbing on the fence. "Do you put words on all the big sheep? The little ones only have dots of paint."

"They're not big enough for the words to fit, but yes, all

the adults receive a word," he said with a quick nod in their direction.

"Can I help you when you put a word on a sheep sometime?" Ollie asked. "I don't know anything about sheep, but if we're going to be here, I should learn something about them, shouldn't I?"

The plea in Angie's eyes told him everything. Yes, she'd been delayed because of her nephew. He wondered where Ollie's mother had gotten to. That she hadn't come to the pub last night wasn't too surprising, he supposed, as she was grieving. Bets' comment about Angie not dancing on the bar even with her sister absent had stayed with him.

He knew what a weight such gloom could be on others. He'd seen it on the faces of his friends and family when they'd come to his door for this or that or to ask him to go to the pub for a pint.

"I'll be shearing the words off the big ones shortly," Carrick said, "but if your mother's on board, you can help me paint them in early fall."

He looked down and kicked the fence board. "She treats me like a baby. I hate it. I told her that this morning, and now she's locked herself in her room. Again. That's why I'm out here with Aunt Angie. She's cool."

Did the boy not realize Angie could hear every word? "Mums are sometimes downright protective of their kids. Sheep are the same way, you know. When they have their lambs in the spring, and a stranger comes upon them, the ewe stomps her foot like a bull. I've seen her charge a person if pushed."

"Do they bite?" Ollie asked, jumping down.

"No, they don't bite. The lambs like to nibble, but it doesn't hurt. Come here and pet one for yourself. There's nothing to be afraid of. I'll lift you over the fence and introduce you to a few. Okay, Angie?"

"That would be great," she said, setting her pad aside. "Actually, I'd like to pet one too. I've been drawing them, and it would help to know what their bodies feel like."

He lifted Ollie into the field as she rose up from her stool and walked toward him. Her legs seemed longer this morning in her paint-splattered jeans with the flowers, and her curves had his mouth going dry. She tucked her shirt around her as if self-conscious, but that only emphasized her tantalizing bustline. God, she was a good-looking woman. Their eyes held. He could see the vulnerability in her gaze, along with the same desire he felt.

When she reached the fencing, the morning light touched her face, and he spied a scatter of fresh freckles on her nose.

"You're getting some of our Irish sun. Watch out for yourself. I've seen visitors sunburn badly even at eight in the morning. Be a shame for your pretty face to fry and peel."

A smile flickered across that very face. "I'll keep that in mind. Let's see. How shall I get over there? I suppose I can figure out how to open the gate."

"No need to walk around." He held out his hand. "If you put your foot on the second rung, I'll haul you over."

When their fingers touched, he felt a zap as surely as if he'd touched an electric fence. Her sharp intake suggested she felt it too, but she simply firmed her mouth and clasped his hand. He pulled her up and lifted her the rest of the way.

She was soft in all the right places, but he was aware of the boy standing nearby. Stepping back, he reminded himself that he and Angie weren't meant for each other, even if their chemistry was undeniable.

"Come on and meet my sheep," he said, leading the way to where the main herd was congregating, some tearing at the grass while others lay in the morning sun.

Ollie ran to keep up with his long strides. Angie stayed back, but he was sharply aware of her. A few of the lone sheep must have sensed something in the air because they came running to him. One marked with *Pleasure* hurried toward him, and he nearly growled as he nudged it off. The boy was getting the romantic words. Good thing his response was *Yuck*. But when a sheep with *Enjoy* arrived, Carrick set aside his ire at Sorcha and held out his hand to the ewe.

"When you meet a sheep, it's best to hold out your hand and let her smell you."

"Are all of these girl sheep?" Ollie asked, slowly extending his little hand to mimic Carrick.

"No, we have some young rams." Probably best not to point out the differences to the boy, but all the local kids could tell them apart. He'd soon learn.

Enjoy came up and nuzzled his hand before turning her head and sniffing him. "She's really big, isn't she? Oh, she licked me!"

"That means she likes you," he told Ollie before turning to look at Angie. "Come on, Yank. Here's your chance to experience a sheep up close."

She took a few more steps, and suddenly she was beside him. Her head only came up to his shoulder, but he knew they'd fit together perfectly. She extended her hand and then gave a delighted laugh as *Enjoy* lavished her skin with a few nibbles.

"Oh, she's feisty!"

"Let me get her settled," Carrick said, resisting the urge to put his hand to the small of her back. "Then you can pet her wool."

He placed his hand on the ewe's head. Her brown eyes rose to him with pure trust, then she nestled herself against his body almost as if hugging him.

Angie glanced over at him sharply. "Have you always been able to do that?"

He knew what she meant. "Yes, since I could walk. My mum said the first time I ran was to a pet lamb a neighbor gave us. Pinkie's mother hadn't taken to her, so Mum took her in. Jamie doesn't like me saying it, but she was my best friend growing up and my first sheep. Usually sheep live about twelve years max, but she made it to fifteen." He'd mourned that sheep when she'd passed. But she'd given them a lot of sheep in her time, which his father had gladly given to him to start his empire. His prize ram, Baron, was from Pinkie, and he knew the gift for what it was.

"I've never heard of anyone having a sheep for a pet," Ollie said with a grin. "That sounds cool."

"We'll have to give you a pet lamb when spring comes back around if you'd like."

He actually wasn't sure when they were leaving. He only knew Bets had said it was temporary. That was for the best, he told himself. Nothing could come of anything.

The wind rolled across the land and the sheep marked with *Thick* streaked by again. Clearly Sorcha wasn't worried about them leaving.

"Go ahead and pet her now." He rubbed the sheep behind the ears. "She won't move."

Ollie and Angie's hands were tentative, but they both stroked her wool.

"She's so soft," Ollie said with wonder.

Angie's eyes were also wide. "I thought she'd be scratchy like a wool sweater."

"Her wool still has lanolin in it," he said, running a hand through her coat. "It's a natural oil that keeps the rain out. I sell my wool to an Irish skincare company that extracts it and sells it. The wool is useless otherwise. We can't get good money for it here in Ireland. Even our famous Irish woolen mills buy their thread from places like China and the like where it's made cheaper."

"You're quite the entrepreneur," she murmured.

He was proud of his expansion. "My next project is to start making cheese from sheep's milk since I'm still figuring out how to make the wool work for us sheep farmers. But that's boring talk."

"Not to me," Angie said. "I've always had an interest in weaving, but painting is my biggest passion."

"How's that going?"

"Terrible." The word hovered in the air before she leaned down to Ollie's level. "What do you think? Pretty cool, huh?"

"Yeah," the boy said with enthusiasm. "I like sheep! Hey, Carrick, if that lano stuff keeps the rain out of their wool, does that mean you can make your hands waterproof by brushing them on a sheep?"

He pursed his lips together, musing on his question. "You know, I haven't tried that. We'll have to experiment. But the lanolin does make your hands soft. That's why I started to use it. My hands get torn up with the work. Check this out."

After running one hand through the wool, he held both out to Ollie. "Can you tell the difference?"

The boy rubbed his fingers over one and then the other.

"Yep," he said with utter conviction. "The other one is smoother. Like you used lotion."

Angie bumped him playfully. "Are you sure?"

"See for yourself, Aunt Angie. Carrick, can I see if any other sheep will let me pet them?"

"Sure, but make sure to let them smell you first," he said, and the boy nodded and ran off.

He faced Angie, his hands still out. "Care to see if you can discern the difference, Yank?"

She looked at his hands as if they were the twin apples of Eve's downfall. He almost called the whole thing off.

She was right to hesitate.

Touching each other again would only inflame their attraction. She glanced back toward the cottage. Her eyes narrowed, and he had the urge to ask why she was vexed.

But all thought left his mind as she took his rough hand in her own. Her fingers caressed the skin, lingering over the calluses and scars. He was aware of how light her skin was against the brown of his as his heart began to beat madly in his chest.

"They *are* rough. Workman's hands. Mine aren't much better. I constantly have paint under my fingernails, and when I use solvent, it dries my skin out."

He hadn't thought about her hands taking a beating from painting. In his mind, there was an elegance to creating art. It surprised him to learn they had this in common.

"Let me feel them," he said, his voice an octave lower than usual.

She let go of his hand and turned hers palm down. He could see the lines of blue, pink, and white under her short nails. The pads of her fingertips were rough and dry as she'd said, and he had the urge to raise them to his mouth and kiss every one of them in benediction. Dangerous, dangerous thoughts.

"They're not what anyone would call pretty hands," she said, trying to withdraw them. "I envy women with nice hands. Megan has nice hands."

"Your hands show your passion for what matters to you," he told her, not letting her go. "That's what you need to remember when you see the paint under your nails and feel the dryness. Besides, some lanolin from my sheep will soothe them. I'll bring you some tomorrow."

Despite himself, he liked the idea of something of his helping her, becoming part of her.

"You really think it works, huh?" She cleared her throat, letting him know their flirting was getting to her. "Let me see your other hand."

He extended it to her, and she traced the back of his hand, running her fingertips over his knuckles up to his nailbeds. When she was finished, she turned it over and stroked his palm before repeating the maneuver.

He'd never known touching a hand could be so arousing.

"You're right about this one being softer," she whispered, lifting her eyes to him. Showing him her desire, her fear.

He understood. He stepped closer, wanting to ease her mind. Her heat washed over him, a powerful draw that had his pulse beating all over his body. "Angie— We said we weren't going to do this."

She glanced over her shoulder again. "I know, but I had a breakthrough this morning as I was sitting here in front of a blank canvas, and I can't let it go. I'm already *not* painting. I'm completely stuck, in fact. What would it hurt if we gave in to this for a while? There's nothing wild about that. It's just plain and simple desire—totally healthy. We both know it wouldn't be forever. That's how we both want it."

Hadn't those very thoughts touched his mind? The wind rose up and blew over them hard enough to ruffle their hair. He couldn't tell in that moment if it was an urging or a warning. He was brushing away the hair that had blown in her face before he realized it. Doing so had been instinctive. Yes, there was something instinctive about the way he reacted to her.

She was smiling at him, he realized with a start. God, she was beautiful when she smiled. He remembered how he'd hated her fake smile last night. This smile, full and radiant, was the one he wanted to see always.

Still, he hesitated, remembering the struggle he'd seen in her at the pub. "What about your art show?"

She made a rude sound. "Bets texted me that we have a huge number of people wanting to take painting classes after yesterday, if you can believe it. Word really spread."

"That's no surprise, considering."

"Best advertisement ever. We might add three more, in fact. I'm going to be busy with classes, which simplifies everything, I've decided. I can focus on Bets' burgeoning arts center for the next month and be with you. This attraction between us can run its course, and then I'll have time to work through some more of my issues. It's the best way to go about it."

The logic was sound, and yet his jaw clenched. He didn't like talking about getting it out of the way, as if it were some bit or bob to discard. Not something that had his body burning and his guts tight.

She glanced toward the cottage again. "I *need* to put myself first. Do some things that I want for a change. I'm going into this with my eyes open. I won't let my old habits with men rise up. It's not like you want or need anyone to take care of you, and you wouldn't try and change me."

My God, what kind of men had she been with? Arse-holes clearly. Still, desire and unease wrapped around each other in his belly, their dance discomfiting. "I want to say yes, Angie."

The wind rushed over them again, and he turned his body to protect her from it. He made sure Ollie was okay, but the boy was laughing, petting his sheep.

She put her hand on his chest. "Then say it."

Why was he hesitating? Because he'd watched her last night. Saw her every morning when she struggled to paint. It wasn't only that she was Bets' relation. Sure, it might complicate things, but they were adults. They could handle this in kind.

Yet, if he took her invitation, he was afraid she was going to stay as stricken on the inside as she'd been last night in the pub. And Bets' allusion to her sister had bothered him fiercely. He didn't want to be another person holding Angie back. "I can't. You're here to find yourself and paint again. You told me I would be in the way. No matter how much we want each other, I don't think that's changed."

He kissed the top of her head and let go of her hands. Stepping away from her took more strength than crossing the fields when the wind was battling him back. He reached for that strength. Felt it come into his heart.

As he walked away from her, he knew he'd turned her down because he cared about her.

Deeply.

And wasn't that what he'd been trying to avoid all along?

CHAPTER SEVENTEEN

H e was the first man to ever turn her down.

Not that she'd thrown out tons of sexual invitations, but somehow this moment seemed different. As she watched Carrick walk away and tell her nephew goodbye with a sweet ruffling of his hair, a sudden warm rain fell upon them. The sun was still shining, and the golden light being showered upon the land along with the rain took her breath away. Yellow shimmered within the crystal diamond showers, and the green fields turned a bright chartreuse.

Wonder stole over her.

A ripple of movement in her chest had her pausing, and she could almost touch an atrophied piece of her heart coming alive. Under her feet, the earth pulsed. Her heartbeat synched to it. Her entire body throbbed in time with everything around her. She'd never experienced such oneness with herself or nature.

Lifting her hands and face to the sky, she welcomed the gentle sprinkle and imagined being cleansed by it.

No questions rose in her mind. In fact, her mind was blessedly quiet. Ollie's laughter reached her, and she looked over as the rain ceased. The wind in the trees made the branches come alive as if waving at her. Her nephew had his hand out to a sheep named *Sweetness* who looked to be nibbling his fingers.

Her eyes tracked to where Carrick had paused beside the gate to the pasture. Even across the wide expanse, she could feel his eyes on her. The strong set of his body communicated his desire, and perhaps it was the communion she felt between her body and the ground beneath her, but it traveled to her. With a slow inhale, she took it into herself. Oh, how she wished they might have made love. But the wanting was so real and powerful, it would have to be enough. A smile touched her lips as the desire stole through her blood and bones, settling in deep. Oh, to be so desired but not to be taken. There was a freedom here she'd never known.

He'd wanted her.

He still did.

But he'd put her first.

No one had ever done that. And it had happened moments after she'd put herself and her needs first, letting go of her self-judgments and Megan's needs. The congruity wasn't lost on her.

He lifted his hand, a hand she had now touched and caressed. A hand that had touched and caressed her. She knew its strength and its toughness as much as she'd experienced its gentleness and passion.

She could deny it no more.

She was going to paint those hands.

She waved to him, and then she was running back to her pad, cresting over the fence with an ease she hadn't experienced in her body in some time. She was weightless. The rain had wet her painting supplies, but she didn't care.

Throwing open the pad to a dry sheet, she drew out yellow ochre and titanium white along with two brushes and went to town.

The picture of his hands was so clear that she didn't have to will the scene to stay alive in her mind—it was there, imprinted. As she painted the outline of his fingers and wrists and then started to fill in the details of the nailbeds and knuckles, she could feel his heartbeat in his hands, the pulse at his wrist throbbing with life.

Her brushstrokes were bold and sweeping in luxurious yellow ochre, depicting the years of sun absorbed into his skin. She painted short, tight lines of titanium white to highlight the age and experience of those hands and to accentuate the practical nailbeds. When she paused to take in what she'd painted, she knew what was missing.

Her hands.

She tore out the page she'd just painted with a care and precision reminiscent of her old self and set it aside.

"That's really good, Aunt Angie," Ollie said, craning to look.

She turned her head to the right, amazed she'd been so entranced she hadn't heard him climb over the fence. "Yes, it is, by God! Did you have fun with the sheep?"

"Uh-huh," he said, coming over to her side. "Can I try and paint one?"

"Of course," she said, pulling out the supplies she kept for him. "You okay to sit on the grass?"

"I'm already wet all over." He touched his damp blue shirt. "I didn't know it could rain when the sun was shining. It was so cool!"

The dampness from the rain still touched her skin, and she felt alive from it. "It sure was. Go, maestro! Paint your sheep."

He giggled—a sound as beautiful as crystal singing—and then sat on the ground, pulling open his art pad. Then she was back to her next painting. Unlike the speed and boldness in her first, her brushstrokes slowed as she painted her and Carrick's hands. Each brush of paint to her pad was a caress. She could feel the paper absorbing the color, much like she'd absorbed Carrick's gentleness and passion.

God, how she'd missed this, the oneness of life and painting.

Their hands depicted a dance. His hands were holding hers as he gently caressed them. Learned their shape. Uncovered their secrets. Honored their experience.

"Wow!" she heard Megan exclaim. "You're painting! And hands. Didn't you once say they're usually one of the most challenging subjects?"

She ground her teeth at the interruption. *Go away, Megan.* "Yes, usually. Not today."

Her voice was crisp, and she was glad when Megan bent over Ollie. Her nephew scooted his butt until his back was away from her sister. Yeah, he was still angry with her.

"You're painting the sheep," her sister said as if that weren't obvious. "Ollie, I brought you a surprise."

"I'm painting," Ollie said in a huff. "With Aunt Angie."

"Okay, but I thought you might want to meet some new friends. The man who gives pony rides made a special trip over with his pony, Winston, just for you."

She'd gone over to see Kade this morning instead of hiding in bed? Angie had to give her credit for that.

Ollie lifted a shoulder. "I suppose I could meet him. To be nice."

"Good," Megan said, standing up. "He also brought a dog, Duke, and he's the cutest thing. I asked if Duke might be able to spend some time at our cottage, and Mr. Donovan

—that's the owner—said he could. I know you've always wanted a dog."

Her nephew finally looked up at Megan. "I'm still mad at you. I want you to promise to stop treating me like a baby. Carrick let me pet his sheep and everything."

Megan's gaze tracked to her, and her sister worried her lip. Terrific. Were they going to fight over Carrick again? She couldn't take it right now.

Angie turned her focus back to her painting, but her inspiration was gone. When she closed her eyes, she couldn't see their hands in her mind anymore. She studied the painting. She had enough that she could finish it later, but she felt deflated. Her sister had brought her down, down to a place she didn't want to be anymore.

Empty.

Maybe Angie's problem wasn't only with men. Maybe it was with everyone around her, everyone she'd put first. Her sister had an all-access pass to her time and attention, and it needed to stop.

"I'm going to head to the studio and paint there," she said, gathering up her things. "Ollie, will you carry my bag back to the cottage so I can carry my paintings?" The acrylic was dry, but she didn't want to tuck them in her bag and risk bending the edges. These paintings were damn good, easily her best work in years.

"Sure," Ollie whispered for her ears only, closing up his art pad and tucking his supplies back into her bag. "Hopefully Mom won't change her mind about letting me ride Winston."

She had a moment of sadness at his mistrust. He'd been so happy with the sheep. She hoped Megan wouldn't thwart his enthusiasm. "You'll like Kade. That's Mr. Donovan. I met him last night, and he's great."

"He is?" Ollie asked, his big eyes hopeful. "Does Liam like him?"

"Liam was the one who took me over to meet him," Megan said before she could answer. "I rode on his motorcycle."

Angie whipped her head around to look at her sister. "You did what?"

Megan shifted on her feet. "It was kinda fun actually."

"Can I ride on Liam's motorcycle too?" Ollie asked, jumping up from the ground and tugging on the hem of her sister's shirt.

Megan's mouth twisted. Yeah, she knew she was in a pickle. "Let's start with a pony ride and see."

Ollie muttered what sounded like, "Figures," and came over to Angie. "I'll take your bag for you. I promise to be real careful."

Megan was always telling him to be careful not to drop things. "There's nothing fragile in there, Ollie. Don't worry about breaking anything. Come on, let's go meet Kade. And Winston and this dog your mom likes."

When they arrived at the cottage, they entered through the back and stowed her things before exiting through the front door. Kade stood on the front lawn holding the leads for two ponies. A Jack Russell terrier took off for Megan, and her sister lifted him up and laughed as the dog licked her face.

Man, Kade really was a miracle worker. Megan hated getting dirty, and she would have thought dog spit would be on her no-no list. She'd even turned down Ollie's repeated wish for a dog. What had happened to her sister after their fight?

"Hiya," Kade said. "You must be Ollie. That's Duke. Come meet Winston and Majestic. Angie, I thought you might enjoy going riding too. It might help unlock your painting mojo."

"I actually painted this morning. Felt like the dam broke clear open."

Yes, that was a good way to put it. Something inside her had given way, and the flood of imagination had poured into her like that gentle, sun-dappled rain. God, she hoped it would still be there when she could be alone again.

"Glad to hear it! If it's not too nosy, what broke it open?"

She was aware of Megan's regard. Yeah, her sister suspected it involved Carrick—her painting had been of a man's hands—but she didn't know any of the details.

"Putting myself first for a change and having someone put me first too," she decided to say, wanting Megan to understand.

She turned her head and met her sister's gaze. Sadness and vulnerability emerged in Megan's eyes. Funny, Angie remembered Megan giving her that same look at her wedding to Tyson. Just before leaving the reception, she'd gazed at Angie with fear in her eyes.

As if she couldn't take the next step without her.

Even then, their pattern had been set, and it had been forged in steel these past eight months. They were both responsible for it, but it had to stop. "Kade, I'll take a raincheck if that's okay. I'm going to keep painting. Ollie, you have a brilliant time riding Winston. If you need me after, I'll be in the studio. See you later."

She waved to Kade, who gave her an encouraging nod and a charming smile. Then she stepped back into the cottage to gather up her supplies.

Angie Newcastle was back in business, and this time it was going to stay that way.

CHAPTER EIGHTEEN

The house didn't look right anymore.

As Carrick stared at the expanse of the open second floor living space, all he could see were the flaws and things he wanted different. The pink rays of dawn couldn't soften the imperfections his mind was cataloguing.

"To think, this design used to be my crowning achievement," he said, gripping his hammer.

"You were visionary to put the parlor, kitchen, and dining area on this floor for the view."

He turned his head. Sorcha stood at one of the large picture windows. Her white dress billowed in a wind he didn't feel, and her brown hair swayed to a rhythm not of his world.

"You've never visited me here before," he said, dropping the hammer and walking to her. "In our house."

"Your house," she corrected, a somber smile on her oval face. "Ah, it's a grand one for sure, but it has to be divorced from me or it will never be finished."

"Fitzgerald's Folly." He swore. "I'm a laughingstock for

it. To think, the Taj Mahal was built by a husband for his deceased wife. No one laughed at Shah Jahan."

"That you know about," Sorcha said gently. "Besides, the Taj Mahal was built as a mausoleum. Not a house."

He gritted his teeth. "Did you come to fight?"

"No, Carrick." She lifted her hand and pointed. "I'm only asking why you're here working when you should be down there talking with Angie like usual. This is the fifth morning in a row you two haven't spoken, and from where I'm standing, you're going backward."

Hadn't he fought the urge to go to her every morning? Especially when a sudden rain pelted her and her art, and he caught sight of her furiously packing up and rushing back to the cottage.

But he'd turned her down, and it had been the right thing. To see her and talk with her would only make it difficult to hold the line. Whenever they were near each other, the temptation to touch, to connect, was too strong. "She needs to paint, for herself and for her gallery show. She's been tearing aside page after page from what I can see. Things are finally going well for her."

"From up here." Sorcha walked to the corner of the parlor, her hand touching the unpainted concrete wall. "You've been watching her—a good sign. That's the only reason I didn't prod you before."

"I'm not a pervert." He stepped back from the windows completely. "I can simply see her when I work up here. That's all. Besides, she's a friend. I want her to be able to paint. Do you think I don't recall how upset it made you when you couldn't write?"

She smiled as she looked over her shoulder. "Seems you've helped Angie as well. It shows the kind of heart you have, the kind of man you are."

"I have no time for such talk," he said, looking around for something to do. He was putting the hardwood floor in, an arduous process at the best of times, which this wasn't. The floor was still not level in many places due to the foundation shifting. "We both know I'm no Prince Charming."

"Aren't you?"

"No," he answered and pounded a nail into the flooring for good measure.

"You'll have more time very soon," Sorcha said, walking toward him on her bare feet. "You'll be shearing the sheep, and then you'll have nothing but time on your hands. Summer is always a good courting time for sheep farmers."

He wished he could turn the table saw on and drown her voice out, but that would be rude. "A lot you know. Once the shearing is done, it's time to catch up on everything else that's been neglected. I'll be working at this house for one, but the other needs some painting. Plus, I have swallows making nests all around the roof."

She clucked her tongue. "Busy work keeping you away from where you really want to be. Spend some time with Angie while she paints and her nephew rides his bicycle. You're companionable like that."

He'd been good at sitting outside once, enjoying his sheep and his land. Soaking in the sweet slowness of that life. "Those days are gone from me. I have pursuits and ambitions."

"So you say—"

"But I'm glad you mentioned her nephew." He could still hear the way Ollie had giggled as he walked through his herd. "Megan is a different sort. She's had a rough time." He'd wondered about paying a call, but what could he say in the face of her grief when he held so tightly on to his own?

"Kade is working his magic there," Sorcha said, weaving her hand in a figure eight. "Didn't you see him giving Ollie a pony ride and the sister playing with the dog behind the cottage?"

He had but demurred to say so.

"She likes Duke more than she cares to let on. That dog was always a little wonder. I hope Megan will let herself heal. It's pained me to see you struggle, Carrick."

"So don't watch." His throat thickened. "You don't like the house. You're pushing me at another woman. Sorcha, this is no comfort."

Her scent of oranges washed over him as she stood in front of him. "Comfort won't heal you. Not when you've calcified on the inside. You're the one who's choosing to break. Carrick, this can't continue."

He turned away from her. "It can, and it will."

"Have you thought of living here all alone? Do you plan to look out these beautiful windows at night and tell yourself you're content? You're building a home for a reason. Because you want one—with a family and everything it entails! Don't be lying to yourself."

She might as well have struck him with a hammer. He wasn't building this house for some future family he didn't intend to have. He was building it for *her*. She was the one lying to herself.

Except she would never live here.

His energy left him.

"You're right about one thing, and one thing only. I have sheep needing shearing." He would call Ned O'Bannon about coming today. Shearing five hundred sheep and then some would keep him distracted a few more days.

"What will your excuse be next, I wonder?" Sorcha appeared in front of him, making him jump. "Carrick, the house *is* beautiful. But it's not for me. It's time you made peace with that. Open your mind to a new vision."

She disappeared.

He sank down on the floor and put his face in his hands. The pain he'd been holding back tore through him like a river swelled by the rain, breaking the levee holding it in place. Hot tears poured out of his eyes. His chest heaved with labored breaths.

She'd said the house was beautiful. At last. But she was right.

It wasn't for her anymore. It couldn't be.

Fitzgerald's Folly was well and truly his own.

CHAPTER NINETEEN

Her excuse was pathetic.

She stared at the brick-red front door of Carrick's cottage, the rose tags in hand. *This is stupid, Angie. He's going to see right through you.*

But he'd enlisted her help, after all, and then proceeded to avoid her every morning this week. She was sick of it. She pounded on the door.

Moments later, she heard him bark, "Jesus, I'm coming."

When it opened, his Payne's grey eyes locked on hers and the look in them said it all. Longing. Delight. Then fear crept into the irises, and he retreated, taking the light in his eyes with him. She'd seen his walls go up before and wasn't pleased to be the cause.

"What did my door ever do to you, Yank?"

"It was blocking my way to you," she said, nerves dancing up her legs. "You enlisted me as a rose spy and then denied all existence of me after I'd completed my mission. How typical of you handlers."

His mouth twitched, and her belly clenched with desire.

"Here! I found out which roses your sheep ate."

She thrust out the tags to him, and he took them with care, making sure their fingers didn't touch. She stared at his hands, the ones she'd painted on a bona fide canvas only today. They had some new nicks and cuts, ones she wanted to bandage and soothe.

"Good work, Yank." His voice was as perfunctory as the look in his eyes. "You have my thanks."

Her anger mushroomed. "Well, I don't want your thanks, Carrick. I want you to stop avoiding me. Just because you turned me down for sex doesn't mean you need to stop seeing your sheep on my account. You don't need to reject all of your girls, and I don't want you to feel sheepish."

Ultramarine blue flecks fired in his eyes. Good. She had his attention. "Being direct, are you, Yank?"

"Yes! You know I don't mind you calling me Yank, but sometimes Angie would do just fine. Now, you didn't answer me. Will you stop avoiding me?"

"No."

"That's it?" That was all he planned to say? "Do you want me to take back what I asked? I'm afraid that's impossible."

He waved as a car went by on the road and honked. "Come around back." His gaze flitted to the drive, empty but for his SUV. "Wait! You rode a bicycle here?"

"It's a standard method of transportation," Angie said, hoping it would help her lose weight as much as the midafternoon walks she took to clear her head after painting. "Are you embarrassed to have me here? I can leave."

She was surprised at the hurt the notion caused. Maybe she *should* leave.

Glaring at her, he charged down the sidewalk to where

she'd set her red bike and hauled it across the yard and around the back.

She stood on the sidewalk.

"Are you coming, Angie?" His shout could be heard across the yard.

He'd used her name, and she touched her heart as the pain changed to warmth. She followed him, taking note of the rose bushes flanking the light gray stone walls. They were bursting with blooms in canary yellow, Persian rose, and titanium white.

When she reached the back, she stopped short at the little stone courtyard decked out with more flowers bursting from the very cracks. "Oh, this is charming."

"You sound surprised. Did you think I lived like an ogre?"

She felt her mouth twitch as he set her bicycle against the wall. "Well, you do act like one from time to time. I brought some money in case I needed to pay to cross the bridge. No, that's a troll, right? And no. You didn't really act like an ogre until I asked you to have sex with me."

"Something I'd prefer we not—"

"I wanted to thank you for turning me down."

He fisted his hands at his hips. *"What?"*

She looked down at her white canvas sneakers before meeting his narrowed gaze. "No one's ever done that before."

"Terrific—"

"And it had an incredible effect on my painting," she continued, rocking on her heels as the scent of oranges touched her nose. "I've been able to paint better than I have in years. Of course, realizing my sister was sucking me dry helped. Not that I don't love her, but—"

"Her continued state of grief brings you down," he

finished for her with a great sigh, his arms going lax.

She went silent a moment. "Sounds like you know what I'm talking about."

Again, she smelled oranges and wondered where it could be coming from. He had no late supper outside. No orange tree stood in the backyard. Maybe it was one of the flowers? Whatever it was, it was delicious, and she felt the urge to paint it. Art that could fire up senses other than sight was one of the most powerful types in her mind, and it would be a sweet challenge.

"Since you've gone quiet again, can I just interrupt this thread and ask you: is there a flower out here that smells like oranges? I want to paint it."

He flinched, going gray. "You smell oranges?"

She hated seeing that color on him. "Yes, don't you?"

His muttering and head shaking didn't portend anything good. He was only getting cross again.

"Never mind." She could ask Bets later about an orange-scented flower. "You were saying about this weight grief-stricken people have?"

His dark brow rose. "Was I? Want a whiskey, Yank? If you're staying, we might as well have one."

He'd drank from her glass before—at the pub—and the memory delighted her as much as his invitation. "I'm glad you're letting me stay. I've...missed you."

His face went from gray to yellow ochre.

"That's not easy for me to say." Her voice was a whisper.

His growl was like the slow burn of a fire. "I've missed you too, Angie, and *that's* not easy for me to say either. Let me get the bottle."

She eyed the circular black wrought iron table and chairs and sat down. His cottage was one story, white like all of them in the countryside, with the old windowpanes and lintels painted the same brick red as his front door.

Their cottage was similar in design, but the terrace and gardens at his place had seen more care. Instead of having a wide-open view as hers did, this place was nestled in trees to protect it from the wind. The hawthorn was flowering, those fragrant white blossoms she loved. When he appeared with a half-empty bottle of Red Breast and two glasses, she smiled. "I like your garden."

"Sorcha's doing," he said, tipping the bottle toward it. "She liked to write her poems out here when the weather was fair."

"How is the building of your other house coming?" She took her whiskey after he poured it. "A few people from the pub say you've been working there more lately. The pub is like the town newspaper. Everybody tells you something about someone else."

"And Fitzgerald's Folly is good fodder for the gossips," he said, taking a drink with a bitter smile.

"People aren't always kind, but most of them don't seem purposefully mean either," she told him, wishing to remove that smile from his face. "I've seen your house sitting on the hill, and I can't imagine the view. I'd love to see it sometime. Maybe I'll find a view I'd like to paint. A new perspective of the land." Another waft of the orange scent drifted over her, tantalizing. "Do you really not smell the oranges?"

"Drink your whiskey and forget about the oranges," he said, nudging her glass closer to the edge of the table with his large hand. "To your health and your paintings. May you become a millionaire from them."

If her heart had been a kite, it would have launched itself into the blue sky above them. "I can and will drink to that."

After they both took a sip, she hoisted her glass into the air again.

"To you finishing your house and it being the grandest in the county."

His mouth tipped up on the right. "Sometimes you surprise me, Yank—Angie. But I thank you. I'll gladly drink to that."

And they did while he studied her. She didn't bring up the orange scent, but it seemed to strengthen. Maybe she was picking up on the notes in the whiskey?

"Now, you asked me a direct question."

"A few, in fact," she said, trying to hide her smile.

He tipped his head back, his wrist lax as it held the whiskey glass. "Let me see if I can recall them. No, I don't want you to apologize to me on that one matter."

Wasn't he going to say it out loud? Well, she sure as hell was. "Sex."

The air sizzled with the word.

"You should spray it on one of your sheep," she said impishly, taking another sip of whiskey, watching as his eyes shifted color from Payne's grey to a deep midnight blue.

Actually, his eyes weren't the only part of him that changed color when she poked at him. Even his strong face had shifted from gray to yellow ochre and now a more crimson red, especially around the nose and cheeks. She knew what that meant as a painter. His skin was changing temperature. Desire did that. Okay, irritation did as well, but that's not what his eyes were conveying right now. When they locked with her own, she could feel heat fan out in her belly.

"Your suggestion is noted," Carrick said, clearing his throat. "As for avoiding you, I thought it best. Angie... We don't want to be tempted."

She raised her hand to her throat. *Tempted.* Now that was a word. "But we are already, and we've discussed it."

"Twice—"

"Both times nothing has happened—"

"Yet," he said emphatically and with a heated, pointed look. "Let's not tempt fate."

Part of her wanted to say *Oh, yes, let's.* The orange scent saturated her. "Do you really not smell that?"

He poured them both another drink. "Have another drink and tell me how the painting is going. I already know your students are loving their classes, my mother included."

"Good to hear what's being said around town. Every student has their own journey, and I do my best to help. We're connecting more as we get to know each other. But are you really serious about my paintings?"

"Of course! I've wondered."

Her bones seemed to liquify. "You have?"

He sliced a hand through the air. "Are you testing my patience? Yank, I know how important it is to you. Do you think I'd have turned you down otherwise? Never mind. Tell me."

His demanding tone oddly didn't bother her. He wasn't trying to control her—not like Randall or Saul had. He was only impatient to know. She rather liked that. "I've been painting up a storm. Mostly outside in the mornings, when it's not raining. And later in the afternoons between classes and sometimes even after Ollie has gone to sleep."

She hadn't wanted her nephew to realize he was staying away from the cottage because of Megan, but the tension was clear around dinnertime and Ollie's bedtime. They mostly talked to Ollie rather than each other, and right now Angie was okay with that. Megan had to find her own answers, and truthfully, so did she.

"You asked about the weight of grief earlier." He brought his whiskey to his lap and studied it. "It's not easy to speak of. But yes, I understand. I haven't been easy to be around. You've met my friends and family. They've tried to pull me out—to the pub or to a concert or even for a pony ride. Kade can be relentless when he wants to be."

She'd realized as much. He'd been giving Ollie a ride every few days, bringing Duke by to play with Megan. Ollie would tell her about the funny things Winston had done—bowing and pooping were his favorite stories. They both seemed happier for the visits, and it hadn't escaped Angie that her sister was happier outside her presence too. She lit up when she talked about Duke sitting on her lap or running to greet her.

They were bringing each other down. Giving each other space seemed to be the key.

"He seems to know what he's about," she agreed. "Kade even offered to give me a pony ride to help bolster my creativity. Fortunately, I didn't need it, but it seems to be helping Ollie. We're buying him his own helmet, in fact."

Bets had offered to pay her more since they'd added three extra painting classes to the schedule. Now she was teaching midmorning, late afternoon, and early evening on Monday, Tuesday, and Thursday. She had another class on Saturday morning as well. They were doing still lifes as well as beginning figurative drawing. In a few weeks, she'd start introducing them to different painting styles, everything from realism to expressionism. As her students learned, they would find or hone their voices.

Much like she herself was doing.

"I'm glad Kade's therapy is helping them," he said, his tone grave. "But it's not something that would help me. Everyone has their own way of dealing with things. I...do my best to keep busy while honoring my promises and the past."

On their very first meeting, he'd told her that he liked to keep his wife's words around him. He was building her a house after her death. "You seem to have made vows to your wife, ones you won't break. Megan isn't like that. She let Tyson become her whole world. She lost herself."

"Like you did with men."

His direct gaze held no reserve now. His eyes were all-seeing. "It's different. She was married."

"So were you—"

"But I didn't have a kid or even think of myself as a wife really," she protested. "I..."

He leaned forward. "Yes?"

She worried her lip. He couldn't be right. They couldn't be the same. She and Megan were completely different. "But I've always taken care of Megan. When I was married, I took care of Randall and then later another guy named Saul."

"What did this Tyson do?" Carrick asked.

"He was a solider and gone most of the time overseas," she said, aware her heart was agitated and beating faster. "We're not alike."

"Aren't you a little? You might take care of everyone around you, and Megan likes to be taken care of—as did those men. But there's a similar thread to all this that I keep hearing."

The deep, persistent thud of her heart seemed to drown out his voice. She didn't want to hear it. The sweet smell of oranges washed over her, relaxing her. She took a breath and leaned forward, sensing a breakthrough. "Okay, tell me. What's the thread?"

"You *both* lost yourselves," he said, taking her hand and rubbing the back of it with his thumb.

Her solar plexus tightened. "Oh, shit. We *are* alike. But we're... I don't know. She's always been the good sister, and I'm the wild one—or so my father dubbed me until I got a day job. I found it rich that my dad only approved of me when I wasn't painting. He wasn't thrilled I wanted to come here and paint, but then again, he always thought Cousin Bets was a bad influence on my mom."

"Ah... The black sheep comment makes sense now."

"The thing is, I don't think I'm wild. I've been reviewing a lot of my life since coming here, and going out, traveling, talking to people, exploring new ideas, and having fun doesn't seem all that wild."

"You like to be free—like a wild horse does," Carrick said with an emphatic shake of his head. "Completely different. You're an artist. You need to be open to life, people, and experience. Otherwise, how could you convey anything powerful in your paintings?"

Tears burned her eyes. "You know, for someone who avoids me, you're turning into one of the best friends I've ever had. No one's ever understood me like you."

He covered her hand and squeezed it. "You're awfully canny yourself, when you have a mind to be."

"Thank you." His hand was warm and comforting, and she could feel the compulsion to paint their hands like this, woven together.

"Where you and your sister are different is that you're struggling like a worm on a hook to be free, to face your problems on your own, and maybe she's not so into struggling. The way your sister's taken to Kade's dog suggests she might need love and affection to get through a crisis. My mother is like that. She always talks about healing in community."

She studied him, sitting there so handsome and yet so wise. She'd never been attracted to a wise man before. Her taste in men improving was a sign of growth. "She mentioned that at our welcome party. My first thought was that it had to be the right community. The right people. Otherwise, you're throwing yourself to the wolves when you're in a vulnerable state."

"Stupid that," he said, squeezing her hand. "Good thing neither of us is stupid."

The scent of oranges touched her nose again, but she didn't say anything since it didn't seem to affect him the way it did her. "The painting is going really well because you turned me down. That's why I thanked you earlier."

He scoffed, a lock of hair falling over his brow. "A jab to my ego for sure, you telling me the prospect of not having sex with me fired up your creative engines."

She rolled her eyes. "Carrick, it wasn't the prospect of not having sex that turned my painting mojo around. It was your decision to put me and my needs first. To not take anything from me. You knew I needed to find my voice again more than I needed to have sex."

The sex wouldn't have been simple, had they attempted such a relationship. They both knew that.

Desire hovered in the air.

"It would have been a distraction to both of us," he said, releasing her hand then. "I'm glad you're painting again. I'd love to see your work, if you're willing."

"And I'd love to see the house you're building sometime. From the outside, it looks like you have an eye for architecture."

His expression grew shuttered. "You don't think I'm

mad to be building a house for a woman who's dead?"

Her throat immediately thickened. Is that what people said? She supposed there was a touch of judgment in the way they spoke of Fitzgerald's Folly. "I don't think it's mad. When you said you made a promise and wanted to keep it, I believe you."

"I promised her a bigger house from the very first we moved in here, shortly after our wedding," he said, drinking his whiskey as if the words had dried out his mouth. "The kitchen was small, and she had to go to the store more often than she would have if there had been more room for food-stuffs. She was killed in a car accident going to the store. I've never forgiven myself for it."

She reached across the table and took his hand. He didn't fight her, and her chest tightened with emotion. "I'm so sorry, Carrick. A million people can tell you the accident wasn't your fault, but they can't know how you feel inside."

His brows shot to his hairline. "You aren't going to try and tell me not to feel guilty and that I need to move on?"

"You already know all that up here." She tapped the side of her head with her pointer finger. "You need to feel it in your heart. I mean, I teach and practice art therapy—or did. I encourage people to draw and paint their feelings. Myself included. Sometimes it isn't pretty. Sometimes our hurts don't make sense, and we might as well draw maze after maze to show how lost we are. I've been there, so I get it. I've blamed myself and others for where I am and what's become of my life. Hell, I'm still avoiding Megan to protect myself and this newfound creativity. Carrick, I'm the last person to tell you what to do."

He squeezed her hand. "You have no idea how glad I am to hear you say all that. A maze is exactly what it feels like sometimes. Angie, you keep on doing what you're doing. You're painting again, and from where I'm sitting, you've found a chainsaw and carved through the hedgerows and briars in your own maze. If you need any more help, you tell me. I have a right fine chainsaw in my own shed out back."

She swallowed the thickness in her throat. "I can borrow one from Liam if you need the same sort of help. Carrick, let's just both try being happy. We all deserve to be, but it's so hard to find it and keep it."

He sat forward, his mouth twisting. "Do you really believe that? That you and I can be happy?"

Lifting her shoulder, she said, "I'm happy when I get into the groove while I'm painting. When I finish a piece that makes my heart soar in my chest. When I hear Ollie giggle with your sheep or with Winston. When something clicks for one of my students, or a client has a breakthrough in their art therapy."

She paused as another image rose in her mind. Maybe it was pushing things to say it, but they'd always been blunt with each other. Why stop now?

"I'm happy when I see you crossing the fields coming to see me and chat in the morning." *I was happy when you opened the door tonight.*

He made a soft sound she couldn't decipher. "If the weather is good tomorrow, and you're out, I will find you in the morning before the sheep shearing starts. Because, Angie, I may be a little rusty on the feeling, but I'm happy when I see you too."

God, why were tears filling her eyes all of a sudden? "Good. How long will it take to shear all your sheep?"

"Three or four days usually. My shearer can shear about a hundred and fifty a day without keeling over dead. It's hard work, the shearing."

"We can talk about a time after you've finished the shearing. I'll show you the paintings I have so far."

His mouth lifted, a rare and gentle smile all for her. "I'll be there. Why don't you come by and see the other house sometime?"

She blinked back the emotion in her eyes. Spending this much time with him wouldn't help her stay away, but it felt so good to share with him. To make plans. "I'd like that."

He lifted her hand and opened it, studying it while he traced the lines. The caress was like delicious warm rain when the sun was shining.

"You know, you do have beautiful hands."

In that moment, she believed it. "I should probably get back. Megan and I might be avoiding each other, but she still keeps tabs on my comings and goings. She's a worrier, especially after losing Tyson, and she might call Liam if—"

"Be bad to have him searching the countryside for you," he finished, giving her hand one last caress before releasing it. "I can drive you back."

"It's not that far, and I'm trying to get back in shape." She patted her hips. "It will be good for me."

"You look fine to me," he said, and the way his heated gaze traveled over her surely confirmed it. "Better than fine, in fact."

Not responding seemed the wiser approach, so she walked to her bike and lifted the kickstand, rolling it to the front yard. He followed behind her, and it was hard not to feel his eyes on her. She was breathless when she faced him on the sidewalk.

"Wait just a moment," he said, holding up a hand and then running off.

What was he doing? Should she get on her bike? She tapped her foot, trying to act like there wasn't a rope strangling her chest. She needed to leave. The thought of kissing him was growing in her mind.

Only a kiss...

Surely that wouldn't mess with her painting mojo.

He appeared, carrying a beautiful white rose he must have plucked from the backyard. "Since you liked it, you should take one home with you. Put it in a vase."

"Thank you," she choked out. "It's beautiful." Would he have given her a daisy if they'd been growing in his front yard? Roses had a very particular meaning in the States, but they grew everywhere in Ireland. Maybe he was only being friendly.

Still, she looked into his eyes for the answer she sought. The gray in them was completely gone, replaced by rich ultramarine blue dotted with gold.

They were the eyes of a lover.

She tried to form a smile. Her mouth moved, but it wouldn't hold. So she rushed forward and kissed his cheek. The bike crashed to the ground, but she was back in a moment, picking it up and hopping on. "See you tomorrow."

Her feet struggled to find the pedals before they finally latched on. She knew if she looked back, she would bobble and fall off the bike. But oh, how she wanted to catch one last glimpse of him.

"See you," he called. Then, a moment later, "Angie." He said it almost as an afterthought, as if it had stuck on his tongue for a moment.

She pedaled faster and realized she still held the rose, clutched to the handlebars. Looking at it, her smile formed and stayed at last.

The scent of oranges followed her home the entire way.

CHAPTER TWENTY

They had five painting classes.

Five! Bets surveyed the new flyer Angie had helped her create. Her plans for a community arts center were taking shape quite well, she thought, kicking back in her new office chair. Mary Kincaid's mean-spirited gossip couldn't touch her now. The streaking had gone over as a bit of craic, and it had ignited a fire of goodwill in the village. Still, she hadn't submitted her proposal for the arts center yet, wanting to collect more details for her proposal. Soon they'd be offering more kinds of creative arts.

She had a list of possible offerings they could expand into once they were greenlit. Siobhan was already game to teach some knitting. And perhaps Megan would agree to hold a ceramics class after all, as Kade—and Liam, she had to admit—continued to work their healing magic on her.

The audience should be there, especially after people heard about the new arts center at the agricultural fair. Best advertising around. Oh, she was pumped.

Bets pushed back from the desk she'd commandeered

from the attic as a car rumbled up the driveway. Walking to the window, she spied the sleek black Mercedes.

Donal.

She thought of ignoring him, but that would be rude. Walking to the front door, she flung it open. "Glad to see you with clothes on."

He gave her an infuriating grin—he cut a fine figure, damn him, nicely dressed in navy dress pants and a white shirt—and then ducked his head in the back seat. When he emerged, she gasped. "Oh, my God! What have you done? Is that Falling in Love?"

"Glad you recognize it," he said, holding the potted beauty up and walking toward her. "I brought you one of the biggest roses in the world."

Five-inch pink blooms! "I'm in love."

He stopped in front of her. "Then it's working and my prayers have been answered. I've reconsidered your proposal. I think we should get married, after all."

She hoped he was kidding, but she couldn't be sure. "You can't mess with my mood, Donal," she said, taking the potted rose from him. "Hello, beautiful. You and I are going to be the best of friends."

"I figured you would win the flower competition at the agricultural fair this year for sure with this rose," he said, fingering the petals. "Best be putting it in the ground. I can do that for you if you'd like."

It was rather nice of him. Still, she said, "I have my own shovel, Donal."

He muttered what sounded like a curse word. "As you wish. I've heard Mary Kincaid found a new hybrid, and she's been feeding it a secret fertilizer since March, hoping to beat you."

"I've heard the same. She's been a pain about my roses

and she's had a go recently at being a pain about my art classes, but I won't be stopped."

"No, you won't," Donal said, looking off in the direction of her rose garden. "I worried my sheep might have harmed your beauties like you said. I thought they'd be safe since the weather was nippy and the roses hadn't started putting on real growth yet. Stupid, I know. Blame it on my singular thoughts of you."

That had her breath freezing in her chest.

"The thought of you not winning troubled me greatly. I want you to win! You had a smile on your face for three weeks at least when you won last year."

He'd noticed that? She heaved out a sigh, as if beleaguered. "I'm touched by the gesture after all your sheep shenanigans."

He snorted. "Bets, I know my way around those fairs. The committees are usually wowed by the bigger and better thing. Sheep or flowers. I hope you'll accept this as an apology if you're still vexed with me."

How could she be after this gesture? Besides, his antics at Angie's painting class had definitely worked out in her favor, in the end. He'd said as much when she'd marched over to his house to give him a talking-to. Later, she'd wondered...had he known, or at least suspected, it would unfold that way? "Wait, I'm trying to bring my rage back."

"Oh, smell the blooms for heaven's sake and let that incident lift from your mind," he said, gesturing to the plant. "Their perfume is strong and sweet—just like you."

She would have shoved him if she hadn't been holding the rose bush. "Don't start that up again."

"Am I not wearing my Sunday best? And on a weekday."

He gestured to himself, and she found her gaze lingering. His fine clothes made his offer to plant the rose more touching. "I might admit you're looking more presentable than usual."

His deep chuckle caught her by surprise. What was he thinking?

"Calling on a lady with a rose is serious courting, Betsy O'Hanlon. I plan to continue paying you calls until you agree to have dinner with me. We can go to another town if you don't want the village nosing into our business."

A date? The temptation was as strong as this rose's fragrance. "If we did it here, people right and left would be coming to our table to talk to us, I imagine. I remember when I first arrived here. I hoped to continue date nights with Bruce. No such thing in Caisleán."

"No, people always come round for a chat if they know you," Donal said, holding her gaze. "Be rude not to, but it isn't always wanted, is it? If I wanted to be alone with Margaret, we'd take a picnic or go to another town. We didn't call it date night—only our night. Bringing her flowers or her favorite tea pleased her, but time alone was good for us both. If you don't mind me saying."

"I don't mind you saying at all." She liked that he and Margaret had continued such traditions. She and Bruce hadn't, and with the boys, she'd let it slide.

As she met Donal's brilliant green eyes, she couldn't deny she felt a pull toward him. He'd brought her a gift—a lovely, thoughtful one—and understood how to have a proper date in the countryside. He even wanted to help her win the flower competition. It felt like a message that he wanted her to succeed and, more, would help her do it. Plus, he was a fine-looking man, dressed up or naked. Dammit. She'd thought about his beautiful form and dreamed about it once or twice.

"We'll try one date," she said, "and we won't tell a soul about it should it end in disaster. And I'll need your word that it won't impact my future application for planning permission for my arts center." She filled him in on her plan, knowing she could trust him.

"That's quite a plan, and one I'd be happy to support." Still, he glared at her. "What kind of man do you take me for, though, asking me for my word about the application?"

"Forget I said it." She didn't want to admit she knew he was honorable. "As for our date... I'll drive my own car and meet you somewhere."

"Done," he said as if they were negotiating over sheep. "Do you prefer a weeknight or weekend?"

He was being conciliatory. "Weeknight. Less people."

His mouth twitched. "Any dietary requirements?"

This time her lips twitched. "The bigger the steak, the better."

"Wonderful!" He clapped his hands together. "I know just the place. And if I may ask one other question, if only to set the stage in my mind."

She wanted to clutch the rose bush to her chest, her delight was so great. Feeling like this, she had to wonder why she'd held back so long. "Ask away."

"Are you in favor of kissing on the first date should things go as well as I hope?"

Her whole body shivered, something she hadn't felt in ages. "It's been a long time since I've dated, but if I recall, it depends on the night and the man."

He made a sound deep in his throat—absolutely sexy to her ears.

"Then I will endeavor to make both the night and myself appealing to you." He nodded toward her, almost courtly. "Well, I won't keep you. Your rose and yourself will wish to become better acquainted. I'll make us a reservation for next Wednesday if that suits."

A smile flickered on her lips. "That will be fine."

"Seven o'clock?"

"Perfect."

Having agreed to go out on a date with Donal, she let her gaze roam up his body more slowly. He *did* have a fine form. Her skin heated as she remembered the look of him without his robe on. *Oh, Bets, you're in for it.*

"Cian's on Bridge Street in Westport work for you? I'll call and make sure they have the finest steak ready for us."

That would be a drive—over an hour—but she loved the town. "Can't wait."

"Neither can I."

"One last thing..." He shoved his large hands in his pockets. "You look absolutely beautiful holding that rose, but if I were the one judging, I'd say you were the more beautiful of the pair. I'll see you, Betsy O'Hanlon."

"You surely will, Donal O'Dwyer," she replied, sounding all Irish.

He made the sign of tipping his hat to her, and then he was striding to his Mercedes. She waved as he drove off and looked down at her rose.

Of all the gifts she'd ever been given, surely this rose was at the top of the list. But what moved her more was that he'd chosen it to help her win the flower competition.

Now *that* was a way to win her heart.

CHAPTER TWENTY-ONE

His sheep had all been sheared. The days had been long and grueling, and he was sitting sprawled in his garden, a cold beer in hand, when his friends rounded the corner.

"I thought Jamie might make an appearance to mollycoddle me but not the lot of you," Carrick said as they made themselves at home, grabbing beers and extra chairs from inside and plunking themselves down around him.

"And miss one of your most depressing moments of the whole year?" Declan stroked his jaw. "I brought my cleaver in case you wanted to cut your heart out at last."

"Of course we came. It's the day when all of Sorcha's words aren't around you anymore," Kade said, setting another beer in front of him after unscrewing the top.

No, they all lay in the discarded wool coats stacked up in the back of his shed. The word on the top of the pile had seemed to light up in bright blue as he finished. *Release.* He'd bit his tongue to keep from frowning.

"How bad is it this year?" Brady asked, flicking his beer cap like a coin in the air. "As a postman, I'm wondering is it a *We're Thinking About You* or *You Have Our Greatest Condolences* kind of card?"

He'd been wrecked other years, the first especially. If he were being honest, this year hadn't been as hard as usual. In fact, he'd been cross with Sorcha for her interference with Angie—for the smell of oranges that had hung in the garden that night—so much so that he'd told himself he was glad her words were being stripped from his sheep.

Still, the sadness had come, as it always did. As more words came off, he'd felt the familiar stinging in his eyes, which he'd explained away as sweat. If his shearer had noticed, he hadn't said a word.

Throughout the long, grueling process, Carrick's thoughts had drifted to Angie. He couldn't wait to see her paintings and have her see his house. Of course, he'd been strolling the fields every morning like usual, and they'd had a chat each morning. In fact, they couldn't seem to stop talking. He'd made a habit of lingering longer than expected, though she hadn't complained.

That night in the garden had changed things. He could feel it in the air between them.

Realizing his friends were waiting for a response, he said, "You got the right card and came tonight, clearly thinking of me. Thank you."

"Well, I'm glad we didn't need to dress up in black," Declan said. "It's a depressing color, it is."

It could be, yes, but the way Angie used it wasn't depressing at all. He'd caught a glimpse of one of her almost finished paintings. A black tree in a bright green field, almost brilliant in its shadow. That black conveyed power. He'd liked it very much.

"You look like an undertaker in black anyway, brother," Brady said, flicking his hand at him. "Your butcher white

221

suits you better, but can you tell me why you wear white when it shows the blood?"

"It's to show we're good at our job," Declan said with a firm nod. "Not gabbing like you, Brady, on your mail runs, or lolling your days away, like you, Jamie."

"Hey! I'm on summer break. Remember?"

"If all that lolling gets to you," Kade said, "come by my place to help out. After Liam finishes painting the fencing in primary colors for the kids."

"Which your dad hates," Brady said, making a scary face.

"Tell me a new story." Kade sighed.

"Where is Liam tonight, by the way?" Jamie asked.

"He had a hot date with an American visiting her relations for the summer over in Foxford," Brady said. "I saw her picture on Facebook. She's a beauty, but alas, she'll be gone soon."

Carrick thought back to the tourists he'd enjoyed. Funny how he'd had no interest in seeking any of them out after Angie's arrival. "Go on with your story, Kade."

He ruffled the brown mop of his hair. "Well, I got to thinking it would be grand to have a couple bridges, which means I'm going to extend the path. You're better at carpentry than Liam."

Everyone went silent. They all knew if Jamie were going to be doing any carpentry, it would be at Fitzgerald's Folly. Carrick met Kade's eyes, which gleamed with knowing. Hadn't Sorcha enlisted his help? She didn't want him to finish the house unless he did it on his own terms—as his house, not hers.

He could let himself get angry, but instead he took a sip of his beer, then said, "Jamie has a good mind for the kind of bridge the kids would like. You'd be lucky to have him, Kade."

Maybe when he finished the house, he could lend Kade a hand. His friend's father certainly wouldn't lift a finger to help. Although he allowed Kade to carry on his business, he had no liking for it. He always talked about not wanting his respectable horse farm turned into a circus.

"Are you serious?" Jamie set his beer down and stared at him. "You'd be all right with me helping Kade and not you?"

"I am," he said, pounding his brother's back heartily in support.

Sorcha appeared suddenly, and he jumped in his chair. Kade put a hand on his arm and smiled in her direction. She clapped, as if applauding him, and then disappeared.

"What's going on?" Brady asked.

"Do you smell oranges?" Declan asked, sniffing in the direction of the house. His tone turned hopeful. "You didn't buy that whole duck on special this week and make it with the orange sauce in the packet? I've had five compliments from some very good customers about it this week."

Kade's mouth moved as he fought laughter.

"When have you ever known me to make a whole chicken, to say nothing of a whole duck?" Carrick asked, still regaining his balance after seeing Sorcha.

Jamie opened his mouth, but Carrick gave him a look. He lifted his beer to his lips instead.

"I've got it," Brady said, tapping the side of his head.

"You've got what, brother?" Declan asked, scoffing. "You're as thick as a fencepost sometimes."

Brady laughed. "Thick, am I? Like I don't know the secrets of every person in this village. I even figured out Mary Kincaid's. She's been awfully odd for a few months, mixing something up in her greenhouse and then laying an old curtain from her house over top of it. For a while I thought she might have finally killed a man—"

"Jesus! It's this secret rose fertilizer everyone in the village has been mumbling about," Declan said. "You're not the only one who knows everyone's secrets."

"Bets will have her hands full with the flower competition this year," Jamie said. "Brother, you'd best not have messed up her chances at victory with your sheep wreaking havoc. You'd never hear the end of it."

He poked Jamie in the shoulder. "And you, brother, are behind on your news. I brought Bets not one but two new rose bushes to replace the ones my sheep nibbled on."

"Nibbled!" Jamie made an anguished cry and crossed himself. "If that's nibbling, then you wouldn't know if a cannibal was eating you alive."

"As a butcher, I've wondered if humans taste like chicken."

Everyone booed Declan, with Brady throwing his beer cap at him, which he batted away like a Roman centurion might have a druid's arrow back in the day.

"God bless us for putting up with you, brother," Brady said, wincing. "Sometimes I think you're more daft than Mum and Dad put together."

"All because I believe in expanding my mind?" Declan made a tsking sound. "And this from a man who only reads the same one hundred addresses every day all year round."

From there, it devolved, as it often did, with Brady telling a story or two about the recent imbroglios he'd witnessed while delivering mail, and Declan chiming in with gossip about a married woman buying an expensive cut of meat for someone other than her spouse.

Finally, Kade put a hand on his shoulder. "Come on,

Carrick. Let's go to the shed. I can help you gather up a few of your young sheep, and we can spray a handful tonight."

This had been their custom for the last few years. After the shearing, Jamie or Kade would help him put words on his growing lambs. Most of their bodies weren't full size quite yet, but they were close enough. This way he didn't have to look at an entire herd of sheep devoid of her poetry.

They both rose, leaving the others, and Kade headed to the pasture closest to the shed to gather up the smaller sheep. Then Sorcha appeared in front of him, and he jumped again.

"You'll always have my words, you know, in the same place I'll always be. In your heart. As someone you once loved very much."

She disappeared in the blink of an eye.

He clenched his jaw. Dammit, why was everyone on him so? Part of him wanted to hurl his bottle at the shed and hear it shatter into a million pieces like he felt inside.

Except he didn't feel that way anymore.

He was tired of feeling fragmented and tortured. He wanted a night out with the guys where no one joked about greeting cards and cleaving out broken hearts. Just a normal night with them.

Or with a special woman who wore paint splatters on her jeans...

Kade was leading a trio of sheep into the shed. He called over his shoulder. "Come on! These seemed the most docile. We can get the guys to help after they've had it out."

Carrick followed his friend into the shed. Kade was already sitting on a stool, petting the lambs, who were nuzzling him with gusto.

"You would be a great sheep farmer," he told him,

walking over to his metal bookshelf and eyeing the spray paint.

He picked up the blue, and it struck him how close in color it was to the sky in the painting Angie had been working on this morning. Frowning, he walked over to where his friend was sitting and knelt on the ground next to the first candidate, who stood nibbling on Kade's jeans.

"So what's the first word to be then?" Kade asked softly.

Carrick hearkened back to one of Sorcha's last poems.

> *The day is gone from us now.*
> *A harsh wind has brought in the*
> *darkness.*
>
> *Yet I am not cold.*
> *I am unafraid.*
>
> *My hands have a fire to ward off the*
> *chill.*
> *My heart is warmed by love.*
>
> *I live in a land of magic.*
> *True darkness can never touch me.*
>
> *I am unafraid.*
> *And so I always will be.*

The poem's simplicity had always appealed to Carrick, even though Sorcha hadn't thought it her best work. Still, for a time, he'd thought the sentiment at the heart of it mistaken. True darkness *could* touch someone. It had touched him. Only she hadn't known it, and he was grateful she'd been spared.

But he hadn't been, and his grief had been his darkness. It had made him feel a cold nothing could warm.

Until recently.

He felt a change in his heart whenever he caught sight of Angie. And on those two sweet occasions—yes, he'd counted—when they'd held each other's hands. His Yank, for that was how he thought of her now, had managed to warm him. In the end, it was her unwillingness to tell him to move on, as everyone had, that had made him want to do it.

He looked at the sheep, his finger poised on the sprayer. If he were to choose a word, it would be *Unafraid*. God, how he wished to be so again, both as a man and as someone who had a heart with a mind of its own.

His gaze drifted to the stack of wool coats in the shed. The last message from Sorcha had been *Release*.

She was right. If he sprayed another sheep, he'd be choosing to live in that darkness. His friends would still come round, but the jokes would continue about mourning clothes and cleavers. They'd come less as they married and had families of their own.

He'd be left behind.

Neither his sheep nor his ambition would warm him. They hadn't been enough for him these past years, and they never would be. It was time to stop pretending.

He lowered the can and set it away from him. Kade lifted his hand from the sheep, his gaze as gentle and understanding as always.

Carrick wiped at the burn in his eyes, a burn he couldn't blame on sweat anymore. His friend put a hand on his shoulder as he cradled his head in his hands.

"You should leave, Kade."

His voice was harsh because of the thickness in his

throat, and he rubbed away tears as they began to run down his cheeks.

"What kind of friend would that make me?" Kade asked softly.

"A good one." He rubbed his nose. "You're the only one I'd do this in front of, you know."

"Nah," Kade said, rubbing his shoulder companionably. "You'd do it with all the rest because you know we love you. And you love us, my friend."

His heart throbbed in his chest as that truth grew inside him. He did have them. They were still here, even if Sorcha wasn't.

Sorcha.

He laid his head on one of his sheep and released the remains of his grief, pushing the darkness away from him at last.

CHAPTER TWENTY-TWO

The words were gone.

Angie studied the sheep in the pasture. God, they almost looked naked without their wool. She almost wanted to throw a blanket over them to preserve their modesty, which was silly.

Her thoughts ran to Carrick. What must he feel when his deceased wife's words were gone?

"The sheep look so funny," Ollie said, running up beside her, his new horse-riding helmet swinging in his hand. "I miss the words."

She put her arm around him. "I do too."

The messages had been uplifting. When Carrick was around, they'd seemed pointed, almost magically so. The sheep with *Pleasure* on her wool came to mind. Now that had been a subconscious nudge if she'd ever seen one.

The sound of a horse riding their way made her turn around. Kade was on Majestic, holding the reins of Winston, who trotted beside him. Duke ruffed, running alongside them.

Ollie raced over to him. "Hi, Kade! I'm ready to go riding. Do you like my new helmet?"

"It's a grand one," the man said, dismounting from Majestic with practiced ease and leading the ponies toward them.

Duke reached Ollie first, licking his face madly when he picked the dog up. Angie looked over to the house. Megan was standing in the open doorway to the kitchen.

Kade lifted his hand and signaled for her to join them before turning his gaze to her. "They're a sight without their coats normally, but Carrick's sheep look even more bereft without the words. Usually he sprays words on the larger lambs who've put on good spring weight. But not this year. If you understand me, Angie..."

She looked at him, sensing a message, and then she smelled it again. Oranges. Jeez, maybe she was crazy, but the scent had been following her, and no one else seemed to smell it. She'd even mentioned it to Megan, who'd said she smelled nothing. Angie liked to think her art had so absorbed her she was experiencing the harmless side effect of seeing—and smelling—beauty everywhere. Still, she wondered about it. She shouldn't ask Kade, but...

The scent saturated her senses suddenly, as if she'd peeled all the oranges in the universe. Okay, surely he smelled *that*.

"Kade, you might think I'm crazy, but do you smell oranges?"

Ollie sniffed the air, lowering Duke back to the ground. "I do, Aunt Angie."

She stared at her nephew in shock. "You do?"

"Yeah, but I didn't realize what it was. The grass smells really sweet sometimes."

"That's why it's called sweetgrass," Kade said, holding

out Winston's reins to him. "How about you take Winston over to say hello to your mother?"

"You'll let me lead him?" Ollie asked, his face alight with wonder. "How do I get him to my mom?"

"Walk over to her." Kade ruffled her nephew's hair. "Winston will come. Duke won't need any encouragement to follow. He loves your mother. Go on, Duke."

The Jack Russell gave a *ruff* and raced off to join Megan. Ollie tugged on the reins, and he and Winston were off.

"The orange scent isn't one everyone can smell," Kade said, "in case you were wondering."

She narrowed her eyes at him. "Why ever not?"

"Because it's from a special realm only a few can connect with." He laughed when the gray pony nudged him in the shoulder. "The orange scent is from Carrick's deceased wife, Sorcha. It's her way of telling you that she approves of you and is trying to help you."

Her hand flew to her throat. A ghost? Carrick's dead wife? Over the past weeks, she'd heard plenty of stories of the supernatural, and of ghosts, but holy Toledo, this was too much. "Help me? Why would she want to help me?" She left her other thought unspoken: *She should help Carrick, shouldn't she?*

Kade smiled mysteriously. "She's helping you and Carrick come together. You're a good match, it seems."

Her legs turned to mush under her. She thought about sitting down on her stool, but she didn't want to give in to that kind of weakness. "Are you saying she's trying to make us a couple?"

"That's the story, and so it is," Kade said, rubbing Majestic behind the ears. "I agree with her. He's been changing for the good since you came, and from the painting I can see on your pad there, you seem to be doing pretty well yourself. It happens that way. We change when love comes into our lives—in whatever form that might be."

The orange scent saturated her again, and she gave in to the urge to sit down after all. "*Love*? We're not..."

"Perhaps not yet, but you're on the way." Kade knelt in the grass beside her. "Angie, I tried to tell you before, but let me be plain. Carrick didn't spray any lambs after the shearing. He let it go. He let *her* go. It was a miracle to behold after these three long tortured years."

She clutched her knees as the impact of what he was saying rolled over her. "But he doesn't want to be with me any more than I do him."

Even as she said it, she knew it wasn't true. They both wanted to be together. Badly.

"I'm no expert, but it's said I am a canny fellow. I think things between you are changing. But, of course, you two would know best."

"He doesn't want anything long-term, and when I get involved with a man, I..." God, it was hard to say out loud. "I lose myself. I lost my voice painting, but I lost so much more."

Kade looked over his shoulder then, and she noted Megan and Ollie were returning. "I only have a moment, and certainly you can talk to me anytime... But I think the changes in both of you might have altered those other patterns. Of course, you can always dip your toes in the shallow end of the pool and see what comes of it."

The shallow end?

"You mean kiss him?" Oh, God, what would that be like?

Good, really good, Angie.

His lips twitched. "I think you can figure it out. Your

family is upon us. Come to the farm if you want to talk more, but from where I'm standing, I think you're finally able to hear what's inside you. Same goes with Carrick."

He turned, leaving her in shock.

"Well, now!" Kade called out, closing the distance between him and her family. "Duke's favorite new friend is up and about. Ready for some fun? I thought we could take a stroll on Bets' private beach this morning. It's low tide and a glorious day. Of course, we'll have to mind the jellyfish that wash up on the sand, but there might be some new sea glass to discover. Do you like sea glass, Megan?"

Her sister glanced her way, holding a wiggling Duke in her arms. There was a question in her brown eyes before she made a show of trying to smile. "I haven't hunted for sea glass since we were kids and used to play along the Chesapeake."

"That's a giant bay close to where we used to live in the States," Ollie told Kade. "I want to hunt for sea glass. Mom hasn't let me go to the beach much."

"The tide was high, Ollie," Megan said, clutching Duke closer to her, "and it's very rocky."

"Irish beaches are notoriously rocky, which is what made Ireland one of the biggest homes in the world for pirates. What do you say about that, Ollie?"

"Cool! I love pirates."

"Well, get settled on Winston and let's go," Kade said, helping her nephew with his helmet before lifting him up onto his horse. "Megan, if you'd like to ride Majestic today, she'd be over the moon with happiness."

She shook her head. "No, I'll walk with you and hold Duke."

"Fine! Let's go then. Angie, it was a pleasure to chat

with you this morning. Have a wonderful time painting. You'll remember what I said?"

Like she could forget. "Thanks for coming by, Kade. Have a great ride."

Ollie and Kade started to walk off. Megan turned to her. "Do you want to go with us? I haven't seen you much."

Her chest tightened. "I've been on a roll painting and with the new classes. I have a show coming up, remember?"

The excuses were heavy on her tongue, but she didn't want to break her momentum. Megan had progressed these last weeks too, and a big part of that was because she hadn't leaned on Angie. Or so Angie liked to think.

Her sister started walking away, Duke barking softly, but then she stopped and looked over her shoulder. "What did Kade mean? Before? What did he say to you?"

Angie had never felt she was allowed to have secrets. To have things she kept just for herself. Old anger surged. When they were kids, Megan had broken the lock on her diary. God, that had happened ages ago, but thinking of it still lit a flame within her. Her mom had told her it was no big deal. They were sisters. They weren't supposed to have secrets.

Angie didn't see it that way.

That diary had been her place to write about—and sketch—her private thoughts and dreams. But after Megan had broken into it, she'd never written or drawn in one again.

Again, she'd allowed someone to stop her from expressing. Maybe it was time for that to stop.

"You know, Megan," she said, trying to say it as neutrally as possible, "it's private—kinda like a diary entry. Nothing to do with you. Only something between me and Kade. All right?"

Megan's mouth parted. "Are you still mad at me for that? For opening your diary?"

Angie nodded, feeling the solidity of the ground under her feet. "You never even apologized. So, yes, I am still a little mad. There's nothing wrong with me wanting privacy and some space."

Duke gave a bark as tears came into Megan's eyes. "Maybe Ollie and I should give you more space. It seems to have helped your painting. Bets has the other cottage, and she offered it in the beginning. We can move there."

Her stomach burned. "Maybe it would be for the best." What had Kade said? "This way you can dip your toes in the shallow end of the pool, living on your own again. I'll be close by still, and Bets and Liam are only up the drive. It has to happen sometime. Wanting space doesn't mean I don't love you and Ollie."

Duke nuzzled Megan's face as she wiped away tears. "No, of course not. It doesn't mean we don't love you either. But you're still mad at me, and I don't really know why. I'm your sister."

Part of her wished one of the sheep would trot over with a word of guidance, but she was on her own. "Megan, you're probably a little mad at me too, right? Being family doesn't mean we can't have those feelings toward each other. Honestly, you've been leaning on me a lot, and I've allowed it. Except it's been taking me down. Hurting my creativity as much as my exes did. I know that can't be easy to hear, but it's time to get it out there. I figure I've been taking you down too."

Her sister gulped. "Are you calling me needy?"

"A little. When was the last decision you made on your own?"

She threw up her hands. "How can I decide anything

235

when everyone has always told me what to do? Or done it better than me?"

"We all have to learn sometime," Angie said, folding her hands together. "I know things have been hard, but I'm rooting for you. Kade just told me Carrick had a big moment of healing, letting go of his wife's words on his sheep. Megan, healing is possible."

She took a step back, going gray. "I don't want to get over Tyson. He was the love of my life. Something you'll never understand."

Angie sighed deeply. "Then I'm sorry for you because he's gone, and you'll be holding on to something that will keep hurting you. Ollie too. Ask Kade if you don't believe me. Or Liam. He's let his father go. It doesn't mean you don't love him, Megan."

She put her hands over her ears as if to blot out Angie's words. "That's your art therapy training talking. You keep talking about me making judgments, but aren't you doing the same? You're still telling me what's good for me."

"You're right," Angie said, shifting on her feet. "I'm sorry if I ever made you feel wrong or bad about it. That's part of the problem, Megan. We've formed this routine where we throw judgment after judgment at each other. There's this push/pull of neediness and resentment. Let's try to just be *nice* to each other. Maybe we might even be friends. Being sisters feels so charged sometimes."

"You've thought an awful lot about this," Megan said, setting Duke down.

"I have. And it's helped me paint again. I can't dismiss that. Not to you or myself."

Her sister brushed aside more tears. Angie didn't like to see her sister hurting. She never did. But she made herself hold her ground and not cross to her and say she was sorry for how she felt. To say so would be a betrayal to her very self. Besides, she truly believed this would be better for both of them in the long run.

"You should go on to the beach with Kade and Ollie," she said gently. "You used to love going to the beach. I always wondered why you stopped."

"Tyson didn't like it," Megan said, clenching her fists. "He didn't think I was a strong swimmer, and he worried about me going with Ollie on my own when he was away."

Which was most of their marriage in a nutshell. Tyson telling, Megan doing.

Oh, Megan.

Then she realized her relationships hadn't been much different.

Oh, Angie.

"I'll see you later," her sister said as Duke pawed at her foot. "We'll move out as soon as I can arrange it with Bets. Come on, Duke."

Megan ran off, the fastest movement Angie had seen from her in years. Only this time she knew Megan wasn't only running from her. She was running away from the memories that had flickered over her face in the end, something Angie couldn't fix.

She eyed the cottage. Living alone again would be good for her too. She'd used her sister and Ollie moving in to distract her from losing her job and the disintegration of her relationship with Saul. She waited for the hurt and anger to rise up inside her now that she was alone, but there wasn't a whisper of it.

Around her the light changed, and she knew coming here had changed her in the best of ways. Hope bloomed in her heart. Her voice was coming back full throttle, on canvas and in life. She wasn't afraid to say what she wanted to say anymore. Not to herself. Her sister. Or the canvas.

She finally felt like she was an artist again.

She thought of Carrick and wondered what he was feeling after letting go of painting his wife's words on his sheep. She would see him soon and show him her work, something she usually never did until it was finished.

Then again, she'd never been afraid to speak her mind to him, and as she smelled oranges again, she realized why. Kade was right.

She *was* falling in love with him.

CHAPTER TWENTY-THREE

C arrick hadn't been sure what to bring to Angie's private art show.

He carried the bottle of champagne awkwardly tucked under his light jacket as he walked up the driveway. He'd decided not to drive in the hopes he could steal past the manor house. Would it be weird to be caught coming after hours to meet with Angie? They'd seen each other just this morning, but this was different.

When he and Bets spotted each other, her in a fine orange dress with pencil-thin heels, he had his answer. She curled in her shoulders and winced, making him want to turn around and leave the way he'd come.

Best get it over and done with.

"Hello, Bets!" he called out, striding toward her. "The Yank invited me to see some of her paintings."

She threw an emerald purse covered in peacock feathers into her red Mini Cooper and faced him, her brows wrinkling. "She's letting you see her paintings?"

Nerves whipped up like a mistral in his belly. "She is."

"Well, that shows the way of things, I guess. She hasn't

shown anyone her final paintings—not even me when I asked. Then again, I did hear tell that you aren't spraying any more words on your sheep."

He was done for. His mother should have given him to the fairies to raise. "Yes, people have been staring at me as if I've grown a bull's own horns."

When he'd gone to town to pick up the champagne, he'd been mobbed with questions about why he hadn't put words on his young sheep yet. When he'd said he was giving it up, using the excuse that it was too much work, they'd protested. Some had volunteered to help him even. He hadn't expected that.

He hadn't seen Sorcha since the other night in the shed, when he'd decided to let her words go. He'd left a bouquet of wildflowers on her grave yesterday. There had been no appearance from her. No smell of oranges. He was moving on, and since that's what she wanted, he didn't imagine she'd be hanging around anymore.

"I think it shows good progress in other quarters," she said, pointing to his jacket. "Especially now that I know who you were buying the champagne for."

"Jesus, you can't do anything in this village without everyone knowing about it." He ran a hand through his hair. "Can we speak of other things? You're dressed mighty fine tonight. Where are you headed?"

She swatted as a fly buzzed around her. "Gads, I shouldn't have worn perfume. I'll be crawling with bugs. Maybe I should head inside and forget the whole thing."

"Forget what thing?"

Her mouth gaped, and he realized she was wearing lipstick in bright red. Holy hell, she had makeup on.

"Remember how you asked to speak of other things?" She swatted a bumblebee this time. "I'm going to follow suit and leave you to yourself. Only... You might be unaware of some news."

The way she said it almost had him leaning out of his shoes.

"Megan and Ollie moved into another cottage yesterday." She placed a hand to her collarbone, her face strained. "I offered it to them in the beginning, but Megan wasn't ready. Seems that's changed. Megan told me they both agreed it was good for her to start living on her own with Ollie again."

The Yank hadn't mentioned it to him. He'd attributed her less talkative mood the past couple of days to her art, but perhaps there was more to it. "I would have gone mad myself if I'd moved in with my parents or Jamie."

Bets uttered a tepid laugh. "Would have driven your mother crazy, no doubt. I'm sure it's been hard on Angie these past eight months, taking care of them like she has, even though Ollie is the sweetest boy. I feel for both of those girls, but I think it's the right decision. You have to carry your own grief, even if it bows you under with its weight."

Carrick certainly understood such weight. "It's never an easy time."

"No," Bets said, her gaze unfocused as if memories were playing through her mind. "Anyway, I'll leave you to yours and go to mine. I know I don't have to tell you, but have a care for Angie, Carrick. You're both getting on track. While I've smelled oranges from time to time and know there's support from other quarters, you don't have to rush."

"Who's rushing?" he asked as Bets got into her car and left.

"Did you see my mum racing off in a state?"

Turning, he spotted Liam coming through the copse of

241

trees. "Jesus, I was hoping to make my way up here without calling on the house, but I've already seen the both of you."

"I was checking on a little surprise for Mum." The man threw his arm around him and started leading him to the path that led to studio. "I'll walk with you and catch up. Mum has a date with Donal, and you with Angie if the champagne is any indication. Brady texted all of us earlier to bet it was for my cousin."

That sounded like Brady. The real surprise was hearing Donal had finally gotten Bets to go out with him. That explained her outfit and why she was driving herself. They'd be going off to another town to keep from the gossips. He rather envied them.

"You have any problem with Donal and your mum making a go of it?"

"Heavens no. He's perfect for her so far as I can tell, but she'll be deciding."

Liam remained one of the most easygoing people Carrick had ever met. Still, he asked, "You have any problem with me visiting the Yank?"

"Not a bit, especially as she's invited you." Liam gave him a winning smile. "You can cheer her up. I juggled some paint and stood on my head, and she only cracked a smile."

"Your mum told me about Megan and Ollie moving to a different cottage."

"It'll be good for all of them. You can understand why, I imagine." Liam pushed aside a tree branch on the path as they walked. "Anyway, Ollie will be fine, although he'd rather spend time with anyone but his mother. Hence why Kade took him camping tonight. That's theirs to work out, but we'll be around for him when he needs us and soften things where we can. Be easier for Megan to live on her own again with so much support around."

Carrick hoped that would be the case. "It was nice of Kade to camp with the boy. But that's Kade."

"It is at that." Liam stopped at the edge of the woods. "Well, this is as far as I'll go. I have a quick hot date and need to be back early for Mum."

"I heard about your new girl." Carrick smiled. "Mind yourself."

"Always." Liam raced off.

He walked along the path to the studio, taking in the scene. The shed had turned into a fine studio. He couldn't wait to see the inside. Looking at how others had built things gave him ideas. Maybe it would inspire him to finally finish his house.

His fire to complete it was on a low burn for sure, and something had to be done.

"Are you going to stand outside all day?"

He looked up, only to see her peeking out the open window, her hair a tumbled mess around her beautiful face. "The day is mostly gone from us," he said, "but there's some left, I expect."

He thought of Sorcha's poem, the one he'd remembered in the shed. As he walked into the studio, he smiled. He was unafraid.

When he saw her standing at the top of the stairs, his heart skipped a beat. The stairs seemed to be raising him up to her, and then he was there, standing in front of her.

She had white paint on the tip of her nose and blue behind her right ear. The brown curls of her hair were wild around her face. The smile on her face had his own mouth forming the same shape. God, she was beautiful. And if she had troubles about her sister's move, they seemed far away. Her art—and him, he hoped—had done that. So he wasn't going to ask about it. She would tell him if she wanted.

"Hiya," he said, sounding younger, more free.

"Hiya, yourself." Her brown eyes lit up as if with warm honey. "Did you have a good sheep shearing?"

"I did," he said, inclining his head. "I even got the sheep tagged without too much protest. I'll have more time for other things now."

"Your building." She seemed to duck her head as if shy.

"My building, yes. I'm eager for you to see it. Here." He held out the bottle. "I didn't know what to bring, but we Irish like to have something when we pay a call."

"Champagne?" She bounced in her paint-splattered white canvas sneakers. "How decadent! I love champagne."

He could feel his chest puff up in response to pleasing her. "Wonderful. Then I'm glad I made a trip into town for some."

"Well..." She twisted her hands, also dotted with splatters of orange and blue. "I'm a little nervous. Come on."

Grabbing his hand, she led the way with the bottle of champagne extended like a sword, carving their path to the easel in the far left corner of the studio. "My God, you have a lovely view of the beach," he said, taking in the view from the windows.

"I do, indeed! Except I'm more drawn to the pasture and the surrounding countryside right now."

He hoped it was partially because of him. "The skylights Liam put in are incredible, as are the old floors."

"Yes, it's wonderful. I'm feeling a little cramped at the moment, because more classes mean more easels. We're going to need more shelving for supplies and the like, but I'm babbling. There's no good way to start, so I'm just going to pull out the first painting I touch. Hold the champagne."

He grasped it as she thrust it at him. Then she bent over

to tug out a canvas, and his gaze dropped to her bottom. God, she had curves to rival the very mountains.

"Ta-dah!"

She turned the canvas around, showing a pair of hands clasped in the center of what looked to be a fairy glen in front of an oak tree. Even though he couldn't see the couple, he knew they were after love play. Sunlight touched their skin, and where their hands met, a molten red outline called to mind passion off-screen.

"God! It's incredible, Angie. I've never imagined hands conveying so much."

She ran a hand over her brow. "Whew! Thank God for that. I started painting landscapes, but I was almost compelled to paint hands. Carrick, I've painted a lot of hands. And eyes... I'm thinking my show will be about what the hands and eyes tell us. The best art shows have a theme."

He came closer, studying her brushstrokes. They were bold in defining the outline of the hands, but inside they were almost soft and gentle. Like lovers taking their time with each other. His body heated at the thought. Truthfully, the painting was quite erotic. Or maybe he was just reacting to standing there alone in the studio with her. The full force of the desire he had for her rose up within him, and instead of pushing it back, forcing it into submission, he welcomed it.

I am unafraid.

"Show me more."

Her mouth tipped up, and then she was bending over again. God, how he wanted to put his hands on her.

When she turned another painting around to him, his breath caught in his throat.

There was nothing but eyes in a cloud of white, and the

245

bleakness and longing in them were emotions he'd seen in the mirror often enough. He started. His gaze tracked to the last painting. Could those be—

"They're your eyes," she said softly. "And our hands. I tried to make them different, but I knew the moment you realized it. Carrick, if it's too private a thing for you, I won't share these paintings. But I don't think anyone but us would know."

He wrestled his gaze from the paintings and looked at her. "I would never ask you to hide something you created. Not even if everyone in the village suspected it was me."

She seemed to wilt like a wild lily beside the road in the heat. "Oh, thank God! I was really hoping you'd say that. I mean, some of your wife's poems had to be about you. I figured you're one hell of an inspiration for us artists."

He chuckled softly. "One hell of an inspiration, huh? Yes, some of Sorcha's poems were about me. How did you know?"

She gulped. "Some of the words on your sheep. *Love. Romance.* You know..."

He was charmed she was rocking on her feet. "It's been a while, but yes, I know them. Am I only inspiring to you then?"

Her throat moved again, slower this time. "That's a very direct question."

"'Tis." His voice had deepened, anticipating her response.

She held up her hand. For a moment he thought she was going to touch him, and his heart quickened with it, but then she turned and pulled out another canvas.

When she showed him this painting, he had his answer. The scene was one he'd described to her some time ago, of lovers in the fairy fort amidst the gorge. This time their

246

hands were in the grass, entwined and clenched in passion, as if the man was inside the woman below him. The couple was off-screen again, but it didn't matter. He and anyone else who viewed it would know they were making love in the sweetgrass as the sunshine played over them.

Sweat broke out in the middle of his back. He should have taken off his jacket. But it wouldn't have mattered. He was heated from within.

"How's that for an answer?" She was breathless.

He strolled forward at last, unscrewing the gold foil and wire holding the champagne cork in place, and popped it against the wall.

She laughed. "Oh, goodie! That sound means fun."

He was sending her a devilish wink and a rakish smile before he could think about it. He laughed. Devilish winks and rakish smiles had seemed gone from him.

She had brought them back, God bless her.

"Have any glasses?" he asked.

Biting her bottom lip, she shook her head. "No. 'Fraid not. I suppose we could drink from the jar I wash my brushes in, but why would we do that when we could drink from the bottle?"

"I like the way you're thinking, Yank."

He held the bottle out to her, and their hands met as she took it. Her head dropped, and she paused, staring down at their hands holding the bottle in perfect unison. He knew she was memorizing the scene. He wanted to give her more.

I am unafraid.

When she lifted her gaze, her brown eyes were full of desire and vulnerability. "Are you ready for another direct question?" she asked, her voice soft as a whisper of grass brushing his skin as he walked the fields.

"Tell me."

Her mouth lifted as she tipped the bottle up and drank. "Kade had this idea..."

Of all the things he'd imagined her mentioning, his friend wasn't one of them. "Keep going."

"You might recall me saying a little something about men ruining my life." She cast a free hand back to her work-space. "Me not being able to paint."

"How could I forget?" He took the bottle from her and drank. "I seem to remember turning you down for sex."

"A very good decision," she said in a rush. "Then."

The word hovered in the air like a feather falling from the sky.

"Then," he repeated, his voice silky smooth as her skin.

"Right!" She drank from the bottle with more gusto this time, wiping her mouth. "So, his idea sounded really inter-esting. Almost scientific. If you'd care to give it a try with me."

He could feel his shoulders shaking in amusement. "Sci-entific, eh? Come then. Tell me this idea."

She took a deep breath and exhaled slowly. "I think we should kiss, then see if I can still paint."

He took the bottle and drank so he wouldn't laugh. Kade *would* come up with something like this. He was all about taking little steps and noting one's feelings afterward. Progress was made this way, his friend was fond of saying.

Then he realized what she was really saying, and all humor left him.

She trusted herself, her very voice, with him.

"You humble me."

Her beautiful eyes gleamed, and she swallowed thickly, nodding. "So what do you think?"

He pulled her to him and pressed his mouth to hers.

CHAPTER TWENTY-FOUR

Desire shot through her body as he wrapped his arm around her back, his lips sizzling against hers. She closed her eyes and welcomed the burn.

My God, he could kiss.

After the first feverish passes, as if they both couldn't believe what was happening, he gentled his mouth and set the champagne down on the floor. She knew what he wanted now. She could all but hear him whisper, *Let's make this count, Angie.*

She softened into the hard lines of his body. His hand came around to cradle the back of her neck. Her arms surrounded him, anchoring him in place against her, and their lips met in short, simple passes. Her heart warmed her chest, along with the rest of her body, until the inside of her felt open and full of light.

She wanted more, and he gave it to her, his tongue seeking entrance. She welcomed him in for the dance, and oh, what a dance. Sounds rose in their throats to accompany it, and their bodies rocked against each other in tune with it.

When he tore his mouth from hers, desire rained from

his eyes, but there was shock there too. Something she felt down to her toes. "My God!" he said.

"I know!"

She leaned up to kiss him again, but he held her back. "Go! Paint something."

"Now?" She blinked as he set her away from him.

"Yes, now! Why would we wait another moment to find out?"

She shook herself. "Right. Where's my drawing pencil? I'll start there."

Rushing to her painting bag, she took out her pad and threw it open. He handed her a pencil from the bag, and she looked up at him.

"I've watched you draw before and saw you put your things away."

That he'd paid such close attention had her very heart lifting, as if angels were trying to carry it from her chest.

"Draw, Angie."

She put the pencil to paper and drew a curve in the middle. Then she drew another on the other side. Suddenly she knew what she was drawing.

She was drawing Carrick's face, the one she'd just kissed, the one she wanted to caress.

His chin needed a strong line, as did his jaw. Feeling it as she had, she knew the bones to be thick and solid. His brows were a similar composition, boldly setting the stage for his deep-set eyes. When she looked up to study them, she was arrested. The color was no longer Payne's grey but a deep midnight blue. Although she'd seen his eyes change color before, this seemed significant...as if this were his natural color, and the other had been the embodiment of his grief. Of the weight he carried.

She lowered her gaze back to the pad and hastily

sketched the rest of his face. Forming his lips made her fingers burn as she traced them in. When she finished, she ripped the drawing from her pad and held it up.

"What do you think?"

"Doesn't matter. What do you think?"

"I think I can still do it!" She lifted up her hands, the sketch flapping in the air.

He picked her up and twirled her around. "Thank God! When he lowered her to the ground, she put the drawing to his chest. From this angle, she could see how well she'd captured him. This sketch would be for her and only her, never to be seen in a gallery. To the end of her days, she would savor this moment, this man.

"Want to go a little further and see if I can keep drawing?" she asked boldly.

They flew at each other again, their hands caressing each other's bodies as their mouths reconnected. God, oh God, oh God! It felt so good to be alive again.

Her fingers learned the shape of his chest. He curved his hands around her bottom and dipped at the knees to let her feel him. She moaned as the hard length of him pressed between her thighs.

"Draw again," he said, wrenching them apart and handing her the pencil again.

Her lines seemed to graze across the pad like the swallows she'd seen in the field, leaving their mark. This time the image inside her was of them—her hand touching his jaw as his heated eyes looked into hers.

"Good," he said when she tore the finished drawing off her pad. "You?"

"Excellent." Her voice was stronger as she held it up. "I feel almost cured. Let's find out."

She drew her top over her head. He shrugged out of his

jacket and then pulled off his shirt. His bare chest was well muscled, and it rippled when she touched it. His hands cupped her breasts through her bra.

She let her head fall back, her eyes closing. "Yes, God, yes." The heat was building, and he seemed to know it because he surprised her by angling his leg between her thighs and pressing it hard to her core. She came in a rush, crying out, clutching his arms. God, that was the first time she'd ever come that quickly, and it only reinforced how powerful their connection was.

When she rested her head against his chest, he hugged her to him, caressing her back in soothing strokes. When she could finally look up at him, his eyes locked with hers.

"Draw again," he said softly, his steady voice belied by passion in his eyes.

She fanned herself and picked up her pad again.

The pencil flew over the paper, and this time, she was drawing herself flying across the pasture, his sheep puffy dots underneath her with a trace of Carrick in the distance. She stopped and looked at it when she was finished.

She'd told him the truth. The beach was stunning in light and shadow, and the water flickered in ever-changing shades—going from golden to diamond to a dangerous blue. But the pasture where she sat in the mornings, where they chatted—that view was the one she loved most.

By God, she did love him.

When she raised her face, he cupped it and gave her a long, lingering kiss. The earlier white heat was now a gentle campfire. She knew he wasn't going to take things further tonight, and she made herself ask why.

"Afraid to find out if I'm cured the whole way?"

He smiled as he pushed the wild strands of hair back from her face. "No, I am unafraid, in fact. We might see how you draw in the morning and for the next few days. Plus, it would be our first time together, and it should have a touch more romance than a cold studio and a hard floor, I'd be thinking. We've both waited a while for it. Seems we might want to set the stage a little for each other. I'd like to awake with you and fill you as dawn stretches out across the land."

She rested her head against his chest, and his arms wrapped around her. Somehow the fact that he didn't want to rush only made her more certain of her feelings. "I'd like to set the stage for you too," she whispered, her voice aching with her newly realized love.

His hand was soft as it brushed her cheek. "But do bring your art supplies just to be safe."

CHAPTER TWENTY-FIVE

H er son hated her.

Megan knew she was being dramatic, but he hadn't liked moving into another cottage. Hadn't she heard what he'd muttered under his breath? *I want to stay with Aunt Angie.*

When Kade had suggested that Ollie and he have a boys' night riding ponies and camping outside, she'd been more than delighted to agree. Still, she didn't want to be alone with her thoughts in a quiet cottage, so she decided to take a walk on the beach. She grabbed a cardigan since the evening was cool. Angie would be painting, per her usual routine. She didn't want to talk to her sister yet, so she took an alternate path to the beach. She'd replayed their argument in her mind *ad nauseam*. But it was her sister's last words that kept getting stuck inside her.

You used to love going to the beach. I always wondered why you stopped.

Surveying the breathtaking expanse of beach, the gentle waves lapping on the shore, she couldn't hold back the hurt any longer. Tyson still wouldn't like her going to the beach alone, except here she was, doing it anyway.

Why had she stopped?

Tyson had always told her he loved her and that she needed to trust him. *My job is to keep you safe, remember? The Army doesn't give special missions to just anyone.*

God, she missed him saying that with his cocky smile. She'd loved that he was stronger than she was, what with his rock-solid frame and his fearlessness about going into hot spots. He knew more than she did and did everything better.

But she hadn't stopped going to the beach only because of that. She'd wanted to please him. She'd thought it would convince him to stay home more.

She was pathetic, and she didn't want to keep being like this. Her son didn't like her most of the time, and she didn't think Angie did either—or her parents, for that matter. In the end, she wasn't sure Tyson had. Why would they?

She didn't like *her.*

She charged down the beach, her footprints deeper tonight. The walk only seemed to stir her up more, like the tide stirred up the remnants of the past onto the sand. All the pieces were broken, like her. All the dreams she'd had for her life might as well be sea glass washed up on the beach. Wanting to be away from the reminders, she left the beach and headed toward the path back to her cottage.

When she met Carrick walking on the main driveway, she stopped short. So did he.

"Evening," he said, clearing his throat. "I've just seen your sister's paintings. They're incredible."

She gaped. "Angie never shows her paintings before a show." She hadn't even done that with Randall.

"I'm fortunate then." A smile fluttered on his face. "You

should know it's very important to me that she's painting again."

Of all the things she'd expected him to say, that surprised her. She must have looked puzzled because he said, "I only want you to know that I understand how vital it is to her, and that I'd never do anything to hurt that."

She believed him. Maybe that was why Angie had formed such a bond with him. Their affection was clear from the way they chatted every morning. She'd seen them from the kitchen window of Angie's cottage as she made breakfast. She'd hoped her sister knew what she was doing. Asking her about it hadn't seem right, especially when Angie was painting so well.

"I'm glad," she said, fiddling with the knot of her cardigan. "I heard you won't be spraying words on your sheep anymore."

His whole chest seemed to lift when he took a deep breath. "No. It was time to move on."

Move. Movement. Move on. Words she'd been hearing a lot of lately.

"Well, I'll be off now. Enjoy your evening." He was striding off before she could say anything.

Coming down the lane to the cottage, she spotted Liam on his motorcycle heading up toward the house.

"Fine night for a ride," he called out as he drew closer.

She thought about Ollie, out with Kade, and wondered if he was enjoying the night—probably so. "Glad you enjoyed it."

"Hey, you want to have a drink?" he asked, pulling his helmet off. "Even though she'd kill me if she knew, I came home early to wait for my mum to come home. She's out for her first date since she met my dad. Bound to be a big night. Moving on tends to unlock lots of emotions."

There was that phrase again. "Bets is dating?"

"Yeah, she doesn't want anyone to know." Liam shook his head ruefully. "I'm imploring the heavens to keep everything steady. She's chosen a good match for herself, but I promised my brothers I'd keep an eye on things."

"You approve?" She wanted to ask who the person was, but held back. Liam was usually very open, so if he wasn't saying, there was a reason.

"He talked to me about dating my mum and asked me to tell my brothers he'd have spoken to them, too, if they weren't abroad. He's also being very good to her. Better than she even knows. We're all glad for them. They're two vital people. Just because they lost their spouses doesn't mean their lives should be over in the romance department."

Why was everyone talking like this? Like there was something wrong with staying loyal to a dead spouse. The earlier agitation she had on the beach rose up within her.

"I don't think not dating someone means you're acting like your life is over. It only means you loved the person you married and can't ever imagine wanting to be with anyone else."

Liam cut the engine and hopped off the bike, unwinding the kickstand. "I can see this talk upsets you. I'm sorry for that. We all heal at different rates. You've only just begun."

Her rage broke like a rotted stick. "I don't want to heal, and I'm sick of everyone telling me it would be good for me. I don't want to move on, dammit. I want my husband back."

I want him to tell me he likes me.

An anguished sound punctuated her sentence, a hot, scary sound. She pressed her hand to her mouth as the pain in her stomach shot through her. She doubled over with it.

Liam had his arm around her before she could do anything and gathered her against his chest.

"There now," he said, his voice soft as he stroked her back. "You cry it out. Scream if you want to. There's no one but me to hear."

She tunneled her face into his chest, tears streaming down her face. The anguished sounds coming from her throat were feral, foreign.

"I know it hurts," he whispered, cradling her gently. "And I know you don't want to let him go."

She shook her head against his chest, the pain squeezing the life from her. "I don't. I can't."

He soothed her hair with his hand, like she would have with Ollie.

Ollie. He had no father. She had no husband.

"Come on, love. Just let it all out."

Ty was gone.

Angie was right.

She unleashed her grief in a single sound, the force of it echoing through her bones. Then she fisted her hands in his shirt and cried her heart out.

CHAPTER TWENTY-SIX

The high heels were a mistake. She knew it as soon as she left the car.

What had she been thinking, wearing fuck-me pumps? No one wore shoes like this in their village. She wore these when she was traveling in Paris or Rome with her boys. Here in County Mayo, she might as well have worn a T-shirt that said *Take Me*. But she'd told herself she wanted to wear clothes she normally didn't. Only that was a lie.

She'd wanted to look good for him.

"You dressed up for me," Donal said with a smile, looking her up and down with slumberous green eyes when she found him waiting for her on the street outside the restaurant.

"You're early, and you dressed up too," she shot back accusingly, gesturing to his navy suit and crisp white shirt. But no tie, a look she preferred. Men in the country only wore them to events like weddings, baptisms, or funerals.

He closed the distance between them, his large body blocking out the bright evening sunlight. "You thought I'd be late for our date? Haven't I told you I've been waiting for this?" His scent, a spicy cologne of pine and citrus, wrapped around her as he lightly kissed her cheek.

The touch was electric and shocking, so she shot back quickly, "Everyone runs on country time, remember? There's always some farm or animal incident."

Bets fisted her hands at her sides as he lingered close.

"You wore perfume too," he said, his face close to her neck. "Good. This is all very encouraging."

Encouraging? "It's bug spray, Donal."

He coughed out a reluctant laugh. "Of course it is. Can we just admit we wanted to look and smell good for each other?"

"No," she said, pushing past him to the door of the restaurant, but he opened it for her before she could do it herself. "You open doors for women?"

"I realize men in Ireland aren't the same as in America, but give me a little credit. I know how to court a woman. What did Bruce do? Throw you over his shoulder in the beginning?"

Pretty much, and truth be told, that twenty-eight-year-old girl had enjoyed the alpha approach. "Bruce wasn't one for opening doors, and neither are most of the Irishmen I know."

"Well, now you know me." He murmured to the hostess about their reservation, and she led them to a table in the corner. "Excuse me. Can we have the table by the window? My date would like the view of the street."

How had he known that? she thought as they settled into their chairs.

"Bets, you look beautiful in your orange dress." He leaned back in his chair as if he were an Irish king. "Like a bird of paradise."

Did she look beautiful? She wasn't a girl anymore. She

was sixty, and that was the woman she'd looked at in the mirror as she'd gotten ready. "An exaggeration, but a kind one."

He took her hand, leaning forward, and shocked her by raising it to his mouth. This wasn't a quick pass of the lips. No, they lingered on the back of her hand. Her body flushed with heat as their eyes held. God, she wanted to fan herself, and from the way his mouth quirked to the right, he knew he was bothering her.

"How was your day at the farm?" she asked.

He shook his head. "No talk about farming or sheep. I actually thought it might be nice if we pretended we were on a blind date."

She blinked. "Donal, you've known me for thirty years."

"I figure there's a million things I don't know about you." He tilted his head to the side, studying her. "You're an open woman, Bets. Being a Lucky Charm proves that. But you're also a private woman. That's the woman I want to know."

Her stomach trembled at the intimacy he wanted—and the sudden urge she felt to give it to him. "Donal, I really think we know everything."

"Did you know I love tropical plants?" He shot her an exaggerated look. "Hence the bird of paradise comment. I love to garden."

"You do not." She narrowed her eyes. "Most farmers hate gardening. If the plant isn't hay or grass for a sheep to eat, you don't have an interest."

"Come see my garden on your way home tonight." His gaze lifted over her shoulder. "Oh, good. Here's a little something to make you smile."

She turned as the server brought over a gift bag. There

was a twinkle in the woman's eyes as she set it down, as if she enjoyed her role in their moment.

The server walked away, and Donal nodded to Bets, who pulled the present toward her. It smelled of roses. When she saw the yellow blossoms with the green edges sitting in a tightly packaged vase, she gasped. "Donal, this is the St. Patrick. I love this rose. Mine died a couple years ago when a tree came down in a storm. I haven't been able to replace it."

"So Liam mentioned." He flashed her a cheeky smile. "Does it please you?"

"Yes, but where did you get it? I know which roses everyone grows in our village. Who let you cut these flowers?"

"That's my little secret," he said, kicking back again. "Are you ready for some champagne?"

"How did you know I liked this variety?" she asked, fingering the petals. "Wait! Did you pump Liam for information for our date?"

"Bets, I canvased everything I do know about you to make you feel special tonight."

Her heart knocked against her ribs. She hadn't done anything like that for him. Suddenly she wished she had. "Do you want me to run over to Super Value and grab you some chocolates?"

He waved their server back over. "You remember I like chocolate, huh?"

"You've been eating my chocolate chip cookies for decades," she said, gaping when their server popped open a bottle of Dom Perignon. "Donal! Are you crazy?"

"He brought the champagne for you after arranging it with us," their server said with a wink. "You're one lucky woman."

Donal gestured for the woman to give her the first taste. "Heaven," she said after taking a sip. She'd only had it once. With Wyatt and Rhys, her wine lovers.

When the woman left, Donal lifted his glass. "To Bets O'Hanlon. The most beautiful woman in the world."

Warmth radiated from the center of her chest. "Donal, you didn't have to do all of this."

He extended his glass toward her, and she tapped it gently with hers. "I wanted to. I like seeing you smile. And frown at me too, wondering what I'm about."

She raised a brow at him. "It's a date. Of course I know what you're about. We both agreed we were horny."

"And I told you sex wasn't all I was interested in," he said, his green eyes direct. "Let me romance you a little."

"What's next? A hot air balloon ride?"

"If you'd like," he said with a grin.

Now she was downright suspicious. She was going to test him. "What if I wanted to fly to Paris next week?"

"I'd ask you what day you wanted to leave and make the arrangements. Would the George V Hotel be okay?"

She had to set her champagne glass down. "How do you even know about that hotel?"

"I've been to Paris, Bets," he said, chuckling. "Something you would know if you'd pretend we were on a blind date and ask me about myself. I used to love to travel, but then the family and the farm took so much of my time."

She knew that story by heart.

"But I traveled every chance I got when I was in university," he said. "Afterward, I even worked in Boston for a year as a server in a pretty posh restaurant. I've always had a fondness for Americans because of that. I met some wonderful people."

She clutched her glass. "How did I not know that?"

"We've always talked about the village stuff or the farm stuff or our families, I suppose. Other pursuits fade with age, but I miss traveling. It's one of the reasons why I know we'd be good together."

Her heart knocked against her ribs as he held her gaze.

"You like to explore and travel, and it's high time I get back to doing the same. I'm sixty-three, and I have a hell of a lot more living to do. Besides, sheep farming is a young man's game, and I've been making plans of my own. But that's talk for another night. So... Do you want to go to Paris next week?"

She had to set her glass down and grip the edge of the table to steel herself against the wave of longing that swept through her. "But your sheep... The farm."

"I've hired a helper to give me some freedom, and Dad can throw a hand in if something major comes up. He might be ninety-three, but he's still spry."

He *was* serious. "Donal, I don't know what to say."

"Think on that while we order." He reached for her clenched hand and put a menu in it. "I'd give you the world, Betsy O'Hanlon."

She was glad she was sitting down. "But why?"

He let out a heavy sigh. "Why wouldn't I? I care for you. It's what you do when you feel like this."

Her diaphragm tightened. Feel like what? She was too afraid to ask.

"Let's order," she said, burying her head in the menu.

She lingered over the choices to give her face some time to cool down from his comments. When the server returned, she ordered roast chicken.

"I thought you wanted a steak," he said.

He'd remembered?

He gave her a look as if reading her mind came as easily

to him as breathing. Scary, really. Still, she changed her order. She *did* fancy a steak.

"Thanks for the reminder," she said afterward, clearing her throat.

"Let's see how else I can romance you," he said, taking her hand and turning it over. "We can pretend I'm reading your palm."

His touch sizzled, and her fingers clenched in response —like somewhere else in her body. Good Lord! She was getting hot at their table. "Stop that! Only a fool would believe you know how to read palms."

He laughed when she tried to pull her hand away. "It was only an excuse to keep touching you. But I could tell you a tale about your life and future even without reading your life line, or whatever it's called."

When he straightened in his chair, tightening their connection, she nearly tore her hand away and ran to the bathroom. But she wasn't a coward. She picked up her champagne with her other hand and met his gaze head-on. "Go ahead then. It's clear you won't be stopped."

His mouth tipped up again. "We'll have fun together and travel together. When you have another business idea, I'll be there to support you or help you build it. I'll love you slowly while the rain soaks the land—and you'll remember how much it rains here."

Her core flushed with heat, and she almost moaned aloud.

"But most of all, Bets," he said, kissing her hand again. "I promise to make you laugh every day—even if it's over something silly. Because you love to laugh. And I do so love to hear it."

Her heart was like a crazy Irish storm, dark in one corner and filled with light in another. One person shouldn't be able to feel so much all at once. "Back where I come from, we'd say you're too good to be true."

"Then I'm glad you came to Ireland, because Baltimore sounds like a miserable place."

The gritty neighborhood she'd grown up in had mostly been miserable, with dirty streets and lots of garbage. Ireland had been a marvel from the beginning, always presenting her with something new to be in awe of. Seems the man before her was its newest offering.

She was afraid to take it, she realized. It felt she was missing something. She'd known Donal forever. He wasn't like this. "Are you saying all this just to get me into bed?"

His mouth twisted, and he set her hand down gently. "No. I thought we'd covered that. It bothers me greatly that you'd still think so."

She almost reached for his hand then. "I'm sorry, Donal."

He nodded crisply. "Okay. Let's eat. Our food is coming."

They ate, but some of the magic was gone. She wanted to kick herself as he chewed his steak slowly, keeping his mouth occupied so he wouldn't have to carry the conversation.

The silence grew awkward, and she felt his challenge in it. Would she start to do her part on their date? She bit the inside of her cheek, unable to hold back. She started talking about the new arts center.

He looked to be fighting a smile when she finally wound down. She forked a cold piece of steak after telling him about the classes she'd like to offer—pottery and knitting and stained glass—and he commented on how much he loved the windows in churches like Chartres or the Rosary Chapel in Vence, designed by Henri Matisse. When he went on about his interest in Matisse's paintings, especially *Woman in a Purple Coat*, she'd drunk her champagne, hoping to disguise her surprise. He liked art?

He was right. This might as well be a blind date. She may have lived near Donal for thirty years, but she didn't know him.

It alarmed her how much she wanted to.

After they left the restaurant, he walked her to her car. She protested, of course, but he didn't fight with her about it. Only continued to walk next to her as she told him she would be fine getting to it alone. When he opened the door for her after she unlocked it, he looked her straight in the eyes and lifted those sexy silver brows.

"Will you come see my tropical garden?"

She fought the urge to swallow under that intense gaze. Her reaction to him unmoored her, but she couldn't deny she was curious. "I'll meet you there."

He started whistling as he walked away.

When she got on the road leading home, she noticed him a few cars behind her. Her heart grew warm again. They pulled into his driveway almost at the same time.

He strode to her car with the single-minded purpose of a man on a mission. She'd hoped for a moment to reapply lipstick, but there was no time. He was already helping her out of the car and taking her hand. "Come."

He led her around the side of the house. All these years of being neighbors, and she'd never once been back here. His yard had a beautiful view of the beach, but what stopped her was the utter glory of his garden. He hadn't lied! It was filled with a gorgeous collection of tropical plants: palm trees, Australian tree ferns, wine-colored cordyline, hakonechloa, and silver, spiky-leaved astelias.

"Did Margaret get you into this?" she asked, glad for the

cool breeze on her flushed cheeks. His very presence made her feel like she was standing inside a boiler room.

He snorted. "No, I love them, and my youngest daughter, Leila, does as well."

Her boys had grown up with his girls, but this was news to her. "It's gorgeous, Donal. I don't think I've seen a finer grouping."

They walked down the windy path of Japanese hardy bananas and False Castor Oil plants, their hands naturally finding each other. Holding hands with him wasn't a bother. In fact, she liked feeling his large hand curl around hers as much as the way his scent enveloped her.

She stopped short when she saw the largest greenhouse she'd ever set eyes on. Pots of white jasmine and black bamboo were visible through the open front door as well as birds of paradise in full bloom. "My God! It's huge."

He snorted. "I believe you discovered that the first day of your art classes, but I'm glad you finally remembered."

That memory rose up, and this time she did pull her hand away to fan herself. "Don't distract me."

"It's a cool night," he said, waiting for her to precede him inside. "Seems you're already distracted."

Was she ever. Suddenly all she could think about was his gorgeous naked body. She made a beeline for the *Yucca gloriosa*. "Everything is so healthy."

"I keep my eyes on things," he said, plucking a spent flowerhead from a tall succulent. "After a long day, this is one of my favorite places. I bring out a cold beer and do what needs doing. Sometimes I simply read a new crime thriller or listen to some music."

She pointed to a cozy corner beside a potted palm. The nook held two outdoor chairs with plush pillows, one in sage green and the other in a bright red. A round table held a few candles and a Moroccan lantern. "Seems you entertain here too."

He put his hands on her shoulders. "I got that chair for you, Bets. I know how you love red."

Her diaphragm clenched again. "Donal, seriously! This is way too much." *And way too fast.* Her heart was racing from it. He'd been open to going to Paris next week!

"Are we back to that?" He tipped up her chin. "Bets—"

"This is all really nice, Donal," she said as she stepped back. "But it's not real. We can't have some crazy fling where we go to Paris or sit in your glass house in the evenings and read and listen to music. That's the kind of thing that only happens in the movies. This is real life. We're sixty, for Pete's sake. And you're a farmer."

"Soon to be retired, remember?"

"Farmers don't retire."

He blew out an aggrieved breath. "Bets, go out with me again and let me show you it can be real between us."

She wanted to. This was staged. It had to be. "I told you I'd give you one date. We've had it."

Resting his hands on his hips, he gave her a look he might give his errant sheep. "I can be patient. Take your time. Your eyes—and your heart—will tell you what they need to know. Will you let me kiss you?"

She sputtered at the unexpected question. "Since this is our last date, you might as well. We can call it a goodbye kiss."

He was in front of her before she could mentally slap herself for her logic. His mouth commanded her attention, and she went weak in the knees as his lips moved over hers. This was no goodbye kiss. This was a *you'll want more* kiss.

His large hands cupped her hips and drew her against him. She was glad for her heels, but he still had to pull her off her toes to kiss her. And he did kiss her. And kiss her. And kiss her some more.

When he finally released her, he pressed her face into his chest. His heart was thundering. The greenhouse. It had to be the greenhouse. It was too humid for her to breathe in here.

"Donal, I—"

"Stop." He kissed her on the top of her head and then led her out to her car.

Confusion warred inside her, especially when she realized he was smiling at her. She'd just told him she wouldn't go out with him again.

"I have something for you," he said, stepping away and heading off.

When he returned, he was carrying a potted bird of paradise. Her breath caught. This was the second plant he'd given her, and this one was from the greenhouse with *her* red chair. That confirmed it. He was way too good to be real. She'd made the right decision.

His gaze held a challenge. "To remind you of how beautiful you looked tonight and to remember our first date."

Like she could forget.

She suspected that was the point as he kissed her goodbye again and put her in her car.

CHAPTER TWENTY-SEVEN

A ngie was coming to his house.

    His house. Not Sorcha's house. Somehow the distinction was critical.

He surveyed his newest accomplishment: the floors were finally installed. The pine boards didn't exactly gleam from his sweeping, but the boards' individual characteristics were visible. He liked that his hands had laid down every one of them, further adding to the foundation of his house. After letting go of Sorcha's words, he'd let go of this being her house.

He'd even altered a few of his plans. Why did the house need a music room? He was going to make it into a home theater instead, like he'd seen in fancy shows on the telly. He liked movies. Why not sit in a comfy theater chair with a big screen and surround sound? He could invite his friends over. The closest cinema was forty minutes away, after all.

He rose as he heard her car drive up.

He'd insisted they wait three long days to make sure she could still paint after their last encounter. No kissing or touching to cloud the experiment, he'd told her jokingly. To ensure there was no kissing or touching, they'd avoided being alone together. When he'd reached her this morning, a grin had spread across her face as she turned her pad to show him her half-finished painting of the dawn. They'd immediately made plans for tonight.

A knock sounded on the door moments later, and he loved the sound of his boots moving across the floor as he moved toward it. He spotted Angie through the sidelight windows around the door, a large blue gift bag in her small hands. Given the cool, rainy weather, she had on a black raincoat over her painter jeans, along with new wellies covered in daisies. Cute. She must have felt his presence because she looked over. Their eyes locked, and his heart was pounding as he opened the door.

"Hi. I asked a few people about the Irish version of a housewarming gift, and they gave me a load of answers I didn't expect. I wasn't even sure where to buy a bag of coal, but I didn't take you for someone who'd want a plaque with Celtic knots and a traditional Irish blessing. This seemed better."

"You didn't have to bring anything." Their fingers touched as she handed the gift to him. "Besides, the house isn't done yet. Please come in."

She crossed the threshold, and he could have sworn he felt a tremor under his feet. He looked at her then. God, he wanted to kiss her. "How are you in the painting department?"

Grinning, she lowered her hood. "Never better. Oh, it feels so wonderful to be painting again and again, whenever I want. Carrick, I can't thank you enough. Is it too bold to ask you to kiss me?"

He caressed her cheek, fingering the ends of her shorter

hair. "I was thinking the same thing. But before I do. You cut your hair after I saw you this morning."

She raised her hands and touched the ends, letting their fingers dance together again. "I needed a change. Maybe it was the Irish wind, but it was tangling all the time. I held back from dying it auburn, though. Liam told me it would be way too Maureen O'Hara of me."

Right. Liam loved classic movies. He'd think Carrick's home theater was savage. "I like it. The style suits you better, I think. And while I know it's dangerous to tell a woman anything about her appearance, I only want to say that I like your hair color as it is."

Her mouth parted. "You do? It's so mousy."

He thought of how he'd first seen her. She'd shrouded herself in some ways. "Maybe it's the Irish wind and sunshine that have brought out your highlights, but there's nothing mousy about it. Your hair is now like the Burren in County Clare. There's browns and yellows and reds. Oh, listen to me. Talking like an eejit when I should be kissing you."

She linked her arms around his neck, her body brushing his. "I love you talking like that, but kiss away. I never want to wait three days again."

He lowered his mouth slowly. The first brush of her lips had him going rock hard. Fighting the urge to cup the back of her neck and sink into her mouth, he kept their contact light. When he leaned back, her eyes were soft.

"You got the memo, huh?" she asked.

He wanted to lean in and kiss her all over again. "What memo?"

"About not kissing too crazy straight off." She fanned herself. "If we carried on like that, we'd never get our tour in, and I came to see your house."

"Since we're talking about memos, you clearly didn't get mine."

Her lips twitched. "No?"

"We're not making love tonight." As much as he wanted to. "We pledged to set the stage. If you'll glance around you, the floors are in and swept, but there's no bed in sight. I did mention wanting to wake with you."

She nodded. "You did. Good to be clear. I was wondering the whole way over. I bought some new underwear and some condoms in Westport since I went off the pill as part of my No Men Ever plan."

"I bought some too. I went to the next village over to preserve our reputations."

"You bought underwear too?" Her lush mouth was fighting a smile.

"No, but maybe you'll show me yours after the tour." They were flirting, and God, it felt good. There'd been so little happiness in this house. "Shall I open your gift first?"

She crossed her feet. "Sure. I hope you like it."

Her nerves were obvious, and when he pulled out the canvas in the gift bag, he understood why. She'd painted him walking in the fields at dawn, his house in the background, his sheep nestled around him. His face wasn't visible, but his body was turned toward the spot where she always set up her painting supplies. Somehow, he knew he was smiling in the painting, and truth be told, he always did smile when he saw her, even before, when he was fighting the pull between them.

"It's beyond beautiful, Angie, and so surprising. I... never expected a gift as treasured as this." He knew exactly where he'd hang it. Over the mantel with the stove in the main room.

"I'm glad you like it." She uncrossed her ankles and stood normally again. "I called it *In His Element*."

His throat grew thick. She saw him, and he was glad of it. Lovers should see each other. "Are you sure it's not too precious a gift? I know you need to sell your paintings, and I expect you could sell this."

She put her hands over his, her grip entreating. "I want you to have it. Carrick, you've given me so much. I want... you to have something from my hands."

He lifted one of those hands and kissed it. She touched his jaw and traced the line of bone and sinew. He wanted to close his eyes and let her explore him before he did the same to her. It took the control of a saint to pull away. "Let me give you the tour, Angie." His voice had dropped an octave.

She drew in a deep breath and nodded. "Lead on."

He laughed. "Well, look around you. It's an open floor plan—more modern than Irish."

"I love the floor-to-ceiling windows," she said as they wandered into the main floor. "Oh, the views you have, Carrick. The light in here must be incredible. Maybe even better than in my studio. I tell you. Windows make all the difference."

He'd never thought about light in that way, but it gave him an odd feeling to learn the house was suited to her painting needs. "You have an open invitation to paint here anytime. You mentioned Bets' studio is bursting, what with all your new classes."

"We'll manage," Angie said, glancing around. "Liam is adding some extra shelves in the closet, and I'm rethinking a few things here and there. But never mind. Tell me what you see here."

He outlined where the rooms would be for sitting, dining, and cooking, and gave her a quick look at the downstairs bathroom before mentioning the new theater room. Oh, she loved that, he was pleased to discover. He took her hand as they walked up the stairs to the second floor. He'd swept those too, making sure there was nothing she could slip upon.

"There are four bedrooms up here," he said, letting go of her hand as she walked down the hallway and peeked into each.

"They're large with big windows," she exclaimed. "I love them. Being in the cottage has me missing big bedrooms. Big bathrooms too. I like that two of your bedrooms have en suite bathrooms. Carrick, it's lovely."

"Thank you, Angie." He eyed the long hallway, suddenly aware of how quiet it sounded. When he was working, he usually kept the radio on, and the sound of a saw or hammer was his accompaniment. Not today. The silence was almost as potent as the wind. Unavoidable.

Lonely, if he were being honest.

He'd planned his bedroom in the west corner and made it the largest with a view of the sycamore tree. Sorcha again. He'd thought she'd love that view. Now he knew she would never sleep in it. Maybe he could use the bedroom for something else. He had an office, too, but it wasn't very big. Didn't the largest sheep farmer in the county need a larger office?

"You look sad, Carrick." She leaned against the doorway. "Is it hard to build this house?"

He blew out a breath. "It was the hardest in the beginning. It's only since I let go of her words on my sheep that I've accepted she won't be living here. Oh, that makes me sound mad, and many in the village think I am mad for building this house. But I made a promise to her. I keep my promises, Angie."

She crossed and put her hand on his arm. "I know you do, Carrick."

When she said no more, he let out more of the pent-up air in his chest. "It's a hard thing, letting go. But I know I need to make this my house now. My mind is starting to move along with the notion." He'd only needed his heart to lead the way, he realized.

"I'm glad." She rubbed his arm before she dropped her hand. "I'm also glad you didn't want to make love here. I didn't know if I could say so earlier, but I feel like I can say it now."

His throat thickened for another reason, hearing that. "Aren't we always direct with each other?"

She opened her hands as if searching for the right words. "This house and the reasons you built it were your own and ones I'd never wish to hurt. Carrick, I didn't want to make love to you here."

"When it was Sorcha's house," he said, meeting her gaze. "You were brave to come at all."

"It's not brave," she said, gesturing down the hallway. "It's part of you, and I happen to like all of you. This house matters to you. That's why I'm here."

He pinched the bridge of his nose. "I like that you're not running to the door."

She touched his arm again. "Oh, Carrick. You're too hard on yourself. Honestly, there's a part of me that admires a man who would keep a promise to the woman he loved. Even after she died. I've never been around a man like that, least of all been attracted to one. What does that say about me? Maybe I'm a little crazy too."

He took her hand and laid it against his heart. "Maybe that makes us perfect for each other."

"Maybe it does," she whispered.

Cradling her head against his chest, he caressed her hair, learning the new shorter shape. "Since we're sharing parts of ourselves, I wanted to ask about Megan. Bets mentioned she and Ollie had moved to a new cottage, and I ran into her after leaving your studio the other night. She didn't seem very talkative, and I've noticed you haven't been as keen to talk in the mornings. Are you all right?"

She blew out a long breath. "When I'm painting, I feel free. I don't have to worry about being home for dinner or to get Ollie a bath and to bed. Not that I don't see him. I do. We go biking and walk the fields and paint. After a lifetime of codependent patterns and living together for eight months, Megan and I are having growing pains. I tell myself Rome wasn't built in a day."

Carrick took her in his arms and stroked her hair. "Tough situation all around. But you've broken out, and hopefully this move will help your sister and Ollie."

"She has been changing too," Angie said. "Her affection for Kade's dog is a good sign. And Ollie loves it here."

He lifted her face. "And you're thriving too. You're painting gallery-worthy pieces again and starting to stand in your own feet, as we say. The new hair is a sign, as are the new wellies."

She finally gave a smile, and it tugged his heart. "You noticed my daisy wellies?"

There were shadows under her eyes from all this talk. He wished they could rub off as easily as some of her paints. But that's not how life worked. "Angie, I notice everything when it comes to you. Also, you're figuring things out pretty well, in my humble opinion."

"I'm here with you, aren't I?" She traced the dent in his jaw. "This is where I want to be. Carrick, you're not like any man I've ever known."

He took her face in his hands. "And you're not like any woman I've known. I think it's something to take care of people as you have. You did it out of love at the core, I expect, before things got twisted. You might remember that, even if things are a little thorny."

Tears appeared in her eyes. "Love. Yeah, there was love. I loved my exes, and I love Megan. I do. Even when I'm upset with her. But while we're on this subject, I should add that I've found a higher version of loving someone, someone I don't feel compelled to take care of. Someone who doesn't even need me."

He knew in his bones who she was talking about. His heart seemed to warm in his chest. That space expanded, until he didn't feel anything but the beat of his heart, a heart that Angie had brought back to life. *Love. Is. Here.* That had been the message in Bets' garden, after his sheep had overrun it. On this, Sorcha had been right. God bless her.

He and Angie had pledged to be direct with each other, hadn't they?

"If you're talking about me, I'm of a similar mind."

Her mouth opened and then closed and then opened again. "You are? But I thought—"

"We've both come around a long bend from our first discussion, Yank." He smiled as he said it. "And we've surprised ourselves a fair bit in the process, have we not? Do you not know yourself and your heart?"

She nodded slowly. "I do. Not that I expect anything."

That was part of the problem. She didn't expect anything because she didn't think she deserved anything. The irony was that her lack of expectations was the very thing that made him feel free to love her. Oh, they were contrary, he and this Yank. Perhaps they could tip the scales back in the other direction and find some balance, both in themselves and with each other.

He pointed to himself. "Even in my stubborn moments, do I strike you as a man who doesn't know himself?"

The left side of her mouth tipped up. "You don't."

He took her hands in his own. "So tell me, and I'll tell you."

She inhaled deeply before saying, "I love you, Carrick."

Some words conveyed promises that were binding, but these words had none of that. They were as pure as a sea-fed stream. "And I love you, Angie."

"Okay, this is one hell of a surprise." She tightened her grip on his hands. "You and I seem to create a lot of surprises together. With our direct talk."

He leaned down and kissed her softly. "We do at that."

"I have some more of it for you then." She looked up at him, her smile stretching across her face. "I think you should come home with me tonight. We can both set the stage there."

He didn't want to wait any longer either. "Lead the way."

CHAPTER TWENTY-EIGHT

Had she ever been this happy before having sex with anyone?

Angie hummed to Rihanna as she drove Carrick back to her cottage, their hands tangling on the gear shift. In times past, there had been an urgent rush to intimacy, sometimes leading to regret afterward, once her mind snapped back into action. Other times, her heart had led her after a few dates, thinking the guy was special, only for her to discover he didn't have any plans to see her again. With her exes, she'd been nervous, wanting to please them after the first weeks of lust-driven madness. But the happiness she felt now was new and invigorating.

"You're smiling, and you have a nice voice," Carrick said, lifting her hand from the gear shift and kissing the palm.

"I was just thinking how happy I am—before sex." She shot him a grin. "It's heady stuff."

"It is," he said, letting go of her hand when she needed to downshift as they reached the cottage. "I think we're likely to manage being happy afterward too. Angie—"

She pulled to a stop and turned the car off, facing him. "What?"

"I haven't been happy in a long time. Before we do this, I want to thank you for that."

"We both have a lot to be thankful for." She cast a glance over her shoulder. "Hurry, let's rush inside before anyone sees you. I'm mostly kidding."

He laughed, exiting the vehicle and striding to the door quickly, and she hurried behind him. She opened the door, and he made a humming sound. "You don't lock your door. You're becoming more Irish by the day."

"Liam said it wasn't needed, and I liked the idea—although Brady opened the door the other day with a package and set it inside without knocking. Totally shocked me."

"That's how the post gets delivered here in the country," Carrick said, closing said door and shrugging out of his jacket. "But we aren't here to talk about the post."

"No, we aren't, but do you have a package for me?" She cocked a hip and then laughed at herself as he rolled his eyes. "Bad joke. How do you feel about candles?"

"I'm good with them," he said, looking around the small parlor, "but they're a pain to blow out after a long night of sex."

"Rookie! Who needs to blow them out? They go out on their own."

He crossed and wrapped his arms around her. "Who's the rookie? You keep lights on all night, and everyone in the village the next day will tease you about your nighttime goings-on."

She leaned back, the lightness in her body making her want to do cartwheels. "Seriously?"

He waggled his brows. "Seriously."

Her mind started to turn. Megan's voice started. *Everyone will know you had sex—*

She stopped the thoughts in their tracks. "I'm going to get the candles."

Pulling her back to him, he cupped her cheek. "Having second thoughts after the candle comment?"

"No." She shook her head emphatically. "Do you ever hear other people's thoughts in your head?"

He narrowed his eyes. "Of course. My mum's especially. I also hear dead people. See them too. You should probably know Sorcha appeared to me the day you arrived and told me this was going to happen."

"Wait a minute. Kade told me Sorcha was helping you and me get together, which blew my mind, but she's been involved since *the first day?*"

"Kade told you about Sorcha?" His face was slack with shock.

"Yes, I asked him about the orange scent in the air. Well, this is... How do you explain it?"

"Maybe it's an Irish thing." He lifted his shoulder. "She wanted me to move on and—be happy. You were the key. Once I got over my own hurt and stubbornness."

"You weren't that stubborn."

"The takeaway is that she approves of you." His smile was soft as he gazed at her. "Not that I needed her to. But I thought you should know. Leave it to Kade to make sure the path was laid. Since directness is our signature, I haven't seen her since I sheared the sheep and let her words go. I also wanted you to know that."

Leaning her head against his chest, she wrapped her arms around him. "It almost makes you believe anything is possible. It's really sweet, her pushing us together. Oh, that's how your sheep got out that first day. I just got it!"

She started laughing, and he joined in. "She blew the gate wide open. Still don't know how, but her dress billows even when there's no wind. Are you sure you don't think I'm mad?"

"If you are, then I'm just as mad. And so is Kade." She smiled as she traced his jaw. "Maybe it's the artist in me. Do you know how many paintings depict mystical things? I've always been of the opinion that those things have to exist for so many people to paint them. I've felt things myself, but have never seen them." Although apparently she'd smelled his dead wife's orange scent.

"Enough of this talk. I only told you because I thought you should know, not knowing you already did."

She caressed the broad lines of his shoulders. This was another way he was telling her he'd let go of the past. She rose on her tiptoes and kissed him lightly on the mouth. "I'm glad you told me yourself. Be right back."

Rushing from the main room into the kitchen, she pulled out the votive candles that she'd spied under the sink. The smell of citronella was subtle. "Hope you don't care that our candles were designed to ward off mosquitos."

"You mean midges, our tiny flies," he said, coming up behind her as she stood up with the candles and shoved them at him. She turned to look for the matches, aware he was behind her.

"You know, the kitchen feels even smaller with you in it," she said as she rummaged through the mess drawer. "Aha. I found them."

Matches in hand, she nodded in the direction of the short hallway leading to her bedroom. His hand settled on her hip as they walked to the back.

"It's not a big room," she explained as he shut the door,

threw some condoms on the bed, and stripped off his shirt. "Oh, my! I guess we're getting right to it."

"We can draw the next one out," he said, unbuckling his pants and shucking off everything else.

"My God!" She fumbled the matches, and they spilled onto the floor. "You're gorgeous. I mean, I knew you would be. But seriously…"

Her mind captured the image of him standing naked in her tiny room. The powerful lines of muscle. The broad shoulders and thick neck. The rock-solid abdomen leading down to the kind of cock she'd only seen depicted in paintings. Thick. Long. Full. And very aroused.

"Are you going to stare at me all night, Yank?" He gestured to his body. "Undress. I want to see *you*."

She looked down at herself, seeing the parts of her that she thought were too full. "I'll light the candles."

Why had she thought they needed light? It was bright out until ten these days. She bent over for a match and grabbed the empty matchbox. His bare feet appeared in her vision.

"Is this about those curves you mentioned?" he asked, pulling her up gently.

She stood, clutching the things to her stomach. "Yes. I'm suddenly feeling self-conscious. Give me a moment. I'll get over it."

He only snorted, grabbing the match and matchbox and throwing it aside. "Later. Come on. Let me help you get over it."

Squeezing her eyes shut, she shook herself. "I'm over it."

He pressed a large hand to her hip with intention, and she felt the answering heat between her legs. "I don't believe you."

When he pressed his mouth to the side of her neck, she

moaned. If this is what he had planned, she could go along with it. "Try the other side. I might need all this help balanced out."

His chuckle was dark as he reached for the hem of her sweater. She raised her hands and he tugged it up and off, throwing it across the room.

"You're a messy kind of guy, right? The kind who doesn't pick clothes up off the floor. The new me wants you to know that you can pick things up yourself."

"Shut up, Yank," he ordered, kneeling in front of her and unbuttoning her jeans and lowering them. "I didn't tell you in the studio, but your breasts are masterpieces. If I could paint you, they would be a prominent feature in the painting. I'm about to find out what else I'd paint."

He paused as the heat in her belly and between her legs grew. "Wait. I just found the other spot."

His hand slipped between her legs, his fingers tracing the edge of her underwear. She widened her stance, giving him better access. That was all it took. He slipped off her underwear and her socks. His hands went around and removed her bra, tossing that aside too. Levering back on his knees, he studied her, his eyes a fiery ultramarine.

"Yank, you take my breath away."

If she hadn't believed him, she would have when he grabbed her bottom in his hands and pressed his mouth to her core. The feel of his tongue and lips had her coming in a rush.

"Oh, God, that was fast," she said, panting. "I'll slow down."

He set her back on the edge of the bed, still on his knees. "I don't want you to slow down. Not. One. Bit."

Her body fired up at his words. "That's the most dangerously delicious invitation I've ever had."

His mouth tipped into a smile as he stroked the backs of her legs. "It wasn't an invitation, Angie. It was an order."

Oh. God.

"Lay back now and let me love you again," he said, pressing a kiss to where she needed him.

This man... Her heart expanded in her chest as their eyes met. "In a minute." She traced his jaw and leaned in to kiss him slowly. Their lips met again and again until she heard him sigh. "I love you," she whispered, wanting to say it again.

He caressed her cheek, holding her gaze as he kissed her deeply and gently. "I love you too. Now do what I tell you."

The order, said with such love, made her smile. She leaned back, opening herself to him in a way she never had with anyone. He seemed to understand as he traced the sides of her legs, the intention as powerful as one of her brushstrokes. Then he placed her legs over his shoulders and kissed her and caressed her until she was arching against his mouth and crying out.

"Yes," he said, "let me hear you."

She didn't hold back, feeling the freedom of her pleasure and of being with him. When she came back to herself, he was lying on his side next to her on the bed, gloriously aroused. The smile on his face was as beautiful as his desire for her.

"Come here," she said, opening her arms to him.

He rose and settled between her legs after putting on a condom, one hand playing with her breast. She'd known the feel of him inside her would be powerful, but they both still moaned as he slid inside. He pressed his forehead against hers.

"Give me a moment." His muscles locked. "I want to feel all of you."

She laid her hands over his hips. Listened to the rapid beat of their hearts. Their breathing mingled. Her body seemed to shift into him, and then she felt a click, one she'd never felt before with a man.

Oneness.

He raised his face, and they gazed at each other. The light coming from his ultramarine eyes was as warm and beautiful as sunshine, and it traveled all the way to her heart, expanding it even more. She flowed with love and him as he began to move inside her, slowly at first. She knew his rhythm and matched him. She knew his pace and followed. They flowed into each other. She pressed her face into his shoulder, clutching him, awash in love sounds and the pleasure of their bodies coming together.

They found a faster pace, moaning brokenly now. Her body turned to molten fire, rising to a dizzying height, and then she was crying out and coming, pulsing around him. He called her name and followed her, clutching her to him.

She couldn't open her eyes, and she couldn't get enough oxygen. But she'd never been more pliant. She'd certainly never felt loved like this.

"Oh, Carrick," she whispered, tunneling her face into his neck.

"I know," he whispered back in awe.

She melted even more, never wanting to let him go. He seemed to be of the same mind since he didn't move from her. Still, he didn't lower all of his weight onto her, which she appreciated since she was trying to get her breath back.

"I probably need to get off you," he said after a time, leveling back to meet her eyes. "The only problem is I don't want to."

"Then stay," she said, her voice shot with emotion. God! She wanted him to stay forever. She closed her eyes. She'd

288

promised herself she wouldn't do this. *Stay in the moment, Angie. Just love him.*

His fingers touched her cheek. "Look at me."

She breathed out her frustration and opened her eyes. His gaze was soft but serious. "Haven't we done well up to now?"

She nodded, her throat thick.

"Then let's keep doing that. Being us. Being direct. Because when you asked me to stay, I heard it too. The promise of things between us."

Her sigh was easier this time. "I can't hide anything from you, can I?"

He studied her. "My question is: why did us making love make you want to?"

The question made her heart knock against her ribs in fear. She tried to chuckle. "Because I'm funny sometimes. Now get off me. I need to breathe."

He shook his head firmly. "Not yet. Answer me. I think this is important. Whatever caused you to stop painting before had its roots here."

Her mouth grew dry as her heart trembled. She knew why, but she'd never told anyone. Only a scary blank piece of white paper when she was sitting in a hard yellow chair in a classroom, being trained in art therapy. "It's hard to say, but fine. I...start to think about this ending. It's like I get a taste of love, and then it's gone. None of the men I've cared about, starting with my father, have loved the real me, so I always try to be what a man wants. Technically it's called a fear of abandonment. And I hate it."

"You're already thinking about us being done?" he asked, his brows slamming together. "About me not loving you? Why would you think that? What just happened between us moved me as powerfully as it did you. I started wondering about what we'll need to do to have you *stay* here so I can keep loving you. If you want to, that is."

Here in Ireland, he meant. Her heart seemed to soar in her chest in joy. To stay here with him... She made herself roll her eyes instead. "It's those words. *Stay here.* I shouldn't have said them."

He cupped her chin, forcing her to look at him. "We love each other. I think it's only natural to think it. Of course, we have some thinking to do about it. But perhaps we can take our time. Everything else has fallen into place for us."

Trust. Her lifetime nemesis. "I tell myself that, and then I have other thoughts."

"So do I." He smiled. "Think we can be easy with each other as those pieces settle into place? I'm willing."

"Me too. Do you want to shake on it?"

He left her a moment, dispensed with the condom, and then put another on. Her mouth was gaping as he gave her a look and slid back inside her. They were redefining arousal as she knew it. "Is this your version of a handshake? I like it."

"I'd rather make love again. Wouldn't you? Unless you want to try and paint to make sure you're still okay."

She wet her lips. "I'm still going to be able to paint." She wouldn't have it any other way.

"Are we of the same mind then?" he asked softly, watching her closely.

"We are," she whispered as he thrust into her. And of the same heart too, it seemed.

They never did get to the candles, and it didn't matter. The waning white light coming in through the windows showed her everything she wanted to see. By the time night finally came, she knew his body well enough to pleasure his every sense, and they only deepened their knowledge of each other until dawn's early light filtered into the room. She laid her head on his chest, love radiating through her every cell. His arms came around her and she remembered one of the first messages from Carrick's sheep.

Love. Is. Here.

She smelled oranges and fell asleep with a smile on her face.

CHAPTER TWENTY-NINE

She was so beautiful.

Carrick watched Angie sleep. How did she not see it? She was a painter. Shouldn't she know beauty? Well, he supposed he had his own blind spots, though none where she was concerned. He'd known their lovemaking was going to be powerful, but nothing could have prepared him for the whole scope. Loving her was like being washed by a waterfall—potent, cleansing, uplifting. Certainly memorable. He caressed the ends of her brown hair resting on the pillow. Oh, how he loved her. He hadn't imagined he could love like this again.

A pocket of fear rose up to clog his throat like a bit of loose gravel inside him, stirred up by traveling forward. He breathed it out like Angie had done. She'd told him the root of her fears: abandonment. He realized his fear was the same. He never wanted to lose someone he loved again. Wasn't that fear of abandonment too?

"What are you thinking about so seriously this morning?" she asked, brushing her hair away from her forehead.

"How similar you and I are, Yank." He leaned in and

kissed her and loved hearing her soft sigh of contentment. "I hope you're all right with me using it as an endearment. I find I can't give it up."

"I don't mind at all. In fact, I rather love it."

She stretched, her glorious curves lifting as if to meet his touch. His body rose in response. The sheet was tangled around her waist, and he was glad to see she didn't pull it up to her chin. After what they'd shared last night, there could be no barriers between them.

"Want to know something else I love?" He rolled her onto her side and settled a hand on her waist.

She tapped her finger to the tantalizing line between her breasts. "Me?"

"Yes, you. In fact, that's why I'm thinking of starting our first morning differently than I might otherwise."

Laughing, she hugged him, the gesture pure delight. "You already started it, remember? Filling me as dawn's light filled the land. I think that's what you said. It was really hot."

Had he said that? God, he was turning into Yeats. "I meant... I think you should paint this morning."

Her brown eyes danced. "Paint? You want to make sure I'm still cured, Dr. Fitzgerald?"

He leaned back to the edge of the bed for her paint bag and lifted it, then plunked it down between them. "Don't joke. This is too important. I want you to be able to paint, Angie. Always."

She put her hand on her straw bag, her hands patting it like she would a child. "Okay. I'll paint because it's important to both of us. But only if you let me paint you."

He pursed his mouth together. "Me, huh? Haven't you already? I seem to remember seeing a few paintings of my eyes, my hands, and my figure in the landscape you gave me. Have another part in mind?"

She leveled a glance at his lower body, and he laughed. "It's as I thought. You secretly want me for a life model." He threw back the sheet. "Have at it."

He put his hand behind his head, looking off like he'd seen some subjects do in paintings. Her snort had him smiling.

"Eyes on me, Carrick," she said, already pulling out her supplies. "Always on me."

There was nowhere else he wanted to look. He watched her as she painted him, sitting cross-legged and leaning back to the nightstand for a paint or a brush as her hand moved rapidly over the paper. At one point she leaned forward and rubbed a mixture of paint on his chest—very arousing—before returning to her pad, occasionally brushing the mixed paint on his chest onto her brush.

"I like being your palette," he said, only to have her mutter, "Flesh tones," and shush him.

He let her work. Her brow wrinkled when she painted, he realized, and she brushed white across her cheek when she pushed a strand of hair out of the way.

He could imagine waking with her every morning and watching her paint this way, especially if she mixed paint on him. It was arousing and endearing, and he felt...happy. God, there it was again, the same feeling he'd had last night and when he'd awoken to hear her breathing next to him, nestled against his side.

He was happy.

The rain started to fall, pinging the metal roof. Her concentration was absolute. She didn't even look up when a knock sounded on the front door.

"You're frowning," she said, her hand moving across the paper. "Why are you frowning?"

"Someone's at the door, love," he said, looking over his shoulder. "I'm rather hoping they don't just walk in, but it's Ireland and—"

"Oh shit!" She grabbed her paper and scooted off the bed, her curves a delight to his senses. Placing the paper on the dresser, she spun around. "Where's my robe? Oh, God, there are matches everywhere."

He laughed, remembering how she'd dropped them the moment he'd dropped his pants. "If they come to the bedroom, I'll tell them we knew a storm was coming this morning. That we were prepared to light candles in case the power went out."

"It's light outside, Carrick." She tugged on the robe, something he wished he could burn with the matches.

"I don't think you should wear clothes again," he said, watching as she cursed on the way to the door, scattering more matches. "I like you better naked."

An insistent pounding punctuated his sentence. She stilled. "That doesn't sound like Megan or Ollie. Thank God. Oh, what time is it?"

He picked up his phone from the floor. "Eight. Latest I've been in bed in years. Yank, I suggest you go to the door and handle whoever is there so you can come back to bed. I told my sheep to behave themselves this morning."

"You did? Oh, hang it! Who is pounding like that? Be right back."

Rolling out of bed, he grabbed his pants and tugged them on. He walked into the kitchen as she opened the door.

"Jamie!" she exclaimed.

Carrick shook his head.

"Kade. Brady. Declan. My God! This is a surprise."

Those interfering arses.

"Forgive me," Angie said unnecessarily. "I didn't know you were coming. I'd have made coffee cake. I'd invite you in from the rain—"

"No bother," Carrick heard his brother say.

She meant it as a joke, you idiot.

"We've come to deliver Carrick some fresh clothes," Jamie said.

"Oh, Jesus," he muttered. "I'm coming out."

He stepped into the parlor and sent his friends a hard smile as he walked toward Angie. She looked up at him, biting her lip.

"Were you painting on him, love?" Brady asked, gesturing to his chest. "I have to admit. That's hot."

"Oh shit." She turned and rubbed the paint with her fingers. "I was painting a real painting of him and needed the right color. Oh, never mind."

"You're right, Brady," Declan said with a grin. "Totally hot."

"Trying to decide whether to laugh or act embarrassed?" Carrick asked, stopping her cleanup and putting his hand to her back to ground her. "I told you how the village was, Yank. As for you eejits... What in the hell are you doing here, knocking on her door?"

Jamie held up a black bag, grinning like the rest of them. "I called you after I didn't find you at the new house, your old house, or walking the fields. I would have worried you were dead, except I spotted the beautiful painting in the sitting room of the new house. I figured you were here and might need some fresh clothes."

"It's what good friends do," Brady said, tugging on his

jacket. "You two look fresh as air-dried laundry. Despite the body paint."

"Oh, for God's sake," Carrick muttered. "Go on. Get it out of your systems."

Jamie extended the bag to him, and their eyes met. "You look happy, brother."

"You really do," Kade said, smiling.

That was all his friends had wanted to see, and he couldn't begrudge them for it. He nodded. "Thanks for bringing these. Although I could have managed."

"I brought you two fresh cowboy steaks," Declan said, handing another plastic bag to them. "For a romantic dinner...or breakfast even."

"That's very...thoughtful," Angie said, taking them.

"Anyone else?" Carrick asked, glaring at them.

"You two look downright savage," Liam said, coming down the drive on a bicycle and pulling to a stop. "Carrick, you look like a bona fide life model. Did you have a great night then? I thought I heard a bunch of sounds up at the house."

"Stop that right now," Carrick ordered as everyone laughed.

Angie bit her lip, trying not to join in. "The cat's out of the bag, Carrick. Might as well go with it. He was incredible."

He turned his head and gazed down at her. She was laughing softly.

"Fine," he said, playing along because she was. "It was epic."

That only made them grin more.

"Jesus! Now off with all of you. Don't you have work?"

"Don't you?" Jamie asked.

"Oh, he's *working* all right," Brady said, heading back to

his postal truck. "See you two later at the pub. I'll buy you both a drink."

"Not before I buy them one first," Declan said, heading to his car, parked behind the mail truck. "Have a good one."

"I'll walk about and see to your sheep," Jamie said, hunching his shoulders against the rain. "Be a good day to stay inside. You look peaked, brother. You need some rest."

"You might be coming down with something," Liam said, his lips twitching.

"You'll be coming down with something if you go for a bike ride in this weather," Angie said. "What are you thinking?"

"This here's Ireland," Liam said, pointing to the sky. "If we waited on the rain, we wouldn't get anywhere. I'll see you at the pub later." He sped off.

Kade gave Angie a wink. "I'll be heading up to see Ollie and your sister while I'm here. I didn't have time to bring the animals, what with Jamie's text saying it was urgent, but I figured he might like to go for a ride at the farm. The rain's not too bad."

The light changed then, as it often did in Ireland. The sun came out, lighting the tops of the trees until they were golden. The rain turned to mist and then disappeared.

Angie pointed in the sky. "Look, there's a rainbow. A double. Oh, it's beautiful. Carrick, isn't it beautiful?"

He was used to rainbows, but he couldn't see her happiness without feeling it. "'Tis one of the most beautiful I've ever seen."

"I agree," Kade said, sending him a knowing wink.

"God, I need to paint this. Excuse me, boys, I'll be right back." She raced out of the room.

"She doesn't know only the tourists love the rainbows, does she?" Jamie suddenly stumbled. His face leached color. "Oh, God! I can see Sorcha. She said not to poke fun at the rainbow she brought."

"It's a gesture she would bring," Kade said with a smile. "Poets like rainbows too, as do I. You have to understand their magic. It's more than just about pots of gold, you know."

Carrick turned his head. She stood at the edge of the trees, a radiant smile on her face. They shared a look. Sorcha had told him double rainbows always appeared when a person made a big life decision. It portended good fortune. He couldn't think of a much bigger life decision than deciding to be with Angie. Putting his hand to his heart, he said *Thank you* silently, knowing she would hear. She nodded and blew him a kiss. He returned it, smiling himself.

"I smell oranges," Jamie muttered. "Oh, God! I think I'm going to faint."

He fell to the ground before either of them could catch him.

"He did that pretty gracefully for a large man, didn't he?" Kade leaned down and opened his jacket to give him air. "He's okay. He'll come around when he's ready."

Carrick heard Sorcha's laughter. Let his eyes rest on her again. He knew this would be the last time he saw her. His heart swelled as she lifted her hand, her smile as beautiful as he remembered. And then she disappeared.

"Not bad for a regular morning, is it?" Kade asked, clapping him on the back.

He surveyed his brother, who had yet to stir.

"No," he answered, hearing Angie coming back into the parlor. "It might be my best morning in quite some time, and I expect it's going to stay that way. Angie, come on! We need to set you up so you can paint this rainbow."

CHAPTER THIRTY

H*ere. Be. Good.*
Angie was living the message every day, a message she now knew was from Sorcha. All of the woman's messages had come true, and Angie had laid a bouquet of wildflowers at the base of her favorite tree—the one they both loved—to offer her thanks. The wind had blown gently, and the smell of sweetgrass had mixed deliciously with oranges. Her heart was happy. Both for herself and Carrick.

Her painting classes were going well. Like with everything, some students were excelling while others felt more challenged by the medium. She understood. She'd been there. It was her job to help them get past their blocks, if she could, something that was easier now that she'd gotten past hers.

Bets was continuing to formalize the art center. She was posting new flyers around town along with the ones advertising Angie's show, something she was growing more excited about as the event approached.

Angie's voice was growing stronger. She painted more

freely. She was less critical of herself. When her brush wanted to fly off in a new direction on the canvas, she let it. When she had the urge to mix a surprising collection of paints for a new color, she did it. She'd never been prouder of her work.

She was so proud, in fact, that she'd contacted a few galleries that used to show her work, telling them she was back after a long teaching sabbatical. Their praise had made her hug herself and dance in the studio, and when one of them had said they'd like to feature some of her new work, she'd jumped up and down.

Carrick had bought more champagne, and they'd had dinner in bed and made love with more joy than she'd ever imagined feeling in her life.

As for her and Megan, she'd concluded they were at a detente. Megan was staying out of her way as much as she was staying out of hers. For the time being, they both seemed to be doing better for it.

Ollie seemed to be thriving too. Megan had stopped babying him and was letting him run free around the manor. The added benefit of his new best friends—Liam, Kade, Duke, and the horses—helped. His bedtime had shifted to ten o'clock with the sun setting so late. He'd been taken to see the spots along the rocky shore where the pirates had landed and the Spanish Armada had crashed, and he was filled with tales of fairies, leprechauns, giants, tree spirits, and other Irish myths from books Liam had given him to devour.

Carrick had done his part to help her nephew, showing him how to look after his sheep and inviting him to walk the fields with him and attend to any holes in the fencing. He'd even taken Ollie with him in the tractor to dress the freshly cut fields with slurry, and her nephew had come back beaming.

She couldn't imagine loving Carrick more.

She painted in his house on some rainy mornings as he worked on nailing down baseboards. When he smiled at her, she felt as light and airy as a cloud. And when he suggested she store some of her paintings there since she was bursting out of her studio space, she thought she might step out of the open window and walk on air.

She was still in the clouds on the day of her Wednesday painting class, the one the Lucky Charms were in. The women weren't only about fun and games, she knew. All of them worked hard—even Carrick's retired mother. While Brigid hadn't said anything about her relationship with Carrick—the whole village knew, of course—she would feel the woman's gaze on her at times and look up only to see a kind smile.

In fact, while his friends might have shown up to check on him their first morning together weeks ago, no one had teased her or pressed her for details. She suspected they were delighted Carrick was happy again—some did remark on his changed nature, he told her.

"Angie!" Nicola called out, waving a paintbrush her way.

She rose from the drawing table, where she'd been sketching as the class painted. After her demo, she let them get to it since they all knew they could ask for help anytime. Her students had been given three objects to choose from today: a charming yellow watering can she'd found in the garden; ceramic blue wellies potted with orange calendulas that Bets had placed beside her front door for color; and, lastly, a stunning red-tipped pink rose Carrick had brought her from his home garden in a simple crystal vase.

"Yes, Nicola..." she said, walking around to look at her easel. "Oh, my Go—"

"I tried to paint a still life, but my hand drew Killian, almost as if guided by the fairies." She tilted her head to the side. "Ever since he streaked in this very room, I've had a hard time not giving in to the urge to paint him nude. I think Kade is right. The men, including my Killian, were expressing some inner desire to be seen as men. Maybe it's their age or maybe I don't look at his body the way I used to. I think drawing him nude will be good for our relationship. What do you think?"

Suddenly Bets was at her side, joined by Siobhan, Brigid, and the other women in the class. Angie thought she needed another of the chocolate chip cookies Bets had brought to class.

"Well, you got his member right, from what I recall," Bets said, elbowing Nicola. "That's pretty good actually. Does it make you want Killian more?"

She fanned herself. "It might as well be a rare scorcher of a day in August for how warm I feel."

"You *do* look flushed," Siobhan said, her round face creasing in concern. "Let me find you some water."

The ladies clustered around Nicola's painting. Angie studied it, her art therapy mind turning in circles. "I think you might soften his shoulders some. Use some thicker brushstrokes to show his muscles."

"He does have nice muscles for his age," Nicola muttered, touching her slender neck. "All the work on the farm."

"Seamus is the same, what with all the meat he hefts around at the butcher shop," Brigid declared while the other students murmured their agreement.

"Gavin is wiry from running back and forth along his

bar, and he's always been tall as a beanpole," Siobhan said, returning with a glass of water and giving it to her friend.

"He never sits down, that man," Bets said with a laugh.

"And what about you, Bets O'Hanlon?" Nicola asked, skewering her with a look. "Are you finally going to come out and say you're seeing Donal O'Dwyer on the sly?"

Since no one gasped, Angie knew the news had never been a secret. She shrugged and admitted, "Even I knew, Bets. I think it was Cormac O'Sullivan whose cousin lives in Westport that broke the news."

"Yes, that's the way of it," Nicola said as the other women nodded. "They saw you at Cian's."

"You can't go anywhere on this island!" Her cousin made a face and stalked back to her station, picking up a paintbrush. "We've only gone out once, and it was a complete disaster."

This was news. "Whyever would you say that?" Siobhan asked.

Bets touched the edge of her canvas. "He was too wonderful for words, that's why. I told him it made me suspicious. I've known him many years, and I never knew he could be so... Oh, never mind."

"So what?" Brigid asked, crossing and rubbing Bets' shoulder.

"Attentive. Fun. Adventurous." She clunked her paint-brush into her water and swirled it around. "I only went out with him because he gave me the most beautiful rose, a prize winner, I might add. I'm going to kick Mary's arse with that rose."

A few women sighed, including Angie. The way to Bets' heart surely was through her roses. The talk in the village was that this year's competition would be bigger than ever.

"You should go out with him more then," Nicola declared. "And paint him nude."

"I've been trying to forget all about that," Bets said. "I figured one date would cure me, but something's not right. He was even game for going to Paris out of the blue."

"*Paris!*" the women shouted.

Her mouth twisted. "Yes, Paris."

"None of our men go anywhere, Angie," Nicola said with a sigh. "It *is* suspicious."

"Except..." She pressed her hand to her heart. "He meant it. He couldn't be that wonderful. Could he?"

Everyone looked at Angie.

"You're new to town and seem to have good judgment about men," Brigid said, as others nodded. "What do you think, Angie? Is Donal too good to be true?"

She touched her chest. "Wait. I'm still stuck on the part where you think I have good judgment in men. I've been terrible at that."

"In the States, dear," Brigid said, taking her hand with a soft smile. "Not in Ireland. You've worked wonders with my son, and he's clearly done the same with you. I'd say you have more wisdom because of your past experience. Wouldn't you, girls?"

They all nodded their heads in agreement, and that feeling of being able to walk on air showed up again. She embraced it. "I've had classes before where all of the students suddenly become a community. I think we've reached that, don't you? So, I'll tell you what I think, Bets. I talked to Donal in the pub the same day of the streaking, and I have to say, I think he's crazy about you. I don't know him, but he seems like a man you could depend on. If he said he'd go to Paris, I suspect he meant it."

"Dammit." Bets looked down at her blue sneakers. "He

told me to take my time getting over my suspicions, if you can believe it. That he was happy to court me without setting another date. He's had his father bringing up little presents for me since he knows I didn't want anyone in the village to know. That clearly didn't work."

"I vote for going out with him again, Bets," Nicola said, "and I think Angie should dedicate a couple classes to nudes. Who else is up for it?"

"I'd need a picture," Siobhan said with a sly smile. "I don't draw well from memory."

"Maybe we can have them show up as real-life models," Angie said with a smirk. She held up a hand when a few people let out a whoop. "I was kidding."

"I'm not," Siobhan said with a wink. "It would help my artistic nature."

"Sure it would. It can't be worse than my first class in college. The life model got an erection suddenly and blurted out, 'Up periscope.' He'd been in the Navy. Girls, you can have Eoghan but no one else."

"You drive a hard bargain, Yank," Nicola said, her lips twitching. "Pictures of our men, it is."

She looked at Bets, who was trying not to laugh. "Up periscope. That's a good one! See, I told you teaching a class on nudes was likely."

Inevitable was more like it. "Are we sure we're good to do this? I don't want it to be a strike against you when you put in the application for the arts center."

"Demand for classes shot up after the streaking," Bets said. "We're good to go. Besides, Donal is on the county council, and he was part of such shenanigans. I think we're safe."

"I agree," Nicola said. "Every shop has posted a flyer about your gallery showing in my bookstore. Bets, people have been complimenting the gorgeous new flyer about our arts center too."

God, she loved this town. Between Carrick and her work, she'd already told Bets she wanted to stay longer than the six months allowed by her visa. Bets had promised they'd figure it out.

Still, the Lucky Charms weren't her only students in the class, just the most outspoken. She knew nudes didn't work for everyone, so she looked around the room and said, "I want everyone to be comfortable. If it's not something that interests you, we can easily arrange for you to attend another class."

"Anyone want to transfer?" Bets asked.

Not a single woman raised her hand. "Fine. Let me talk a little about drawing and painting anatomy since the still lifes don't seem to be capturing your imagination."

Truly, she couldn't blame them. Wasn't it Carrick who'd awoken something in her? She thought about all the rainy mornings she'd painted him. She had a whole paint pad full of him, and they were as good as they were sizzling. His body was stupendous, both as a subject and as a lover.

"Need a glass of water too, dear?" Siobhan asked with a laugh. "You look a bit flushed."

A blush spread across her cheeks. She'd been thinking about Brigid's son in the buff right in front of the woman! "I'm fine. Let's talk about the human body."

She fell back into a more clinical recitation, and some of the women's eyes seemed to cross. When she ditched the academic routine and pulled up a vintage photo of a male nude and started to paint it as a demonstration, she had them enthralled. Given all her recent practice with Carrick, she was in her element. When she finished, the whole class cheered.

"My God, Angie," Bets exclaimed, crowding the painting with everyone else. "You need to have some nudes in your gallery showing."

"It's only two weeks away," she said, biting her lip. "I have a theme. Hands and eyes—"

"And cocks," Nicola breathed. "The non-rooster kind. Oh, to see Mary Kincaid's face."

Her students burst out laughing, but she studied the painting. The man filled the canvas almost as if he owned it, the brushstrokes powerful and bold. His green eyes commanded attention—like someone else she knew—and his body seemed to assert itself. Even she couldn't look away.

"Next show for sure." Because she didn't doubt there would be one. She rubbed her fingers together, wanting to paint more. "I'd want to have the time to paint properly."

"You did that nude in fifteen minutes," Bets said. "I'd say you're on a roll."

"I've had a lot of practice—" Oh shit, had she said that out loud? "Never mind."

A few of the women grinned as Bets patted her on the back. "Good for you, dear."

She held her cousin's gaze. She pointedly did not look at Brigid. "You might try it yourself."

"I might at that." She turned her head swiftly. "Do you hear that?"

Angie cocked her ear. "Sounds like thunder." Except Ireland didn't really have thunder to accompany the rain. Plus, it wasn't raining. Sunlight was streaming in the skylights.

"Oh, no, Bets!" Nicola said, running to the window. "I'd know that sound anywhere—"

"Sheep!" Bets cried out, running for the stairs. "My roses!"

Everyone followed her, racing toward the manor house. Angie heard the bleating and increased her pace. When they reached the edge of her rose garden, she stopped cold. There had to be a hundred sheep feasting away. And Megan was standing with a golf club lifted overhead, shouting at the herd of aggressive sheep tearing off Bets' large flower heads!

"Help!" her sister cried as she poked a bleating ewe. "There're too many of them."

Angie did a double take and then raced after Bets to grab more clubs from the house. They each grabbed a few and thrust them at the other women as they ran back out.

"I'm calling Donal," Brigid called, holding up her cell phone. "And Carrick. He can help."

"They might be too late," Bets shouted. "Come on, girls. After me. Push them back."

Angie was more experienced with sheep this time, and she managed to frighten eight of them clear away. But the sheer number was intimidating, and while they battled the sheep and tried to push them back, the pull of the perfectly symmetrical dinner-plate roses was too strong for the other sheep to ignore. They ripped off Bets' flower heads, chomping quickly before going for another. Angie fought the sheep alongside the other women, but the more roses the sheep ate, the more determined they seemed to have more.

When Donal and Carrick finally arrived on the tails of each other and jumped out of their vehicles to wrangle the sheep, Angie lowered her weapon and surveyed the damage.

Bets' award-winning roses were gone.

CHAPTER THIRTY-ONE

Earlier, in the art class, Bets had decided to hell with it. She'd give Donal a chance all the way, just like the girls had suggested. But her excitement had vanished.

He'd given her his word that his sheep wouldn't touch her roses, and she'd believed him. While she knew it was unreasonable—sheep had minds of their own—she felt he'd betrayed her.

The somber look that man had given her as he left with his infernal bleating sheep wouldn't sway her. Carrick didn't help by saying, "I can't imagine how Donal's sheep got out like this. I went by his pasture on my way here, and his gate was flung wide open. Usually, he has it locked up tighter than a duck's arse, especially after the last incident."

She didn't care that he was sorry. She was sick to her stomach, and she had the odd urge to cry. They were roses, sure. But they were her babies. She wouldn't be entering the rose competition this year. Mary Kincaid would be giddy when she heard she'd have an easy pass to the large gold trophy. Mostly, though, she was struggling with the feeling that Donal had let her down. There would be no more romantic evenings or kisses in his greenhouse. Forget mad trips to Paris.

It was over before it had begun.

Liam showed up, and it only took a moment for him to see the way of it. "Oh, Mum," he said, putting his arm around her. "I'm so sorry."

Leaning in for a moment, she took his comfort and then stood as tall as she could for a petite woman and surveyed her friends. The rest of the Lucky Charms and her painting classmates were all huddled together, their faces gray. Did she look that bad? Probably worse. "I won't say it doesn't feel like a huge loss."

Ollie ran over, a single Gemini rose in his small hand. The damn sheep must have torn it off and forgotten to eat it. "Maybe you can put this one in water and save it for the competition."

His voice was eager, his gesture sweet, but with the fair two weeks away, it was a pipe dream. "Thanks, sweetheart. Your mom was quite the warrior today. Megan, I thank you."

The dear girl rested on her golf club. "I didn't know I had it in me. I only wish I could have stopped them."

"How could you?" She ran a shaky hand through her short hair. "Listen, everyone, I feel like I should hand out chocolate chip cookies for a good effort, but I just can't muster it right now. If you'll excuse me..."

She headed inside to her room and was grateful no one followed. Her friends knew she liked her quiet time after a loss. From her window, she watched as Liam led the way to clean up the mess in the yard. She closed the curtains and lay down on her bed.

When she started to cry, her roses swam in her mind as much as Donal's face.

The light changed in her room, touching the western wall. Liam knocked on the door and said he'd left a tray outside if she wanted to eat. She didn't rise. Sometime later, another knock intruded on her quiet, and she pulled a pillow over her head. Had Angie decided to breach her sanctuary? Given the boldness her cousin had regained these past weeks, she was the most likely to try.

The creak of the old doorframe caught her attention, and she looked over to see Donal striding across her bedroom.

"Get out of here," she said, sitting up. "I don't want to see you."

He set his weight. "I know what happened today was horrible, but I need to show you something. Come with me. *Please*."

His deep-set green eyes entreated her. He was heartsick too—it was evident in his eyes—and in the thick of her grief she couldn't take it. Her throat thickened, and she pressed her face into the pillow.

Strong arms wrapped around her and pulled her against his big muscular body. "Don't do this, Bets. I know I gave my word to you, but if you come with me, I promise you'll feel better."

"It's all destroyed," she whispered, fighting his warmth.

"No, *mo ghrá*," he said, kissing the top of her head.

She gripped his arms at the endearment. *My love.* "Don't call me that. Please."

"To call you anything else would be a lie to my own heart, and I won't have that on my conscience. Now. Let's go. Don't make me haul you out of this bed."

Turning around, she shoved at his chest. "Liam wouldn't let you."

His thick silver brows rose. "Let me? Woman, he was

the one who let me inside and then some. You should know I spoke with Liam before I started courting you, and he and your other boys all approved of me."

That made her sit up straight. "They did not!" How could they not have told her?

"They did indeed." He set his hands on her arms and rubbed them gently. "I know you have your suspicions, Bets, but I won't have you cutting me out of your heart without a fair showing, and I certainly won't lose you over something like this. Come with me now. I don't want to be tough with you, but this is too important. I saw the way you looked at me when I left with my sheep."

She pushed off the bed, swayed as much by the emotion in his voice as by his argument. "Fine, I'm fair-minded. Where are we going?"

"First, to my pasture and then to a special place." He extended his large hand. "If you want a chaperone, I can ask my father to join us."

A bubble of humor worked its way up inside her. "We're both over sixty. I doubt we need a chaperone. But where's this special place?"

"I'm keeping its location secret until the last moment, but it's my solution to today's problem." He shook his hand at her. "Now, are you going to take my hand or continue to stand there looking cross at me? It's time to trust me, Betsy O'Hanlon."

She took his hand.

He squeezed it and then ventured closer, until he was towering over her. Such a large man should make her feel smaller, but he didn't. His size was as comforting as his tender gaze. "Thank you. I'll drive."

They ventured down the stairs, holding hands. Liam appeared in the main hall holding a bottle of beer. "Good.

You have her up. Mum, I was hoping you wouldn't be that stubborn. Listen to what Donal has to say."

"You already know? How is that?"

"Because he and I have an understanding, Mum." Liam inclined his chin. "Now that the cat's out of the bag, so to speak, I've no problem telling you Wyatt and Rhys are of the same mind."

She was huffing as Donal drew her toward his Mercedes. "Bets, you raised right fine boys. Now let's have a pleasant ride, shall we?"

"Your pasture is just around the corner."

"I plan to drive slow." He hit the touchscreen for the music, and Bon Jovi's "Always" came on. "I've been listening to the band since you love it. This song seemed a good choice for this moment."

He couldn't be serious? This song was about loving someone. Always. She turned her head, studying his tight jaw. "You *are* serious."

"I told I wouldn't lose you over this, Bets O'Hanlon."

The music continued, Jon singing about loving someone forever. When Donal said no more, she pressed back into the leather seat in shock. He'd talked to her boys, and they were in favor of him. If that wasn't monumental enough, he'd called her *mo ghrá*. He'd been listening to her favorite songs...

He parked in front of the pasture gate when they arrived, and his scowl was fearsome as they got out and faced each other over his car. Why was he so angry?

"Come see." He strode to the gate. "Someone cut my rope."

She put her hand on his car to steady herself. "What?"

He thrust a pointer finger in its direction. "When I realized how stupid I was to let my sheep out to get your attention, especially with your roses starting to bloom, I increased my fencing. You might not know it, but I have interlocking fences. Usually that's good enough, but I wanted to be extra sure—especially after Carrick's sheep got out on a whim. I thought that was strange."

He wasn't wrong. It had been strange. But he clearly didn't know about Sorcha's involvement from beyond. Probably not the time to mention it.

"I added this blue polybraid gate rope, which is as sturdy as an ox. I had to climb my own gate to get to my sheep, but I was willing to do it for you. Come take a look at the sabotage."

She wandered over and examined the rope's threads. "But who would do such a thing?"

His jaw ticked. "Teenagers maybe? If I pissed anyone else off, they'd tell me to my face. No farmer around here would do it."

No, they wouldn't. "Donal, this is incredible. You don't think Mary Kincaid would go this far?"

"She's been decidedly single-minded, but I'm not sure we'll ever know the culprit."

He was right, and wasn't that a bitter brew? Mary was the only person who made sense, but by God, Bets had never imagined she'd stoop to it.

Taking her shoulders in his hands, Donal studied her. "Do you believe it wasn't my fault?"

Her anger was gone, as was the sadness pulling at her. The worst of it, she realized, had been thinking he'd let her down. She nodded crisply. "I believe someone cut it. I'm sorry for acting like you were at fault. It wasn't very fair of me to make assumptions without knowing the facts."

His brows lifted. "You sure?"

"Yes. I love my roses. I was upset you could have been

an agent for hurting something I love so much, especially after everything you've said to me. It felt like a betrayal."

He hugged her to him. "I'd never betray you, *mo ghrá*."

Oh, his arms felt so good around her, but then he was pushing her toward the car, albeit gently.

"All right, we've seen this sabotage. Now we're going to the special place. I have something else to show you."

She was silent on the short journey—back to her very own house. "Why are we back here?"

When he parked in her driveway, he strode out of the car with the single-minded purpose of a man on a mission. Only he didn't walk to her front door. He went around the side of the house. She followed, wondering where in the world he was going.

He took the overgrown path she'd been after Liam to trim, leading to an even more overgrown part of their property, which her son had told her to stay away from since there was a hornet's nest he'd yet to take down. She frowned, pushing away briars and branches.

Donal led her to the edge of the clearing. "Jesus, Mary, Joseph, I hope this won't make you cross, but I want you to know Liam helped, if that's any consolation. My dad too."

A beautiful view of the beach came into sight as she stepped into the clearing. Then her gaze took in the garden before her. "What's this?"

"Your new rose garden." He didn't need to gesture to the rows of giant hybrid tea roses, blooming in a variety of jaw-dropping colors. Her nose had already caught their inviting fragrance.

"What in the world?"

She pressed her hand to her aching heart as she took the sight in. The hot pink showstoppers Hot Princess, Zach Nobles, and Dublin made her mouth water. Celebritynamed winners, Randy Scott and Marilyn Monroe, were loaded with blooms. And glory be, this was where he'd gotten the St. Patrick rose cuttings from.

But it was the captivating sight of the lusciously fragrant Love's Magic roses that had her heart beating faster.

"I thought you needed another rose garden well away from where any sheep could find them, especially after Carrick's got out. Something told me to do it. Seems I was right."

"But that was two months ago!" she gasped. "Before I'd even agreed to go out with you."

He lifted a shoulder. "I was hoping to give you one rose at a time as we dated, starting with Falling in Love, but I decided to plant them all and pray this helped the message sink in at the right time. I enlisted Liam's help to find a sheltered place and to keep you away, and then we came here and planted these beauties."

"Oh, my God, Donal! I can't believe you did this." She made a beeline for Love's Magic, fingering its giant five-inch red blooms and leaning forward to sniff. God, the perfume was decadent.

"I'd like to put some fencing around them, although I know it will be an eyesore," he said, coming up beside her. "But if we have a saboteur, we need to take precautions. I'm thinking about getting a GoPro just in case our culprit hears about this place and puts in a repeat performance— although I think you should keep it a secret as long as you can. We should probably grow a few roses in your glass house too. We need to build in redundancies, Bets."

He'd said "we." She looked up at him and put her hand on his chest. "I still can't believe this. You bought all of these for me? Donal, I can't imagine the time and energy it took to find them. It's not like they're regular run-of-the-mill roses.

These varieties are so prized, they're often out of stock if carried at all."

"I started with nothing but hope in my heart." He cupped her face gently, a smile touching his beautiful mouth. "They're rare, but not as rare as you, Betsy O'Hanlon."

His touch had her leaning into him, and she put her hand on his massive chest. "Donal, I don't know what to say."

His mouth drifted into another glorious smile. "Good. Actions speak louder than words anyway."

He was right. Actions did speak louder than words, and the roses seemed to wrap their scent around her.

"I think I should put up some fencing today. It'll take me fifteen minutes to gather some supplies. Bets, no one is going to hurt your chances at winning the rose competition while I'm around. I hope you have a sturdy shovel to dig the posts—"

She grabbed his collar and brought him in for a kiss.

CHAPTER THIRTY-TWO

U sually, Angie was ill for days leading up to a gallery showing and then for several days afterward.

Today her stomach wasn't burning with nerves. As she held Carrick's hand, surveying her paintings displayed on the second floor of Nicola's bookshop, One More Chapter, she was filled with pride and that new and familiar happiness she treasured. She didn't know how today would turn out, but her heart felt fulfilled.

"They look really good, Aunt Angie!" Ollie said, taking her other hand. "You're going to make loads of money today. I just know it."

"I think so too," Megan said softly.

She looked over her shoulder, and they shared a tentative smile. Her sister had given her space, and it had been good for both of them. Megan's color wasn't gray anymore. While her grief was still present, it wasn't full-time, and Angie was glad for her. Ollie was tanned from all his time outdoors, and Megan had red cheeks from the wind.

Angie turned back and looked at Carrick, remembering how his eyes had been a barren Payne's grey when they'd first met. Now they were a warm, bright ultramarine filled with love. "Carrick did a great job framing them, don't you think? That's going to make a huge difference."

He kissed her cheek, his solid presence a welcome anchor. "It was a small thing, and I was happy to help."

Framing had been out of her budget, and she'd been stressed until she'd shared her worry with him as they were lying in bed one night. When he'd offered, she'd launched herself at him. Hadn't she seen evidence of his expert woodworking at his house? And Carrick being Carrick, he hadn't settled for some half-hearted effort. He'd scoured the countryside for special kinds of wood, and they'd gone to a beach known for driftwood aged by the sea's potent waves. "They're the best frames I've ever had."

She also couldn't dismiss he'd been the first person to put in that kind of an effort to support her showing her work. Randall certainly never had, and it only cemented what she knew. She and Carrick were at a new level of love, one she was starting to think might last for a lifetime.

"I think they're cool," Ollie said, dancing in place to a tune all his own, like he was seen doing a lot these days. "Kade says you can find all sorts of surprises where you least suspect them if you pay attention."

"It's 'where you least expect them,'" Megan corrected. "Oh, never mind. You said it better, Ollie."

That was a good show of progress between them. Ollie had needed space too, and people in his life besides Megan and Angie.

"How's everything going up here?" Bets asked, coming up the stairs holding Donal's hand.

"Looks pretty good from here," Donal said, "although I'm no judge." He presented her with a bottle of champagne he'd had tucked under his arm. "To pop later, after a successful day, Angie."

"We'll drink it together to celebrate everyone's good fortune," Angie said, flashing him a smile.

Oh, she liked him. She was delighted Bets had gone out with him in the village shortly after the sheep incident two weeks ago, making their relationship official, saying a good man was even harder to find than prize roses. Angie couldn't agree more. She felt the same way about Carrick.

"My roses should be safe. Donal flagged down a lookout and even locked the car to make sure my entries have no mishaps," Bets said.

"I love not locking the doors," Ollie announced, rushing over to Bets and hugging her. "We could never do that in Baltimore. I never want to leave Ireland! It's the best place on earth."

Kade often said that, she knew. Ollie quoted him and Liam a lot. She met her sister's eyes. Megan hadn't talked about leaving anymore, but Angie wondered how she planned to keep busy. Ollie would be going to school in a few weeks. Well, her sister would figure it out.

"Your roses look beautiful," Angie said, remembering how Bets had shown her the prize cuttings last night, swearing her to secrecy about their origin. No one knew whether Mary had been part of the sheep incident, but the woman had been suspiciously reclusive of late, with only Orla visiting—and Brady, for the post. He said she only cracked the door a bit when he brought the mail by.

"You should see the Love's Magic rose this morning," Bets said with a sigh. "It's opened up perfectly and is emitting the most glorious scent. It might be the winner."

"I'm so sorry I'll miss that competition," Angie said, "but I know for certain you're going to win."

"I can't wait to face off against Mary Kincaid," Bets said. "But I'm ready for her. I'll text you with the outcome either way."

"I wish you good luck today, Bets," Carrick said with a nod. His grin turned wicked. "But not you, Donal. How's your ram looking? Not as good as my Baron, I've heard. Cormac O'Sullivan has me beating you according to the tallies in his book."

"Your *ram* is down to beat me," Donal said with an amused glance. "Not yourself. Right, Bets?"

"Oh, you men! You want to compare... You know. Come on, Donal. We need to get to the fairgrounds."

"I'll see you two later," Carrick said, putting his arm around her. "I plan to stay with the Yank a little while. I want to see all the jackeens from Dublin fawn over Angie's artwork and pull out their wallets."

"I thought they were known as townies," Angie said. "Oh, I don't care so long as they buy my art."

"Kade says we're *culchies*," Ollie said, saying the word slowly. "He's teaching me Gaelic, you know."

"He is?" Donal asked, touching his nose. "You'll have to tell me what you've learned sometime. Let's see if you know this one, for when you're older. Come, *mo ghrá.*" He looked at Bets with eyes full of warmth. "See you later, everyone."

"Good luck, Angie," Bets called, waving. "Nicola will be luring people in right and left for you, and so will the other shopkeepers, don't you worry. Oh, I can't wait to spread the word about the arts center. What a day!"

This village was the best in the world as far as Angie was concerned. She'd never had so much support.

"What does *mo ghrá* mean?" Ollie asked. "Mr. O'Dwyer left without telling me."

"It means 'my love,'" Angie answered, holding Carrick's eyes. "You use it when you're in love with someone."

Megan smiled then. "It's a very lucky thing when you find someone like that, Ollie, and your aunt looks pretty lucky."

Carrick had invited Megan out to dinner with them last week, and she'd declined, saying she was still working on herself. Angie had respected it. But her sister's smile gave her hope she would join them next time—and support Carrick's presence in her life.

"Aunt Angie has the luck of the Irish now, Mom." Ollie scratched his chin. "But Mr. O'Dwyer is right. I won't need that word until I'm older. Like Kade or Liam's age."

"Ancient," Megan said with a laugh. "We're going to head to the fairgrounds. Be good to cheer on Bets. Kade is picking us up."

"He's going to enter his new pony into the competition," Ollie said, bouncing in his wellies. "Her name is Blaze. Have you seen her? She's the color of caramel apples and rides like the wind. Mom, do you think they'll have caramel apples at the fair?"

"I don't know, but they'll have lots of food and music, I hear." Megan walked over and hugged her briefly. "Good luck, Angie. Carrick, thanks for helping my sister with the frames. I meant to tell you how beautiful they are. Let's go, Ollie."

Ollie squeezed her leg. "Knock them dead."

"Ollie!" Megan exclaimed before letting out a breath. "Come on."

He shot her a grin and then ran down the stairs, Megan following at a sedate pace. That she didn't call him out for running was a good sign.

"Your sister is doing well, I think," Carrick said, rubbing her arms. "Now, how about we get you a coffee?"

"Water. If I have more coffee, I'll be buzzed."

A well-dressed portly man appeared at the top of the stairs. "I heard there was an art showing upstairs. My goodness, they're incredible. Are you the artist?"

She nodded even though he wasn't looking at her. He'd made a direct line to the painting of the couple's hands against the tree. "Yes, I am. I'm from the States but am here for a six-month stint teaching locally."

"I saw that art classes were being offered in town." He moved to the next painting. "Goodness, I love your brush-strokes and your framing of the subject. Your depiction of their hands is so real. How much is this one?"

He was looking at the one of the couple's hands in a passionate embrace on the ground. She named her price, her stomach doing its first flip.

"I'd like this one," the man said with a smile. "Now, who do I pay, and can you have it wrapped and ready for me after I leave the fair on my way out of town?"

Carrick elbowed her gently. "Nicola, the proprietor of the shop, will handle all of that downstairs for you."

"Grand, thanks." The man took another look at the art before heading to the stairs. "Imagine. Finding art like this outside of Dublin. I wouldn't have thought it possible, but there were flyers all over town. I've been coming to the fair for years and they've never done that."

"Caisleán is a special place," Angie said, trying to keep her smile in the non-grin stratosphere. "Have a wonderful day at the fair."

"I will, thanks. I always find excellent horses here. Have a grand day yourself."

When he left, Carrick kissed her cheek and grabbed the champagne and popped it.

"We were supposed to save that for later," she said, laughing as he pressed the bottle into her hands and indicated she should take a sip.

"I have one chilling in the fridge at my house," he said, grinning. "Oh, Angie, it's a grand day to see you so happy and have people appreciate your art. I'm glad for you, *mo cuishle*."

My darling. She tipped the bottle up and took another drink. The bubbles danced in her mouth. Oh, it *was* a happy day. Her first sale in ages! "You drink too. You'll have the money to buy that land from Bets after the fair is done. Carrick, we have so much to celebrate."

He'd told her that even if he didn't win first prize, he'd have enough interest in his prize ram, Baron, to sell him for a lofty sum. Baron already had a reputation in the sheep community, as much for his own qualities as Carrick's reputation as a competitive sheep breeder.

"We do, indeed." He drank the champagne, watching her. "I plan to celebrate in private with you. After the dance. You're going to be a popular woman tonight, so I'd best keep you close or dance every dance with you."

"I would love that," she said, holding out her high-heeled wedged foot. "My feet are going to be exhausted tonight. I'm not used to wearing shoes like this, but I thought they would look more fashionable. Plus, Bets pointed out that I could wear them at the fairground on grass."

"Practical." He waggled his brows. "I like them greatly, if that counts at all."

"It does." She put her hand on his chest and kissed him,

pouring into him how much he mattered to her. "I love you, you know."

"And I love you," he responded, kissing her back softly.

"You'd better go. I hear footsteps on the stairs."

"I do too." He kissed her one last time and took the bottle over to set beside her purse on the small table in the corner. "For after your next sale. I hope you get tipsy from all the toasts you drink today."

She did too and blew him a kiss as he left.

Her next toast came forty minutes later and the next one after only fifteen minutes. An hour later, she toasted Bets' victory at taking the top prize in the rose competition. She drank another when she sold another painting and then two more back-to-back. In only three hours, she sold all twelve of her paintings. And by God, she finished that bottle and was happily tipsy when she went downstairs.

Nicola danced behind the cash register as she totaled up Angie's payday. When she heard the number, she cried out and they hugged each other. "Thank you so much for letting me show here!"

"My pleasure, dear," Nicola said, shimmying her hips. "We did well today too!"

Nicola's daughter came over, grinning. "Yeah, we sold more books today than ever. Angie, you're a good luck charm. When would you like to do another showing?"

"Yes, when?" Nicola asked.

She sputtered. "Whenever you want. I feel like I'm flying. I haven't sold my art in forever, and it feels like I've come back home to myself. I mean, I love painting for its own sake, but there's something downright satisfying about having people love my work enough to buy it and hang it in their home or office."

"I can't imagine," Nicola said, fingering her silver Celtic cross necklace. "Next time, we'll do the nudes, if you'd like."

"I'd like," Angie said, doing a little dance at the thought. "Some Nordic galleries have expressed an interest in them too."

Her life as a painter was beginning again.

"I'm joining your next class," Shannon said, pushing her straight brown hair over her shoulder. "If I'd known you were going to teach nudes, I would have signed up straightaway."

"Your mother is a natural at them," Angie said, winking at her mother. "Maybe you should show some of your art too."

"Killian would love that," Nicola said, pressing her hand to her mouth. "Right now, I'm happy, and he's happy. In private."

"Oh, Mum, you and Dad are glowing." Shannon gestured to the nearly blushing woman. "Kade was right. You two needed to express some things."

Nicola only hummed. "It's time for you to take yourself off to the fair, Angie. There's loads to see. Bets will be so happy to show you her trophy. Plus, I imagine Carrick would like you by his side. There are bets too on whether you'll be the one to live in that house of his since he's finally buying the land from Bets today. I thought you should know."

She stilled. "You're kidding. We haven't talked about—"

"Would it bother you to live in a house he built for another woman?" Shannon asked, tilting her head. "The very Irish and the old tales say it's bad luck."

She felt a lurch in her stomach, the champagne turning sour. "Bad luck?"

"That's what they say in the myths." Shannon gestured

327

to that corner of the bookshop. "We Irish are dramatic in our myths, but love isn't for the fainthearted, is it?"

"Like you'd know with all your boyfriends," her mom said with a pointed glance.

"Why can't women play the field?" Shannon asked.

"It threatens the male order?" Angie postulated. "But back to this bad luck."

"Enough of that. Angie, you forget what anyone says. Your and Carrick's opinions are the only ones that matter on the subject. You remember that."

She wanted to agree, but they *did* have a ghost working on their behalf, which meant at least some of the old myths were true. The other part of her mind was still trying to process the way the village bet on everything. Did Carrick know? What did he think about that? Heck, what did she think?

They hadn't talked about long-term, but she wanted to be with him.

Oh, Angie, hold the phone.

She left shortly thereafter and headed to the shuttle buses to the fairground, trying to tap back into the victorious feeling she'd had after selling all her paintings. But she still couldn't dismiss what Shannon had said to her about bad luck. That was the last thing she needed or wanted.

The faint smell of oranges around her as she rode to the fairground didn't assure her.

CHAPTER THIRTY-THREE

C arrick had his money and then some.

Baron didn't disappoint, and his new owner was overjoyed to be buying his coveted, six-month-old Texel ram, a breed known for its muscular build and lean meat. The ram had won the top prize as predicted. His perfection —in the shape of his head, body, and golden color—was unassailable. God bless his first sheep, Pinky. It had all started with his longtime friend.

Angie had arrived just in time to see the end of the bidding. Seven bidders had engaged in a heated battle, until a well-known sheep farmer from County Meath had outbid them all.

"One hundred and eighty thousand euros!" Angie had sputtered alongside his mother, who was crying. "Oh, Carrick, I'm so happy for you."

He hugged his mother, who had a tissue pressed to her eyes, and then turned to his father, who also had rare tears in his eyes. "You made it happen, son. By God, I'm proud of you."

"Is that a lot of money?" Ollie asked, making them all laugh.

Megan tousled his hair. "Yes, it's a whole bunch of money. Congratulations."

"Yes, congratulations, man," Kade said, hugging him.

Ollie jumped in the air and cried, "You're rich, Mr. Fitzgerald."

"He's always been rich," Jamie said, wrapping an arm around him and grinning. "But today he might as well be sheep royalty."

Carrick laughed heartily. He was rich, and he'd grow richer still after word spread. Oh, the plans he could make. "I've found the right breeding formula, and the fairies have blessed me with luck." Perhaps Sorcha had even intervened. "Bets, you'll have the money I owe you as soon as it hits my bank account."

"Whenever." She grabbed his arm, and they shared a look. "I knew you could do it. My God, I should go into sheep."

Donal groaned. "Did you forget what they did to your roses?"

She pressed her gold trophy to her chest. "Right! But it all turned out well in the end because of you. You should have seen Mary Kincaid's face when I set my roses out. She turned green! Oh, we have so much to celebrate."

Yes, they did. He wanted to toast with Angie and then drink with his family and friends. She'd had such a grand day herself, selling all her paintings. He was overjoyed for her. For him. For *them*. Putting his arm around her, he reflected that it was a day neither of them was likely to forget.

He'd fulfilled a promise from his past.

She'd put to rest demons from her own.

They'd both started anew, and now they could truly start on their life together.

"My God, man," Donal said, slapping him on the back. "You set a record today. Soon your sheep will be selling for the likes of Double Diamond."

"Who's that?" Ollie asked, bouncing up and down in the showing yard.

"A sheep that sold for almost five hundred thousand euros in Scotland," Carrick said, laughing as Brady and Declan hoisted him up onto their shoulders. He punched a fist into the air, and they carried him through the crowd, Liam clearing the path.

Someone sent up a cheer, and others joined in. He looked back to yell at Angie, "I'll see you at the pub. We'll do the dance next year." Yes, she'd be there for it, if he had a say.

Her eyes seemed to glow with understanding, and she blew him a kiss, making him think of Sorcha. Wherever she was, she'd be happy for him too.

The moment he reached the pub, a pint was placed in his hand. The first Guinness went down real smooth, as did the next three Gavin pulled. He received more congratulations, and his hand hurt from all the shaking it had done with the men about town. His friends commandeered two large tables for their friends and family, keeping him at the table's end for well-wishers.

When Angie arrived with the Lucky Charms minus Megan and Ollie, he pulled her onto his lap and gave her the rest of his Guinness. He was sure someone would find her a pint, but there was something primal about seeing her drinking from his very own glass while perched on his knee. She was his, and he was glad everyone in Caisleán knew that was the way of it.

"When are you two getting married?" someone called out from the bar, making Angie cough on his beer. "I'm betting against you and the Yank living at either of your houses. Old or new. Bad luck that. Don't have me losing money, Carrick."

"Oh, shut your trap, Niall McGuire," Gavin said, glancing over sharply at the rangy man. "Drink your drink and let the man enjoy his moment."

Carrick tensed as others looked over, everyone from neighbors to strangers. They were all wondering, it seemed, now that he had the money for the land. Angie was so still she might as well have been made of stone on his lap. Her face was stricken. He wanted to punch Niall for spoiling their celebration.

"They're betting on whether we'll move into the new house," Angie said, leaning down and whispering in his ear. "I only heard today."

He reared back. Fitzgerald's Folly had always been the butt of plenty of jokes, but this was too much.

"Everyone needs to mind their own business," he said loudly.

"Hear, hear," Brady said, standing up. "Dad, turn up the music, will you?"

Bets shoved her chair back. "Wait! We've got this. Don't we, girls?"

The Lucky Charms stood. Some in the pub groaned. He only had eyes for his Yank.

"You and I need to have a toast to celebrate your good fortune today," Carrick said, putting his arm around her, hoping to assure her.

They hadn't spoken of long-term commitments, but he knew what he wanted. They would speak about it when the time was right—for them, not for the village. As for the house he'd built...

His heart beat faster. Would he need to sell it when he'd only just finished it? The more traditional Irish would think it bad luck to move into a house he'd built for his dead wife, but he wasn't of that mind. Then again, he didn't know what Angie thought. They'd never spent a single night at either of his houses, as if by silent agreement. Had he been wrong not to bring this up before?

"I had plenty of champagne earlier," she told him, "so I'm good with a little of your beer. To us."

"To us," he said, cupping her face, not caring that his entire family was watching.

She took a sip of his drink and then held the glass out to him, their eyes holding as he drank too.

Oh, he couldn't wait to have her all to himself. They were going to have a time of it. He was going to love her until well after dawn.

"Angie!" Bets called as Bon Jovi came over the loud-speakers. "Come on. It's your time, girl!"

The other women yelled their encouragement as Gavin helped them climb onto the bar. Carrick lifted a brow. "What will you do today, Yank?"

She gave a saucy smile, and he knew she'd shaken off the rude comment. "After today, I'm going to celebrate and dance on the damn bar."

"That's my girl," he said, patting her bottom as she stood up.

He realized she'd need help getting up there, but when he started to get to his feet, Gavin waved him off.

"Dad's right," Brady said, tapping his shoulder. "He'll help her. Plus, your view will be better from here."

Yes, it sure as hell was. He kicked back and smiled as

Gavin hoisted her up at the end of the bar. Angie wiggled her hips, bobbling a little until Gavin steadied her, but she found her footing. Yeah, those shoes weren't the smartest for dancing, but boy did they look good on her. Bets gave her a high five, and all the women laughed as they started to dance to the loud, throbbing music.

"She's a winner, son," his father said, pulling his head close with a large hand and grinning as he watched the show. "You're richer today than you've been in a long time. Don't forget that."

Like he could. He knew fate had given him a second chance at life, and he was going to take it with both hands.

Angie turned on the bar with a half step, wobbling again. He had the split-second thought she should take those shoes off, but all thought was obliterated when she lifted her hair and wiggled her bottom in the sexiest move he'd ever seen.

"Jesus, she can dance," Brady said, clapping him on the back. "You're the luckiest man in the world, Fitzgerald."

Yeah, he surely was. He put his fingers to his lips and gave an ear-splitting whistle. The crowd started to clap, and Bets, ever the leader, started to kick her legs like a Vegas showgirl. The other Lucky Charms joined in, and Angie missed a few beats, laughing.

God, she was beautiful. Her hair was bouncing around her shoulders. Her eyes were lit up like a sunburst. She lifted her leg in a kick.

Then she was falling backward, flailing her arms in the air.

He shot out of his chair. *"Angie!"*

Gavin dropped the Guinness he was pulling, but not soon enough. Angie fell and disappeared from sight.

Carrick rushed forward as the Lucky Charms jumped off the bar to where she'd fallen.

"Get out of my way," he yelled, pushing people aside to reach her.

When he reached the bar and hopped onto it, he saw her lying on the floor, still as death. Her head was bleeding.

"Call an ambulance!" Bets shouted.

"Calling," Nicola said, pressing a phone to her ear.

Carrick crawled over the bar, crouching next to Angie as Gavin made room for him.

"I'm sorry," the older man said, his expression stricken. "I couldn't get to her."

Carrick touched her face and found it cold. Watched a drop of blood drip down from her temple to her cheek. Bets dabbed at it with her shirt.

"Angie," he said, pain stabbing his heart. "*Mo ghrá.*"

She didn't move. Didn't wake.

She was dying.

Just like Sorcha.

He sank onto the ground and pulled her gently onto his lap.

"She's stirring," Bets announced. "Oh, thank God!"

Her eyes opened, her expression hazy. "My head hurts. And my arm."

He clutched her to him gently, gazing straight ahead. She went lax in his arms again, stealing his hope.

"Best not to move her, Carrick," Bets said, taking her away from him carefully and laying her back on the cold cement floor. "Gavin, I need a blanket."

"Right," the man said, pushing up and disappearing.

As Carrick stared down at her, the pain in his chest went dark, replaced by a familiar numbness.

Taking her hand, he willed her to open her eyes again,

but she was still unconscious when the ambulance arrived. He stepped back as they came in, assessing her and then lifting her onto the stretcher. They strapped her in.

She still didn't move.

Someone put a firm hand on his shoulder. "She'll be okay, Carrick."

His dad's voice.

A soft hand cupped his waist.

His mother.

They'd comforted him like this when Sorcha had died. He'd gotten the call to come to the hospital. He'd rushed over, knowing only that she'd been in an accident. When he arrived, his parents had been there waiting—to tell him she was dead.

They started to wheel Angie out. He followed her, barely registering that he was moving. It seemed everyone in the bar went with them.

"Who's her family?" the medical tech asked.

"I am," Bets said, rushing forward. "Carrick, I'll see you at the hospital."

He watched as they loaded her into the ambulance. The sirens tore at his ears as they drove off.

"*Carrick.*"

Jamie's voice.

He bent over and vomited in the street.

CHAPTER THIRTY-FOUR

Everything was throbbing.

Angie cracked open her eyes and winced at the light, moaning. Her cousin and sister lurched out of the chairs they were sitting in on either side of her hospital bed.

She was in the *hospital*?

"Good," Bets said, touching her face gently. "You're finally awake."

"Thank God," Megan said, taking her hand covered in plastic tubes. "I was so worried."

She squinted, the pain searing her temple. "I fell off the bar. Those shoes..."

"Yes," Bets said. "Plus, the excitement and my idiot dance moves."

"And the champagne..." Megan said.

"It could have happened to anyone," Bets insisted.

But it had happened to her. She looked down at her white hospital gown covered in millions of tiny blue dots, like a tube of paint had exploded uniformly. She had an IV and a hospital bracelet. She didn't feel connected to her body. The meds? Then she saw the black sleeve on her right arm. "Oh, my God! Did I break my arm?"

She painted with that arm!

"No, thank God." Bets blew out a breath, moving her short bangs. "You'll be black and blue from the fall for a while. The doctor wants you in the sling for at least ten days, but if it hurts to move it, another week. Then you need to do some exercises."

"The biggest concern is your concussion," Megan said, her voice strained. "That's why they want to keep you overnight. You're going to have to rest for a while, Angie. No screen time. No bright light or loud noise. No—"

"No painting for a while then." The thought depressed her. Painting had become a daily thing again, something she needed as much as food and water.

"No art classes either," Megan said softly. "Since you hit your head so hard. You needed ten stitches. Mom says you're lucky it wasn't worse after she watched the video of you falling."

Angie looked at her sister. She was that pale gray again. "I'm sorry I scared you."

Megan nodded. "Ollie was scared too."

Her heart clutched. "I hate that. Where is he?"

"Kade and Liam have him out picking wildflowers for you even though it's late," Bets said. "We thought giving him a task was better than having him here at the hospital."

She made herself ask. "Where's Carrick?"

If Megan and Ollie were scared, how must he have reacted?

Megan cast a look at Bets, and her cousin said, "He's very upset. No surprise. Jamie and some of the boys are sitting with him in the waiting area. Brigid and I thought it might be better if he didn't see you in here while you were unconscious. He...has bad memories of this place."

Her body seemed heavy suddenly, and she lay back. "His wife died here, didn't she?"

"Yes," Bets said, worrying her lip. "Angie, I know you're hurting, but you might send him home. He didn't want to leave you. In fact, he told me to tell him the moment you woke up. I should..."

Angie didn't have the energy to wave her to the door. Bets tried to smile, patted her good hand, and then rushed out.

"Why were you dancing on the bar?" Megan asked, her brow crinkling. "If you'd only listened to me, this never would have happened."

She made herself sit up, gritting her teeth at the pain. "Megan, this was an accident. It really sucks, and I'm probably going to bitch about not painting and teaching for a while, but I would dance on that bar again."

"*Angie!*"

"I wanted to do it." She squinted at her sister. "I'm not worried about what other people might think. Besides, it made me happy. I sold all my paintings today. Do you have any idea what that felt like? After all this time?"

Megan remained silent.

"I *wanted* to celebrate. I wished you'd come with us to celebrate."

"But—"

"The Lucky Charms inviting me up there wasn't something I was going to miss a second time."

She thought about Carrick and how she'd looked forward to being alone with him to toast his big day. That all seemed ruined now.

The door opened, and Carrick entered. His body was

bowed as if he were battling a strong wind to cross his pasture. She made herself look into his eyes, knowing they would tell her all the answers.

The bright, loving light and ultramarine color was gone. They were Payne's grey again and desolate. Even if he hadn't stayed beside the door and not crossed to her, she would have known the truth.

She'd lost him.

CHAPTER THIRTY-FIVE

H e didn't have the strength.

As he gazed at Angie lying in the hospital bed, he had to admit that to himself. Every muscle in his body had tensed up when he'd gotten into the car with Jamie and the McGrath twins and rode to the hospital, the same one where his wife had died. Memories of traveling that road to see Sorcha, only to learn she was dead, wouldn't leave him.

The smell of death had assaulted him when he'd arrived, and he'd rushed to the bathroom to vomit again. This time he'd stared into the mirror at his sweating face before washing his mouth out with water and splashing his face. He'd locked his body up tight and headed out to the waiting area, eyes staring straight ahead, trying to banish all noise and thought. He'd gone numb, but the smell couldn't be ignored.

Death saturated his senses.

He prayed it wouldn't take Angie.

His friends tried to tell him she would be all right, but he'd seen the blood and her unresponsiveness. Her brain could be bleeding, the doctors unable to stop it. He couldn't stop the thoughts of her dying, of him standing with roses beside her graveside, the freshly tunneled dirt an abomination to life.

"It looks worse than it is," his beloved Yank said, her face nearly as white as his sheep. "That's what happens when I wear heels and drink too much champagne. Easily solved. I won't do that again."

"I'll leave you two," her sister muttered and edged around him to exit through the door.

"Carrick, I can't imagine what you must be feeling."

He stared at her beloved face, recoiling at seeing the shaved area on the right side of her head where she'd been stitched. "Don't worry about me," he murmured. "You focus on healing yourself."

Get out of here, Yank.

"I will," she said, making a brave showing at a smile. "As for you, I think you should go home with your friends. Toast your victory and mine. Carrick, you had such a great day! I don't want this to spoil it."

Her voice was hoarse, and when their gazes met, he knew she could see into his very soul. She knew he wasn't strong enough to move on with her after this.

He was going to go home and work until this pain and fear left him. There was new fencing he could put in and briars to be cut back.

He would go back to how he was before he met her.

"You mind yourself," he said, forcing his legs to move.

Crossing to her hospital bed was torture. Even in here, the smell wound around him, pulling at him. Leaning down to kiss her cheek was the worst kind of pain, a pain he remembered all too well. It was the kind of pain that drove a man to the brink, a place he wasn't sure he could come back from a second time.

"I love you, Carrick," she whispered.

He lingered a moment before saying, "I love you too."

Then he made himself walk out.

CHAPTER THIRTY-SIX

Tough times challenged even the toughest spirits.

Angie was home, thank God, with Megan hovering around her for a change. Might be good for their relationship. Sometimes role reversals helped the other person see a fresh perspective. Frankly, Bets needed that for herself, after being disqualified from the rose competition.

She yanked out another weed strangling the roses in her front garden. She'd already seen to her secret garden. She'd cried a little while tending to Love's Magic, the one she'd won the competition with only yesterday. In the blink of an eye, a weed could pop out of nowhere and start destroying something beautiful. Mary Kincaid was that weed, and Bets wished she could pluck her up and toss her out of the village right now.

Donal's Mercedes purred up her driveway, and the man who had found purchase in her heart got out and slammed the door of his precious car. "I only just heard. They disqualified you because of me? Bets, I won't stand for it!"

She grabbed the sticky stem of a cleaver and plopped it in her rubbish pail. "There's nothing to be done about it.

Mary somehow found out you'd given me the rose bushes and planted them only a few months ago. Even though there is nothing in the contest rules about a rose being purchased by another person or the length of time it needs to be in the ground, the committee decided it wasn't fair for me to win."

He marched over in his long strides. "The rules are the rules, and if it doesn't say it—"

"It gets better," she said, ripping out another weed. "When I told them that someone had cut the rope on your fencing, which made us suspect foul play, do you know what they said? They said someone in the village claims there's a ghost around. While they're right about that—"

"*What?*"

"Sorcha is back—"

"Sorcha! Bets, I'm Irish as anyone, but you'd better tell me this tale from start to finish."

By the time she finished, his face was pale. "I didn't know the myths were true about such things. Makes me wonder why my Margaret or your Bruce didn't try the same thing as Sorcha."

Bets scratched her head. "I hadn't thought of that." Oddly, she was rather sad Bruce hadn't.

"Maybe we didn't need the kind of help Carrick did." He rubbed the back of his neck. "God, I need a whiskey. Bets, I'll take them on for their rubbish. Imagine that, blaming a ghost. Especially Sorcha, who wouldn't hurt a soul."

"She wasn't named, Donal, and given the state of Carrick right now, it's best not to say anything." He would be upset to have anyone slander her name, and rightfully so.

"Like a ghost can cut a rope. Jesus. How would Mary have even fathomed something like this?"

Bets had her suspicions. Mainly, she wondered if, like Bruce, Mary Kincaid had the gift of seeing spirits. "Let's set this aside for now. Promise me you won't mention the ghost thing to anyone else." She couldn't imagine the judges would say anything either after telling her what they'd heard—from an unnamed source, no less. They'd be laughingstocks. This nugget she would keep to herself, but she would watch Mary from now on. She knew this wasn't over.

"Fine." His shadow shaded her from the afternoon sun. "But I still have a mind to pop by each and every one of their houses and tell them—"

"It's not worth it, Donal. I'm yanking weeds, imagining they're Mary, and telling myself everyone in the village will still think I won anyway. Seems she didn't just stop at growing her Black Magic rose. No, she had to get out her cauldron and go all witchy on me. Dammit, I hate that. Black Magic shouldn't beat Love's Magic. Ever."

Donal knelt down beside her and yanked out more weeds, his large hands moving efficiently in time with hers. "I've heard of jealousy—"

Bets set her hands on her knees. "She was jealous the moment I arrived married and pregnant, and it only got worse as the village embraced me. The Lucky Charms most of all, I think. She wants to live here, in my house, and with Bruce gone, it's only gotten worse."

"There might be another reason," Donal said, rubbing her shoulder. "You should know she flirted with me after Margaret died and a reasonable time had passed. Bets, her lemon curd was so sweet I thought my teeth might fall out."

That made her laugh. "So she and I have the same taste in men? God, who would have imagined it? Oh, hell. It's like Caisleán's PG-13 version of *Fatal Attraction*."

"God, I hope not! I like bunnies and hares."

He elbowed her, and they both started to laugh. "It's only a rose competition, and we'll be watching her, won't we? Your GoPro is our secret. Not even Liam knows."

"You'll win next year," he said, "and I'll hoist you onto my shoulders with your trophy in front of the whole town."

She could see that image all too clearly in her mind. "The important thing is that Angie is home and doing great according to the doctors."

"You're right about Carrick," Donal said with a frown. "After I left you at the hospital last night, I passed by his place as I usually do."

"Seeing how you live on the same road..."

"The lights in his house and shed were on. He was working at three in the morning. I don't think he'd been to bed."

Just as she'd thought. "He must have been thinking about Sorcha. Not the ghost."

"Right." Donal plucked another weed. "Be hard not to. Even I had a bad moment when Angie fell. It could have gone another way, Bets."

She stood and brushed the dirt off on her pants. "I know it. The Lucky Charms and I agreed to never dance on the bar again. We'll dance on the floor and be happy for it. I thought about blaming myself—her sister isn't too pleased with me, mind you—but accidents happen. We get up. We can't live our lives carrying that kind of guilt around. At least I don't want to."

"Sound advice," he said, looking over as a blue Berlingo drove up. "That's Tom MacKenna. Why are my balls twitching all of the sudden?"

She rose. "Probably because of Mary Kincaid and all the time she'd been spending with Tom's wife, Orla, behind closed doors. It's an odd time to be paying a call after a relation was released from the hospital."

Donal took her hand as Tom exited the car, and she understood he was telling Tom he was on her side. "Hi, Tom. Nice weather we're having, isn't it?"

He was a short, thin man with a receding hairline, and he didn't do anything but nod. "Bets, I'm sorry to do this after what happened last night, but some felt an urgency. Donal, we didn't call you for the meeting as you had a clear conflict given your relationship with Bets here."

Holy freaking hell.

Donal leveled him a glance. "You decided to exclude me without talking to me straight to my face?"

"I'm telling you now, aren't I?" Tom's eyes fired. "The county council passed a cease and desist for your art classes, Bets."

"What?" She felt Donal tighten his hold on her. *"Why?"*

"Yes, why, Tom? The village is behind this arts center one hundred percent. Didn't you see every business in the village proudly displaying the Bets' flyer about art classes? And it's not like she needs planning permission. She's registered for taxes and is only using a shed on her property, which is allowed."

"For agricultural use only," Tom said, his narrow eyes unrelenting. "Don't make me quote the rule book for you."

She had to bite her lip. *The same rule book the rose judges used? Oh, Mary, you have reached a new level of bitchy.*

"There's a rule book?" Donal's muffled laughter echoed through the yard.

Tom rubbed the sunburn on his head. "We can't abide nudes being taught here. It's indecent. Donal, we were willing to look the other way when you and the guys had a little craic with the streaking, and what with you on the city council—"

"If this is how you plan to have things go, I'm resigning."

"Donal," Bets said, turning to look at him.

"As you like," Tom said, "but some are starting to wonder what's going on here in these so-called art classes."

"Painting nudes is a common practice in art," Bets said. "Can you tell me who's behind the complaint, Tom?"

He shifted on his feet, not making eye contact. "It's public record, so I'll tell you that it was Mary Kincaid. I know it's tough news, but that's the way of it."

"And your wife being Mary's closest friend didn't disqualify *you* from the vote?" Donal asked, his voice soft and a little dangerous.

"A romantic relationship is different than a personal one," Tom said. "I'll be going now."

When he turned to leave, Donal grabbed his arm. "What if Bets agrees not to have nudes taught here anymore?"

Give in to them? "Wait, I—"

"Let him answer, Bets." Donal shot her a look, and she held her tongue, trusting him.

He rubbed his head again, then shook it. "There's concern you're stirring things up. Making our young people get ideas."

She couldn't believe this. "About what? The human body? What's so wrong with that?"

"They're dirty paintings, aren't they?" Tom's face began to turn red as well.

"You have got to be—"

"These are pretty strong accusations, Tom," Donal said, staring the man down.

He only lifted his weak chin. "Gives me no pleasure to say it. Bets, it doesn't take a genius to know why you ladies want to draw naked men."

Donal snorted over Bets' gasp. "And what if I want to draw a naked woman, Tom?"

The man coughed loudly before saying, "That's your business, I suppose, but the county council doesn't plan to sanction it—even with you being a member."

"Something I'll be seeing to after this, you can bet," Donal said. "Is this a decision we can appeal?"

"No." His tone was emphatic. "I'll be off now."

Bets stomped her feet as he sped away. "This is unbelievable. Mary's been busy. Dammit! I can take losing the rose competition because I'll have another shot, but I can't let her close down my arts center. I love it, Donal. Expanding it is my dream."

"I know that," he said, taking her hands. "We'll figure something out."

"You don't have to give up your place on the council over this," she said, leaning into his chest.

"I'm tired of all the bullshit anyway. Besides, he's right. If you put in a planning permission application for expanding the center, I would have had to recuse myself."

"Because we're in a relationship?" she asked, the only silver lining at the moment.

"We are." He traced her cheek. "This won't be easy, Bets. But I'm with you all the way."

She didn't doubt him, not anymore. In fact, she was starting to see how they could fit into each other's lives. "You know, Donal. If I had a rose to name, I'd call it Love's Promise. After you."

This time he pulled her to him and kissed her senseless.

CHAPTER THIRTY-SEVEN

Hearing the news about the arts center had ramped up the pain in Angie's head.

"That's it then," she said, falling back into the pillows. "There's nothing for us here."

Her sister gasped from her seat in the corner of the room, a spot she'd rarely left since Angie had been released from the hospital yesterday.

"Don't say that!" Bets said, sitting on the side of her bed. "Donal and I will think of something. People in the village are outraged, and I've a mind to tell Mary Kincaid to meet me with pistols at dawn."

"Bets," Angie said, patting her hand. "Don't kid a kidder. Not everyone will be in favor of me teaching nudes."

Megan was shaking her head. "Imagine if I'd taught how to make nude sculptures."

Had Megan ever made one of those? Angie would have paid to see it.

"Forget about those numbskulls." Bets waved a hand, her gold bracelets clacking. "We deal with one problem at a time. The first agenda item is putting pressure on the county manager, who appoints the city council—"

"He won't get involved," Donal said, appearing in the doorway. "Sorry to interrupt. Liam told me you were down here. Hello, Angie. How are you feeling?"

She'd lost a job she loved—again—and the love of her life. "Wretched."

"That's about right then." Donal rubbed his brows. "Davey was our last hope, Bets. I made the rounds with my fellow council members, and they've all dug in. Me resigning hasn't helped, nor have the calls they've gotten from people in the village—"

"The Lucky Charms and their husbands as well as some of our students," Bets said, her mouth tight. "We shared the news with them, of course. They're all horrified."

"Well, the council members didn't take kindly to being called stupid or ridiculous." Donal lifted a massive shoulder. "Irishmen hate being called that."

"So they're being stubborn." Bets threw up her hands. "How typical. Oh, this is awful."

Angie's head pounded with her heart. "I'm sorry, Bets. I know how much this meant to you. People don't value art anymore. Maybe they never did. I'm tired of trying to fight it, and politics only makes everything worse. I'm just going to head back to the States and paint there. At least I have that to fall back on once my head heals."

Her heart was another matter. Carrick had visited her yesterday—briefly—bringing wildflowers, not roses for love. She hadn't expected it after the moment of understanding that had passed between them at the hospital. His gray gaze and coloring had been tough to look at, and she'd almost asked him to say it out loud—that they were done—but it would have been cruel to them both.

Talking about breaking up wasn't always the best way, especially when it was so clearly over, so she hadn't broached the subject. What would come of being direct this time? Of having him tell her the accident had traumatized him all over again, and he couldn't bring himself to love her and go on? Why would she want to hear that or make him utter such terrible words?

"But Ollie is so happy here," Megan said, her hands fisted in her lap. "And I..."

They waited for her sister to finish her sentence, but she only looked out the window.

"You can stay with Ollie until your visa is up, Megan," Bets said. "Angie, I understand why you want to leave. Is there no hope with Carrick?"

Her throat closed, and it took her a moment to respond. "No, it doesn't seem so."

His visit had proved that. He'd been all but paying his respects, and she couldn't stay around for that. The village was too small. If he came again, she was going to have Megan tell him she was napping. She wasn't going through the motions with him.

No breakup she'd ever had before had ever hurt this much. One would have thought a marriage ending would have been worse, but no, it hadn't been.

"I'm sorry for you both," Bets said. "Do you want me to try and talk to him?"

Oh, this is why she loved it here. Nicola had been right when she'd said that people heal in community—or at least that was true of the right community. She had. Now she would have to do it again. Somewhere else. Maybe life was a series of hurts and healings. She closed her eyes. God, she was tired of it.

A phoenix rose up in mind, its glorious body covered in

naphthol red and cadmium orange flames. She should paint the mythical bird. Did it ever grow weary of dying and being reborn over and over again? Her fingertips burned like the flames, wanting to paint. But she couldn't do that yet with her injured arm and damn concussion.

"I imagine his friends have probably talked to him." She would miss them too. "If that didn't help, nothing will." And maybe it was better it had happened now. What if they'd gotten married and had a couple of kids and then one day she'd fallen off their kitchen island dancing, and he'd shut down like this?

"I could talk to him," Donal said, leaning back against the wall. "Man to man. I know what it's like to lose a wife."

"But it's not about that," Angie said softly. "It's about fear. Oh, can we cut this talk short? My head is splitting."

Megan's chair squeaked as she left it. "We should let her rest. The doctor said stress isn't good for her."

If she'd been able to laugh, she might have. Stress? What else was there?

"Angie, I know it seems hopeless," Bets said. "But if I figure out a way to reopen the arts center, will you stay?"

Pain seared her heart like it was on fire, as if that damn phoenix were inside her chest. Now that would be a great painting. "I don't know, Bets. Honestly."

"I'll teach pottery," Megan blurted out.

Angie's brow rose, which immediately shot pain through her temple. "Seriously?"

Her sister gulped and then nodded her head slowly. "Yes. I... It's peaceful here, and Ollie is happy. He loves Liam and Kade and the animals so much. I would hate to take that away from him. There's nothing for us in the States. Don't get me wrong. I love Mom and Dad. But I

could never live with them. And I don't want to see them...
for a while."

"Well," Bets said, pursing her lips. "I'll be sharing
around the village that we'll be having ceramics classes once
we're back up and running. Angie, I'll leave you. Donal, we
have some brainstorming to do. I won't give up."

Megan remained in the room. She stood at the end of
the bed, in fact. Angie wanted to close her eyes, but she
waited to see if her sister would say something.

"I think you should fight for what you want," Megan
said. "Don't run away from this place. Angie, you've never
been happier."

Tears filled her eyes, and she closed them so her sister
wouldn't see them. But one leaked out anyway, damn it,
trailing down her cheek. "I'm not running away. I'm being
practical."

"You could paint here," Megan said. "Ollie would miss
you."

Oh, God. More tears leaked. "I would miss him too."

"And so would I," Megan said softly.

She had to look at her sister then. Tears were streaming
down Megan's face too.

"I'm sorry, Angie." Her fisted hand rose to her chest.
"I've done a lot of thinking since I moved to the other
cottage, and I've watched you and the people around me.
I've even read a few books Liam gave me on grief and
starting over."

Liam, the wandering philosopher. "That's good, Meg.
That's really good."

She nodded. "You can't solve things only by reading
books. I realize that. And I want to thank you for taking care
of me and Ollie like you did. I know I was depressed before
and that we fell into our old pattern, but that's no excuse."

How long had she hoped for Megan to say such things? "I'm sorry too, Megan. For everything."

Her sister was quiet a moment, and then she nodded. "I only wanted you to know that I plan to take care of me and Ollie, even if it's scary and even if I don't always know what to do."

"Who does?" Angie said, feeling a breakthrough with her sister. "I don't. I mean, I was on top of the world, and I literally fell off."

"Not funny," her sister said, crossing her arms.

"It is." Angie's mouth started to tip up on the right, and she pointed to it. "See, even though my head and heart hurt like hell, I'm starting to smile. Shit, Meg, life can be so hard, but there's so much beauty in it too. I'm glad I experienced the beautiful part again here. I'll always be grateful for it. But staying here would be too hard now. There has to be another beautiful place for me. Maybe Baltimore isn't right anymore. Maybe I should go to Florence or Provence and paint again. I was happy there. I can leave when the doctor gives me the go-ahead to travel."

That would give her enough time to put things in order. Oh, it was going to be hard to go. She'd fallen in love with the people—one literally—as much as the land. How she would miss the light and her spot in the mornings. Yet it wasn't her spot anymore, not next to Carrick's sheep or the view of his house. Her heart would be crying if she sat there.

Megan looked down. "You need to do what's best for you, and since we're done telling each other what that is, I won't say any more on the subject. It seems better that way, doesn't it?"

The pain in her head was easing. Smiling and honesty

were good for the soul. "Yes, it does, although it's hard to say and do after years of ingrained habit."

"Habits keep us in chains," Megan said flatly. "I read that...somewhere."

"I like it." She liked hearing her sister talk like this, in fact. "You'll have to tell me what else you've discovered."

Megan coughed and held up a finger. "This one seems to stick in my throat. I loved Tyson, but I wasn't very happy with him. I told you that once and regretted ever saying it, especially after he died."

Angie shifted on the pillows, wanting to sit up for this.

"You were right," she said, the golds in her brown eyes growing brighter. "He...wasn't home much for me or for Ollie, and when he was, he was out catching up with his buddies. He cared more about soldiering. He took us...for granted. That's not easy to say. I see how Liam and Kade are with us—Ollie especially. They always have time for us. They always ask about us. And they always seem to be there when we need them. I even think they like me—us."

Angie coughed again, tears filling her eyes. *Oh, Megan.*

"It's like you said about your relationships. All the trying... I *tried* to be a better wife and a better mother so he'd—"

"Love you and stay?" she asked when her sister broke off again.

"Stay home more, anyway, because that would mean he loved us more." Megan nodded. "Our issues with Mom and Dad cast long shadows, don't they?"

Angie held out her hand to her sister. Megan's gray color seemed to change before her very eyes, turning a bright porcelain pink. "We were living out Mom and Dad's relationship," she said, "and ours with them. I mean, I love them, but I don't want to keep falling into the same rut.

That's one thing I'll be grateful to Carrick for—even though losing him hurts like hell. He showed me that I didn't have to do anything for him to love me."

Her voice broke. He had loved her. So much.

"Well, that's not true," she finally continued. "Apparently falling down and getting hurt was a deal breaker. Bad joke."

"The worst," Megan said, squeezing her hand. "I'm sorry he acted that way, although I understand. Remember how overprotective I was with Ollie after Tyson died? I was afraid to lose him. And I've hovered a little over you since you scared me with your fall. Angie, I didn't like seeing you in the hospital."

Her mouth tipped up again. "On that we agree. I hated being there. You might have been a little right about not dancing on the bar. Or at least dancing in wedges. Now that *was* stupid."

"I was being a busybody." Megan made a face. "Next time you dance on the bar, hold on to someone like Liam or Kade. They would never let you fall."

If Carrick had been close, he'd wouldn't have let her fall either. But he hadn't been, and that one moment had changed everything. Her chest tightened with the pain again. She was going to have a good cry when Megan left.

"I'm glad you stayed and talked to me, Meg. I've hated the distance between us."

Her sister squeezed her hand. "I have too. Once I got over my anger and self-pity. Angie, I...don't really like who I am."

She pointed to her dresser. "I hear you. Megan, I need new clothes. I hate the ones I've been wearing. I like my old jeans and shirts and coat with paint and patches on them."

Her sister let out a short laugh. "You look better in them actually. Less frumpy."

"Thanks! I *hate* frumpy."

"But I wasn't only talking about clothes," Megan said softly.

She met her sister's gaze. "I know. You'll figure it out. Seems you have good helpers around. Liam and Kade."

Megan smiled fully this time. "Yes, they're pretty wonderful. Oh, Angie! I forgot to tell you one positive thing that's come out of you going to the hospital."

"They had good ice cream?" she asked.

Her pointed look was so sisterlike. "I'd pinch you if you weren't convalescing. Be serious!"

She laughed. "I am! The ice cream in our area is terrible."

"Your blood pressure is picture perfect. The doctor couldn't believe you'd had any trouble with it when I mentioned it."

Lying back against the pillows, she snuggled in. "See! I knew letting loose was the answer."

"I'll have to try it," Megan said.

They shared a smile, and Angie could feel things lightening up in both of them.

"I can't wait," she said. "Now, come here and hug me. Then I'm going to nap."

Her sister scooted closer and embraced her. She put her arms around her and closed her eyes.

It felt like a new beginning between them.

"Are you two making up finally?" she heard Ollie ask.

Megan leveled back but kept her hand sweetly on Angie. "Yes," they both said.

"Good!" He blew out an exaggerated breath. "Liam and

Kade said you would get there, but man, you were mad at each other a long time."

She chuckled as he came over to the bed, his short dark hair windblown.

"Are you still mad at me, Ollie?" Megan asked, tilting her head to the side. "It's okay if you are."

He lifted his shoulder. "Not too much. Liam and Kade said it's okay to be angry. You just don't want to roll around in it, like the cows do in the mud. They're disgusting when they're that dirty. People get like that too, you know, but we have clothes on, so you can't always see. That's why you have to listen to people's words and actions, Kade says. It tells you the full picture."

Liam and Kade were regular life coaches, and Angie was grateful they were working wonders with her sister and nephew.

"Goodness!" Megan laughed. "Was I a dirty cow?"

Ollie laughed and made a mooing sound. "But you're pretty clean now. Aunt Angie, how are you feeling?"

"Much better," she said, glancing at Megan.

"She's going to nap," her sister said, standing up.

"I was going to bring your paints," Ollie said. "When I told Liam you couldn't paint, he said you can, only you might need to finger paint with your good hand or your toes. Wouldn't that be funny? To paint with your feet? Some Irish guy did that, Liam said."

She was glad to be reminded of Christy Brown. "When you're older, we'll watch *My Left Foot*. It's about an Irish painter and writer who did his art with his left foot because he was disabled."

"He should go on a pony ride at Kade's farm," Ollie said. "He can help anyone."

Angie nodded. "How about we paint for a while, and then I'll nap?"

Megan ran her hand over Ollie's head. "Sounds like a plan. You two can have a paint fest. I think I'll bike over to Kade's and see Duke while you're working. I love that dog."

"Mom, we need our own dog," Ollie said as they left the room.

Angie lay back. The image she wanted to paint was crystal clear in her mind. The frumpy, fallen phoenix's body would be muddy brown with vibrant canary yellow, cadmium orange, and naphthol red flames burning at the edges. Its death was going to be beautiful, and in her heart, she would imagine another painting, one where the new phoenix rose from the ashes bright and radiant in chromium green and phthalo blue with scales of golden light—reminiscent of the colors in Ireland that had helped her find her voice.

Then she was going to burn the paintings. She wasn't going to do this die and be reborn shit anymore.

She was just going to be a beautiful, happy, larger-than-life bird, content with herself.

CHAPTER THIRTY-EIGHT

No one came to visit.

Carrick stewed for days after he'd gone to see Angie, recovering in the cottage. He'd needed to know she was out of danger, and he'd gone with a trumped-up reason and a passel of meaningless flowers to make sure. She'd already known the truth, of course. The Yank had seen it in his eyes in the hospital. Then again, they'd always understood each other. He was glad she hadn't demanded explanations from him. Such a conversation would only hurt them both.

But his family and friends were different. He'd braced himself for interference. But no one bothered him over the next five days as he worked much of the day and night.

Not even Sorcha.

He didn't know what that meant. He didn't know how to take that. They'd always encouraged him to move forward, and the Yank had certainly looked to be the way for him. How could they have simply stopped?

Something had to be wrong.

Hell, part of him wanted them to poke at him, fight with him.

He drove to Kade's first, around the time his friend usually fed the horses. Duke ran over to him, followed by Ollie. The boy could give him an update on Angie. Didn't he wonder how she was? Didn't he miss seeing her sitting beside the tree every morning painting even though he knew she was hurt so badly she couldn't paint now?

And what was he supposed to do with all of the paint supplies and finished paintings she had at his new house? He'd have to deliver them, he supposed. Except she didn't have space in her current studio. Maybe she could still paint at his house when he wasn't working there?

"Hi, Mr. Fitzgerald," Ollie said mournfully, kicking the ground.

The kid didn't seem happy to see him. Did he know about he and Angie going their separate ways? Correction. About him deciding they were finished? "Hi, Ollie. How's it going for you?"

He lifted his shoulder. "Okay. I was getting Duke."

"Hey, Carrick," Kade called, setting aside a pitchfork. "Ollie, can you run up to the house and get another bottle of water for us? I'm dying of thirst."

"Sure thing, Kade," Ollie said, giving him a somber look and running off.

"He knows about me and Angie, I take it," Carrick said, planting his feet.

Kade rubbed his hands on his brown pants. "He's a smart kid. Well, enough gossip. How are you? Did you get your money for Baron and pay Bets?"

"Gossip, is it?" Carrick swore. "Why aren't you poking at me? Offering me a pony ride? Why aren't any of you coming by my houses or pastures to kick me in the arse?"

Kade bent over and petted Duke when the dog pawed his foot. "We decided against it. We did that before, and it didn't work. I don't believe kicking anyone produces much result anyway. In the end, we all have to make our own way. We figured you know you have friends who care about you."

He was so off-balance he took a step back. "Sorcha hasn't visited you?"

"No," his friend said crisply.

He sniffed the air for oranges, but only came away with odorous farm smells. "Not once?" Hadn't she been all up in his business about being with Angie? "She put messages on my sheep about love being here and the like. She's never been one to give up."

"Maybe she gave up because you both did," Kade said, patting him on the shoulder.

"Both? What do you mean?"

Kade made a sound before saying, "I thought you'd have heard. It's all the village can talk about. The county council shut down Bets' arts center because Mary Kincaid spewed a bunch of bullshit about Angie teaching nudes on-site and it being indecent. So the Yank is leaving once she's well enough to travel. She's going to paint somewhere else."

He reared back, causing Duke to bark sharply. She was leaving?

"What? How could this happen? Why isn't Bets fixing it?"

"She, Donal, and most of the village tried, but the council dug its feet in." Kade patted him on the shoulder again. "Donal has even resigned over it. Look, Ollie will be back shortly, and I'm trying to keep his spirits up. He and his mom are staying, which I'm glad about. They've both done well here."

Shock roiled through him. Her sister was staying, but

she wasn't? "*Angie* has done well here. She can't simply leave."

"Be hard to have you both in the village, I imagine. We agree, Declan particularly. He thought of going to Dublin after his engagement ended. But then herself left and he stayed. Remember?"

The waning sun came out from behind the shed and struck him in the eyes. He couldn't see for a moment. He lifted his hands to shade them. "I don't like this, Kade. Not one bit."

His friend's mouth lifted. "Then do something." Kade slapped him in the shoulder this time, and then he was striding toward the house, leaving Carrick alone in the yard.

He pulled out his phone and made a few calls, as much to hear how the wind was blowing around the closure as whether there was any way to overturn it. He hit a stone wall. The county council had never reversed a decision, and there were plenty of hard feelings in the mix because of Donal leaving and people calling them thick for the decision. The only way to handle the situation, a good source said, was to create an entirely new center, which was as ridiculous as this mess.

Leaving, he let his head hang in his car before he drove off. He wandered up the roads he'd driven his whole life. The fields were turning that golden color Angie loved. Pain shot through his heart as he thought of her.

He didn't want her to leave where she'd thrived. When he reached the pasture to the west of Bets' land, he parked and got out. He patted a few sheep as he walked the fields. There were no messages to guide him, and he'd never felt so lost or alone.

He looked around, hoping Sorcha would give him some other sign. The sky was a rich blue dotted with clouds, ones he wouldn't have noticed if Angie hadn't exclaimed over their beauty. She'd helped him see the richness of life again.

God, it was hard to go back to the bareness. The numbness that had lingered over him for days had lifted. The hurt was there, at them breaking, but the wonder she'd helped him recover was still present. It made the pain worse because she wasn't here to share it with him.

He looked at the cottage, wondering how she was, wishing with all his being that he was stronger in spirit.

To love her had been a joy. To fear losing her an agony.

But to know she'd left because of him...that he'd been the cause of her losing something good, something vital. That would be a new kind of hell.

He couldn't let that happen.

Looking across the land, he asked Sorcha and all the angels in heaven for help to find a way to keep Angie here. For a way for Bets to have her arts center to uplift everyone in the community. Sorcha would have loved a place like that. She might have even taught poetry there if she'd lived.

The ground under his feet seemed to move. His sheared sheep jolted and started to run. He looked around for a reason but found none. He was on to something... He had to be. This was a sign. He started walking again and felt pulled to his new house on the hill.

When he reached it, he noticed an envelope taped on the front door. He pulled the papers out of it and looked at the deed, freshly stamped with his name on it. Bets had moved fast, but then again, she always did. He started to shove the papers back in, but a ray of sunlight landed on the first paragraph. He read the language, and his heart started to pound in his chest.

Venturing inside, he looked over what he'd built. Thought about *why* he'd built it. Let himself feel the pride of having achieved what he'd set out to do—even if the old dream would never be. Then he let it all go and walked over to where Angie had set up her painting things. He traced the edge of her easel and then made himself look at her work.

She told the story of him in all of them, from the early wariness in his eyes to the love she'd brought to them.

He had changed.

She had changed him.

He couldn't let her leave without at least trying. Maybe she wouldn't be able to get past his decision to step away from her when she'd needed him. Maybe she'd leave anyway. But that would be for her to decide. If she could believe he loved her enough—and he did—and was willing to hold his hands through those awful moments, then he would sink to bended knee and apologize and ask for another chance to love her for the rest of his life.

As he shut the front door, he braced himself for the path ahead.

Carrick Fitzgerald knew what he had to do.

CHAPTER THIRTY-NINE

Being greeted by her dog friend always put a smile on her face.

Megan bent down to pet Duke as he gave a delighted bark. "Know what? I'm going to be around a little longer. I just couldn't leave you."

"I heard," Kade said, leading Majestic out of the barn. "You got an early start."

"Angie was finger-painting, and Liam took Ollie with him to learn how to build a fence." She flexed her muscles and almost laughed at herself. "Man stuff."

He smiled like he always did. She'd never known a man to smile so much. "Man stuff is good. We're all on the journey of learning what it means to be a man—or a woman."

"You seem to have it down." She sputtered, her face turning red. "The man stuff... I didn't mean it like that." But it was hard to ignore how handsome and wonderful he was. Forget about cloning sheep. The world needed more men like Kade: kind, handsome, dependable.

Majestic neighed, and Kade laughed. "See. This one agrees. I'm still learning. Every day."

She thought about Carrick and how he'd broken Angie's heart. Should she ask? Duke nudged her leg and barked, and she took it as a sign. "What about Carrick? Is there any hope of *him* learning? Oh, that sounds harsh, especially with me being a widow myself. But it's kinda ironic. Angie's accident has made me appreciate her more, and it's made Carrick back away. It's only... Angie really loves him. I hate seeing her so upset, and to be honest, I really don't want her to leave. We're in a good place."

He led Majestic across the yard, signaling for her to join him. She fell in step with him. When he handed her the lead rope, she didn't object even though her stomach flipped. He'd never had her take charge of a pony—not that his ponies needed it. They were all well behaved from his care and training.

"I told Carrick it's for him to decide," Kade said as they walked down the lane where he gave the pony rides.

The wildflowers were so bright, they might have been painted by Angie's own hand. "I thought about going to see him, but I didn't know what to say. Her fall scared me too."

"Scared everyone. Someday I'll tell you why it scared me. But not today. The sun is shining, and it's another glorious day in Ireland. I think it's a good time for you to have a ride yourself."

She faltered, and Majestic looked at her, the horse's eyes filled with the same care as she saw in Kade's soulful gaze. "Me? Oh, I don't know."

He halted, and Majestic stopped as well. "I think it's time. Do you trust me, Megan?"

Had she said soulful eyes? They were both looking at her now. "I do trust you. Completely."

"Then hold on to the top of the saddle and give me your foot."

He leaned over and cupped both hands, and she put her shoe in them. Then she was being lifted in the air, and he helped her mount. She settled her bottom until she was more comfortable.

He handed her the reins. "Well done. You're a natural. Now hold the reins like this, and we're going to walk. Shoulders back. Check out the horizon."

She scanned the view. The dirt road tracked through grassy pastureland lined with flowers. On either side in the distance, large hills towered over the land. "Everything looks different from up here." She'd thought it would be scary, but she felt powerful. Like the world was at her feet.

"Sometimes we need to see things from a new perspective," Kade said, walking beside her. "Ollie will be going to school soon. What are your plans?"

She tightened her hands on the reins. "I'm on a marathon run of reading self-help books and listening to the podcasts Liam recommends. He thought I might like to learn how to meditate, but I'm not sure I can sit still for that long." Of course, she'd lain around tons, so that wasn't true. She just wasn't sure she could be silent like that, and what if she didn't hear anything? Worse, what if she heard something she didn't like?

"No one is as well versed in such things as Liam, and he's a wiser man for it," Kade said, patting the gray pony on the mane. "Life can be a meditation too. You engage with everything around you. The land. The people. The animals. Don't you feel a connection to them?"

Suddenly she felt newly aware of the sun warming her head and shoulders, of Majestic moving under her. The wind came up, rustling the grass. She looked over at Kade, who was gazing at her like he always did, an easy smile on his face. Her heart warmed. "I do. Thank you, Kade."

"Oh, that's all you, Megan," he said, patting Majestic again. "You're waking up after a long sleep."

That was a good way of putting it, she thought.

"I wondered..." he started. "You're so good with the animals. I wanted to see if you'd be interested in helping me with them."

She dropped the reins, and he only fitted her hands around them again. "Here at the farm?"

He nodded. "Yeah. I need a helper. I have more people coming for rides than ever before. It would be a joy to have you around, and I know Duke especially would love it. He likes to think he's my helper too, and honestly, I couldn't do without him. I'd pay you a fair wage, of course, and this way, you could stay here longer, under a different visa. I looked into it. How does that sound?"

Tears filled her eyes, and she had to look away.

"Are you crying, love?"

Megan knew Irishmen called people *love* all the time, and she thought it was dear. But every time Kade used that endearment, her heart seemed to swell in her chest.

"Yes, I'm sorry. It's only. Your kindness is sometimes..."

He touched her hand for a moment. "Kindness is part of the reason we're here. We're here for each other. I'm glad you're starting to accept more of it."

She wiped away the tears and turned her head. There he was, waiting for her like always. "I'd love to be your helper."

"Good." He sent her a delighted wink. "Now, how about we trot a little?"

Her hands gripped the reins. "Trot? Oh, I don't know."

"Do you trust me?" he asked again.

His smile was as bright as the sun above. *With my life.* "Let's try it."

Her shoulders tensed as Kade started to run, Majestic picking up his gait. She bounced against the saddle a few times until the gray pony seemed to settle under her. She got the rhythm. Then she was moving in tune with Majestic, smiling as Kade ran on. Oh, it was a good name for the pony.

"How is it?" he asked, looking over his shoulder.

A surge of happiness rose up inside her. She welcomed it, drawing it close to herself. Had she ever felt this free?

"I love it."

Thank God she'd come to Ireland.

CHAPTER FORTY

Bets was running down the driveway, yelling, Liam thundering behind her on his motorbike.

Angie and Megan stood up from the settee as Ollie rushed to the door and opened it.

"Are you okay, Cousin Bets?"

Their cousin breezed in, breathing hard. "Ollie, I'm grand, as the Irish say. In shock. But grand. Oh, Angie! Donal just called me. The news is all over the village."

"What is it?" she asked as Liam came in and plucked Ollie up off the ground.

"He's done it!" Liam spun Ollie around. "We all hoped he'd find his way out, and he did, by God! The pub's going to be madness tonight."

Angie looked at Megan, who made a face. "What are you talking about?"

Bets crossed and grabbed her shoulders. "Prepare yourself. It's the grandest gesture I've ever heard of."

Her entire body went still. *"Carrick."*

"Yes! He donated his new house to the village."

She was glad her cousin was holding her in place because she rocked back. "Why would he do that?"

"As an arts center!" Bets exclaimed, throwing her hands up. "Oh, he's a clever one. Told them he wanted it to be called the Sorcha Fitzgerald Community Arts Center. The village was always proud of Sorcha. Named me as the executive director and negotiated hard to ensure the art school could teach any form of art—nudes included. Donal said the gossip was that he shamed them a little, asking if they would have told Yeats and other poets not to write love poems or Christy Brown himself not to draw something. Were they Irish in their very hearts or not?"

"This means you have a job, cousin," Liam said, lifting Ollie over his head, making the boy cry out in joy. "If you wish to stay."

Angie sank down onto the settee, touching her head.

"Is it throbbing?" Megan asked, sitting beside her.

She thought about it. "No, it's not hurting. It's blank. I think I'm in shock."

"I know," Bets said, dancing around the room. "It's the most incredible thing. He's been working on that house for years, and then he gets the money to buy the land sitting under it and up and donates it all for an arts center for the village. Oh, I can't wait to buy him a drink."

Megan took her hand. "What do you think, Angie? Just because he donated it doesn't mean you have to do anything about it."

Liam set Ollie down. "That's true, but if this is a cultural issue, let me clear it up. This is an act of love, cousin. A million times over."

Her heart sped up. "It doesn't—"

"*It does*," Bets said, putting her hands on her hips. "Probably there's an apology in it too. Look, I've been with

Irishmen for the last three decades. Trust me. He's all but telling everyone he messed up and wants you to stay in the grandest way possible."

The speed of her heart must be the cause of the pain spreading inside her. "Why didn't he tell *me*?"

"Because the news spread through the village faster than a fire," a familiar voice said as he stepped through the open front door. "Are you well enough to walk with me, Yank? I thought we needed a proper direct talk."

Her gaze lifted immediately to his eyes. They were back to ultramarine, and a hesitant love was shining in them. She stood up immediately at the sight and crossed to him.

"Told ya, cuz," Liam said with a clever grin. "Way to go, Carrick. The guys and I are as relieved as we are happy for you. It was hard not to come by and kick your arse."

His mouth tipped up. "Kade said I had to come to it on my own. As usual, he was right. Well, Yank. Are you fit enough for a short stroll? I have much to say to you, if you'll listen."

She nodded, hope and hurt rising within her, and he gestured to the door after grabbing her portable stool. They walked down the sidewalk, animated sounds following them from the cottage.

"Care to walk to your favorite spot with me?" Carrick asked, slowing his gait for her. "If we stay on the road, we'll be mobbed by cars. I suspect the Lucky Charms, Donal, and my friends are on the way over. Probably more from the village too. The Irish love to party, as you know."

"They certainly have something to party about." They detoured to the pasture, the wind caressing them. "So you gave away your house."

"I gave away *Sorcha's* house to the village to create an arts center where you can work and paint, if you're willing

375

to stay," he said, opening the stool when they reached the sycamore tree. "But that's not what I wanted to discuss with you."

No, that wasn't the crux of their problems, and they both knew it.

He helped her sit and lowered himself to the ground. "I don't know if there's an apology great enough for how I hurt you. Angie, I'm sorry I stepped back from you. I could try to explain what it did to me to see you fall like that. I could tell you how agonizing it was to go to that hospital again and smell death and see you there. To fear it might take you too."

His words easily painted the scenes in her mind. She'd known, but hearing it from him only sharpened the picture. "Oh, Carrick."

"But trying to account for my behavior doesn't move us forward," he said, plucking a blade of grass from the ground, "and that's what I wish for with all my heart. Still, I'll ask if you can ever forgive me."

The hurt shimmered inside her, and then it seemed to rise out of her as if on the wings of butterflies. "How could I not forgive you? I knew you didn't step away because you didn't love me. Doesn't mean that it didn't hurt like hell though."

He sighed and threw the blade of grass away, turning to her. "I'm sorry for that the most. It hurt me too, but I couldn't seem to step around the fear with all those feelings fresh and looming like a specter in my mind. But it lessened, you see, and it felt different than last time. I knew you were alive. I knew you were lying in that cottage, and I ached for you. That kind of pain was agonizing too, especially knowing I'd caused it."

Agonizing was a good way to describe it, and she held out her hand to him.

He clasped it, his blue eyes brightening. "When I heard you were leaving, it was the worst kind of lash. How was I to live knowing you were somewhere else, apart from me? Angie, I couldn't bear that."

She'd wondered how she was going to bear it too, and she'd cried herself to sleep.

"I love you too much to lose you," he said, rising up on one knee before her, "and I'm hoping with a little time, you might give me a second chance to show you I can stand beside you—through anything that comes. *Anything.*"

The power of his promise as much as his direct gaze seemed to echo in her very bones.

"I'm not a perfect man. I might even be an emotionally scarred one, although I'll never step away from you again if I have a bad moment. No, *mo ghrá*, I'll grab you to me and hold you until it passes."

She believed him. Somewhere deep inside, she'd needed to hear that.

"And I'll love you all my days," he said, holding her gaze, "and I'm hoping you'll do the honor of letting me."

Her heart swelled in her chest, and her mind framed the truth. The light in his ultramarine eyes shone brightly, along with the love he spoke of. No, he wasn't perfect. He was unexpected, in fact. And she loved him and trusted his word.

She leaned into him and wrapped her arms around him, her throat too thick to speak. He nestled her closely to him, the wind swirling around them both.

"I don't want to be without you either," she whispered against him.

The light falling on the land shifted, the grass turning

her favorite shade of golden. She ran her hand up his back, marveling at the way things had changed for her.

She'd come to Ireland to find her voice and paint again, and she had.

She'd never imagined she'd find the most unexpected of Prince Charmings.

And she certainly hadn't expected to fall in love with him beside a golden Irish field.

Here. Be. Good. That had been her first message, arriving in Ireland.

Sorcha had gotten that right, and she sent up a kind thought to thank her for her help.

The scent of oranges came moments later, and she smiled.

CHAPTER FORTY-ONE

Fitzgerald's Folly was no more.

Giving it to the village had made them embrace it, and Carrick was shocked and amazed to have volunteer after volunteer show up to help him finish the final touches.

Angie had given her thoughts on some easy changes to make it more suitable as an arts center, and his friends had assisted him on their days off and after working hours to implement them. The Lucky Charms had selected bright paint colors and painted the walls, along with other members of Angie's painting classes.

But the most surprising development, perhaps, was Megan agreeing to follow through on her offer to teach ceramics. They'd opened the class up to see how many students might register, and twenty had signed up straight-away, some of his friends included. He'd installed a kiln with the help of the town electrician, as well as some more industrial sinks. The village had agreed to pay for the paving of the road and a makeshift parking lot.

Bets had planted roses while Donal had installed tropicals to beautify the surrounding area. Those two were coming along fine, Carrick thought.

On the day of the opening only a month later, the village packed the place. Carrick kissed Angie on the cheek as he made his way to the dais they'd set up. Everyone quieted.

"I'm not much of a speaker, but I wanted to thank you for coming to open the Sorcha Fitzgerald Community Arts Center. I know it will be a place for many an artist to learn and grow."

When he spied Mary Kincaid in the crowd, he was sure the shock was visible on his face before he coughed to clear it. She hadn't been seen in town since the announcement, but of course she'd come today. The village would be talking about this for years. She had to show her face, even if her nose was in the air like she didn't smell the stink she'd caused. Some people lived their whole lives in bitterness. He was glad he'd decided on a different course for himself. He looked over to Angie as he continued.

"We're lucky to have a well-known painter teaching here—Angie Newcastle—one I am happy to see stay here for the rest of her life. We've all come to love her. Me most of all."

It felt right to be honoring the two women he loved. Everyone was smiling, and some were even wiping tears, his own mother included. He was glad they understood.

"I'd like to finish by reading a short poem by Sorcha, one I hope sets the tone for this center." He started to recite.

> *The land calls us to her.*
> *We strain to tell what she whispers.*
> *But how can we fully share the*
> *mystery around us?*

Then our friends come and give us a
story,
And we hear the mystery through
them.
Our words paint the picture.

When he finished, the applause started, and his heart expanded as the sound crescendoed. The poem had seemed the obvious choice. Sorcha had used the words. Angie painted the picture. They were both part of this heart of his, and he was a better man for it.

"Thank you, friends. Now I'd like to introduce the executive director. Our one and only Betsy O'Hanlon."

More cheering and whistling ushered Bets to the dais, where she hugged him.

"You did good," she told him. "Real good."

He nodded and stepped away to join Angie and take her hand. She was smiling at him, a smile he understood. Soon he would ask her to marry him, and he would design and build a home with her. But he wouldn't think about that today. He was going to celebrate this moment.

"Well, friends, we still have an arts center," Bets said, her pale blue eyes dancing with delight.

There was more cheering and whistling, including from Angie next to him. He laughed. There were still plenty of hard feelings in the village from what people felt was the council's overstepping, and leave it to Bets to get people riled up again.

When the noise died down, Bets put her hands on her hips and looked over the crowd. "Apparently we have enough artists in this town that we can't be kept down."

Oh, Jesus, Bets, why don't you shove it in their face?

But the cheering was stronger this time, and Angie was

one of the ones whistling. Ollie was jumping up and down, and his mother was clapping loudly. Megan's turnaround was a wonder to behold, and he caught Kade's look as his friend inclined his chin toward them all. Kade was a miracle worker, and now Megan was working at his farm. Would wonders never cease?

"I'm still on call for the life modeling, Bets," Eoghan O'Dwyer called out, adjusting his red bow tie, making everyone laugh.

"We just might take you up on it, Eoghan," Bets said with a look in Mary's direction before continuing. "This place is for the community, after all, and I'm proud to call Carrick Fitzgerald my friend and a friend to this village. His gift will have a lasting impact because when we give ourselves and our children the gift of expression, we give them a deeper understanding of their very selves and motivations."

Carrick couldn't agree more, and he cuddled Angie close when she rested her head against his shoulder.

"I for one am excited to have more people support this community through the arts, and I'm excited to see where it takes us all. Thanks to my wonderful American cousins, Angie Newcastle and Megan Bennet, and our own Siobhan McGrath for being our first teachers. I can't wait to see what other teachers we might attract to this glorious space. Thank you."

Donal was at the ready to wrap his arm around her, and the Lucky Charms surrounded her, talking animatedly. Someone clapped Carrick on the back, and he turned to see his friends behind him.

"Nice speech," Brady said, jostling him.

"Short is always sweetest," Declan said, his mouth in a wry smile. "The place looks really good. I might even sign up for a class. Hey, Angie. Has anyone ever painted with a cleaver?"

"You'd cut the canvas open, you eejit," Liam said, laughing.

"Declan might manage it," Kade said, putting his arm around Ollie when the boy grabbed his leg in a hug.

Jamie arrived, a tray of whiskeys in hand. "Your dad can't stop being the publican. He's serving up drinks right and left."

"People in the arts love drinks," Angie said as she took the first one.

The adults in their group took one, including Megan, which had everyone staring. "I'm trying something new every day. It's my first whiskey."

"Saints preserve us," Declan said, crossing himself. "I'll be bringing you a bottle then to keep you going. It's un-Irish not to drink whiskey and with you living here now—"

"Do I get some?" Ollie asked. "I'm living here."

"When you're older," Liam said, hoisting Ollie onto his shoulders. "To Carrick," he added, lifting his glass. "For being a good man."

"Hear, hear," his friends shouted.

Carrick held Angie's gaze as he said, "*Slainte*."

"*Slainte*," she said back with a wink.

"Oh, the lovebirds are cooing," Declan said, downing his drink. "You should find a happy little corner for yourselves, or the village will talk your ear off."

It was good advice, and Carrick had had his fill of ignoring wisdom, so he grabbed her hand and took her to a mostly vacant corner and tugged her close. "Well, what did you think? Do you understand why I chose that poem?"

She brushed the lapel of his blue suit before laying her

hand there. "I do. Did you see the painting I did this morning?"

"You mean after I fell asleep after you had your way with me? Or right before that, when you asked if I ever count sheep to go to sleep?"

"I was curious!"

Now that had been downright funny. "No, I didn't see your painting. Bets called me about picking up the decorations for today." He fingered her waist, set off by her formfitting blue dress, embroidered with red and white flowers trailing up the sleeves. Her clothes were slowly changing as she found styles to suit the new her, and he loved seeing this further expression of her essence.

She brought up her phone. "It won't have the same energy or size, but I think you'll get it."

The painting was of him alone, mostly in blue tones save his face, standing tall yet somehow relaxed, if the way she'd drawn his shoulders was any indication. He looked years younger than he'd looked before. "This is how you appear to me today. I wanted to commemorate it. In the States, we'd say, 'You've come a long way, baby.'"

"So have you," he said, holding her close.

"I'm glad you're at peace with everything, Carrick."

He inhaled the feeling. "It's a prized way of being after so many years of struggle. In fact, the best part of the way I'm feeling these days is standing right in front of me."

"Right back at you, *a stór*."

He fought a grin, but she hit him anyway. "Hey, your Gaelic is getting better," he said, lifting his hands. "But really you should call me *my treasure* in English. I rather like it when you do."

"I call one part of you that," she said, looking down

briefly and then giving him a saucy wink. "Thanks to you, I'll be able to paint all of you here in the arts center."

"Oh, happy day," he said, pulling her to him. "Maybe Declan is right. We should cut out of here before—"

"I've been looking for the two of you," Cormac O'Sullivan said, arriving in his best suit and a top hat.

"You're looking very dashing today," Angie said.

"Biggest gift to the village since we were founded, and it's being commemorated with pictures left and right. A man has to look his best. Now about yourselves..."

Carrick groaned as the small man brought out his black book.

Angie started laughing. "Let me guess? They're betting on how soon I'll be teaching an official nudes class."

"Yes, but that's not why I interrupted your kissing," he said, lowering his gaze. "I'm wondering—as is the village— when the good news will be announced."

Angie's brow knit, but Carrick only glared at the man. "When it's time, man. Now be off with you."

"What good news?" She gasped then. "You mean when I'm pregnant?"

Carrick startled at that, while Cormac crossed himself and said, "Jesus, if that's the way you want to go, but here I was thinking you might be official and such before such a happy event."

"We will be official before then," Carrick said, glaring at him.

"Ah... So it's in the works then." Cormac waved his book in the air. "Good. One more question."

"No," Carrick said flatly.

"It's of interest to many in the village if you'll be buying another piece of land, an already built place, or constructing your own."

"Oh, feck off, little man," Carrick said, turning him around and shoving him gently away.

He waved at the people in the crowd watching the spectacle, then positioned himself and Angie away from prying eyes. "Will they never cease to butt in?"

She put her hand to her mouth, but he could still see she was laughing. "It appears our future plans are of interest to the village. You know, it's actually kind of nice. I've never had anyone care about me like that. Or bet on me, for that matter."

He brought her close to him. "Well, since there are questions in the air... You mentioned us having a baby in the future. Is that something that's swirling in your mind then?"

He had the ring. He'd only been waiting for a sign she was ready to take the next step. Yes, she'd forgiven him and given him another chance, but he'd wanted to make sure she trusted him the whole way.

She took her sweet time answering. "If we're being direct—"

"Yank, it's our way," he said, caressing her cheek.

Fingering his lapel again, she inched her fingers up and traced his jawline. "Then yes, the frame of it is so crystal clear in my mind, I could paint it in an instant."

"Good," he said, kissing her softly, not caring that everyone was watching and likely placing more bets with Cormac. They were part of the village, and she was right. They were loved. But he knew something Cormac couldn't guess at.

He was proposing tomorrow.

EPILOGUE

Marriage was in the air.

When Kade left the building, the cheers and whistles over Carrick kissing Angie followed him out. So did Jamie. As soon as his friend set his foot on the short stone terrace, he laughed. "My ears are still ringing. Oh, but I'm over the moon for my brother. *Jesus!*"

Jamie's cry didn't startle him. He'd smelled oranges inside and had followed the scent out onto the portico, sensing he should.

"Hello, Sorcha," he said, looking over to where she stood against the backdrop of the sky, her white dress billowing, a radiant smile on her face.

"Hello, Kade."

"Oh, no," Jamie said with a moan. "I can still see her. I don't *want* to see her."

"Enough, Jamie," Sorcha said, crossing to stand before them. "You're going to see me plenty, so you might as well embrace the idea."

"I'm going to faint," Jamie said, mopping his brow with his handkerchief.

Kade steadied him with a hand before saying, "You should go inside then and splash your face with cold water."

"Good idea." He lifted a finger in the air. "Ah... Good-bye, Sorcha."

"You should pick up Carrick's bar tab more," she called after him, laughing. "Oh, he's going to be fun to mess with."

"Are you hanging around to mess with us then?" Kade asked. "I thought you might have gone on when we didn't see you after Angie's accident."

"It wasn't for me to help then. It's like you knew. Carrick had to take that final step himself. And he did, by God. I'm so very proud of him."

Kade had the urge to touch her arm, but he knew his hand would only pass through. "Do you want me to tell him for you?"

She shook her brown curls. "No, he knows. He and Angie are going to be very happy together. Now it's your turn."

He wasn't surprised somehow. "Do all of you ghosts know what's about then? I don't think any of my family or friends have guessed it, but I knew she was coming months ago."

Sorcha inhaled deeply, almost like she was enjoying the fragrant roses in the courtyard. "And then she did."

He didn't need confirmation, but still he said, "Say her name."

"*Megan.*"

He nodded, glancing over his shoulder, through the open door. She was talking to Brady, who could bring anyone out of their shell at a party. She didn't know as many people as Angie, but she was meeting more of the village as she emerged from the chrysalis she'd been in. Only he understood she'd been in it for longer than her marriage, which was why he was being extra patient and taking his time.

"You're going to need help," Sorcha said, resting her invisible hand on his shoulder.

He looked her straight in the eye. "I'll take it."

———

Every time you leave a kind review, a rainbow appears in the sky.

Leave a review for this book and get ready for a splash of color!

———

Love Angie and Carrick? Immerse yourself in their romance with the audiobook. Listen to Beside Golden Irish Fields, read by legendary narrator Emily Woo Zeller.

———

Surround yourself with more magic with Megan and Kade in the next Unexpected Prince Charming novel, *Beneath Pearly Irish Skies*.

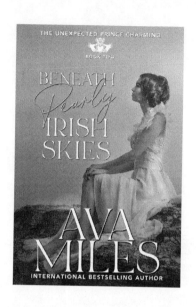

Beneath Pearly Irish Skies
The Unexpected Prince Charming Book 2

A feel-good tale about a single mom starting over in Ireland and the unexpected Prince Charming who helps her find her purpose and happiness.

Scan to dive into *Beneath Pearly Irish Skies* now!

ABOUT THE AUTHOR

Millions of readers have discovered International Bestselling Author Ava Miles and her powerful fiction and non-fiction books about love, happiness, and transformation. Her novels have received praise and accolades from *USA Today*, *Publisher's Weekly*, and *Women's World Magazine* in addition to being chosen as Best Books of the Year and Top Editor's picks. Translated into multiple languages, Ava's strongest praise comes directly from her readers, who call her books and characters unforgettable.

If you'd like to connect with Ava or hear more about her upcoming books, scan this code:

Visit Ava on social media:

facebook.com/AuthorAvaMiles

twitter.com/authoravamiles

instagram.com/avamiles

bookbub.com/authors/ava-miles

pinterest.com/authoravamiles

Made in the USA
Middletown, DE
11 September 2023